D1382834

A DREAM SO REAL

She was so perfect. He could feel her shiver as his fingers trailed along her side from her shoulder to her hip, yet she made no move to withdraw.

"The curve of your body is flawless. I would know it anywhere by touch. You're the one I've dreamed of all my life, but you've never been so real in my arms. Did I die in the balloon crash? If you are heaven, then I'd fall a thousand times to have you near." He leaned forward and kissed her forehead. "How can you feel so warm and wonderful in my arms and be only a dream?"

He slid his hand past the white cotton gown she wore and touched the silk of her thigh. Her body arched to his touch just as he'd known it would. He moved his hand higher to her hip. She moved slightly, bending one knee over his leg in an intimate gesture that warmed his blood as no fever ever could . . .

NORTHERN STAR

Jodi Thomas

CHARTER/DIAMOND BOOKS, NEW YORK

NORTHERN STAR

A Charter/Diamond Book / published by arrangement with
the author

PRINTING HISTORY
Charter/Diamond edition / October 1990

All rights reserved.
Copyright © 1990 by Jodi Koumalats.
This book may not be reproduced in whole or in part, by
mimeograph or any other means, without permission. For
information address: The Berkley Publishing Group, 200
Madison Avenue, New York, New York 10016.

ISBN: 1-55773-396-1

Charter/Diamond Books are published by The Berkley Publishing
Group, 200 Madison Avenue, New York, New York 10016.
The name ''CHARTER/DIAMOND'' and its logo are trademarks
belonging to Charter Communications, Inc.

PRINTED IN THE UNITED STATES OF AMERICA

10 9 8 7 6 5 4 3 2

To Jean Price,
who believed in this book enough to help
make a sister's dream come true

Chapter 1

Hunter Kirkland collapsed in the damp, dusty hay of the abandoned loft. The wind blew over him, unhampered by rotting boards that marked the aging barn walls. The roof stood firm above, like a stubborn old man refusing to bow to the wrath of the storm. Slowly, with pain showing in his tired gray eyes, Hunter removed his uniform jacket. He laid it in the hay tenderly, not seeing the blood and dust of the present, only the pride of three years past when he'd been commissioned in the Union Army. The coat, like its wearer, had aged and suffered since that first day and bore little resemblance to its earlier self. Hunter covered the uniform with straw, hiding it along with his identity. His life would be worthless if the jacket were found.

Resting his head on the musty hay, Hunter tried to ignore the throbbing in his shoulder long enough to sleep. Rest was vital if he was ever going to make it back through the lines to camp. However, sleep eluded him as the pain washed over his body in long, icy waves.

Damn the Rebels. What if they've captured the Star? His foggy mind filled with visions of his beloved *Northern Star*, riddled with bullets, falling from the sky. *I shouldn't have listened to Wade. Storms and balloons never mix.* Was he hallucinating or had the *Star* truly fallen? The an-

1

swer lay just out of reach in the reality he could no longer touch.

In the dampness of the loft Hunter felt suddenly warm, and his thoughts grew cloudy. His last ounce of consciousness faded as he heard the barn door creak slowly open. He lay silent, beyond action, beyond caring, and drifting beyond life.

A ragged figure emerged from between sheets of rain through the cracked barn door. A bolt of lightning briefly illuminated a youth resembling countless others washed aside in the wake of war. The thin-faced, wide-eyed child seemed old enough to survive yet too young to serve either army.

The youth tugged at the oversize clothes that hung wet on his exhausted body. With the next roll of thunder a larger figure, neatly dressed in black, slipped through the ancient door. Her chocolate-colored face filled with fear as her eyes darted around the barn.

The slave whispered to her ragged companion, "I think we best stay here, Miz Perry. We can't make it much farther in this rain." She shook her shawl. "Smells like rotten death in here."

"Anything's better than being out there," Perry Mc-Lain replied as she pulled off her soggy hat, allowing her hair to fall free. Tangled ebony curls surrounded her small oval face. The boy's clothing she wore had adequately concealed a small-framed woman of twenty.

"If this storm slowed us down, it surely stopped Captain Williams. We'll rest here. In an hour it'll be morning." Perry wished her soft tone would calm her own nerves as well as it reassured Noma.

As Perry's eyes grew accustomed to the darkness, Noma headed toward an overturned bucket. The middle-aged slave sat her considerable bulk upon it and complained, "Wish we could build a fire." Unexpectedly, a bubble of laughter erupted from the black woman. "Guess we had enough fire for a spell, though."

Perry smiled. "I'm amazed you can laugh," she said. Moving beside Noma, Perry placed her arm protectively around her shoulders. Noma was the closest friend Perry had, more family than slave.

"Ain't no use crying about it. What's done is done," Noma answered. "But I do wish that devil Captain Williams would stop nipping at our heels. Ain't nothing worse than a Johnny Reb turn Yankee, and he took what you done so personal."

Visions of flames as high as hundred-year-old elms flashed through Perry's mind. She'd never dreamed the fire would spread from the fields to the barns and finally to Ravenwood. "I had to burn the fields," she whispered to some invisible judge before her. "No matter what the danger. I couldn't just give up." Even before the fires were under control, Captain Williams had issued a warrant for her arrest.

Noma wasn't listening. She'd begun exploring their dilapidated shelter like an old miner who'd found a new tunnel. "I wish your brother was here. All that boy's life he's thought he was your protector. I miss that bossy, red-headed man."

Perry nodded. Her brother was a surgeon with General Lee's army near Raleigh. They'd heard a few weeks earlier that he was moving toward them and hoped he might get to come home for a few days. But the fighting had grown worse for the South, with the number of wounded climbing daily. Andrew McLain's letters were only short notes written in an exhausted hand. He could've been within a few hours' ride of Ravenwood and not been able to cross lines to get home. If Lee moved south, he'd be trapped between Sherman and Grant.

Perry straightened her tired muscles slightly. "Andrew would have done the same thing. We couldn't let Yankees

have our harvest. I'll hang first.'' Her choice had been
simple—stay and fight or burn the fields and run.

Noma kicked something in the shadows. "And hang
you will, Miz Perry, if that devil Captain Williams catches
you. He'll have that rope around you faster than I wring a
chicken's neck on Sunday.''

Noma's remark sent a sudden chill through Perry's body.
She knew the law, as did everyone in the South. Destroying crops was an act of treason. A tear rolled unchecked
down her dirty face. She forced herself to swallow her
doubts. "We'll make it to Granddad's old place and hide
out there. I'll find some way to get word to Andrew. Then
all we have to do is wait until he comes.''

"Wish we could go farther south. That farm ain't far
enough away from them Yankees. And it's so old, there's
probably more varmints living in that house than are staying in here.'' Both women glanced around nervously.

"Well, look there,'' Noma squealed.

Perry's glance followed the point of Noma's finger. A
loft stood half hidden in the dark corner. Only the extend-
ing ladder gave away its presence. They both scrambled
up, hoping for a dry bed.

Perry stepped from the ladder, testing the loft. It was
not only dry, but also sturdy enough for both women. The
aging wood cried under the weight of Noma's awkward
bulk as she followed a few steps behind.

"This might not be a bad night's sleep, after all,'' Perry
said, unbuttoning her damp coat. The garment was too
big, but it had felt wonderful when the rain began. Now
the damp material felt like lead molded to her shoulders.
"I never thought curling up in a blanket on the hay would
be so inviting.''

Perry's sleepy gaze fell on a dark bundle in the far corner. Hoping someone had left bedding in the loft, she
hurried forward.

Kneeling, she reached for the bundle. The mass rolled
an inch forward and she gasped as the object came alive.

Thunder rattled the barn and lightning turned night into an instant of day. Perry screamed as a hand fell with a lifeless thud across her boot.

She fought down another scream and stepped back, her eyes fixed on the pale open palm lying atop the hay. Noma moved closer, whirling the bundle she carried like a weapon. But there was no one to battle. The form on the loft floor remained still. Cautiously Noma knelt as Perry slipped a small knife from her pocket.

"Is he dead?" Perry whispered as the smell of blood assaulted her senses.

The storm cooperated, lending Noma a flash of lightning by which she could examine the man. "He's pretty near gone, from what I can tell," Noma whispered. "He's a soldier; blue or gray, I can't say. There's blood and mud everywhere." She rose slowly to her feet. "He'll be dead before morning."

"No!" Perry said bitterly. "No." The hopelessness of her own plight was momentarily forgotten. She was sick to the core of all the dying. "Noma, we must do something. I don't want to see another man die as long as I live."

The mighty heave of Noma's chest told Perry that the slave didn't share her concern for this man's life, but Noma nodded. "I hear you, Miz Perry. There ain't no use to argue when you use that stubborn tone with me. Sometimes I think you and your brother were fathered by a mule and nursed by the Angel of Mercy, the way you carry on about folks who are sick and dying." Noma pulled off her wool scarf. "If you'll get that bucket downstairs and fill it with rainwater, I'll clean off some of this blood and see what we can do for this soldier boy."

All fatigue was forgotten as Perry fetched the water. *This time I'll fight,* she thought. Death followed her like a shadow. Always there; always taking those around her. Perry often felt she was playing some morbid game without knowing the rules. Death had taken every member of her family in the past few years, except Andrew. "But not this time," she kept repeating in her mind. "This time I'll fight death and win."

As Perry returned with the water Noma was already hard at work. The black woman had often helped Andrew with the doctoring before the war. Other slaves said Noma had healing hands, even if her heart was sometimes cold. This stranger was in good care.

"Dig that knife outa that pouch you brought with your mother's papers and things." Noma was too busy to look up. "Cut me some bandages outa what's left of his shirt."

Perry followed instructions. By the time Noma had the blood cleaned off, a stack of bandages lay waiting.

As she knelt a few feet away, watching Noma work, Perry absentmindedly braided her black hair into one long chain of silky ebony. Her hair had always been a source of joy to her father. Perry knew he would have frowned to see how it had been twisted and hidden under her dirty hat. But a lady didn't travel alone, especially if she was wanted for treason. The old clothes were her only hope of escaping Captain Williams and his band of Yankees that rode across the Carolinas. She knew she'd traveled far enough south to be well behind the lines. Within another day she would be completely out of any Yankee's reach. Yet this man before her fought a battle within, and for him there was no safe ground.

The stranger's chest, stripped of shirt and blood, seemed like only muscle pulled over bone with no softness. Though his face was a shadow, Perry wondered about his identity. He might be a poor Southern farm boy running away from more fighting, or maybe one of the many Northern spies infiltrating the South. Watching his life ebb, Perry concluded that it didn't matter. Maybe Noma was right: Stubbornness and mercy were both her strengths and her curse. If this man died, she'd feel the pain of his loss without even knowing his name.

Noma shook her head as she leaned back from her patient. "Without a fire it's going to be hard keeping this fella alive." She rubbed the small of her back and waddled to the far side of the loft. "I'm going to curl up and let this old body get a few hours' sleep. Unless it stops raining, we ain't going anywhere come morning."

Perry noticed the first hint of daybreak. "I'll sit by him awhile. You get some sleep." She covered an already snoring Noma with their only blanket.

Slowly she crawled to the sleeping soldier, studying him closely. His hair grew lighter with the morning. Sunny blond strands covered his forehead and brushed his sleeping eyes. His jawline was strong and covered with sandy, short whiskers; his mouth was generous, relaxed in sleep. Gently Perry touched a curl hanging across his forehead. With a will of its own the curl wrapped around her finger, surprising her with its tender gesture.

In the early dawn light the sleeping man's lips thinned, and his face contracted in pain. A sudden chill overtook him and he shook violently, as though the entire earth were unsteady beneath him. War raged within him, a war of life over death.

Sliding down beside him in the hay, Perry pressed against his body while pulling her large coat over them both in a tight cocoon. He was hard and muscular in her arms, but she felt death's cold hands chilling him from within. Her body was all that warmed him.

His unharmed arm encircled her, pulling her closer to his lean frame. His fingers slid down her back, molding her close, as though he craved the feel of another human being in his last moments of life.

Perry knew she should pull away, but she couldn't deny this man the comfort he desperately seemed to need. His fingers moved slowly along her body, touching her as no other ever would have dared. Her shirt and trousers did little to buffer the boldness of his touch as his hand traced lightly across her.

The stranger's action seemed easy, almost casual, as if

he were merely assuring himself of her presence. But Perry burned with each of his strokes. Many times she'd longed to be held as a woman, but the war never allowed the luxury of romance. This man's touch caused a storm inside her, where only calmness had resided. A turmoil swirled within her blood like a whispering wind that warns of a raging tempest to come.

Any moment she might be caught by the Yankees and never know the touch of a lover's hands. She wanted his gentle movements to continue, telling her of a closeness she'd never known before and might never know again.

He pulled her against him and nestled his head beside her hair. His arm remained protectively across her as his breathing slowed slightly. A sense of belonging, of home-coming, drifted over Perry.

As the minutes passed, she could feel the heat within her body moving to him. Perry relaxed. The shared warmth, combined with her lack of sleep, drew a curtain of drowsiness about her. She slept soundly for the first time in three days, her arms around a man about whom she knew nothing, not even his name.

Afternoon crept upon them as silently as a dream steals between thoughts. The rain slowed to a drizzle and the March wind faded to a low whine. Light seeped through the cracks of the barn walls, erasing the shadow's domain. Noma stretched out in the corner. Perry rolled a foot from the stranger and sat up, surprised she'd lain so close to him. Noma stood, mumbling something about breakfast as she joined Perry.

"How bad was he shot?" Perry finally spoke the question that had haunted her during the hours she'd held him.

The black woman yawned and answered. "Near as I can figure, he weren't shot at all. Looks like somethin' heavy crashed into his shoulder and ripped his muscles apart. It puzzles me how he was hurt. On the right side of his neck and both his hands, there's marks like a rope burn I saw once. It don't make much sense at all."

Looking intently at Perry, she continued. "But one thing's for sure, Miz Perry. If he does come around, you better keep your hat pulled low. We don't know what kind of man he is, and better he thinks you're a boy."

Perry smiled to herself. Unless the man was totally void of the sense of touch, he already knew her gender. Just the memory of his hand moving over her made her blush.

Noma wrapped her shawl around her bulk. "If he makes it, we'll have to feed him. I'll be back shortly. I'll walk till I find food and maybe information. There's bound to be folks around here somewhere. That thunder sounds like cannon fire. If I don't check it out, we may end up in the middle of this damn war yet." She continued mumbling as she left the loft, grunting in rhythm with the ladder.

Calling up quietly, Noma instructed, "Pull the ladder up so no one will notice the loft if they should wander in."

"Be careful," Perry answered.

Noma shoved the barn door open. "Don't worry about me. Ain't nobody interested in an old black woman. If I see any soldiers, I'll just hide till they pass."

Perry watched her leave, then pulled the ladder up, feeling as if she'd been abandoned. She sat beside the stranger, trying to understand why she felt somehow tied to him. He looked to be in his mid-twenties, about the same age as her brother. His tan was deep and the tiny wrinkles around his eyes indicated he spent a great deal of time in the sun. Judging from his sun-bleached hair, it seemed he'd done so without a hat. The whisker stubble and dirt couldn't conceal the fact that he was by far the most handsome man she'd ever seen.

The warmth of the stranger's body drew her close. His breathing had a slow, regular rhythm. One determined ray of sun splashed planes of light and shadow across his face. Her eyes drifted past his strong chin to the bandages Noma had wrapped around his shoulder.

Something glimmered at his neck, twinkling in a mo-

ment of sun like a slender gold cord. Curiosity forced her
to tug at the fine yellow rope. A round gold disk appeared
from behind his neck and slid lazily along the chain into
Perry's fingers. She turned it slowly from side to side,
examining the disk in the dingy light. One side bore a
crest unlike any Perry had ever seen. On the other side it
was engraved, simply, Hunter Kirkland.

Perry smiled to herself. She now knew the injured man's
name. Hunter. He was no longer an unknown soldier. Filling the only cup with water, she knelt by his head and
whispered, ''Hunter.'' She waited. ''Hunter, swallow a
little water. Please!''

Hunter didn't respond. Perry removed her bulky hat and
coat. Kneeling beside him once again, she cradled his head
in her arms. ''Hunter, please swallow.'' Water trickled
down his chin, but again no response came.

Perry wiped the spilled water from his face with her
sleeve. He has to drink, she thought, or he'll never live.
She cradled his head close to her, holding him in a gentle
vise between her breast and arm while she tried to force
his mouth open. Again water trickled down his lips.

''Hunter, please swallow!'' Again and again she begged.
The water in the cup was half gone, and Perry's arm ached
from supporting the soldier's head. Putting her finger into
the cup, she touched Hunter's eyes lightly with the cool
water. His eyelashes seemed longer and darker when wet.
The tips of her fingers touched his cheek and traveled to
his lips. His short growth of beard tickled her fingertips
as she stroked his face. She marveled at the softness of
his lips.

''Hunter, please drink,'' she whispered. This time, to
her surprise, his eyes opened. Piercing gray eyes looked
directly at her. A touch of alarm and an ounce of uncertainty blended in the smoky depths of his riveting gaze.

He stared at her, searching her face as though looking
into her very soul. The gray intensity seemed to hold her
frozen for a moment. Suddenly an invisible rumbling of

pain twisted his face, forcing his eyes closed. Torment echoed through her as she watched his agony.

A determined note rang in her voice as she said, ''Hunter, drink this.''

Nodding slightly, he swallowed the remaining water in the cup. As though the effort were too much for him, he fell back, collapsing into sleep once more, his head still resting in her arms. She cradled him gently to her and felt a sense of accomplishment. She'd won the first battle with death but the war was not over. He was still very weak, and blood continued to seep from his shoulder. She lay his head down lovingly, as a mother puts a sleeping newborn to rest. Covering him with the blanket, she slid beside him once more.

Yet as she curled around him, Perry found it impossible to relax. She couldn't erase his gray eyes from her mind. Their boldness and honesty had touched her, whirling her insides like a speeding merry-go-round.

As before, Hunter reached in his sleep to pull her near. His arm encircled her. His hand moved in the slow, familiar strokes of one who'd held her in his dreams all his life.

Perry was wide-awake now and totally aware that they were alone. She responded to his touch, molding willingly against his side as his fingers applied slight pressure along her spine. If the morning brought death, at least she would not have spent her last moments alone. He might not know it, but Hunter Kirkland might be her only taste of love.

Carefully she rested her hand on his unharmed shoulder, her fingertips touching the chain about his neck. Unbeckoned feelings were running through her veins, warming her blood and awakening a longing she'd never known. How could just a moment's look into his eyes affect her so? Why was the feel of his hand surveying her body addictive at first touch?

She brushed her fingertips over his skin. Touching him excited and frightened her. Her heart pounded from the feel of his flesh beneath her touch. Though her mind told her she shouldn't, her senses danced with a timeless awakening. Somehow she knew that this time was special, secret and apart from the rest of the world.

Perry had spent many nights dreaming of how it would feel to have a man by her side. She pressed her body against Hunter's full length as her hands continued to brush his skin lightly. She could feel his smooth muscles underneath the warm flesh. A tear drifted down her cheek as she thought of the bandaged shoulder, already stained anew with blood.

Hunter mumbled, and Perry leaned closer to understand his words. "Hold on, Abram!" he whispered. "Don't let go. Hold on! The balloon's going down. Hold on longer!"

Pain ripped through him; shaking Perry's heart with sympathy. From the depth of his cry she knew his pain was both physical and emotional. She reached up, cupping his face with her hands and whispered softly, "Hush, Hunter. It's all right now."

Yet his agonized words tore through her as he continued to call softly, "Hold on, Abram!"

Perry attempted to steady Hunter's large frame in her small arms. She caressed his sweating face, cooing words of reassurance. When her lips brushed his forehead, she could feel the high fever within him. Tears spilled onto her cheeks as she pulled him closer. "Please, please," she begged. "Please, Hunter, don't die." Her words brushed his warm lips as she pleaded.

Then, like a storm that had blown itself at full gale, he relaxed. His body fell against her and he whispered, "Stay near." His uninjured arm pulled her close, as if holding on to life itself.

Perry brushed his hair from his closed eyes. Her lips trailed light kisses across his temple. Dear Lord, she thought, his nearness was intoxicating. Touching him brought her a reckless pleasure, a deep gulp of life when she'd only taken sips before.

Her breath whispered against his ear as his hand slid up
to brush the material covering her breast. He pulled her
collar open enough for his fingers to caress the soft flesh
of her neck. The top button pulled free, making her shirt
slip from her shoulder and allowing Hunger's fingers the
freedom to slide her camisole strap off her shoulder.

As his hand brushed her warm flesh Perry's mind raced.
He might only be holding on to life, but she was living it
for the first time. Every part of her was alive. As his thumb
traced the lace of her camisole to the dip between her
breasts, Perry knew she wouldn't withdraw even if his
hand explored further.

Hunter moved his face into her hair. "Don't leave me,
my angel, don't leave me." His voice was rich and deep,
stirring her no less than his gray eyes and warm touch had.

Tears ran down her cheeks as she whispered, "I'm
here." He might only be dreaming, but the memory of
this moment would stay within her forever.

Hunter relaxed in sleep, his arm around Perry.

"Live," she whispered, moving her lips against his
cheek. "You must live."

The memory of his touch haunted Perry's sleep as she
dreamed of a tomorrow that might not come for Hunter.

Chapter 2

As dawn glistened through the cracks and danced on the far wall, Perry awoke with a start. Noma had not returned. Slowly, Perry's groggy mind realized that the constant thunder around her was cannon fire, not a storm. She crawled to the window and looked out. She could see nothing but blackness, but judging from the sound, the fight could be no more than a mile away. Noma was easily frightened. She was probably hiding somewhere, waiting for a chance to get back.

Now Perry felt not only fear but guilt as well. She'd spent the night dreaming of the way Hunter had touched her so tenderly and looked into her very soul with his gray eyes, while Noma had been somewhere outside, hiding. For one night Perry had been removed from the war, with no rules or fears to inhibit her. She'd cherished each moment. Now, in the morning light, she feared their time together might end before nightfall and she would be unable to spend another night in his arms.

The bandage across Hunter's shoulder was a bloody reminder of death's waiting vigil. Some spots along the white cloth were bright red, and others were already drying to a dark purple. The bandage had to be changed before the material stuck to his flesh and caused more damage.

Perry felt bonded to Hunter. Though they'd never talked,

his life was as vital to her as her own. She would do whatever was necessary to see that he lived; then she would try to find Noma.

Afraid of seeing the searing pain in his eyes again, she pulled off the soiled dressing as slowly and gently as she could. Blood oozed from the torn tissue on his right shoulder, calling an abrupt halt to Perry's progress. She took a deep breath, fighting to control her nausea. She knew that the hot redness, spreading like scarlet weeds beneath the skin from the bloody injury, meant infection.

Hunter slept, unaware of her touch. She slowly bathed his shoulder, remembering how he'd touched hers in the darkness. Whether he lived or died would depend on her keeping the wound clean until a doctor could be found. The jagged rip in his skin and muscles stood in sharp contrast to the other smooth shoulder. Perry watched as his chest rose and fell slightly with each breath. In the light his undamaged skin shone golden to his waist.

She wrapped his arm where sections of the skin were rubbed away. Hunter moved in pain, clenching his teeth, yet made no sound. Perry finished her work as rapidly as possible, binding him with clean strips. She lifted his head gently as he accepted the water she offered. Even as Hunter's fever raged, anger boiled in her own veins. Dear God, how she hated this war! How she hated not being able to help him. She longed to see those gray eyes filled with something other than pain.

Hunter held out a hand toward her. "Angel, where's the *Star*?" he mumbled. "Angel . . . my angel, was the *Star* captured? Is Abram alive?"

Perry grabbed his long fingers and pulled them to her cheek, wishing she could answer his questions, but they made no sense. "I'm here," she whispered as she moved his fingers along her face.

Hunter looked up, his eyes half closed, his mouth tight with struggle. His hand slowly crossed her cheek and circled to the back of her neck, as though touching her were the medicine he craved. His fingers caressed her flowing black hair as he pulled her face near his own. "My angel, you are so . . ."

Pain clouded his eyes. Perry lowered him to the hay and reached for a scrap of cloth to bathe his feverish face. She wrapped the only blanket around him, softly whispering words of care, though she knew he could no longer hear her.

She sat, chin resting on her knees, watching Hunter for most of the morning and wondering what he'd been about to say. She was lost in thought and didn't react at first to the creaking sound of the old barn door. In her mind the sound seemed faraway, unreal. When the noise did register, she would have bolted to the edge of the loft to welcome Noma, but panic's cold fingers gripped her. It might not be Noma, and the visitor might not be welcome.

Pulling her hat down securely, Perry inched her way to the loft's edge. Lying on her stomach, she slid over the stored ladder and pulled herself close enough to peer down at the intruders below.

Three soldiers milled around beneath her. They poked, inspecting the hay, searching every corner of the dusty floor. Luckily not one bothered to look up. With the ladder removed, the tiny loft rose unnoticed in the late-morning shadows. Perry stared at the three blue uniforms moving beneath. Blue! They were wearing blue. Her mind raced. Somehow, since dawn, her haven had changed hands. She was no longer in Southern territory but in Northern-occupied land.

Perry glanced at Hunter, then back at the men below. He had to have a doctor. If she couldn't tell which side he was on, neither could they. The fact that she'd found him hiding should be strong evidence to any Southerner that he was a Yankee.

Scrambling like a mouse at daybreak, she moved across the loft and shoved a small pouch of valuables between two rafters. Her tiny treasures would be safer in this loft than on her body. Then, with a sigh of resolution, she lifted the ladder and shoved it through the opening before she had time to change her mind. Blue or gray, Hunter needed help.

As the ladder hit the floor with a thud, the three men bolted into a defensive action. They moved swiftly and cautiously, with catlike grace. Each showed the skilled training one obtains only with years of practice and war. They wielded their weapons as if the metal were an extension of their arms. The trio seemed more like animals of prey than men. Perry pulled her hat low and set her mind to enlisting their help.

All three were staring, guns cocked, as Perry slowly descended the ladder. Her own personality vanished like an actor's must as he steps into a role with each curtain's rising. "You dirty Yanks haven't started killin' kids yet, have ya?" Perry's voice was low and rough. "Y'all wouldn't want to kill me, anyway. I've done you blue bellies a favor."

She reached the bottom of the ladder, squared her shoulders in the oversize jacket, and faced the men with all her mustered bravery. She kicked at the dust, as she'd often seen young boys do when they spoke to their elders around the churchyard. Perry didn't look the men in the face for fear one might suspect her gender. She cleared her throat. "Like I say, I done you boys a big favor, and I'm hopin' you'll be grateful."

One man, larger and stockier in build than the other two, moved forward. His large bulk seemed caked with enough layers of dirt to cultivate a crop. Perry curled her nose at his odor, but she forced herself to stand firm. The man grunted and smiled with a mouthful of yellowed teeth. "Well, little Johnny Reb, what have you done to make us all grateful? Did you stay out of the war so we'd have a chance to win?"

His two companions laughed at his joke and lowered their guns. They, too, were dressed in worn, dirty uniforms of faded blue. Both had slim, weasel-like bodies and dull eyes that reflected no love of life. Like men Perry had seen in the South, they'd done too much killing and not enough living.

Perry rubbed her nose on her sleeve and purposefully boasted, "I've been keeping one of your Yankee officers alive all day, sir. Found him nearly dead, I did. Knew he be one of your officers, so I thought somebody might just come lookin' for him. Figured if I kept him alive, there might be somethin' in it for me," she lied.

The huge soldier's eyebrows raised questioningly as he surveyed the room. Perry pointed upward. "He be up there, sir. I figured it was drier. He needs a doctor bad, 'cause he's lost a lot of blood."

The stout soldier motioned for his comrades to watch Perry while he climbed the ladder. Sweat beaded across her forehead as her heart thumped past the minutes. Her hands were in tight fists inside her huge pockets, her right fingers gripping her small knife. If this lie didn't work, maybe she could run for the door. Her heart pounded as she realized what nonsense that would be. A woman with a four-inch knife was no match for three men with guns. If they didn't shoot her, they'd surely discover her to be female in the scuffle. Perry had heard stories of lone women found by soldiers, and these three looked capable of any crime.

A booming voice echoed down the ladder. "The kid's right. There *is* a wounded man up here. Looks half dead." The stout man appeared at the edge of the loft. "Catch, Jack," he yelled, throwing his rifle down at the same time. "I'll carry him down."

"Fine, Luke," the man who caught the gun answered in a hollow, dead tone. Perry studied the two men before her and realized neither cared if Hunter lived or died. They must see men die daily; one more was of no consequence.

Brusquely descending the steps, the huge man returned with Hunter flung over his shoulder. Perry cringed as blood once more stained the outside of Hunter's dressing. She wanted to yell out for the man named Luke to be careful but was afraid her voice would give too much away. As she saw Hunter's pale face she blinked threatening tears away. How she wanted to comfort him. If only she could tell him that soon he would have a real doctor. If only she could brush the blond hair from his face—but there was no time, and three men were watching.

Luke turned to face Perry as he stepped off the ladder. He seemed unhampered by the burden on his shoulder. "Where's his uniform jacket and cap, kid?" he demanded gruffly.

Swallowing hard, she tried to think of an answer. She lowered her head and kicked at the dirt again. "Well, sir . . . well," she said, stammering, stalling for time.

"Well, what?" Luke demanded, moving within a foot of her. His breath fouled the air between them.

Perry tried to make her voice whine as she whispered, "I sold 'em to a Negra woman for food." She closed her eyes, praying she sounded convincing. If Hunter was a Union soldier, he would be safe. If not, maybe he could get doctoring before anyone discovered otherwise.

Perry's eyes flew open as she heard the soldier's laugh. "Enterprising little bastard, ain't he, fellows? Sonny, you may come out of this war rich, after all," Luke said, chuckling. "Well, come along with us, Johnny Reb. If this officer of yours does live, maybe you will get somethin' out of it. In the meantime, reckon we've got enough grub in camp to feed the likes of you a meal. Lookin' at those puny arms, I'd say you haven't been fed in weeks."

The other two men glanced at each other, as though wondering why Luke was bothering with a wounded man and a kid, but they didn't seem to find it worth the effort to comment.

With Hunter still folded over his shoulder, Luke moved out of the old barn that had been Hunter's refuge for two days. Perry followed quietly behind the men. She knew they glanced back often to ensure her progress. It would be foolish to run. Where would she go? How could she leave Hunter now without knowing if he lived or died? Her best plan of action seemed to be to follow along, then backtrack when she wasn't being watched. Luke was a gruff fellow, but he cared enough to carry a wounded man to camp, which was more than she could say for the other two.

Conflicting thoughts battled in Perry's mind as her feet plodded in the oversize boots. Maybe the camp wasn't too far from the barn and she could sneak back tomorrow to see if Noma had returned. Surely Noma would wait in the barn, or would she? Perry pictured Noma arriving, finding both Perry and Hunter missing. She wasn't sure Noma would remember to go to Granddad's old place. As one mile turned into another, then another, Perry planned.

Cannon fire rumbled around her in low moans. At first it seemed as harmless as the thin trails of smoke that drifted slowly into the clouds. Then the smell of impending death blended with the odor of a campfire. Early spring was paled by the winter of war.

Bodies scattered like litter beside the muddy path. They lay as a silent reminder of earlier battles. Blue and gray, with their blood blending together in death. Ragged, ghostlike characters knelt over the remains. Whether they were mourning or robbing, Perry could only wonder. Somehow the vulture or mourner brought the same sadness to her. The sight of the twisted bodies only strengthened her determination to help Hunter. She was a fighter and she'd fight to the death for this man who'd touched her soul with his gray eyes. Somehow for her there was nothing left but this one quest. If she lost it, she'd snap and vanish as quickly as the puffs of smoke from a gun blast.

His bandage was bright red now, and his face the yellowy paleness of lye soap. As she moved closer to check his breathing, they entered a clearing and the temporary Union camp. She looked up and froze for a moment. The

Stars and Stripes flew above them. She hadn't seen a Union flag in years, but after her long walk it was somehow a homecoming sight.

Luke marched past the tents and mess wagon to the back of the clearing. Perry had no choice but to follow. The campgrounds melted into a shady, wooded area. Wounded men lay everywhere under the shade of the trees. Most were asleep or unconscious. A few moaned or cried in pain. Perry's heart ached for them. She could hardly bear to look at the field of suffering surrounding her. Men were bleeding where limbs had been torn from them. The dying were all around, and no one was helping to ease their pain. Perry wondered how Hunter could possibly be better off here than in the loft. At least there he could die in silence, without the stench of rotting flesh around him. He could sleep until death without the cries of another's agony ringing in his ears.

Luke bellowed at a lone man moving among the bodies. "Where's the doctor?" he inquired.

The thin, overworked soldier moved toward them. His limp was pronounced and his slow stride showed exhaustion. His voice was dull and lifeless. "Doc left just before the last battle with a load of wounded. I'm the orderly in charge till he returns." As he spoke, he lifted Hunter's head with only passing interest. "Anyway, this one probably won't make it till Doc gets back. Put him over there with the worst." He pointed with his bony finger.

Perry guessed the orderly was too old to serve as a soldier and wasn't particularly fond of his duties among the wounded. How could they assign such an uncaring man to this job? But then she realized the position would drive a caring man mad.

Luke nodded to the old man and motioned for Perry to follow. She admired the way Luke had carried Hunter all this way, seemingly unmindful of the extra load. His stockiness was due to a wealth of muscles. Though she noticed his two companions had complained several times during the walk and dropped in exhaustion as soon as they'd entered camp, Luke hadn't said a word about his burden.

They moved among the dying men until Luke found an empty spot near the edge of the clearing. He laid Hunter next to a large elm, showing more gentleness than Perry thought him capable of. Turning to Perry, he said, "You can stay with him if you'd like, kid, but don't see much use myself. About dark, if you wander back over to that mess tent, I'll see you get some grub."

As she knelt beside Hunter in the grassy shade Perry nodded and muttered, "Thanks." She watched Luke pick his way through the wounded and disappear into the distance. Tears rolled down her cheeks and fell on the damp grass. What a mess she was in! Perry had never felt so lost. A few days ago Captain Williams had issued orders for her arrest, and now she found herself surrounded by Union troops.

Hunter's bandage was blood-soaked and dirty, his face ghost-white beneath sweaty blond hair.

The old orderly moved toward her, a half-filled bucket of water sloshing at his side and a ledger book under his arm. Setting the bucket at Hunter's head, he opened the ledger. "Kid, you know this soldier's name?" he asked without interest.

Perry nodded as she drew the dipper from the bucket and gently lifted Hunter's head to give him a drink. "Hunter Kirkland is his name. He needs a doctor bad," she blurted in one breath.

The old man scribbled in the ledger book as he shook his head. "Ain't no doctor around, I already told you. I got me hands full with nearly fifty wounded to care for. You'll have to tend him best you can. You're welcome to use any bandages you find over yonder in the wagon." He waved his bony hand in the general direction of a supply wagon. "But as for me, I'm not wastin' my time on any that looks as bad off as him." He rumbled with an ugly chuckle. ''I hear tell there's a Johnny Reb sawbones over among the prisoners, but any man'd be better off dead than to let one of them boys work on him.''

Perry fought off the quick surge of defensiveness that filled her. When she made no reply, the old man closed his ledger and moved away.

For a few minutes Perry sat like stone. Hunter was dying, and she'd done nothing to help him. She was miles away from Noma and not sure she could locate the barn again, even if she did find a way to slip back. She had no friend to turn to, and her only valuables were hidden away in the barn loft.

Hunter's low moaning jerked Perry back from self-pity. His head moved slowly from side to side, each moan tearing at the roots of her heart. With a sense of urgency she ran to the wagon and rummaged for bandages and blankets. To her surprise there seemed an abundant supply. She thought of her brother and how he'd written about the shortage of supplies in Lee's army. This war seemed so unfair.

Minutes later she returned, loaded with a blanket and fresh bandages. For more than an hour she worked to make Hunter more comfortable. First she removed the dusty, blood-soaked wrappings and gently bathed the swollen flesh, now more infected than before. She rubbed the damp rag over his chest and face, hoping to cool him down. Carefully she wrapped his shoulder in clean cloth and covered him with the blanket. Hunter's hand covered her own as she pulled the blanket across his chest. He was now in too much pain to speak or open his eyes, but the feel of her hand within his relaxed him as no medicine could. His breathing slowed and he slept, now much weaker from loss of blood than before he'd been moved.

Perry sat back, exhausted, as the sun melted into the hills to her left. Men silently moved in the twilight, building small fires among the wounded. As more men returned to the camp, Perry noticed several helping the wounded around her.

The last rays of daylight disappeared. Smelling the cook fires, she felt strong hunger pains batting like crows in the pit of her stomach. She decided to follow the smell to the mess tent. Reluctantly she moved away from Hunter toward the campfire in the center of the clearing. Without much effort she found Luke squatting by the fire with a mug in one huge hand. He smiled at her and signaled her to fill a plate. He was the only one who paid any attention to her as she filled a tin with beans and bread. The meal wasn't much to tempt the taste buds, but in her famished state, any food would seem wonderful.

Moving to the edge of the campfire light, Perry devoured the meal like a hungry animal. Wiping her fingers on her pant leg, she smiled at her own behavior. She was a far cry from the Southern lady she'd been raised to be.

A shadow moved between her and the fire. Perry stared up at the black outline in the darkness, every muscle tense as the huge, blackened form moved toward her. She slowly pushed her hand into her pocket and gripped the knife. The mountain of blackness stood above her, only a foot away when he spoke. "Get enough to eat, boy?" Luke inquired, his face entirely hidden in darkness.

Perry let out a long breath and relaxed her grip on the knife. As she nodded, she decided maybe Luke wasn't as evil as she had first marked him to be. After all, he'd carried Hunter to camp. Maybe he'd help again. She ventured a question. "Sir, the orderly says there's a Confederate doctor in camp. Think you could get him to look at my officer? Reckon I'll never get nothin' if he up and dies on me."

Luke chuckled. "Don't see any harm in asking, kid. But are you sure you trust a Confederate doctor not to butcher him up even worse?"

Perry bit her bottom lip before replying softly, "Way I

see it . . . he's gonna die if'n he don't get some doctoring. Might as well take the chance.''

Luke nodded. "All right, kid. I'll check around. You go on back to your soldier and I'll meet with you later. And by the way, if I ever get shot in this damn war, I hope you find me." He disappeared, making her blink as the firelight danced where he'd stood.

She stood and moved unnoticed back toward Hunter. Small fires placed every thirty feet between the wounded did little to add warmth or light. There was no mistaking the foul smell of dying as she walked among these men. The orderly had placed a blanket over each patient. Perry carefully edged toward the huge elm, knowing its shadow lay across Hunter.

Within a few feet from where she had left him, Perry glanced up from the path to observe a man kneeling over Hunter's body. He was a large black man with one arm in a sling. Light played across his face from the fire a few feet away. The firelight also reflected the gold disk he turned in his fingers. Hunter's disk. Perry's emotions exploded as she realized Hunter was about to be robbed of his only possession.

In one animallike spring she threw her body full force into the bulk of the black man, throwing him backward into the brush. Catching him off-guard, Perry plunged her arms and legs into his mass on the ground. She fought wildly. The man groaned in pain and shielded himself with his good arm.

"You filthy Yankee. Stealin' from a dying man. May your soul rot in hell. You scum." Perry spit out the words as she continued to rain blows on him.

Slowly one huge arm encircled her small waist and pulled her down. Using a leg to still her kicks, the black man pinned her to the ground. "Stop. Enough," he said in an educated voice that shocked her.

Perry stopped. He could break her back with a little more pressure.

"I don't know who you are, or what Hunter is to you, but I assure you, I wasn't stealing from him. I was only trying to make sure of his identity in the darkness, without forcing his face to the light. He's my commanding officer and my friend." With this the black man released her legs and pulled her into a sitting position. He studied her quietly for a moment as Perry quickly stuffed loose strands of hair back up under her hat. "The orderly said a dirty kid came into camp with Hunter. Said the boy nursed him all afternoon." The emphasis he put on the word *boy* left no doubt that he knew her secret. "What's your name, boy?" he asked quietly, amusement in his voice.

Perry stared directly into his eyes. She might as well use her own name; it was a boy's, anyway. "I'm Perry, and I found this here Yankee almost dead."

"Pleased to meet you, Perry. I'm Abram Johnson. I thank you for helping my friend. I owe my life many times over to him." Abram spoke as an equal to Hunter, not as a slave.

Suddenly his name registered in her memory. "Abram. That's the name Hunter kept saying, 'Hold on Abram.' You must be the one he keeps calling for."

Abram nodded. She saw kindness in his smile as he looked toward Hunter's sleeping form. "We were separated during a storm. We're balloon surveyors. We were up, just over into Confederate territory, when the storm broke. The cable holding us snapped, then the wire whipped into us mightily and tore Hunter's shoulder wide open. I was thrown out and Hunter tried to pull me back in the basket, but with his shoulder hurt, it's a wonder he held himself in. I landed safe enough in a muddy field, but Hunter drifted another few miles with our balloon, the *Northern Star*. I'd about given up hope he was alive."

Both were silent for a moment as understanding passed between them. Both knew the other desperately wanted Hunter to live. Abram had been impressed by the small woman's fire as she'd fought for Hunter, and Perry could almost see the intensity of Abram's feelings toward his friend.

Abram offered his hand. "Thank you for helping Hunter. Let me know if I can return the favor."

Raising her hand slowly, she looked past Abram and noticed Luke's form moving toward them. Quickly she leaned close to Abram and whispered, "There's the soldier who found us and brought us here. I sent him after a doctor in the prisoner camp."

Both turned to watch Luke's approach. Perry's tears reflected the firelight in the warm brown depths of her eyes. Luke was alone! She knew without asking that no doctor was coming. Her hope for Hunter dimmed. Abram, watching her out of the corner of his eye, saw the pain she felt.

"You want Hunter to live very badly, don't you?" Abram whispered.

Before Perry could answer, Luke waved toward them. Abram stood to address him. "The kid said you were bringing a doctor."

Luke frowned. "Wouldn't come, said he had all he could handle with what we shot up of his men."

Perry's heart sank as he continued, "Don't know as it would do any good to try and push him. Might end your friend's sufferin' earlier. Besides, the redheaded bastard hates Yankees. He took great delight in tellin' me where to go for just suggestin' he leave his men and come doctor one of us."

Perry's heart quickened for a moment. The doctor was redheaded. Could her brother be the Confederate doctor Luke had talked with? She hadn't seen Andrew for so long, but she'd heard he was near. Could he be this close?

"Sorry about him, boy." Luke shook his head and moved away.

Perry stepped forward, timidly reaching to touch Luke's arm. "Did ya get the doctor's name, sir?"

"Nope, didn't see it mattered none, anyway," Luke replied with a wave of his mighty hand.

As soon as Luke was out of sight, Perry turned to Abram, her face filled with hope. "I may know the doctor. Abram, he'd come if he knew I was here. You've got to get to him and ask him to help." Perry realized how desperate she sounded to this huge black man. All Perry knew of Abram was that he called Hunter his friend. Her only prayer lay in a hope that he cared a great deal about Hunter's life.

Abram backed off, skeptical of her plot. "First I need a few answers before I get in league with the likes of you. You're no boy, but I guess I can understand why you'd want to hide that. Also, your speech goes from being illiterate to refined. You give me some answers and I'll decide whether to trust you."

Perry plopped in an unladylike manner beside Hunter's sleeping form and waited for Abram to join her. She had no choice but to trust Abram. He knew too much already, so why not?

Softly she began her story of the past three days. She described to him how she had burned her fields to keep the Yankees from getting her crops. In so doing, she'd marked herself for hanging as a traitor. When she told of walking for a day and night before finding the barn and discovering Hunter, Perry omitted Noma from her story. She might have to trust this man, but Noma could remain unknown. In this small way Perry felt she was protecting Noma. She ended by telling him the redheaded doctor might be her brother, Andrew.

Unshed tears floated in her brown eyes as she whispered, "You have to swear to tell no one who I am or that I'm a woman. If the doctor is Andrew, I know he'll come when he finds out I'm here."

Both were silent for several minutes before Abram spoke. "I'll keep your secret. Don't want to do you any more harm than this war has already done you. Appears to me you're in need of a friend, and I do owe you something. But for God's sake, don't go jumping on anyone else; one feel of you gives you away as a girl.''

Perry blushed as Abram continued. "I'll go have a talk with the doctor, and if he's your brother, maybe I can convince him to take a look at Hunter." With this resolution Abram stood and dusted his blue uniform. "Don't know what Captain Williams would have to say about this if he got wind of it."

Perry's heart turned to ice inside her breast. "Captain Williams?"

Abram nodded. "He's the officer here, though he spends most of his time chasing traitors." His last words were a whisper as he looked into Perry's frightened face. "He's the one after you, isn't he?"

There was no need for Perry to answer. Abram was making a statement, not asking a question.

"Stay with Hunter, boy." Again he placed the emphasis on the word *boy*. "We'll see about Hunter, then worry about getting you out of this place fast. I don't want to think what Captain Williams would do if he caught you here." Abram walked away, shaking his head.

Perry tried to curl into the darkness behind Hunter. Every muscle in her body was tense, ready to run. Somehow she'd walked right into Williams's hands. He'd never seen her, and she wasn't sure she'd know him if he walked up. All she knew about him was from what she'd heard, and it was all bad. She'd been told he was handsome enough, except for a small scar over one eye and a love for hanging Southerners.

The evening grew cooler as the hours passed. She spread out on the ground a foot from Hunter, longing for the privacy they'd had in the loft. Tired and frightened, she longed to move nearer and feel Hunter's touch along her flesh. As her eyelids grew heavy, Perry placed a protective arm over Hunter's undamaged shoulder.

Finally sleep covered her, and she became oblivious to everything around her. She no longer heard the moans of the wounded or the soft hoof falls of horses against the muddy ground as the camp's officers arrived.

Chapter 3

Fires were burning low, in need of tending, as Perry snuggled deep into her blanket. Voices mumbled softly in the darkness, drawing her from sleep. Opening her eyes slowly, she saw three blurred figures standing above her. One she recognized as Abram's dark bulk. As her eyes adjusted, she realized that the second figure was a Union officer, impeccably dressed in his blue uniform. The officer shouted at Abram while a third man waited a few feet away. He was a shabbily dressed Confederate soldier, clutching a worn bag under his arm. As he turned toward her Perry caught her breath in sudden recognition of her brother, Andrew.

He seemed much older and thinner than he'd been a year ago. His hair was unkempt and badly in need of trimming. A dark red mass of beard covered his face. Her first instinct was to leap up and run into his arms, but before she could respond, he moved the short distance between them and gripped her shoulder.

In a demanding and authoritative voice he asked, "Are you the boy who found this wounded man?"

Her senses jumped alive both at Andrew's question and from the pain of his hand digging into her shoulder. Did he still think her a child to be reminded of the danger she faced?

Fighting for control, she pierced the darkness to see his
face. The warm and loving eyes of her older brother
pleaded with her to remain silent. Her anger cooled. His
eyes looked so tired. The war had destroyed the hopes and
dreams of a young man. He'd had only enough time for
school before the war. The once bright spark within him
had faded to dull shades of indifferent gray. Andrew's soul
was as ragged and muted as his clothes.

Not trusting her voice, Perry nodded her head in answer
to his question. He relaxed his grip on her shoulder. She
stood slowly, pulling her hat low to hide any loose strands
of hair and let her shoulders slouch to ensure that the baggy
clothes concealed her breasts. The officer's hand unconsciously traveled to his holstered gun handle in a silent
reminder to both Andrew and Perry. She watched him
with growing fear. He was a handsome man, but there
was something cold, even heartless, about him. Then she
saw it: the scar over his left eye. Terror gripped her. The
officer not three feet from her was Captain Wade Williams.

He knelt beside Hunter. "If this is Captain Kirkland,
we'd better get him fixed up fast or Professor Lowe will
see there's hell to pay." He jerked away Hunter's blanket
and tried to force his face toward the campfire light.

Wade's voice was cold and aloof as he stood, not bothering to replace the blanket over Hunter. As if Andrew
were deaf, the officer said, "Abram, tell the doctor I agree
to provide extra supplies to the prisoners in exchange. I
want no part in this directly. It's your idea to have this so-
called doctor help Hunter. If Hunter dies, I'll see the authorities are informed of your plan. If he lives, I want no
one in camp to know we made a deal with the filthy likes
of this Confederate."

Perry's hands balled into fists within the folds of her
pockets. How could Andrew allow this man to talk to him
so degradingly? She glanced at her brother and realized
he had no choice. What could be gained by a fight here

and now? She vowed to live in order to repay Wade Williams's insult.

Abram spat his reply out, as though even he found talking with the officer distasteful. "I understand, Captain Williams. I've always understood you."

She found his reply much to Abram's credit. She both liked and trusted this huge mountain of a man and wondered what Hunter must be like to have such a man as Abram for a friend. An educated black man was a rare individual. His voice as well as his proud postures told all that he considered himself an equal.

The officer shot orders in rapid fire as if to brush away Abram's insult. He ended with "Let's be done with this. I have more important matters waiting."

Minutes later Perry saw the pain in the huge black man's eyes as he lifted Hunter in his arms. His efforts were costing him dearly as he strained already injured muscles, but he allowed no other to carry his friend. Abram took Hunter across the campground, with Captain Williams and Andrew leading the way. Perry followed close behind. They marched to an isolated area a few hundred feet from the edge of the main camp. Following an overgrown path through the trees, Abram swayed, avoiding branches as he rocked Hunter in his arms. The moon appeared for a few minutes, shedding silvery light upon the trees, which hung heavy with growth and rain. Nature's beauty seemed shrouded in evil tonight.

The path halted abruptly before a moonlit clearing. In the center of the clearing awaited a burned-out hull of a farmhouse. Where once a family had lived, now only charred walls stood. The small band waded through thick brush toward the structure. The forest was fighting to reclaim this small spot, and winning.

Perry watched Abram fold his huge bulk and Hunter's limp body through the aging door frame. A table with clean sheets was waiting in the center of the roofless room. Lanterns hung from each corner, casting a collision of shadows on the walls. From the opening Perry saw Abram gently place Hunter on the table. A drama unfolded as her eyes adjusted to the light. A sense of secrecy enveloped this meeting. She had the feeling that no one other than those present knew of this late-night call from the doctor.

Officer Williams paced, one hand absently patting the handle of his revolver.

Andrew passed Perry. For a moment, in the door frame, he faced his little sister. "Your eyes look huge with the lamplight dancing in them," he whispered. "You seem to care for this man. I'll do the best I can to save his life, but only because of you. I wish I could tell you all will be fine, but I no longer believe it myself." Without another word he moved to the table and opened his bag.

She sank into the damp grass beside the smoke-blackened stone. She melted into the shadows, constantly aware of Williams's presence and the danger he presented. The shadowy figures danced along the inside walls as Andrew and Abram worked over Hunter's body. After what seemed an eternity, the shadows began to blur and Perry curled up in the cold grass, a prayer for Hunter's life on her lips.

She felt warm and dreamy as she heard someone saying her name. Opening her eyes, she saw Andrew's hand stretching toward her. She rose to greet him as an army blanket fell from around her shoulders.

Suddenly Andrew was pulling her behind the ruins and into the thick wooded area just beyond. He glanced around until satisfied they were alone, then dropped low in the brush.

Perry knelt to hear him whisper, "Perry, we only have a few minutes. Abram is standing watch for us." His eyes were filled with concern. "I heard about what you did to the fields. You've got to get out of here fast. Williams has half his men looking for you."

"Noma and I were trying to get to Granddad's old place when I was caught behind the lines."

"Where's Noma?"

The anger in his voice surprised her. "I don't know," she whispered.

Andrew rubbed his red beard. "If Williams finds her, it won't take him long to figure out where you are. I wouldn't hold much hope in Noma keeping a secret."

"Of course she will." Perry only wished her words were spoken from her head and not her heart.

Her brother sighed. "I've seen strong men break in a blink."

She wouldn't give thought to his doubts about Noma. She'd face the problem at hand. "Did you help Hunter?"

Andrew studied his sister, her face revealing she already cared for this Yankee. Gently he whispered, "I did the best I could. He's in bad shape. Don't know who he is, but several people are awful interested in him staying alive. He's got one hell of a will to live. I'll say that for the blue leg." Andrew ran an exhausted hand through his shaggy hair. "I worked most of the night with that black giant beside me. Got the feeling he'd have snapped me in two if I'd failed. He did some fast talkin' to get me to come. We agreed it might look suspicious unless I got something for my work. Abram got the captain to agree to give me plenty of medical supplies. It's just a hunch, but I think you were right to trust Abram. Maybe Hunter is worth saving if he's got a friend as loyal as Abram."

Andrew paused, his face full of sadness. "Perry, I've got to get back to my men, but I made Abram swear to see you somewhere safe. This war has got to end soon; it can't last much longer. I'll come for you when it's over and we'll go home."

Perry opened her mouth to tell him that more than Ravenwood's land had burned, but the urgency of their time together overwhelmed her. Andrew swept her up in a desperate hug, grabbing one moment of life. Perry longed to stay in the protection of his arms. If only he could make all the sadness go away, as he used to do when she was a child. Andrew had always been more of a father to her than a brother. His embrace, though comforting, also reminded her of her loneliness. The man before her was far removed from the laughing big brother who had left for war, but he was her only family.

She stiffened as she heard movement among the leaves and knew they were no longer alone. Abram stepped from the morning shadows.

"Perry, Abram promised," Andrew whispered, more to himself than to her. "He promised to see you safe. I've got to get back to my men. Remember, when this ends, I'll come for you at Granddad's place."

"I'm not even sure the old man is still alive. We haven't heard from him except once."

Andrew tried to sound reassuring. "He's still alive or we'd have heard. Dad used to say the old guy was meaner than a two-headed rattlesnake." Andrew kissed her forehead. "You'll handle him, little sister."

Before Perry could express any of her fears, Andrew was past her, moving toward Abram. The last band that tied her to Ravenwood was stretching and breaking as Andrew disappeared into the woods. She was alone.

Hunter seemed to be resting quietly, his shoulder expertly bandaged now. His blond hair shone in the morning sun. To Perry's relief Captain Williams had disappeared. She hoped never to see him again. Just the memory of him hung like a bad odor in the air.

She pushed her own problems aside and tried to help Abram give Hunter a shave. Clean-shaven, he looked younger. His fever was low and his color seemed a touch better. Having completed all her tasks, Perry slid into a corner of the wall and relaxed. Abram moved in a slow, easy pace around Hunter, favoring his left arm as he worked. Abram was injured, but he'd made light of her concern. He merely said he'd twisted the muscle when he fell from the balloon.

Hunter's low moan brought both Abram and Perry to his side. His right hand reached up to pull at the bandages around his shoulder, as though he wanted to pull away the pain. Perry grabbed at his waving arm with both hands to stop him. Abram spoke to his friend in a low, steady voice. "Ease up. Hunter, you're all right. Just rest easy."

Hunter's body relaxed. Slowly his eyes opened and focused on Abram. Hunter's lips moved, trying to form words. A smile touched them and he whispered, "Abram, you're alive." Each word seemed an effort.

"Why, sure, takes more than one little fall from the sky to kill me," Abram said with a laugh. "You know, I figured you were a goner for sure. Didn't anybody ever explain to you that you can't catch a five-hundred-foot grounding wire with your shoulder?"

Perry watched a mischievous sparkle in Hunter's gray eyes. Slowly he whispered, "Well, once I let you out, someone had to stay with the balloon." Both men laughed.

Hunter shook his head. "That was one storm! I should have known better than to try to fly up into it. Of course, I don't remember having much of a choice. Our beloved Captain Williams was making it pretty plain we would go up or be shot as deserters."

The disgust in Hunter's voice as he brought up Captain Williams's name was evident to Perry. Abram glanced her way, as though suddenly remembering her existence. He sobered and said, "Captain Kirkland, this boy saved your life. Near as I can tell, I think you owe him thanks."

Hunter looked at Perry. For an instant bewilderment clouded his face. Then he smiled warmly and glanced at his arm, which Perry was still holding. "Thanks, boy." His voice was friendly and Perry found it thrilling.

"I promise not to hurt myself. You can let go," Hunter laughed.

Self-consciously Perry released his arm and jumped back. She found it hard to think rationally with Hunter's eyes fascinating her so. They seemed to be drawing her like a magnet to him.

"Don't jump, boy, I'm in no condition to hurt you, and I'm not in the habit of hitting someone who saved my life." Hunter studied her. "What's your name?"

She cleared her throat in panic. She had to control her voice enough to sound like a boy. "Perry," she whispered.

"Well, Perry," he continued, "I appreciate what you've done, and I hope I can repay the favor someday."

She liked the way her name sounded in his Northern accent. His smile reflected a reckless side of him, yet his eyes told of a man who could be very caring. This man was dangerous when awake, perhaps more so than Captain Williams. For Hunter's kindness could be disarming and as deadly as Wade's revolver if she wasn't careful.

Abram interrupted her thoughts. "Seems we can repay the favor right now, Hunter. We've got to get this Confederate kid back across the front line."

"What?" Hunter glanced from Abram to Perry.

"Way I see it," Abram continued, "it's the least we can do. The kid crossed lines taking care of you, with you half dead. Even jumped me when he thought I was going to steal your crest last night."

"Is that true, boy?" The look of puzzlement returned briefly to his face.

Perry lowered her eyes and answered, "Well, I figured you had enough problems without somebody stealing from you." Frustration shook her small frame. Why was she allowing this man to affect her so? She was no child to be dumbfounded by a man's gaze. Things far more important than the color of a soldier's eyes were at stake.

"Come here, kid." Hunter reached with his left hand and awkwardly removed the necklace from around his neck. "It took some guts for a half-pint like you to tackle a mountain like Abram." He dropped the chain into Perry's hand. "Take it. It's yours. Not as payment, but as a promise. If ever you need a favor, use this to remind me of the great debt I owe you. No matter what happens, you'll always know I owe you one." Hunter leaned back and drifted into sleep, exhausted by his short conversation.

Abram smiled at her and nodded, giving his seal of approval to Hunter's actions. He turned and began moving toward the door, calling back over his shoulder, "I'll get lunch, you stay with him, boy."

Moving over to a log that served as the only furnishing among the ruins, Perry couldn't stop staring at the gold in her hand. The precious metal caught the sunlight, as bright and shining as the promise it stood for. She hung the chain around her neck, and the gold pressed hotly between her breasts, warming her soul with its presence. Somehow she felt protected by this small round disk.

Hunter slept until the shadows were long into evening. Abram managed to get him to eat a few bites, but Hunter kept requesting more and more water. Perry helped Abram change the bandage and noticed less bleeding than before. While working, she could feel Hunter's eyes watching her, studying her, analyzing each of her movements. She wondered how long, at close range, she could maintain her disguise. She must keep her head low so the old hat would obstruct Hunter's view of her face. Could he be remembering the woman who held him in the loft? Did he think his mind had played a trick on him?

After dark Captain Williams appeared. His uniform was crisp and new, in sharp contrast to the attire of the men he commanded. As he stepped within the walls he instantly began pacing like a caged animal. He was even more fidgety than he'd been the night before. He greeted Hunter and Abram, yet ignored Perry completely. Perry thought she saw a glimpse of disappointment in his face when he noticed Hunter's improvement. Though he was nice-looking, Perry saw a coldness in his gaze, a look of evil, as though the devil walked beside him.

He addressed Hunter. "We must talk. You have to get

to Philadelphia as soon as possible. Professor Lowe wants you back at headquarters. Can you move out tonight?''

"No, Captain Williams," Abram interjected. "It's too soon to move him. We'd be risking Hunter's life."

Captain Williams gave Abram a look of disdain. "There are doctors in Philadelphia."

Abram glanced at Hunter for support.

Hunter touched Abram's arm. "I have to get to Professor Lowe quickly, Abram. Wade, find me some clothes." Captain Williams bristled at the order, but Hunter, ignoring him, continued. "Is there any chance of repairing the balloon? Could we fly?"

"No, not by tomorrow. But I've arranged a buckboard that can transport you," Wade replied. "I'll send the balloon as soon as we can get it loaded and shipped by train." Then, to Perry's shock, he headed to the door and added, "Good-bye, Cousin."

Just before he left, Captain Williams glanced at Perry. "Can the kid be trusted?" he snapped. "I can keep him in with the prisoners till you're safely away."

"No!" Abram and Hunter responded in unison. "Perry goes with us," Hunter said in a tone that left no room for argument.

Frustration crossed Captain Williams's face before he shrugged, mumbling, "Balloons . . . kids . . . hell of a bother in war." Then to the men he said, "I'll have the wagon ready in one hour." Williams left no time for discussion as he disappeared into the darkness outside the threshold.

Hunter glanced first at Perry, then at Abram, and said, "One hour and we move."

Abram nodded, resigning himself to the trip, and started collecting what they would need.

Perry tried to sit calmly, hiding her overwhelming curiosity. Wade Williams's feathers certainly ruffled when he was in Hunter's presence. What lay between Hunter and

Wade, other than a shared bloodline? Perhaps in time she would know. Right now she had to adjust to the fact that in one hour she would be on her way farther north—with two Yankees.

Chapter 4

The night was foggy and moonless. The three moved out of the Union camp onto a road that faded to invisibility only inches ahead of them. Abram sat alone on the bench seat, straining every muscle, alert to any danger that might spring out of the darkness. Hunter lay cradled among blankets and supplies, a new Union jacket folded over him. Perry rested against the sideboard as she sat curled up in the back of the wagon, her eyes fixed on Hunter. She could see the pain in his face each time the wagon swayed from side to side and wondered if he would survive yet another move.

Captain Williams had made certain everything was packed and ready by the time Abram had dressed and carried Hunter the few hundred feet from the ruins to the wagon. The captain seemed to be pushing the mismatched threesome out of the camp. Yet at the same time he carefully saw to every detail. Perry wondered what lay behind the curt captain's attitude and behavior.

Now, with the jostle of the wagon, Hunter's eyes grew heavy and he whispered, "Boy, better hang on. Hate for you to fall out when we hit a bump." Then all she heard was his rhythmic breathing as he slept.

Cuddling among the supplies for warmth, she longed for home. The fighting seemed endless. She'd been only a child when it had erupted, yet the war had hastened her steps into adulthood. When Andrew left, Perry willingly assumed more responsibility at Ravenwood. By the time her father died, she was able to run the large plantation effectively by herself. Now, riding in a wagon with two men she'd only known a few days, she felt far from home and somehow like a child again . . . as if she no longer had any control over her life.

Perry's thoughts drifted to her grandfather. She remembered very little about him. Though he came to Ravenwood before the war, she'd never been invited to visit him. The old man had always seemed saddened in Perry's presence. She was a painful reminder of his only daughter, who died giving birth to Perry. Andrew jokingly referred to him as "our crazy old grandpa," but she'd seen a lifetime of heartbreak in the wrinkles of his face. If he did behave a bit oddly, perhaps it was because the pain of life had been too great for him.

Now he was Perry's only living kin except Andrew. He was her one hope of refuge. She wondered how she would be received when she turned up penniless on his doorstep. Times were hard, but he was her grandfather. Surely he would take her in. If he was dead, she'd find some way to stay at his home until Andrew found her.

Perry turned her worried eyes skyward in desperation. The gold disk Hunter had given her moved between her breasts, and she felt oddly comforted by its presence. She wrapped her arms around her knees and fell asleep as the wagon rolled northward at a slow clip.

Just after dawn, Abram drew the horses to a halt in front of a small water crossing. Walking around to the back of the wagon, he offered Perry a hand down. "We'll rest the horses a few hours and I'll fix some breakfast." Then, as if reading her mind, he added, "You can probably find a spot to wash up over yonder."

Smiling warmly, Perry rubbed her sleepy eyes and nodded her approval at his suggestion. It had been days since she had washed properly. As she stretched toward the warming sun Perry's spirits lightened.

Before leaving, she turned to check Hunter. He lay sleeping peacefully among the blankets, his disorderly blond hair covering half of his tan face. She pictured what he would look like in his uniform. He was the most handsome man she'd ever seen—even now as he lay dangerously near death. He reminded her of a sleeping prince in a fairy tale. Never could she picture him as a soldier killing others.

"He's all right. Sleep's the best thing for him," Abram said, as if reading her thoughts. "I'll keep an eye on him. You run along."

Grabbing a towel and washcloth from a stash of supplies, she disappeared around the first bend in the shallow stream. She walked along the grassy bank, enjoying the peaceful surroundings. The air smelled clean and new. The stream looked untouched by man and beckoned invitingly. Here there was no war, no killing, no dying. She passed between large rocks that were strewn amid the grass, as if God had deliberately tried to confuse the stream in its path to the sea. Between two such rocks, Perry nestled.

Throwing her hat off, she lay in the velvety grass, stretching her muscles after her long, cramped ride. The soft earth felt wonderful against her back. She watched the white clouds above her as they drifted to nowhere. Languidly she rose and removed her coat, shirt, and boots. The rush of the water called to her and she hastily ripped off her pants, leaving only her light camisole to cover her.

As she pranced knee-deep in the water, a shot rang out from the direction of the wagon, rattling the quiet air and filling Perry with dread. She splashed toward the bank, all thoughts of the bath forgotten, rolled onto the grassy bank, and pulled on the rough pants. Running, she buttoned her shirt and shoved her hair into the hat.

Could it be that Abram had been shooting game? Or

was the sound a signal of approaching danger? Fear was
a parasite within her eating away all the peace she'd felt
only moments before.

Just before turning the last bend, Perry slowed to ensure
that her hat completely camouflaged her hair. She froze in
mid-stride as unfamiliar voices drifted through the brush.

Perry trod silently, crouching beside the brush, strain-
ing her eyes to see between the leaves.

Two strangers were with Hunter and Abram. One was
unhitching the team while his companion held a rifle point-
blank at Hunter's chest. Their dress told Perry they were
probably two of the thousands of men who had grown sick
of fighting and deserted. They were men without a cause,
without a country. Their dirty blue uniforms were stained
with the blood of others and the dust of a hundred miles
of marching.

Searching the small camp for Abram, she finally spotted
his legs on the far side of the wagon. The men had tied
him to the wagon wheel. Judging from the fresh blood on
both deserters' faces, Abram hadn't been bound without a
fight.

The deserter nearest Hunter pushed the rifle barrel into
Hunter's gut and said, ''Now, Captain, 'pears you're bein'
sensible. We ain't meanin' to hurt you or your man, but
we're powerful tired of walkin' and thought we'd borrow
your horses.'' He flashed a smile at his partner, who was
approaching with both horses. ''This blackie of yours must
think somethin' of you. Only thing that kept him from
breakin' both of us in half was my pokin' this gun in your
gut. So I suppose you'll return the favor and sit real still
while we go through your supplies.''

She could only see the back of Hunter's head, yet she
noticed he held it high.

''Now, since you were real neighborly in offerin' us a
ride when we strolled up,'' the deserter continued, ''Tim
and me's gonna leave you some grub and the wagon. Not

that it'll do you much good without horses. At least you got your life.''

Abram's low voice cut the air. ''Unless you leave us one horse, the captain won't live. He's been hurt bad.''

Hunter's voice was ice cold. ''Forget it, Abram. They'll not reason, and we'll not ask anything from them.''

Perry heard no fear or panic in Hunter's voice, only a deadly calculated calm. She could tell from his tone that he was a man who set his standards and would never beg. Even though he was very near death, he wouldn't lower himself to plead with these men.

The stranger continued, ''How right you are about that, Captain. Why should we ride double? We're in a bit of a hurry. Might as well be shot for stealing two horses as one.'' Both robbers laughed.

Perry listened to their talk as she lowered to her stomach and crawled to the back of the wagon. She had to do something immediately or they would be stranded. She had to reach the wagon and slide under. Her only hope was to get to Abram.

As Perry crawled forward, rocks scraped her arms and legs through her rough clothes. The sun was at her back, so it would be in the strangers' eyes should they chance to look in her direction. Without a sound Perry rolled onto the road and slid under the wagon. Inching her way, she crept toward Abram's back as it rested against the wheel.

The two intruders were discussing what they should take. She could see their legs only a few feet away as she slid behind Abram's bulk. Perry touched his shoulder softly to indicate her presence. She felt his muscles tense, yet he made no move. Frantically she examined the rope, but all the knots were tied out of her reach. She rummaged in her pockets for her knife.

Finding her weapon, Perry's fingers molded around its smooth handle as she removed it from her baggy pocket. Jerking the knife from its concealment, she rapidly opened it and applied the small sharp blade to the thick rope. The two men were mounting their stolen horses and panic seized her. Frantic now at her labor, she placed her hand firmly behind the rope to steady her work. With all her strength she slid the silver blade back and forth across the coarse rope.

Suddenly the knife slashed free through the rope and dug into Perry's palm. A crimson line formed across her hand as she heard Abram jerk free. Relief and pain struck her as one. Tears clouded her vision, making the scene above her more a dream than reality.

Abram bounded in smooth pantherlike strides toward both men. They were busy loading the horses down with the stolen provisions and were unprepared to face an attack. Abram managed to land a heavy blow upon each before either could react. The two thin soldiers were no match for this angry mountain of muscle. He knocked the rifle from one intruder's arms and sent it crashing among the rocks.

Perry cradled her hand to her chest and slowly crawled from beneath the wagon. She stood watching as Abram slammed his fist into one deserter's face, sending him flying backward into unconsciousness. Turning, Abram began his thunderous assault upon the other.

Blood spilled from the soldier's mouth as Hunter's voice interrupted the attack. "Enough, Abram, enough," he said calmly.

Without even a glance back, Abram dropped the deserter's body in the dirt. Perry turned to Hunter, amazed at his control over Abram. He hadn't commanded, only requested. Few words seemed necessary between these two men. Wide-eyed, with tears dribbling down both cheeks, she looked into Hunter's gray eyes. She saw again the puzzlement in his face she'd seen when he regained consciousness back at camp. He was searching for something or someone. He looked deep into her eyes, as if looking for a piece of a puzzle.

Finally he glanced down at her bloody hand. For an

instant Perry watched sorrow cross his face, as though he could feel her pain as well as his own. "My God, boy, what happened to your hand? Abram, get a bandage."

Perry stared at Hunter as he frowned at her bloody hand. She marveled how only moments before, when he'd faced two desperate men, his voice was without emotion; however, anger and concern echoed now in his words. Caring had replaced courage in a blink of his gray eyes.

Within seconds Abram was at her side, examining the knife cut. He lifted Perry effortlessly into the wagon beside Hunter so the captain could examine her hand.

"Your palm's as soft as a girl's." Hunter laughed as he supervised the bandaging.

Abram grunted at Hunter's remark but said nothing. The cut wasn't deep, and soon the pain subsided as Hunter talked to her. He seemed to be rambling to keep her mind busy while Abram cleaned the blood away.

"Boy, have you ever seen one of our balloons?" Hunter asked.

Perry shook her head. She'd read about the North using balloons to observe battles but had never seen one.

"The only thing greater than watching them drift into the sky is being in one as it lifts. I first saw one six years ago in the summer of '59. Abram and I traveled over two weeks to watch Professor Wise launch his balloon, *Atlantic*. It beat anything I'd ever seen. It was a huge balloon, bordered on either side by smaller ones, lifting a gondola with four men inside. Just think, kid, it covered over eight hundred miles in less than twenty hours.

"Old Professor Wise plans to cross the Atlantic soon, if Lowe doesn't beat him. When the war's over, I bet Lowe tries again." Hunter was speaking half to himself as he watched Abram wrap Perry's hand.

Perry raised her head. She remembered hearing the name Lowe before. Captain Williams had said something about a Professor Lowe needing Hunter back fast. She'd known by the tone of Williams's voice that Professor Lowe must be someone important. "Who is this crazy man, Lowe, who wants to cross the ocean in a bubble?" she asked, hoping to encourage Hunter, for his face was already tight with fatigue.

"I wouldn't call the chief of our Army's aeronautical division a crazy man. He's a genius. He put a telegraph up in a balloon in '61. He attached it to a cable holding the balloon. We can send information down from five thousand feet up."

Abram said, "It was a telegraph cable that almost got us killed a few days ago."

Hunter laughed, forgetting his own pain for a moment. "Maybe so, but it's not usually dangerous. Men have been going up in balloons for almost a hundred years now. I've heard Marie Antoinette watched the first test flight in 1783."

Perry was fascinated by Hunter's story as he told of early ballooning. He examined Abram's work on her hand while he talked. She saw that tiny lines wrinkled the corners of his eyes.

"Fine job, Abram. You may have missed your calling. Instead of floating around with me, maybe you should have tried doctorin'." Hunter's voice was light as he teased Abram.

Abram agreed. "I'd have had plenty of patients traveling with you."

Hunter smiled at his old friend. "We'd better get the horses hitched up before our friends wake up." Then, to Perry, he added softly, "Why don't you strip that shirt off and wash the blood out of it before we start moving."

Hunter leaned back, and within seconds his eyes closed in sleep, as though his few sentences had exhausted all his energy. Perry watched him curiously, studying the lines of his face for any signs of laughter. Could he have suspected her gender? Perry smiled to herself, thinking of the shock Hunter would have if she did remove her shirt. She wondered if the sight of her bare chest would stir his blood, as his had warmed hers. It was an outrageous thought, for he was a Union officer and she was wanted for treason. Yet she couldn't stop watching him. His facial muscles were relaxed, his lips slightly open, giving his mouth a slight pouting expression. His strong character showed even in the lines of his sleeping face.

Perry climbed carefully out of the wagon, nursing her bandaged hand. She moved to Abram and the horses, watching idly as he hitched the team. She knew the blood would remain on her shirt, for she had no intention of undressing. Glancing at the two unconscious bodies in the dirt, she asked, "What about them?"

"Oh, they'll come around in a few hours. They'll be mighty sore when they do." Abram chuckled to himself. "Thanks for cutting me free, boy." Again emphasizing *boy*, as though it were a private joke he found greatly amusing. "I may have to teach you something about using knives."

The knife! Perry whirled and ran to the wagon. Bending down, she retrieved her pearl-handled treasure from the dust where she had slung it. Very carefully she bent the blade into its case, using only her good hand and her leg as a brace. Caressing the knife gently, she slid it into her pocket. She prayed she wouldn't have to use it again, but somehow the hope seemed lean as she moved deeper and deeper behind Union lines.

Chapter 5

As Hunter's party traveled north, the early spring air grew cool with evening and a mournful, silent fog crept around them. Abram finally turned the horses toward a cluster of trees in the distance. "There's a plantation up the road where we might get that hand doctored properly. Maybe we could even spend the night there. Looks like we're in for a storm."

Perry didn't comment. Every bone in her body ached from bumping around in the wagon. She watched the last bit of watery yellow light pass from the horizon and hoped she could stay awake long enough to find a corner to curl into for the night. The brooding sky blended with her mood. She felt that if the wagon hit another bump, her weary bones would snap in two.

They passed through the gates of the large plantation. The grounds were massive but the house looked old and in need of repair, even from a distance. A brick kitchen and one ancient barn huddled behind the dilapidated main house. It looked as though someone were slowly removing the walls and fences for firewood.

Abram maneuvered the wagon with tireless skill. "During the first part of the war hundreds of troops were housed here. Before we were soldiers, Hunter and I came over to watch a balloon ascent. Now it looks like no one's around.''

Abram slowed beside the deteriorating back steps. A soldier, not out of his teens, bounded from the kitchen. He struggled awkwardly, trying to put his coat on and hold his rifle at the same time. "Who goes there?" he yelled as his rifle twirled like a baton and fell in the dirt before him.

"Captain Hunter Kirkland and party," Abram answered formally with no hint of laughter in his tone. "We need a doctor."

The soldier picked up his gun and straightened to a formal stance. The tiny smile on his pimply face told of his thanks for Abram's kind disregard of his clumsiness. "Don't have no doctor, but you're welcome to come in. Me and the boys were left behind last week to guard this place, and we haven't seen more'n a jackrabbit. If you got news, we'd be glad to share our grub."

Abram climbed down from the wagon. "Have you a dry bed for the captain? He needs to be out of this damp weather."

"Beds are all full. We're sleeping four to a room upstairs. The only fireplaces that work are downstairs. Those rooms are reserved for officers' meetings, but we ain't got any here now." The guard looked at Hunter. Perry could see by the curiosity in the boy's eyes that he'd never seen the pain of battle. "There's a formal dining room. Reckon we could put a mattress over the table for a night. Ain't no bigwigs here to eat off it." The soldier seemed fascinated by the red spot on Hunter's bandage. "We leave a guard on duty in the hall, so you don't need to worry about some deserter killin' him in his sleep. We can build a fire big enough to warm his bones."

Abram nodded. "Thanks for your kindness. I'll sleep with the horses in the barn. We've already had them almost stolen once. I'm not giving anyone another chance. Do you have a warm place for the boy?'' He pointed at Perry. ''He's been feeling poorly lately.''

The guard glanced at Perry. ''Reckon he could sleep in the kitchen. There's a cook and her grandson in there now, but she goes to her place at night.''

Perry was amazed at how fast they settled inside. In a little over an hour Hunter was resting in his bed on a huge formal dining table, and Abram disappeared into the barn for his first sleep in two days.

She helped all she could, then took a blanket from the wagon and headed for a corner in the kitchen. The old cook and a boy of about seven were banking the fire for the night when she opened the kitchen door. Without a word the cook filled two bowls with butter beans and ham. She gave one to her grandson with instructions to take it to the man in the barn and handed the other to Perry.

While Perry ate, the woman mumbled, ''When you finish, there's a medicine kit if that bandaged hand needs care. I wanta head home before the storm starts pouring and I get stuck here for the night.''

''Thanks,'' Perry said between bites. The old woman's face remained as cold as a three-day-old corpse until her grandson returned. She managed a half smile for the boy but huffed her disapproval when he sat down next to Perry and began rattling away.

''Wanta see somethin' really fine?'' The boy's eyes sparkled.

Perry couldn't help but smile and mentally braced herself for a frog, or whatever the child might consider a wonder in this world.

The boy danced over to a corner of the kitchen and lifted a trapdoor. ''This here's a tunnel from the kitchen to the main house. Goes right into the dining room. Before the war, we carried tray after tray of food over to the fine folks and never had to worry about rain or snow. They always made us whistle when going through the tunnel so's none of us would try having a snack on the way. Plus, I think it scared fine folks to have kids appearing in the corner of the dining room without notice. We call it Whistling Tunnel.''

The cook waddled closer, pulling on her coat. She nodded a slight farewell to Perry. "You can use it to check on that wounded captain during the night." Her words were matter-of-fact, as though she had long ago lost interest in anything this world had to offer. "If you try going outside and up the back steps, you're likely to be shot as a prowler."

"Thanks," Perry answered sincerely, though the advice was not given with any kindness.

The old woman shuffled and tied her ragged wool scarf around her neck. "Just don't wanta clean your blood off the steps come morning. Plus it looks like it's really gonna rain, and I don't relish you tracking mud all over the dining room and my kitchen if you make a trip." She pointed toward the corner near the fire. "There's a hip tub over there if you want a bath. From the looks of ya, you might be doing the world a favor to have one. Don't reckon nobody be coming in here if you bolt the door after us."

Perry couldn't help but smile. The old cook was trying to be kind, but lack of practice left her rusty.

The woman pulled her boy toward the door. "There's clean clothes in that basket. You might find something to sleep in besides those bloody rags you're wearin', and I doubt if any one of them soldiers got sense enough to notice somethin' gone."

Perry would've hugged the cook if she hadn't vanished through the doorway an instant later. Her suggestion sounded too good to pass up. Perry locked the door and put water on to boil. She stripped off her clothes and took a long bath to the music of a heavy spring thunderstorm outside. She scrubbed her skin almost raw and washed her hair until her arms ached. Her problems seemed far more bearable as she dried before the fire. With salve and a fresh bandage across her palm, she felt not only human but a lady again.

She found a huge white shirt with ruffles down the front in the clean laundry. The shirt was long enough to be a nightgown, and with the sleeves rolled up it looked almost elegant. Her hair curled and waved around her in a black cloud of silk. She couldn't bear to bind it up, though she knew she should.

Laying Hunter's necklace atop her pile of dirty clothes, she noticed how foreign it looked there, as foreign as a Southern lady in a northern camp. The only gold in this mess was the chance to be near Hunter. During the idle times of the ride she'd let herself imagine what it would be like to be loved by such a man.

Perry lit a candle and decided to try the passageway. She'd seen all the lights go out in the main house an hour before and knew all the soldiers were asleep, except for the guard on duty in the main hall.

She told herself she only wanted to check on Hunter's health, but she knew that was only half the truth. She longed to touch him once more before she had to disappear from his life. One memory of being in his arms would carry her the rest of her life . . . one last moment of being totally alive.

The tunnel was dry and brick-lined. There were no spiders or mice, only the earthy smell of the damp dirt above her. The brick slanted upward until she came to a stairway. She blew out the light, not wanting to announce her presence until she was certain Hunter was alone in the dining room.

Hunter tried to sleep, but the thunder pounded against the dining room's long windows like cannon fire, and the lightning flashed, reminding him of battle. He hated being too weak to move more than a few inches. He hated the constant pain that throbbed in his shoulder. He hated being alone in this old room. But most of all he hated admitting to his weakness.

He closed his eyes and cursed the war for the hundredth time. He wanted a life outside of a uniform. He wanted rest. He wanted to feel more than hate and duty before he was too old to feel anything but pain. The fever always seemed worse at night, making him light-headed and confused.

A creaking sound came from the corner. Hunter's senses came alert. He slowly turned his head toward the noise as his one good arm reached for the holstered revolver above his pillow.

The sound came again, like aging hedges crying with movement. He searched the darkness.

Lightning flashed against the windows as bright as day. Hunter turned his stare for a moment toward the curtains. The yellowed lace looked aflame, then darkened back into pale stillness. The thunder that followed sounded like the heavens were falling upon the house.

Hunter looked back at the corner of the room, but nothing was there. He had only imagined the noise, as he'd imagined so many other things since his fall a few days ago. The corner was as bare as the rest of the room . . . as the rest of his life.

He sighed heavily and pressed his palm against his forehead. Sleep seemed his only escape from the pain, and it was a welcome comfort. He wouldn't think of the loneliness or the throbbing in his shoulder. He would only relax and dream.

A soft hand covered his own in the darkness. Hunter didn't move, knowing his feverish mind was playing yet another trick on him.

His fingers slid from his face, but the soft pressure of a woman's hand remained against his forehead. "I knew you'd come in my dreams again," he said without surprise.

The hand trembled slightly, as if debating vanishing, then hesitantly stroked his hair back from his face.

"Tell me, my angel, are you the angel of life or death?"

"Your fever is no longer high." Her voice whispered, as soft as the palest hue, reminding him of his mother's Southern tones. "I think you'll live."

Hunter's fingers circled her wrist and pulled her nearer. "Lie with me. I don't want to be alone . . . even if my companion is only a dream."

The woman he'd thought of so often climbed atop the table with him. He could see the velvety black hair surrounding her face, which was still in shadow. Hunter moved his fingers and trailed the lines of her jaw. "I can only see your outline, yet I can sense your beauty with my touch. Lie beside me as you did in the loft."

He knew he couldn't stop her if she pulled away, for though her frame was petite, his bandages were chains of restraint about him.

She moved close without hesitation, her body needing his warmth as deeply as he needed hers. She laid a soft cheek atop his unharmed shoulder and her hair circled near his face in heaven-spun softness. "I can't stay long," she whispered.

Hunter moved the back of his fingers along her arm. He would almost chance ripping his wound open to make love to her. But tonight the loving would have to be with his words.

She was so perfect. He could feel her shiver as his fingers trailed along her side from her shoulder to her hip, yet she made no move to withdraw.

"The curve of your body is flawless. I would know it anywhere by touch. You're the one I've dreamed of all my life, but you've never been so real in my arms. Did I die in the balloon crash? If you are heaven, then I'd fall a thousand times to have you near." He leaned forward and kissed her forehead. "How can you feel so warm and wonderful in my arms and be only a dream?"

He slid his hand past the white cotton gown she wore

and touched the silk of her thigh. Her body arched to his touch just as he'd known it would. He moved his hand higher to her hip. She moved slightly, bending one knee over his leg in an intimate gesture that warmed his blood as no fever ever could.

He kissed the tip of her nose, then moved down on his pillows until their lips were close. "I've longed each night to hold you like this." His lips moved lightly along her cheek, brushing the corner of her mouth.

She pushed against his chest. "You must be careful. I would not cause you pain." Her voice had the flavor of the South, exciting him as no Northern girl's could.

Hunter's laughter was low against her hair. "You are causing me much pain, my angel, but not to my injury." His lips touched her lightly as he whispered, "Grant me at least the taste of your mouth."

His kiss covered her lips, lightly tasting. Her head moved slightly from side to side, brushing his shoulder with her hair as his mouth explored. He couldn't stop a moan as she parted her lips to allow him entry. His hand slid up beneath her gown to the soft curve of her waist. Her flesh was like a velvet wonder beneath his touch. As his impatient hand ventured upward, she stopped his exploring fingers with the gentle pressure of her hand over his.

Hunter's action stilled and he pulled his mouth free of her honeyed lips. His words were low and ragged between breaths. "Do you wish me to stop? Does an angel withhold the ecstasy of heaven?" He tried to see into the shadows that hid her eyes from him. Was her hesitance withdrawal or shyness?

Her words feathered against his ear. "I have never . . ."

Hunter smiled and pulled her close against him. Shyness he could accept, but her withdrawal would wound him mortally. He kissed her cheek and whispered, "It's all right—even fitting, perhaps—that my dream love be so shy. Love has played a game with me all my life; why should it vary in my dreams?'' He moved his jaw gently against her cheek as he breathed against her ear. ''Don't be afraid. If I harmed you, I'd damn myself to an eternity in hell.''

Her hand slowly raised from his and she leaned toward him with a sigh as his fingers moved hesitantly up to cup the fullness of her breast. It swelled beneath his touch as though begging to be caressed. His lips covered hers once more, and he tasted passion in her mouth.

When he moved away again, it was to taste the warmth of her slender throat and bury his face in the ebony curls. He could feel her rapid breathing and knew their single kiss had affected her as deeply as it had him.

Hunter brushed her silken hair off her shoulder. ''I could do that all night.'' He moved his hand to unbutton the front of her shirt. ''How can my lady be only a shadow? How can you feel so real in my arms?'' He pushed the cotton aside and blanketed her breast with his hand. ''If I live forever or die tonight, I'll never forget the feel of you. Promise me, my angel, that you'll come to me when I'm well and let me love you with more than a few kisses and words.''

She hesitantly kissed his cheek. ''I can only promise tonight, and I will only stay longer if you rest and sleep.''

Hunter pulled her under his protective arm. ''The promise is easily made, for I am asleep even now. I've been so alone for so long, I wouldn't even frighten a dream away. But I'll not promise to rest unless you swear by all earth and heaven to return to me when I can love you without restraint. I wish to hold you when there is no fever to cloud my brain and no fire within me but the fire I have for you.''

She reached and touched the strips of cotton. ''You feel alone?'' That soft Southern accent touched her words.

''Sometimes I think the loneliness will drive me mad. Or maybe it already has, for I've been waiting to fall asleep all day so I can dream you're here with me and forget the

insanity of the world." He combed his long fingers through
her hair.

"You promised to sleep," she whispered.

Hunter raised her chin gently with one finger. His lips
brushed hers with a feathery kiss. His words were low in
her ear. "If I am to die of these injuries, let me die with
the feel of your mouth against mine."

Before she could protest, Hunter captured her lips once
more. It was a gentle kiss, for he feared she might yet
vanish in his arms.

But this time she returned his kiss with more fire than
he'd ever have hoped. Her hand moved along his shoulder,
leaving tiny sparks of pleasure against his flesh. He caught
her fingers and pulled them to his lips. When he tried to
draw her other hand forward, she jerked away once more,
as if suddenly afraid.

She rose quickly with the grace of a beautiful deer.

"Don't go!" he yelled. What had he done or said that
had frightened her so? "Don't leave me, my angel."

She knelt before him, her back straight and proud, her
hair touching her hips. She held her hands behind her,
which pulled apart the unbuttoned nightshirt even more.
"I will not leave you. I'll be near, but you must sleep."

"How can I sleep when you are so close? And if you
leave me, I'll never sleep from the longing to be with
you."

Hunter's fingers moved up to part her shirt more. The
button at her bust line gave way to his tugging, and he
touched her warm flesh from her throat to her waist. "Your
skin is as soft as fine silk." His hand replaced the few
fingers and retraced the path.

Hunter brushed long ebony strands of hair away from her
shoulder. "You are the best of every woman in the world
rolled into one." He moved his hand to her throat and pushed
the ruffles of her shirt open enough to reveal the swell of her
breasts. She didn't pull away as he ran his fingers tenderly
down between her breasts and made tiny circles in the valley

where her creamy mounds met. "You are God's perfection in creation." He only saw her outline, yet his other senses could not lie. She knelt above him in royal splendor as he worshiped her with his touch, wishing he could find words to express her beauty and his desire.

The door rattled like noisy thunder in the quiet room. Hunter reached for his gun above the pillows. When he looked back, his angel had vanished as quickly as if she'd slid beneath the table. A beam of light widened from the hallway as a man entered clumsily. Hunter lowered his weapon. No attacker could be so awkward. The intruder must be the guard on duty.

"I see you're awake, Captain," a crisp voice said. "I'm on night watch and thought I heard you yell out."

"I must have been dreaming." Hunter didn't try to keep the pain from his voice. The sudden twisting for his weapon had cost him.

"The cook said for you to drink some of her spiced tea if I saw you awake." The soldier lifted a cup from beside the hearth. "What with the cook's herbs and a touch of brandy, it'll make you sleep like a baby and keep those nightmares at bay."

Hunter suddenly felt very tired and confused. If he'd been talking aloud, could she also be as real as his words? "Did anyone come in or out of this room just now?"

"No, sir. I've been standing not three feet from your door all evening. Anybody who'd get past me would have to be a ghost."

"Or an angel," Hunter answered, then drank the tea in long gulps.

"Pleasant dreams, Captain."

"Thanks." Hunter barely had the energy to hand the guard his drained cup. "I plan to."

He leaned back against the pillows and thought of the way she'd felt in his arms, of how sweet her mouth had tasted. He tried to remember her soft voice. She was still near; he could feel it.

Chapter 6

An hour before dawn, Perry climbed back into her dirty old clothes. She took great care to rub a thin layer of mud over her hands and face. She even smeared a few smudges of rancid lard across her shoulders to ensure that Hunter would no longer think she smelled nice. Remembering the feelings he'd awakened in her had robbed her of sleep. After much thought she'd come to one firm conclusion: She couldn't allow Hunter to be part of a crime. If he knew she was a traitor and didn't turn her in, he would be just as guilty as she. He was not the kind of man to take his honor lightly.

Abram was waiting for her at dawn with the wagon ready. Hunter was awake and looked rested, but his gaze watched the sunrise. He was silent, but his eyes showed longing.

Perry climbed onto the seat and looked over her shoulder at Hunter. Her heart tore apart as she saw the sadness in his stormy gray eyes. A sadness not from his injured arm and shoulder but from his heart. She knew he was remembering last night and longing for the feel of her in his arms, and she equally longed to be there. A part of her wanted to crawl into the back of the wagon and hold him forever, but she'd seen the strength in his character. The question weighed heavy in her mind. Would he accept her if he knew the truth? Would she still see the loving warmth in his eyes if he learned that they fought on different sides? She'd seen no weakness, no compromise in him when he'd faced the deserters the day before. Would he be as unyielding to her if he discovered what she had done?

The cook hurried to the wagon and handed Hunter another cup of her hot herb tea. "You drink this, Captain. You'll sleep for several hours and wake up feeling a mite better."

His words for the old woman were kind, but the sadness never left his gray eyes. Almost before he'd finished the last drop, he was sound asleep. The cook pulled the blankets close around his shoulder as Perry watched, wishing she could do the chore for him.

Abram thanked the soldiers and slapped the team's rumps to start them moving down the muddy road. He seemed in high spirits and unmindful of Perry's quiet mood. "We've a long ride to Philadelphia. Soon we'll have Hunter where he can get proper care, not that your brother didn't do his best under the circumstances." Abram urged the horses forward. He glanced back to make sure Hunter was asleep. "I promised your brother I'd see you safe on the road to your grandfather's, and I will, too, as soon as I get Hunter tucked away."

"If I had some money, I could get back on my own." She remembered the one piece of jewelry she'd taken with her when she'd left home. Unfortunately it was in the packet with her mother's papers. The papers were miles away in a loft she doubted she'd ever find again.

"Hunter's got some folks not more than thirty or forty miles from where your brother told me your grandpa lives. He can lend you money, and you could pay him back after the war," Abram said matter-of-factly. "Just look at it as a loan from a neighbor."

Perry's brow wrinkled in thought. She hated to take money from anyone. However, she felt her grandfather would make it good. At least she hoped he would. Her correspondence with him had been sparse, but he was a Southern gentleman. Perry suspected a brooding feud between her father and her mother's father, though neither ever spoke about it. The one time she'd seen the two men together, there had been a coldness in the air.

Turning her attention back to Abram, Perry asked, "Isn't Hunter a Yankee?"

" 'Course he is. But his mom was a Southern lady. Her folks still live in the South. I suppose that's why Hunter hates this war so badly, feeling a part of himself on both sides. He told me more than once about visiting his mom's folks when he was a boy. She died years before the war. Maybe it was for the best; don't know if she could have stood seeing her world divided. Anyway, Hunter's not been back in years, but ever once in a while he gets a letter smuggled through from his grandpa. If this fighting ever ends, I have a feeling that will be the first place he heads."

"Abram, will you go back with him?" Perry asked.

"Guess I will. Though my memory of the South isn't nearly as fond as Hunter's. I was born in Virginia, and from the time I walked, I don't remember much except beatings. I ran away the first time when I was about six. Didn't make it free till I was nineteen." Abram pushed his hat back and continued. "No, can't say I look forward to going back below the Mason-Dixon line, but I will if Hunter goes. I've been with him so long, can't see changing now."

Abram paused, deep in private thoughts of his own. Perry watched the countryside slowly rolling past them. The trees lined the road in thick huddles, as if they'd gathered to watch people pass. Everything was turning green with spring. As the buckboard moved farther north, Perry saw fewer signs of war. Here the farms were peaceful and quiet. She saw no hastily abandoned campsites or burned farmhouses. The war seemed far away, almost unreal in this countryside.

Perhaps an hour went by in silence before Abram broke

in abruptly. He seemed to be in a mood to talk, and Perry was a willing listener. "You remember Captain Wade Williams, back at camp?" he asked.

Perry nodded, knowing she'd never forget the disagreeable young officer. She remembered the feeling of evil that shadowed him and fouled the air when he spoke.

Abram continued, "Guess you could say he was the first person I met when I came north. I was nineteen and turned loose in Philly with three dollars and a good-luck pat on the back.

"I remember the town showing another black boy very little kindness. Within a month I was well on my way to starving and stealing.

"Well, one night I was walking along, looking for a dark corner to sleep in. This young kid yelled at me, 'Hey, nigger, I'll give you two bits to hold my horse here till I return.' The kid was Wade Williams. He was only a college boy then, but as sharp-tongued as he is now. I could tell at a glance he'd been drinking. I didn't know it at the time, but he was planning to play a prank on someone. So he needed his horse ready to be able to get away fast.

"Next thing I knew, up galloped this other fellow, dressed pretty much like the first, only he was sober. They got in a bitter argument right there in the street. Wade kept wanting to fight, while the other kept trying to reason.

"Finally, madder than hell, Wade turned away and grabbed the reins of his horse. Now I was powerful hungry, so I stepped out to remind him of the two bits. Lord! Fire showed in his eyes as he pulled his horse up and trampled me down like I was grass.

"Next thing I knew, I woke up with the other boy staring at me. His gray eyes were filled with worry. I'd never seen a white man care anything about me. Seems he'd stopped Wade from killing me. In the process he scarred Wade's face over the eye. There's been bad blood between the cousins ever since."

"The boy was Hunter?" she asked, remembering the way his gray eyes looked at her.

"Yes—only he was no more than seventeen then," Abram answered.

Perry found the story fascinating. "Then you went to work for him?"

"Not really. I went back to his house. There he was, a kid living all alone. His mother had just died and his dad was off in Europe. He nursed me the best he could, and fed me. I've been with him ever since, but not as his employee. For eight years now we've just helped each other out. You may not understand this, Miss Perry, but we are friends. Closer than most family. He even taught me to read. I've got a room in his house with more books in it than most men my color see in a lifetime."

Perry understood Abram better than he knew. She'd heard Noma talk of what a joy it would be to read, and Perry had started teaching her before the war broke out. Silence fell once again between the huge black man and Perry as they each moved into the cocoons of their own thoughts.

The miles passed slowly as they traveled closer to Philadelphia. Abram stopped only briefly to check Hunter and unwrap food from a small supply box. He made no further attempt to build a fire and cook. Perhaps he had no wish of a repeat of the ambush scene. Hunter slept as they traveled, waking only occasionally to ask for a drink. She tried to assist him, but with her bandaged hand she was almost useless. After a few unsuccessful tries Perry and Hunter found they could work as a team fairly well. She poured the water with her good hand and Hunter held the cup. She watched as the wind softly brushed his blond hair, and longing to remove her filthy hat and loosen her curls in the breeze. Only two people would see her. One, Abram, already knew she was a girl. Yet Perry knew she must continue her disguise, if only to protect Hunter. She sighed softly, resigning herself to her awful clothes.

The following days passed rapidly. Abram drove the team almost continually, stopping only to rest the horses. During these breaks Abram would stretch his huge body out under a tree and sleep.

Perry and Hunter usually spent the time talking. Hunter enjoyed telling about his ballooning adventures, and Perry found this a safe subject. As long as she asked a few questions now and then, Hunter would continue talking.

He told her of one of the first balloon ascents in Paris, in 1783. "The balloon only went six miles," he said, "but it was the first hydrogen balloon to go up. A young physicist named Charles invented it. When it landed in a small village, it frightened the locals, who mistook it for a monster. The farmers attacked it with pitchforks, destroying it. They didn't know they were attacking such an important discovery."

Over her laughter he continued. "Ben Franklin was in France at the time, and it is said he and four thousand others watched the next ascent six months later."

Hunter smiled. "You know, boy, if I could, I'd introduce you to a good friend of mine. He's on leave from the German army to check out ballooning for the military. He's been crazy about it ever since he went up for the first time in Minneapolis. He's a count, you know. Name's Count Ferdinand von Zeppelin. I lend Count Zeppelin my lodgings in Washington whenever he needs them. He junks them up with maps worse than I do." Hunter laughed and Perry noticed a tiredness in his eyes.

Perry and Hunter's conversations were usually short, for Hunter was still very weak. When they talked, the warmth in his smile never reached his eyes. He was a private man. Even when he grew excited about ballooning, there still was a silent wall that seemed to keep all others pushed slightly away.

As Philadelphia drew nearer, Hunter's bleeding lessened. He was growing stronger, and so were Perry's feelings toward him.

Chapter 7

Darkness fell on the weary threesome as they moved through the outskirts of Philadelphia. Perry marveled at Abram's stamina. He'd hardly slept over the long trip. Now he carefully maneuvered the tired team down the narrow streets of the second largest town in America.

Philadelphia was dirtier than most towns Perry had seen. A menagerie of people wandered the streets, as though they were waiting for adventure to dance into their hum-drum lives. Beggars huddled in corners, while soldiers milled aimlessly around, searching for excitement to dis-pel their nervous energy. The crowd added a carnival-like atmosphere to the town. The aroma of food being cooked over open fires blended with the odors of too many people and animals stabled in close quarters. She heard several conversations at once without understanding any of them.

Abram urged the horses past a carriage pulled to the curb. The black coach was polished until light sparkled off it, giving it a charmed quality in the night. Two women alighted from the rich inner folds and strolled into the yellow glow of the streetlight. Both were lavishly dressed in yards of colorful silk. Perry had seen little fine silk over the past four years, and to see so much at once was almost an assault on her eyes. The ladies looked like huge, beau-tiful moths fluttering in the lamplight.

The women's loud laughter drifted through the street like a bell clanging off-key. Perry's gaze darted suddenly from the bright material they wore to their faces. Her eyes widened as she saw, not two fine ladies but rough women of the streets. Their hair shone an unnatural copper in the light of the lamp, and their faces were covered with makeup thick enough to plow a row through. Their eyes were painted and outlined in black, in sharp contrast to the powder-white of their skin. Each had overemphasized her lips in bright red.

Perry felt the wagon lurch forward. Abram's mumbling caught her full attention. "Abram, did you see them?" Perry tried to control the excitement in her voice. "Did you see those ladies?"

Abram let out an uneasy laugh. "Them are no ladies. No ladies at all."

He would have ended the discussion, but Perry persisted. "Did you see the silk? I haven't seen silk like that in years. It was lovely. But their eyes and lips—I've never seen women so made-up. Have you, Abram?" She wiggled in the seat, hoping for another look. The women surely must be as rare as white buffalo.

He seemed reluctant to speak, and when he did, his voice was stern. "They aren't the type of women you should be seeing. They aren't proper ladies. No amount of silk will make them ladies, just like no amount of mud will make you less of one. They're the vultures in a war. They feed off both sides. Don't matter to them who wins, just as long as whoever does has money."

Perry remembered hearing Noma talk about women who sold themselves for the night. Women who were not respected by any man.

"Abram, are they whores?" she asked.

Abram's eyes darted to her face. "Where'd you learn a word like that?"

"They were, weren't they?" Perry laughed. "I'm not a child. I've heard of such women."

Abram grunted and continued driving the tired team. "My bet is they are worse than any you've ever heard of." He slapped the rump of one horse lightly with the end of the reins as he shook his head, ending the discussion.

Perry checked Hunter. He was sleeping in the wagon bed behind them, his body covered with blankets. He was still very weak. The trip had been hard on him, though he never complained. Perry was glad he would sleep in a hospital tonight, but a part of her would miss being with him.

She studied Hunter's hand as it rested outside his blankets. Heat trailed over her body as she remembered the way his strong fingers had touched her so gently. He'd spoken of longing and needing her, but she knew his strength of character would never accept her. To love her in reality would dishonor him. They were separated by an ocean of war, with her on one side and him on the other. She'd seen the strong sense of honor in his eyes when he'd talked with his cousin in camp, heard it in his voice when the deserters had tried to rob them. If his sense of honor had been strong enough to put him in a war he hated, surely it would make him turn her over for trial.

Perry glanced at Abram. How much of a lady would he think she was if he knew the game she played with Hunter?

Abram slowed before a large square building, void of any style or color. All was quiet around them. This street stood deserted, in sharp contrast to the hustle and bustle only a few blocks away.

As Abram stepped from the wagon he warned, "You better stay in the background while I get Hunter checked in. Wait for me over there on the steps. I'll find you a place to sleep later."

Perry followed Abram's instructions as he disappeared with Hunter into the hospital. She pulled her jacket tightly around her. The night was cool, even for early spring. She huddled in the corner by the steps like a homeless child. Clouds slowly gathered above the chimneys, promising yet another April shower. Tucking her knees beneath her, Perry curled into a ball and melted into the corner shadows. The few people who passed paid her little heed. She closed her eyes in exhausted sleep.

Perry was awakened by a man calling her name. For a moment, location and time had no meaning. She jumped up to find a hospital orderly only a few feet from her. He was a youth not much older than herself with a bored expression permanently tattooed on his face.

"You the boy that came in with Captain Kirkland and that huge blackie?" he barked, annoyed that she'd startled him.

"Yeah," Perry answered, trying to lower her voice to match his. She pulled her hat over her face.

"Well, that one called Abram said they'll be a long while. I've been told to offer you somethin' to eat if you're hungry. There's a kitchen, second door on the right. Nobody'll be there this late, but you can eat somethin'. You can sleep on the table there. I told the blackie I'd see about you. I reckon the kitchen quarters are good enough for a rag like you." He snickered, pulling at a few chin hairs that struggled to serve as a beard.

Though Perry was hungry, she could see the boy thought she was a bother. "No, I'm fine right here," she answered. "Go away and let a guy sleep."

The young orderly needed no further encouragement. He vanished, leaving Perry behind on the cold steps.

Huddling back into her corner, she tried to get comfortable once again. It must be after midnight, she thought as she longed for a real bed. The cloudy sky hung menacingly above her. Where before only a few clouds gathered, now a stormy mob rumbled, waiting to unleash its rage upon the night. The wind whipped between the buildings, whispering an unwelcome melody.

Perry watched a lone figure in the distance moving toward her, fading in and out of sight as she ran from one circle of yellow light to another. The woman was large, but she moved rapidly, like a beetle scurrying across a busy sidewalk.

As the bundle of woman approached, Perry saw half of her aging face. Gray hair sprouted in all directions from beneath her colorful shawl. One of her hands held her shawl together, while the other hand pushed a scarf to the cheek. As the old lady hurried closer, Perry noticed that the scarf pressed against her face was soaked with blood.

The old woman didn't see Perry as her blood-covered hand opened the entrance door of the hospital and she darted inside. Perry sat frozen in her dark corner. The woman's face was bleeding! Someone—or something—had ripped into her flesh. Perry reminded herself that this was a hospital. Anyone hurt would come to this door. A hundred accidents could have caused such a cut. But what if it hadn't been an accident? What if someone in the shadows had jumped out at the woman? Perry glanced up and down the lonely street and wished she had another place to wait.

Several minutes passed. Perry watched every shadow, waiting for one to take human form, but no one came near. Her head ached from listening for any sound.

The hospital door suddenly flung open with a loud pop. The young orderly and the old woman twirled before her like dancers without a pattern to follow. The orderly held the woman's elbow as he hissed into her face. Perry rose to her feet, pressing her back into the building, trying to remain out of their sight. An instant hatred solidified in her veins for anyone who would treat an aging woman so unkindly. Her knuckles whitened into fists with the knowledge that she could do nothing to stop him.

Though he whispered, Perry heard his words. "We've no time to treat the likes of you. There are dying soldiers in here. We have no place for old whores. Be gone with you, Old Molly, before you get blood all over the steps."

With this he shoved the aging woman in disgust. She

stumbled backward into Perry's corner, toppling them both onto the sidewalk.

The orderly disappeared and Perry found herself staring into the face of the old creature. Perry saw pain in the woman's eyes, along with something else buried beneath her tears. There was a pride within her, and kindness, as she tried to smile at Perry. Even in the midst of her problems this old lady seemed to feel sorry for Perry, sleeping in a cold corner. Perry watched her try to gather scraps of dignity, along with her shawl, around her.

Standing, Perry clenched the woman's elbow and pulled her up. "May I help you?" Perry asked, seeing the gash on Molly's cheek and neck. The blood oozed out with each pulse beat, spreading into a crimson pool at her collar.

"Thanks, but I just needed someone to treat this cut. I've seen a cut fester and I was afraid. Seems I've come to the wrong hospital, though." Molly tried to smile as she spoke but only succeeded in making blood drip from the cut into her mouth. "I can't read so well and didn't know this were only for soldiers."

Anger mounted in Perry. What if it was a military hospital? Surely the orderly could have spared the time to clean and bandage a cut. He had no right treating anyone as she saw him treat this old woman.

Fire flashed in Perry's eyes, and determination set her chin. "Come with me, ma'am," she ordered as she opened the hospital door. "I'll do what I can for you."

Though reluctant, Molly followed Perry into the hall. At the second door on the right Perry turned where the orderly had said the kitchen would be. She hesitated at the open door as she observed the filth within. Rotting food lay everywhere. Dishes and pots were obviously used over and over without proper cleaning. If a man were not ill upon entering this hospital, he soon would be.

Perry steadied herself before moving forward. The large woman followed in her wake. Perry struck a piece of kindling in the fireplace and lit several stubby candles on the table. She helped Molly onto a stool near the new fire and added another log before speaking. "Stay here, I'll get some bandages." Seeing the concern in the old woman's face, she added, "Don't worry, everything will be fine. I can clean your cut."

Molly's hands were shaking, but she held them tightly in her lap and nodded.

Finding bandages proved easier than Perry had anticipated. Only two doors down from the kitchen was the supply room, its door ajar. She saw no sign of the young orderly. It was probably his good fortune not to have encountered her. She felt she easily could have snapped his head off in her fury. She gathered all the things she needed and returned to the frightened old woman.

Working very carefully, she tried not to inflict any more pain than necessary. She cleaned the blood away and found one deep cut. It looked as if someone had deliberately tried to slice the old woman's face.

As Perry worked, Molly seemed to be studying her with great interest. "I may be past my prime, but little misses these old eyes." She seemed to be dissecting Perry's bone structure. Her accent bore a Scottish flare as she relaxed. "I've spent my life sizin' up people. Underneath them rags I'd say there be quality."

Perry was busy working and made no comment to the woman's chatter. She'd watched her brother close a cut wound many times. Pulling the flesh neatly together, she hoped it would heal with the least scar possible. Carefully tearing thin strips of cloth, Perry dipped each strip into the hot wax of a fat candle. Just before the wax cooled, she pulled Molly's cut together and lay the warm, waxy strip across her cheek. Perry smoothed each strip until the wax cooled, sticking the cloth to Molly's face and holding the cut together. Perry knew this method wouldn't hold long, but if it held until the bleeding stopped, Molly would only have a thin scar to blend among her wrinkles.

As she finished, Perry smiled, saying, "I think it will heal nicely, ma'am."

"I thank you very much." The old woman returned Perry's smile. "My name's Molly. What be yours?"

Perry nodded, welcoming her friendliness. "I'm Perry McLain."

"You're from the South," Molly stated.

Perry nodded again. She liked this old woman with her warm open smile and bright mischievous eyes. Perry was glad she could help her.

"I want to pay you for fixing me up." Molly began rummaging through her pockets.

"No, no." Perry waved her hands. "I'll take no pay for helping someone in pain."

Leaning back for a closer look at Perry, Molly pressed her lips together a moment before asking, "Could you do with a meal and maybe a nice warm bath?"

Perry's eyes brightened at the mention of a bath. She hadn't had a real bath since the night they'd spent at the plantation.

Molly smiled, obviously pleased she'd hit her mark. "I thought anyone as dirty as you would like the idea of a bath."

Wrapping her bloody scarf in a towel, she jumped off the stool. "I've got a house only three blocks away, Number Fourteen Willow Road. Nobody's there except me and my cat. You come home with Molly and I'll see you get a bath and some food. You're welcome to stay the night."

Anything would be better than spending the night on the hospital steps or in this kitchen, Perry thought as she ran toward the door. "Wait a minute, I'll be right back."

Perry moved silently down the winding corridor to a large desk. The orderly she'd spoken to earlier sat sleeping in a chair, his feet propped on the cluttered desk. She picked up a pen and paper in front of him and scribbled Molly's address.

She poked the orderly in the arm with the blunt end of

the pen as sharply as she dared. He shrugged away and opened one eye. "Whatcha want, kid?" he asked.

"Give this to Captain Kirkland or Abram." Perry knew better than to move away and trust him. "*Now,* please."

"Well, what makes you think I have time to be a messenger boy?" the orderly hissed.

"If you don't, Abram will be very upset." Perry hoped her threat was believable.

The orderly slowly took the paper. He tapped it against his bottom lip as he debated. Finally making up his mind, he reluctantly stood. "All right, I'll take it to him." Then, as an afterthought, he glared back at her. "You wait right here. Can't go any farther than this desk, understand, boy?" The orderly was obviously trying to gain back some of his authority. He didn't like being given an order by her. However, Perry knew, Abram's size gave her order some merit.

She nodded and watched him shuffle off down the dimly lit hall. As the moments dragged by, she had second thoughts about going with Molly. After all, she knew nothing of the old woman or what her place would be like. Her home could look the same as the kitchen she'd just been in. Finally, the thought of relaxing in a hot bath outweighed any reservations.

The orderly returned carrying another message. He handed it to Perry without interest and resumed his seat. He propped his feet back up, dismissing her as he closed his eyes.

Perry walked back to the kitchen, slowly unfolding the note. Written in a neat hand was simply, "Have address. Will come for you tomorrow night. Hunter is resting but must see Lowe at dawn."

Perry smiled as she pulled open the kitchen door. "I'm ready, Molly." She couldn't miss the joy in the old woman's eyes as she straightened slightly and led the way out of the hospital.

They walked out together and moved down the street,

now silent, with even the wind asleep. The night air hung in icy stillness around them. Perry thought the hospital steps would have been very uncomfortable by this time. She smiled and slowed her pace slightly to match the old woman's step. Molly seemed in high spirits to have company.

"I think you'll like my house." Molly linked her arm with Perry's. "But to start off with, I believe in being honest. You should know who and what I am before you walk with me. I may have been called a great many things, but dishonest ain't one of them. So to be straight with you, I'm a retired lady of the streets. Worked for over thirty years, I did. Two years ago, one of my oldest and best . . . ah"—she hesitated, choosing her words carefully— "men friends died and left me his big house. I think he probably drank all his money away. Ever'one knows a huge old house won't sell during the war. I had a little money saved away, so I retired and have been living there ever since."

Perry was careful to reveal no shock at Molly's occupation. She had to fight to keep the laughter from bubbling from her. How could a Southerner deep in Union country, who was wanted for treason, ever judge another's past life?

As they passed another block Perry noticed they were in an older part of town. Many of the homes had been left vacant or utilized as storage buildings. At one time this must have been an affluent neighborhood. Now trees and shrubs circled in junglelike thickness around boarded-up houses.

Molly continued talking, as if Perry were asking questions. "Henry—that was my . . . ah . . . man friend—had no family that cared about him. After I moved in, up shows these two nephews of his, claiming they should have the house. Well, I ran them off, no mistake about that. But lately things been happenin'. I know it's those two.

"Last month I found a dead cat on my steps. A week ago someone rode through my garden, trampling down half my plants. Tonight I went out to dump my mop water. This slimy scum jumped out of nowhere. Tried to slit my throat, he did.'' She chuckled. ''Guess he didn't plan on my still carrying the mop. I hit him so hard between the legs, he's probably still holding his breath.''

Perry laughed at Molly's free, open talk. Part of her found it shocking, but mostly she found the honesty refreshing.

Molly laughed with her. ''Oh, you think that's funny, missy? Well, I hope your mom told you about where to hit a man you didn't want gettin' too close.''

Perry froze in mid-step. ''You know I'm a girl?'' she whispered.

''Of course.'' Molly patted Perry's arm. ''I may be old, but I'm no fool. I never would have lived long at what I did if I hadn't been able to tell what gender folks were.'' She chuckled with a snorting sound. ''Now, honey, you don't have to explain nothin' to me, nothin' at all. I know all I need to know about you. You're a kind soul and welcome in my house for as long as you wanta stay. No questions asked.''

Tears sparkled in Perry's eyes, not for herself but for Molly. She thought of how starved this old woman must be for simple kindness. ''Thank you,'' Perry whispered.

''Wait till you taste me cookin'.'' Molly lifted her chin proudly. ''I could have been a cook but couldn't see standing on my feet all day.'' A jolly, rolling laugh bubbled from her, the kind of laugh that makes all those it touches smile.

They walked another half block, thick with eerie shadows, before Molly turned and stepped over a broken-down fence gate. Perry followed, amazed at the size of the house they were moving toward. It was a large old brick home with ivy growing up all the sides. The house stood two stories, with a long wide porch running the length of its front. Once rich latticework trimmed all the windows, and massive oak doors guarded the front entrance, but now a wilderness of green embraced the aging brick.

Molly moved along a path at the side of the house. "I don't have no use for all these rooms. I live in the kitchen out back. It's big enough for me."

They walked through a small breezeway to the kitchen. As Molly opened the door Perry saw a welcoming fire. Molly motioned Perry in and followed, locking the door behind her.

The kitchen was huge and spotlessly clean. A bed stood in one corner, a wardrobe beside it. A long table divided the room in half. As Perry's eyes adjusted to the light she saw a rocker pulled close to the hearth and the table set for one. Molly must have very little company. A sewing basket and a few paintings were the room's only decorations. A huge black cat stretched and rose to greet them.

Molly removed her shawl and motioned Perry to be seated in the rocker. "You rest yourself and I'll draw the water for your bath. It's nice to have someone to talk with besides Herschel there." She tilted her head to indicate the cat. "He's not too friendly. Sometimes I wonder if he even likes me. He kind of come with the house."

Molly pulled a large tin tub from a corner and put water on to heat while Perry removed her hat and relaxed. Molly hummed as she worked, happy to have company. In a few minutes she returned to Perry with her sewing scissors. Perry silently held out her bandaged hand and allowed Molly to cut off the dirty dressing. The cut was healing nicely, and Perry doubted if she would need to bandage it again. Molly smiled at her without asking how the cut had happened. "While you bathe here by the fire I'll fix up a little snack."

In sudden haste Perry stripped off the rough boy's clothes and climbed into the tub. Molly poured steaming water into the half-filled tub, then moved away to another part of the kitchen. Perry felt she must be in heaven as she soaked. Breathing in the steam rising from the bathwater, she allowed the tension of the week to pass from her.

They ate, Perry wrapped in a blanket and Molly talking continually. She explained how she had a garden and a small henhouse out back that provided all her needs. The food was, as Molly promised, quite good. Perry's spirits rose as a feeling of being warm, clean, and full slowed her blood like wine.

After the meal Molly produced a worn but clean cotton nightgown for Perry. Its size swallowed her, but Perry didn't mind. The feeling of soft cloth touching her body was wonderful after so many days in the rough boy's clothing.

Perry curled in front of the fire and listened to Molly's chatter. Molly told of the fear she'd felt here alone in her huge house. She produced an old, dust-covered box. "I found this when I was rummaging in the attic the other day. I wouldn't know how to use them, but they were so nice, I brought them down, anyway."

She opened the box to reveal a beautiful pair of dueling pistols. Perry examined the guns resting on Molly's ample lap. "My father used to have a pair almost like them. The handles were not so fine, though."

Perry lifted one from the case. "I know how to load and fire them. I could show you tomorrow if you like."

Molly smiled. "That would be grand. I wouldn't want to shoot anyone, but I bet I could scare those vultures away with these." Molly held one in the air and pretended to shoot. "Come on, nephews, I'll shoot your ears off if you come around here bothering me again."

Both women laughed. Molly put the guns away, touching her bandaged cheek gingerly as she returned to her rocking.

"Does it hurt much, Molly?" Perry asked.

"Now, don't you worry about this little cut. I've been cut and beat up many times over the years. Kind of a hazard of the business. I ain't complainin' none. I had some bad times, but looking back, it was an interestin' life. Never got the clap, thank God.'' Molly rocked as she talked. ''Went to a doctor once to be checked. He said I never got it because I must've had some natural immunity. Well, I don't know about that, but I've had a great many men. Maybe I had a few of them natural immunities some time or another.''

Perry laughed into her mug of coffee. Molly may have been a whore, but Perry couldn't help but like her. Perry wondered how the polite ladies who came to tea would have reacted to Molly's topic of conversation.

''Guess we'd better get some sleep. I could stay up all night. I used to all the time. But you look tired. Help me lift one of my mattresses off the bed and we'll move it close to the fire for you.''

After making Perry a bed they put all of Molly's bloody clothes and Perry's dirty ones in a pot of water to soak. The aging hands gently rubbed the scarf, as though if this one item of clothing were ruined, it would be a great loss to her.

''Thanks for inviting me to stay.'' Perry leaned over and kissed the old woman's unharmed cheek.

A tear twisted its way down her wrinkled face. ''Was my pleasure,'' Molly mumbled, and pushed the tear away with the back of her hand.

Perry fought the urge to hold the old woman close and protect her from any more pain in her life. But Perry had her doubts that she could get herself out of the mess she was in, much less protect another. However, she couldn't deny the bond that had solidified between them with a single tear.

Chapter 8

The sound of gunfire rattling the kitchen windows woke Perry with a violent start. She jumped up and ran across the cold floor to stand beside Molly at the window. They could see little, except the garden, but they could hear yelling and the frightening noises of people running frantically. Though the garden stood peaceful in the first light of day, the sounds of chaos raged just beyond the wall, threatening like Gabriel's horn to crumble all barriers.

"Molly, are they fighting in the streets?" Perry shouted over the noise. Panic gripped her. After everything else, was she to be caught in the middle of this war?

Molly's face was gray with fright, but she chewed at her lip with a curiosity no fear could contain. "I'll go find out. Stay here, child," Molly ordered as she wrapped a colorful shawl around her bulk and hurried out the door.

Perry dressed quickly and began braiding her long black hair. If there was fighting, it would be better to be ready to move as soon as Molly returned. Perry's mind was racing, trying to think of somewhere to run. She knew nothing of this town or where safety might lie. If war was in the streets, could she make it the three blocks to Hunter, or would her odds be better if she stayed with Molly? If the South took Philadelphia, Hunter would need her, but if the North won, she might need him. A thousand ques-

tions ran through her mind. How could the army be so
close? How could they be strong enough to take a city of
this size? She needed time to think, but the noise outside
made rational thought impossible.

Perry was stuffing her hair into her hat when the door
burst open. Molly stumbled in, out of breath and dragging
her shawl behind her. Her white gown was covered with
splattered mud. Holding a hand over her chest and taking
a few gulps of air, she let out a howl that would have put
a lumberjack to shame. Then she plopped atop Perry's
mattress and shouted, "The war's over, honey. Lee surrendered at Appomattox yesterday."

The war was over! She could go home. She hugged
Molly and they danced around the kitchen, both laughing
and crying at the same time. Her brother would be coming
home! Somehow they would rebuild Ravenwood.

As she danced, Perry realized there was no need for her
to hide behind this horrid disguise. She threw her hat
across the room and shouted for joy. Both women danced
and hugged until they fell back exhausted on the bed. They
knew there had been no winner in this war within their
nation. The joy of this day lay in the ending of the misery.

Molly made a delicious breakfast. She fried a mound of
eggs in fresh butter, exclaiming repeatedly that there would
no longer be shortages. She cut thick slices of salted pork
and chopped it into the eggs, making a feast.

As they ate, Perry found herself doing all the talking.
She told Molly all about the past week and her travels.
She described Hunter in detail and in so doing felt a sud-
den longing to see him. When she finally slowed down,
Molly stood up abruptly.

She folded her arms over her ample breasts and smiled
down at Perry. "Well, now that you don't have to wear
them clothes, why don't we make you somethin' to wear
when this Hunter comes for you?" She grabbed Perry's
hand and pulled her toward the main house. "I was rummaging through some trunks up in Henry's attic the other

day and saw dresses that might give us somethin' to start with. They must have belonged to his wife. She died several years ago, so they ain't doing nothing but rotting up there."

"Are you sure you can spare the clothes, Molly?" Perry asked, wishing she could offer to buy them.

"Lord, child, I have no need for a dress with a waist as big around as my leg. Henry always said I was twice the woman his wife was. After seeing her clothes I'd have to agree." Molly laughed as she unlocked the back door to the main house.

Molly moved inside. "Folks 'round here used to call him Haunted Henry, him livin' in this big house all alone. He wouldn't even have servants after his wife died. In his youth he ran a slave ship. Folks say he was haunted by all those slaves that never survived the crossing with him. They say the evil he and his partner did drove his partner so crazy, he disappeared.

"I, myself, never called him Haunted Henry, though." Molly laughed. "I used to call him Horny Henry, but toward the end that, I'm afraid, was only a haunting memory too." A chuckle babbled from Molly.

Perry laughed as she stepped inside the main house. To her surprise the rooms were fully furnished. Cobwebs hung everywhere, draping the interior in gray. Many of the larger pieces of furniture were covered with white sheets, giving each room a ghostly appearance. The thick drapes and fine, imported rugs were rotting and layered with dust. This had once been a lovely home, before years of neglect had slowly smothered each room, robbing the wood of any glow and stealing strength from the colors.

Dusting webs away, Molly moved to the stairs. "I let my Herschel in here every now and then. He keeps the mice away." A dreamy look of longing crept into her face as she added, "You'll think I'm a fool, but I come in here sometimes and pretend I'm a grand lady waiting for a dinner guest to come."

Perry stated, matter-of-factly, "You *are* a grand lady, Molly."

Molly smiled down at her from the stairs. "Thank you, child. I'll treasure them words." Then she was gone in a whirl of dust.

Perry hurried to keep up with her as they climbed to the attic. For an old woman, Molly had a light step, and her arm was strong as she pulled the attic door open. As Perry stepped through the opening she was shocked to see trunks everywhere. Most of them looked as if they had sat unopened for years. The large attic was covered with a lifetime of clutter.

Moving to a trunk, she jerked up the lid. Within minutes both women were surrounded with dresses and laughter. Old Henry's wife must have loved spending money on clothes, Perry thought, for she had more than ten women needed.

They spent the morning trying on outfits and sewing. They found a few dresses in good shape. The styles were classic, so they needed little alteration.

By mid-afternoon, three clean dresses and a light coat hung in the kitchen in front of Perry. Freshly washed underclothes lay on the table with a pair of black boots that fit Perry as if they had been made for her. Even before the war her father never allowed more than one or two dresses each season. These were more clothes than Perry could ever remember seeing at one time.

Molly giggled like an old maid when the orchestra leader announces ladies' choice. "Let's try them out, honey. I wish we could've found some bright colors, but these will do. Put this green one on and go visit your handsome captain at the hospital." She lifted the dark forest-green dress and lay it across the bed. The rich folds were made to fit snugly at the waist and blouse wide at each elbow, reminding Perry of a dress a lady might have worn in the days of knights and dragons. They'd polished the row of gold buttons decorating the front and each sleeve.

An hour later Perry stared at herself in a small mirror
that hung on the wall. The dark green velvet flattered her
lovely ivory skin and brought out the brown in her eyes.
Molly had arranged her tresses in braids encircling her
head, a green velvet ribbon woven into her dark halo of
hair. Perry could hardly believe her reflection. For the past
few years she'd been too worried about money and crops
to think of frills.

Molly beamed with pride. "I knew you was a lady the
minute I got close to you. You look wonderful. As grand
as any I've ever seen. I'll walk with you as far as the
hospital doors. Wouldn't be proper for a lady like yourself
to walk alone."

Perry nodded, laughing inwardly at Molly's sudden concern about respectability. She'd spent the past week in the
unchaperoned company of men, but now, in a dress, she
was a lady.

Before leaving, Perry slipped her knife into her dress
pocket. She knew she would carry it until she was safe at
home once more. Somehow, like Hunter's necklace, the
knife had become a part of her.

The two women made an interesting sight as they
strolled the twilight streets. Molly walked tall, proud to
be with Perry, but at the hospital steps she refused to go
any farther. She wanted to wait outside and walk Perry
back home, but Perry convinced her that Abram would
see her safely through the streets. She didn't know how
long she would be visiting Hunter, and the streets were
too wild tonight for Molly to wait by the hospital door.

Molly disappeared into the evening shadows as Perry
walked alone from the front door to the main desk. Tonight the desk was cluttered with bottles and empty glasses
from the morning's celebration. The same young orderly
who'd been on duty last night stood politely as she neared.
She noted he'd been drinking his share, and more. His
smile was lopsided, and he kept trying to straighten it with
a hand that refused to cooperate.

He half bowed as he spoke. "May I help you, m'lady?"

Perry refused to offer even a small smile to the lad. "I wish to see Captain Hunter Kirkland."

"Yes, miss." The orderly hurried to usher her down the hall. "You'll have to excuse the mess. We've been celebrating the war's end, you know."

Perry said nothing, hoping to discourage conversation. She didn't want to talk to this half-drunk young man. He might be polite now, but she remembered his cruel words to Molly all too clearly. As she turned the corner she saw Abram leaving a room. He held his hat in one hand and several envelopes in the other.

"Thank you, orderly, I'll be fine from here." Perry dismissed him before moving closer to Abram. The huge black man stood still, studying Perry as she approached.

"Good evening, Abram," she whispered, watching his face for the reaction to her new clothes.

"Good evening, Miss Perry." Abram spoke as he kept an eye on the orderly, slowly moving out of earshot. The huge black man calmly slid the envelopes he carried into his breast pocket and patted them softly as if ensuring their safety.

With the orderly gone, a smile widened to cover Abram's face. "You're a beauty, Miss Perry, a real beauty," he said as he watched her turn before him. There was almost a fatherly pride in his statement. "I never would have dreamed you'd clean up so nice."

"I've met the nicest woman, Abram. She gave me all this," Perry answered, thinking he was referring to the clothes, "just so I could come to the hospital tonight."

"I wanted to bring you this tonight," Abram whispered as he pulled a pouch from his pants pocket. "There's enough money to get you by a few days until we can decide what to do."

"Oh, no! I can't accept money from you."

"Consider it a loan from Hunter. Just till you're back home." Abram wouldn't take no for an answer. He knew

she would need some money, and he wasn't about to
see her beg on the streets until he could keep his promise
to her brother and get her safely home. "If Hunter were
able, he'd say the same thing."

Concern filled her, washing her cheeks pale against her
dark eyes. "How is Hunter?"

"He's been awake most of the day, talking with some
top brass. I just left him sleeping," Abram answered.

A sigh of disappointment escaped from Perry. "May I
look in on him for a moment?"

"Of course, Miss Perry. As soon as you slip this in
your pocket." He held the money out to her once more
and smiled as she did as he'd instructed. "Hunter's been
given a drug to help him sleep, but you're welcome to
visit." Abram opened the door and stepped aside, allowing her to enter. "I'll see that you're not disturbed. Take
as long as you like." He slowly closed the door, leaving
her and Hunter alone.

Timidly Perry moved to Hunter's bed. A single candle
threw its yellow glow around the room. She watched Hunter's chest rise and fall in sleep. His hair half covered his
sleeping eyes. She reached up and softly brushed it away
so she could study his face one last time.

How could any man be so handsome? she thought. She
may have saved his life, yet he added something new to
hers. She'd never met a man who so fascinated her, whose
slightest touch could make her blood run hot. She remembered the rainy night they'd spent in the plantation and
how his words had made love to her. He'd given her one
thing she'd never had: someone to dream about. Her body
ached even now from the need to touch him.

Perry let her fingers drift down Hunter's cheek and touch
his lips. Leaning over silently, she touched her lips to his
lightly and the excitement thrilled her. She moved her palm
to cup the side of his face, allowing her fingertips to brush
his hair. He'd never know how much he'd added to her
life. How in a moment of nightmares he'd given her the

strength to go on, the hope to believe, the will to dream of another time besides war, another emotion besides hate.

Hunter moaned and his eyes opened slightly. Sleepy gray pools looked up at her as his lips thinned into a smile. He whispered, "Good night, my angel." Then he drifted back into sleep, as if her kiss were a nightly occurrence.

Perry's eyes widened in surprise. She remained only an inch from Hunter as she thought, *He still doesn't think I'm real. He thinks he's dreaming.* The idea intrigued her. She bent down again, touching her lips to his. Again she felt the warmth of his mouth, and a fire ran through her. She felt she was opening a door ever so slightly. If this were only a peek inside, think what must lie within. She allowed her lips to move slowly across his strong jawline. This night she must remember, for she might never see so clearly again.

Smiling, Perry lifted her head to look once again at Hunter's face. She couldn't say good-bye to him, for he would always be in her thoughts and dreams.

"Someday," she whispered in his ear. "Someday I'll lie next to you again. I know it in my heart."

Hunter gave no answer and Perry grew braver. "I'll visit you every day until I prove that I'm a real woman and not a dream." She slid her fingers along his bare shoulder, loving the feel of his tanned skin. "Someday you'll touch me with more than just your words."

As she leaned to brush her cheek against his, a knock sounded at the door. She reached the knob as the orderly met her. She avoided his eyes, not wanting him to interfere with her thoughts. "Where's Abram?" she whispered before he could speak, wondering why Abram had left his guard post.

"He got called away by some captain who stormed in like the devil were on his tail. They went off to yell at each other in the front office."

A tiny quiver of panic touched Perry's heart and she glanced around, half expecting to see Captain Wade Williams storming toward her with a hangman's noose swinging from his belt.

The orderly misread her frown and smiled a silly grin. "Now don't worry, miss. We'll have him ready to move to your house first thing tomorrow morning. When the doctor told me Captain Kirkland's fiancée was going to take him to her parents' home to recover, I never thought you'd come tonight."

Looking at the orderly for the first time, she stated, "Sir, I'm not Captain Kirkland's fiancée." Her words seemed to slap the orderly sober. His eyebrows raised in surprise and interest.

A commotion at the front desk saved Perry from any questions. A young woman and a man were arguing loudly in the center of the hallway. Their shouts echoed up and down the quiet halls likes cries through a canyon. As the orderly approached, the woman raised delicate gloved fingers toward him.

"Sir," she said, addressing the orderly, "would you be so kind as to show me Captain Kirkland's room." Sugar dripped from her words, a sharp contrast to what Perry had heard only moments before when she was arguing with her companion. The young woman was very beautiful, blond curls encircling her face. She was richly dressed and carried herself as one accustomed to luxury. Perry was reminded of a china doll she once had. All beauty and no warmth.

"You can't do this!" the man beside her yelled. "I won't have it, do you hear me? Not tonight."

The young lady turned on him. "I'm going to see Hunter. You have no right to tell me what you will and won't have. Tonight or any other night."

The man made an exasperated sigh. "All right, Jennifer, go see him. I'll wait for you in the carriage."

Jennifer smiled at him. "You always do, Richard." Though her voice was sweet, her words were venomous.

Perry slipped past the desk and the young couple. She

was sure they could hear her heart breaking or see the tears bubbling from her eyes. Yet the two seemed wrapped in their own private war as Perry ran unnoticed the few feet to the entrance hall.

She didn't notice a young captain step from an office where he'd been talking to Abram. The captain raised a scarred eyebrow and followed her out of the hospital.

Chapter 9

The April wind whistled between the abandoned buildings in a night song of sorrow. Perry's throat constricted, imprisoning a sob.

"You've been a fool," she told herself. "A fool for believing you meant more to him than a dream means after dawn." Why had she allowed herself to believe there was a future? Hadn't her dreams been swept away from her often enough to teach her that fate was as heartless as a stone?

The evening shadows hid her heartbreak as she passed an intersection crowded with celebrating soldiers and vendors plying their trades. Perry saw the people only as obstacles to be maneuvered around, for in her mind she was alone. Always and forever alone! She built on Hunter's words until she'd believed they'd have a future someday. She'd been a naïve child to heap her hopes atop a wounded man's dreams. The love he felt toward her was only the passion he manufactured in a daydream, nothing more. Tonight the last threads of innocence snapped inside Perry and she vowed that rational thought would forever replace childish fantasy. She'd live without passion, both in her dreams and in her life.

The thunder of horses' hooves rumbled behind her. Perry lifted her skirt an inch and hurried toward Molly's place. The steady fall of hooves seemed to pound into her heart the same words, over and over. Hunter loves another. He loves another.

From deep within her came a pride that had always carried her through. She'd lived before she met Hunter and she would survive now. Yet his lies had stung her deeply. He'd whispered to her of loneliness and longing when he'd planned to marry another. He'd held her as though she were as vital to him as his own blood, and she'd believed she belonged to him. But he had held another close as well.

Perry rushed on, paying little attention as a carriage drew nearer. She turned down the side street half a block from Molly's gate. The buildings were large and close to the street, making the road seem like a tunnel through brick. The thundering horses grew louder. The clicking sounds echoed off the buildings like rapid gunfire. She glanced back, suddenly fearing being trampled.

The creak of the carriage door screamed in the darkness. Perry jumped back, pushing herself against the brick as a man bounded out of the speeding coach. He was dressed in black and carried a dark cape.

Perry screamed as he advanced. For a moment her feet seemed unable to move. She pushed harder against the wall, as if a hidden door would suddenly swallow her. The shadowy figure moved toward her with swift, intentional steps. Her sorrow was forgotten as fear climbed her spine. She glanced around the narrow street for help or an escape. Before she could move two steps, the huge cape came around her like the curtain of death and smothered out all light.

"No!" Perry shouted as thin, strong arms grabbed her and lifted her cocooned body into the carriage. She kicked with all her strength, but the thick folds of the cape muffled any damage. Her knife was only a few inches from her grasp, but the arms around her prevented her from reaching it. Wool-thick air robbed her of the breath to scream.

The carriage lunged forward as she was dropped hard on the floor between the seats. With the arms around her removed, Perry fought hard to free herself of the cape. She shoved the material off her face and twisted away from the shadowy figure on the seat as her fingers clawed through her pocket for the knife.

After a moment, which ticked by like an eternity, her hand encircled the ivory handle, pulling it from hiding as she faced her attacker. In the pale light she froze, her sudden bravado evaporating. A gun's long silver barrel pointed directly at her head. The faint smell of gunpowder warned her of the weapon's frequent use. Her eyes narrowed slightly in anticipation of the flash that would signal the end of her life.

A cold, steely voice came from the blackness of the carriage. "Don't make a move, Perry McLain, or you won't live to know why you've been abducted."

Icy terror slid across the back of her neck. The voice could belong to no other. She didn't need to see his face. Captain Wade Williams pointed the weapon. She could feel his evil impregnate the carriage air, as thick as a skunk's scent in a damp cellar.

"What do you want?"

"What do you think a Union officer would want with a Southern traitor like yourself? You burned half the crops in South Carolina. That's a hanging offense."

Perry fought to keep her body from trembling. "The war's over!" She stated the fact, somehow knowing it would make little difference to this man.

"So it is. And a shame, too, since I trailed you all the way here. But, you see, I always win. No one ever gets the better of me in the end. Not even Hunter." Wade lifted his boots to the seat across from him and folded his legs casually at the ankle.

Perry's eyes widened in horror as he lit a thin cheroot

with deceptive placidity. The flash of light danced off his scarred eyebrow as he turned cold, iron-hard eyes toward her. His voice was low, and when he spoke, she felt as if a rope was being slowly tightened around her throat. "A former slave of yours traded her freedom for the information about you when I convinced her you were in great danger traveling alone. The moment I learned you were dressed as a boy, I knew that you'd tricked me. I had to come personally and see that you and my cousin pay for your treachery."

"Hunter had nothing to do with my escape."

The carriage picked up speed, but Wade's gun never moved. "How nice of you to say such a thing, but you needn't protect him. He'll be dishonorably discharged for this if I have anything to say, and I'll be named commanding officer over the very land where your and Hunter's grandparents live. He'll be discharged in the North and, should he turn to the South, I'll be waiting for him there."

"But the war is over! You can't just take me back."

Wade's laugh sent a shiver of fear down her spine. His voice was a deep rumble as he leaned forward, blowing smoke in her face with each word. "Oh, I'm not going to take you back to Carolina, my dear. You're going to be shot escaping later tonight. Much later."

She huddled into the corner, praying that somehow the shadows would protect her. The door handle was within her reach, but she knew Wade would easily stop her. The knife in her right hand was useless against his gun, but if he turned his aim away from her head for only a moment, she could lash out. Perry forced her eyes to remain open as he leaned closer. Her gaze fixed on his weapon, waiting for what might be her one chance.

Wade's thin fingers slowly unbuttoned her jacket at the collar. His touch was as repulsive as an insect crawling at her throat. "You're so tiny," he whispered. "I must be careful not to kill you too soon." He ripped open her jacket with a sudden, impassioned jerk, spilling golden buttons on the carriage floor. ''I do hope you've a woman's body and not a child's, for I like my Southern whores petite but ripe.''

Perry remained still, waiting for her chance. ''I'm not your whore.''

A thin hand encircled her throat. ''You will be,'' he whispered as his fingers tightened. ''When I'm finished with you, traitor, you'll beg for the bullet that awaits you.'' He slid the barrel of his gun along her temple as his other hand moved along the silk of her blouse, testing the development of her curves.

Forcing herself to remain frozen, Perry clenched the knife at her side and waited. She fought to keep from crying out as he moved the barrel of his weapon slowly down the side of her face and along her throat. He pulled her blouse aside until the cold steel rested between her breasts. Then, as before, his thin fingers slowly began unbuttoning her blouse as he hissed, ''You are so still, little one. Could it be you've bedded men many times before—or are you like all Rebs, great talkers but poor fighters?''

Perry didn't answer, even though bile rose in her throat, along with every profanity she'd ever heard.

Wade's hand slithered between her blouse and camisole. ''A coward, I think.'' He straightened and threw the gun behind him. ''I won't need that until later.''

Perry doubled her knees up in the darkness. As he leaned toward her, she kicked with all her might, knocking him several inches away. The growl that followed sounded more like a rabid dog than a human. As she raised her knife, his hands twisted around her legs with such power that she felt he might snap her bones at any moment. He jerked her forward, sending her knife flying against the seat.

His knees slammed into her chest with the force of a

cannonball, shoving the air from her lungs and knocking her head back against the carriage floor.

All energy passed from her body as sparks exploded in her brain. The sudden jerk of the carriage barely registered in her mind.

"Captain!" came a shout from outside. "Captain, there's trouble in the streets!"

Perry felt she was drifting in muddy water as Wade raised off her body. "I'll finish with you in a moment." He lifted her arm and jerked it above her, tying her left wrist to the door window. "That should keep you inside if this doesn't." With his final word he slammed his fist into her side, laughing at the sound of her ribs cracking.

A long moment of pain later, Perry realized she was alone in the carriage. Her insides blazed each time she moved her chest to breathe. She wanted to close her eyes and dream of Hunter. She wanted to rest and forget all the pain she now suffered—and all that was to come. But she couldn't. She'd never give up as long as she was still breathing.

Groping in the blackness, she found her knife. With a tight grip on the ivory handle she raised the blade. Using the last bit of strength in her, she slashed at the rope that bound her hand. As the blade passed through the air above her head, missing the rope in her blind swipe, Perry felt the pain of Wade's blow once more in her side. Biting back the fire, she tried again and again.

Suddenly the blade met its mark. The thin rope snapped, freeing her arm. Perry twisted the remaining rope from her wrist as if it were a live snake curling around her flesh. She crawled to the door and opened the latch. As she fell out of the carriage she made no attempt to brace herself. Her only thought was to be free.

Powerful arms broke her fall, pulling her up against a massive chest. She pushed away for a moment before a low, educated voice whispered, "Hold on, Miss Perry, and I'll get you out of here."

Perry held as tightly as a baby possum to its mother. She was aware of Abram mounting a horse and riding. Vaguely she saw a drunken mob fighting in the street, then she closed her eyes and trusted in Abram.

Her mind floated above her pain. She was drifting in a balloon with Hunter at her side. They were safe and happy. His face was a warm, golden tan and his jacket fit snugly over his broad shoulders. His gray eyes looked down with love that could only have been meant for her.

Molly's voice brought Perry back to earth. "My Lord, honey, what happened?"

Abram lowered her to Molly's arms. "I have to make sure I wasn't followed. Can you see to her?"

Molly pulled Perry into the house and began mothering her like a hen with only one chick. "I knew I should have stayed and walked you home. There's all amount of drunken meanness out there this time of night."

Perry allowed herself to be undressed. Molly carefully wrapped her ribs, swearing continuously against whoever might have done such a thing.

An hour later, when they heard a horse, both women reached for a gun from the box of dueling pistols. Perry crossed the floor and looked outside, then turned to Molly. "It's all right. It's only Abram. I'll talk with him."

Molly stood guard as Perry stepped into the dark garden.

"Thank you," she whispered, hugging her side to still the throbbing pain of her injuries.

"Are you all right?"

"I feel as though I've been kicked by a mule, but Molly says I'll heal in a few weeks. How did you find me?"

"I followed Captain Williams out of the hospital, but I couldn't catch the carriage until that bunch of drunken soldiers blocked the street." Abram patted his horse. "I've let you down. I promised to get you to safety, and I almost got you killed."

"It wasn't your fault, but I must get away as soon as

possible." She knew Abram would think it was because of Wade, but she couldn't bear to stay, knowing Hunter was with another woman.

"Can you travel?"

"Yes," she answered, realizing that if she didn't, Wade might find her.

"I'll arrange passage for you on a ship leaving at dawn. After you've left, I'll wire a message to your grandfather that should reach him long before you do. If they can't get to him, Hunter's grandparents will come for you and drive you out to his place."

"I'll be ready before dawn."

Leather creaked as Abram mounted his horse. "I'll send a carriage for you."

She watched his outline disappear into the blackness beyond the garden. He believed her safe tonight, or Abram never would have left; but Perry wondered if her knife and the two guns would be enough in the future.

Chapter 10

Clouds hung heavy in the April sky, curtaining the morning in soft gray mist as Perry boarded the small sailing ship called the *West Wind*. The sailboat was beautifully designed for speed, but today it seemed cumbersome with all the people and supplies loaded on deck. Folks stood in small groups saying their good-byes as men tried to move around them to load everything into place.

Abram had made all the arrangements for her trip to her grandfather's home in North Carolina. He had promised her brother he would get her back, and he'd achieved a miracle by getting her a ticket when there must have been hundreds of people wishing to go south now that the war was over.

Perry turned to hug Molly one last time. "I'll write," she promised.

Molly was fighting tears that threatened to fall. "I'll treasure every letter. There's a priest downtown that will read them to me."

"Take care of yourself."

Molly patted Perry's arm. "I'll be fine, honey. I'm as tough as an old boot left out all winter. It's a wisp of a woman like yourself we got to worry about."

"Thanks for all you've done for me." Perry knew she'd

found a friend she'd think of often for the rest of her life, even if they never saw each other again.

"Weren't nothing. Now you run along." Molly wrapped her shawl tighter around her thick waist and hurried off. Her hand waved behind her, but she didn't look back at Perry as her other hand kept wiping her face.

Perry stared after her until someone on board the *West Wind* called her name. She twisted and searched the crowd, her fingers sliding into her pocket and encircling her knife. Finally she spotted Abram's large bulk unfolding from a seat among the supplies. As she slowly walked toward him he took long, steady steps forward.

"I've been waiting for you, Miss Perry. I planned to speak to you before you left the hospital," he said with an air of formality.

"Yes, w-well," Perry said, stammering, "I didn't know Captain Hunter's fiancée was arriving." Perry avoided Abram's eyes. She didn't want him to know that she was heartbroken by the thought of Hunter's engagement. Even the physical pain she'd suffered at Wade's hands was not as great as the ache in her heart. She'd thought about it most of the night. It wouldn't be fair for her to come between two people who were planning to marry.

"Miss Perry . . ." Abram paused. "That woman you saw—"

Perry interrupted. "It's all right, Abram. Hunter doesn't even know me. Don't worry about it."

Abram continued. "That woman has known Hunter all his life. He has grown up with everyone always thinking they'd marry." Abram stopped, searching for the right words. "I wanted to tell you that he thinks you are part of a dream. He can't stop talking about the beautiful woman in his dreams. I'd like to tell him who you are, but I gave my word to you."

"No, Abram," Perry said. "Positively not!" It would be better if she remained part of a dream. He was engaged to be married to someone he loved. Even if she did tell

Hunter and he broke his engagement, there would still be Wade. No. It was better that she disappeared.

Abram's face showed a great sadness Perry didn't understand. Placing her hand on his arm, she added earnestly, "Thank you for all you've done for me, Abram. I wish there was some way I could repay all your kindness."

Abram shuffled his huge feet. "If you would, Miss Perry, I'd greatly appreciate your taking a few papers to Hunter's grandfather."

"I'd be happy to." She looked at him now, wondering why he'd been so hesitant to ask such a small favor.

Abram's face was sweaty, as if he'd been working in the hot sun. "Promise you won't give them to anyone except John Williams. If you can't get them to him, burn them. Promise!"

She couldn't imagine why a grandson's letters could have been so vital. "I promise," she whispered.

Abram wiped his forehead. "And don't let anyone see you give them to him. No one!"

"No one," she repeated as she stuffed the envelope into her purse.

"Thank you, Miss Perry," Abram said. "If you ever need anything, remember we owe you a great debt."

Perry could tell from the way Abram shifted that he was a landlubber, in a great hurry to be off the ship before they sailed. "I'll be fine, Abram, I'll be home soon." Perry turned from him and moved below. She could hear the crew getting the ship under way. She couldn't watch with the others on deck as the ship left the city . . . as she left the terror of Wade Williams . . . as she left Hunter forever.

The ship was rocking by the time Perry reached the plain little cabin where her trunk had been deposited. Somehow all that had happened since she'd left Ravenwood seemed unreal. Maybe Hunter was right, she thought. Reaching up to her throat, she tugged at Hunter's chain around her neck. She held the small medallion tightly in her fist. If it were not for this necklace and the thin scar along her left palm, Hunter could have been only a dream.

Perry spent the days aboard the ship in a thoughtful mood. She took her meals alone in her cabin and walked on deck only a few times each day. The other travelers were a mixture of Northern and Southern families who seemed content to stay within their own small groups. The war might be over, but bitter feelings died hard. No one on board, including the captain, talked to her. She could feel their eyes watching her as she walked on deck, but she kept to herself. The ship was carrying her from one way of life to another. The South she'd known was dead. When she returned home, it would be to a new era, and Perry knew she must face the change.

Three days later Perry stood alone on the sandy beach with her one small trunk beside her. She guessed she was over the Virginia line into North Carolina as she watched the ship pass out of sight beyond the rocks. Only a few passengers had even been curious enough to come on deck when she'd left. They all had their own lives and destinations to think about.

Perry felt abandoned, even though the captain of the *West Wind* assured her this was the place Abram had instructed she be left. The captain explained how the dock must have been blown up to prevent Confederate shipments. Before the war, ships often stopped here to pick up cotton from the local plantations.

He'd set her ashore and rowed back to his ship without giving her another thought. A vacant road stretched ahead of her, a wooded area spilling toward the water, now behind her. As she stood alone, Perry wondered if something could have gone wrong and her grandfather hadn't been notified of her coming. What if he knew and did not want to see her?

Ignoring the ache in her side, Perry lifted her trunk with one hand and her skirt with the other. She moved onto the road. There was nothing to do but walk. According to the captain, her grandfather's farm was ten to fifteen miles due west. She could walk every step if she had to.

Before her slippers were even dirty, Perry lifted her head to see a buggy approaching far off in the distance. At first she was overjoyed, then she realized she knew neither of the elderly people moving toward her.

The old buggy stopped a few feet from her. An aging man slowly climbed down, unfolding his body with the care one might use opening yellowed paper. He was tall and thin, his white hair combed neatly back away from his tan face. "Are you Perry McLain, miss?" he asked, then laughed. "Well, of course you are. Who else would be standing out on this abandoned road?" His rich laughter spread to the lady in the buggy.

Perry nodded and found herself unable to speak as she stared into the old man's gray eyes. It was as though forty years had gone by and an aging Hunter stood before her.

"I'm John Williams, Miss Perry. I live a few miles northwest. My grandson, Hunter, sent me a message to get in touch with your grandfather. I'm sorry to say, my man reported that your grandfather is ill. My wife and I would be honored if you'd allow us to drive you to his home." His thin lips spread into a wide smile that couldn't have been anything but honest. He lifted her trunk into the buggy. Perry didn't miss the strength in his aging frame.

"This is my wife, Mary." John Williams winked at the small woman sitting in the buggy.

She was short and plump, with eyes that danced in her wrinkled face. Her voice was musical as she spoke. "Nice to meet you, Miss Perry. We don't see many pretty young ladies in the country. Now you climb right in beside me so we can talk."

Within an hour Perry felt she had known the Williamses

for years. They were warm, friendly Southern people with
the skill to make her feel at home. They were both in their
late sixties and in good health. John attributed this totally
to his wife's great cooking. John Williams had retired and
sold most of his farmland three years before the war.
Though they felt the war deeply, in their isolated home
they had seen very little fighting.

Mary Williams asked, ''Do you know our grandson
well, Miss Perry?''

''No, ma'am,'' Perry lied. ''Abram, his friend, probably sent you the message. I only met them a week ago.''

''Abram. I remember Hunter writing of a man by that
name. He's a self-educated black who lives with Hunter.''
As Perry nodded, Mary continued. ''My dear, we may
sound curious, but we are starved for news of our grandson. We haven't seen him since he was a boy, and very
few letters have reached us during the war.''

Perry smiled. ''I'll tell you what I know of him. He
was a balloon surveyor in the Union Army, with Abram
at his side. I understand there were only four such balloons in use.''

John Williams interrupted and said, ''Hunter always did
like the adventurous life.

''You know, the South had one of them air balloons,''
John continued as he tapped his chin with his index finger.
''We built a balloon out of ladies' old ball gowns, we did.
I think it was named the *Silk Dress*. Never flew that I know
of. It was on its way to the front line on the tugboat *Teaser*.
The boat ran aground on a sandbar in the James River.
That ironclad *Monitor* finished them off, as I remember.''

Mary Williams spoke up. ''John, please, Miss Perry
was telling us about Hunter.'' Turning to Perry, she said,
''You'll have to excuse my John, he always remembers
details. When Hunter was a boy with us, he and John had
such fun playing games to see who could remember the
most about this or that.''

Perry wiped the perspiration from her forehead. "I guess a mind for detail would be an asset to a surveyor."

Mary's head bobbled up and down. "Right. See, John, Hunter inherited more than your gray eyes. Perry tell us what Hunter looks like now that he's full grown."

"He's tall and slim with blond curly hair, and you're right: He has the most wonderful gray eyes." Perry paused to look at John. She was about to say Hunter looked much like a younger John Williams. However, turning toward them, she realized they were both smiling at her.

Perry's face reddened. They must think her a silly, moonstruck schoolgirl.

Mary Williams patted Perry's hand softly. "It's all right, dear. Don't be embarrassed. There is nothing wrong with admiring a handsome man. I've been doing it for almost fifty years."

Perry glanced up in time to see her wink at John. She realized these two sweet old people were still very much in love, living in a special world of their own where all others were outsiders.

For the remainder of the drive she told them all the stories Hunter told her about ballooning. If they had heard the tales, they were both too polite to say so.

She fell silent for a few minutes, thinking of those few days with Hunter and his stories. She remembered one of their conversations, which had ended in laughter and waking Abram, who had looked at them as if they had both gone insane. Hunter had been telling her about the first big balloon ascent. A pair of brothers named Montgolfier were going to demonstrate their skill to King Louis XVII. They wanted to go up as passengers, but the king was violently opposed. The brothers had to pass the honor of becoming the first air travelers to a sheep, a rooster, and a duck.

Perry remembered Hunter's laughter as he speculated about which of those animals he was descended from. He had told her everyone thought him crazy with his love for balloons.

Glancing back at John and Mary, Wade Williams's name crossed her mind and she decided to ask about him. "I met a Captain Wade Williams once. Is he any kin to you?"

Mary's sunny smile dimmed slightly. She didn't answer. However, after a pause, John spoke. "Wade is my brother's son. My brother, Adam, remarried after his first wife died. All his children were grown and he wanted a companion. His second wife was twenty years younger than he was. So Adam became a father when he was almost fifty. Wade was raised like an only child and given everything. They even sent him North to the best schools. In his teens he was wild and caused my brother much heartache. But he matured. The army did much for him, even though joining the Union Army broke his father's heart. We received word yesterday that he'll be stationed in this area now, helping to get everything back in order."

John paused in thought before adding, "He plans to stay with us some. His parents are both dead."

Perry decided not to ask about Hunter and Wade's relationship. She could tell the Williamses were too polite to say more than they already had, so Wade Williams was dropped from the conversation.

The miles passed rapidly and Perry enjoyed the company greatly. Finally John slowed the horses, and pointed to a huge plantation nestled among three old oaks. "There's your grandfather's place, Three Oaks. I've only been here a few times myself. Your grandfather likes to keep to himself. I believe a man has that right."

Perry smiled. "I've never been here. I was only a girl the last time I saw him. How well do you know him?"

John shrugged. "I don't know much about him. People say his wife died in childbirth. They say he was devoted to his only child. There used to be parties all the time up here. When the daughter left, he closed the doors to his home. To my knowledge no one has been in there since, except servants. The few times I've been over to talk business, we sat on the porch.''

Almost to herself Perry whispered, ''I hope he'll be glad to see me.''

Mary smiled and patted Perry's hand. ''Of course he will.''

They entered her grandfather's drive. The oaks seemed to be protecting the house, warning all people to stay back. The drive was overgrown, telling Perry that very few carriages came to or left this place. A flock of birds flew screaming over their heads, frightening Perry with their sudden unwelcoming call. No other signs of life surrounded the house. The empty corrals and dilapidated stables seemed to be telling her silently to stay away.

Chapter 11

The Williamses refused to come in for refreshments as they pulled up in front of Perry's grandfather's house. She was thankful, for she had no idea what awaited her behind the closed doors. She hugged them both good-bye, promising to visit soon. When John stepped back to lift her trunk down, she handed him the envelope Abram had given her. He looked confused for a moment, then slipped the letter into his breast pocket.

Perry stretched and kissed his thin cheek. "Thank you for meeting me and bringing me here."

Aging gray eyes turned serious. "It is I who am in your debt." He patted the papers beneath his jacket.

She opened her mouth to deny his statement, but his eyes encouraged her to remain silent.

Perry turned and climbed the steps to the double-doored entrance of her grandfather's house. She threaded her way across a large porch cluttered with wicker furniture. Glancing back over her shoulder, she saw John and Mary Williams waiting at the buggy to ensure she was inside before leaving. In a few minutes Perry could stop asking herself whether or not her grandfather would welcome her. For soon she would know one way or the other.

Determination raised her chin as she lifted the knocker

and rapped three times. The brass settled back against a door badly in need of painting.

Seconds passed. Footsteps somewhere within crept toward the door. She waited. Her journey had been so long, but these last few moments seemed endless.

The door creaked open, revealing an ancient servant in worn clothes. His thin black hand shielded his eyes from the bright sun, as though it had been years since he'd ventured into the bright light.

Deciding she'd be well into her thirties before he greeted her, Perry announced, "I'm Perry McLain. May I please speak with my grandfather?"

Shock registered on the old man's face as his eyes adjusted. He seemed like a figure carved in granite. She debated stepping around him, until he finally found his voice. "Yes, miz. We've been expecting you. Your maid, Noma, arrived more than a week ago."

He hesitated before continuing, "Miz, you sure is the image of your mama. If I didn't know better, I'd swear you was the ghost of Miz Allison." With this he stepped back to allow her to enter. "I'll get your bags. You'll find your grandfather in the study." A twitch of a smile cracked the dark stone of his face. "Study's the second door on your left."

"Thank you."

The old man moved onto the porch. "James, Miz. Ever'body just calls me Old James."

Perry followed him down the steps to say a last good-bye to the Williamses.

As she followed him back up the steps James lowered his head. "Your grandpa, he hasn't been feelin' too well, Miz Perry." His words were little more than a mumble as he struggled with her trunk.

Perry wondered if his statement was an apology or a warning. She hesitated a second before entering the cool darkness of the entry hall. All the shutters were drawn, giving the house a cavelike dampness. She moved slowly down the hall to her left, allowing herself time to study each room. It was obvious that no energy had been spent cleaning or dusting in years. Once beautiful furnishings were now covered with the dull hue of neglect.

The study door stood ajar, not wide enough to be welcoming. Perry straightened her jacket and lifted her chin and her hopes as she stepped inside. Stale smoke hung in the room like a low cloud, assaulting her senses. Papers and books littered every table and chair, in no apparent order. Discarded clothing and empty bottles cluttered the floor. An old man relaxed by a dying fire, his feet propped on a stool. For an instant Perry thought she was looking at a dusty painting. Everything about him and his surroundings was faded. His hair was a dull gray and his clothes a washed-out blue. He stared at her with watery, colorless eyes.

As Perry's presence registered on the old gentleman he stood slowly, holding the arm of his tattered chair for support. "Allison, you've come home," he whispered as a tear weaved through the lines of his wrinkled cheek. "Allison, my dear," he whispered again as a glass fell from his hand and shattered.

Perry ran toward him, tears spilling over freely as she realized his mistake. "No, Grandfather, I'm Perry. Allison was my mother." Her words didn't reach him. "I'm Perry, Grandfather," she cried again.

A flood of tears came to his eyes, along with a degree of awareness. He held his hands up to her. "Perry. You're Perry? Welcome, Granddaughter."

Perry moved into his arms, hugging him tightly. He smelled, as he had years before, of dust and tobacco. She didn't remember the smell of brandy, which now clung to him as thickly as a layer of sweat.

He patted her on the back as he held her. "I'm so glad you're home," he mumbled again and again.

Perry was uncertain if he thought he held her or her

mother, but at this moment she didn't care. It was good to be welcomed.

In an explosion of noise the door flew open and Noma appeared, wailing and waving her arms like an overstuffed scarecrow in a tornado. She ran to Perry, tears streaming down her brown cheeks. "My baby, you're all right!" she yelled. "I knew Captain Williams would find you and send you here safely. He promised he would, but I was worried sick."

Perry left her grandfather's arms to be swallowed up in Noma's hug. As the slave cried, Perry tried to comfort her. "Oh, Noma, it's all over. We're together now, nothing else matters." What Noma had done suddenly didn't matter, now that she was safe. Perry thought of telling her the truth about Wade, but that would only torture Noma's thoughts.

Turning once again to her grandfather, she kissed him lightly on the cheek. "Please excuse me while I change. It's been a long journey." The weariness of the trip was lightened by the knowledge that she now had a place to stay and a grandfather who, if somewhat loose in his grip on reality, nevertheless welcomed her.

"Yes, yes, dear." The old man waved his wrinkled hand as though it were a rag attached to his arm. "I'll see you at dinner. Noma will show you to your room." As he spoke the last few words, he lowered himself back into his chair, exhausted.

Perry followed Noma up the stairs. They moved down the long hall to the last room in silence. The dark, brooding atmosphere of the house whispered through the hallway and clung to the pictures and ornaments in moody shadows.

The door hinges to the last room screamed from neglect as Noma forced it wide. "This was your mother's room, Miz Perry. I cleaned it for you. I'll have James oil the door tomorrow."

Perry hesitantly slipped inside, half fearing what she

might see, but the room was bright and lacy, decorated in shades of blue. Everything, from the bed to the dressing table, seemed to have been built to Perry's height. If rooms had arms, this one's would be open wide. "Oh, Noma, I love it. Look, there's even a room for a lady's maid over here." Perry ran around the room, clasping her hands in delight. A feeling of welcome seemed to touch her, a warm greeting from a mother she'd never known.

Noma swelled with pride. "Everything's just as it was when your mother left. I even washed a few of her dresses and hung them up for you, thinking you'd be showin' up with no clothes."

Perry touched a porcelain statue of a cat and thought of Molly. "I was very lucky to meet a nice lady." Then, remembering her grandfather, she asked, "Noma tell me, was my grandfather really glad to hear I was coming?"

"He seemed happy, Miz Perry. Only he do drink. I worry about where his mind goes from time to time." Noma shook her head. "He's more in the past than in the here-'n-now."

Noma sat down on a midnight-blue velvet-covered stool in front of a beautifully carved triple-mirrored dressing table. "The other blackies told me that after your mother left, your grandfather had this room locked. He had it opened when he heard you were coming. Old James told me hisself your mom went over that very balcony the night she ran away with your father."

"I never knew Mother ran away. That does sound romantic." As she spoke, Perry moved through French doors to a tiny balcony. She looked out over an overgrown, forgotten garden as she continued, "That might explain why Papa and Grandfather never were friendly." She thought of the time she'd seen the two men together and could never remember either of them speaking directly to the other.

Perry's mood lightened suddenly. She was safe and the war was over. She ran back to Noma and placed a protective arm around the old woman's shoulder. "Tell me, what happened to you after you left the barn?"

Noma stared at their triple reflections in the mirrors in front of her. "I hadn't gone a mile when I saw bluecoats everwhere. I hid out in the woods for two days before they caught me. I was plum figuring myself for coyote meat when this captain appeared. He questioned me pretty hard at first, till he learned I was from Ravenwood. Then he got real nice and said he was worried about you. He said his folks were from around here and he'd find you and see that you were taken care of."

Turning her face to the windows, Perry answered, "He found me, but I'd already made plans to come back."

Noma wiped her eyes on her apron. "I were so worried."

Perry smiled kindly at Noma. Worry had aged the old woman in the short time they'd been apart. Having raised Perry, Noma felt responsible for her, as if Perry were a child. But Perry was no longer a child, and now she fought resentment for being thought of as such. Noma's mothering had almost cost her her life. Perry made a mental note to be more careful about what she shared with Noma in the future. As they talked, Perry told Noma little of her travels. The people she'd met and grown to love these past days would remain in her memory and her dreams.

The weeks settled into a pleasant routine. Perry and Noma spent most of their days cleaning and airing out the house. James and his wife, Sarah, who served as cook, were the only servants. All the others had run away during the war. James and Sarah were too old to change. They'd spent a lifetime at Three Oaks. It was home to them. The elderly black couple drew great pleasure from telling Perry all they knew of the history of the place.

In the afternoons Perry sat in the cool, overgrown garden and wrote letters to Molly. After the horrors of the war it was pleasant to relax while waiting for Andrew to return. Rumors circulated that many prisoners were still being held.

As the days grew warmer and life slowed to a crawl, Perry spent more time in the garden dreaming of Hunter and what might have been. She couldn't explain why, but even when talking with Noma she held back all information of Hunter and Abram.

Every evening Perry dressed for dinner in one of her mother's gowns and dined with her grandfather. The huge dining room had long windows facing the front of the house. She would watch the oak trees swaying gently in the summer breeze as her grandfather called her by her mother's name. He always called her Allison when he had been drinking heavily. On the evening they received news of Lincoln's murder, he drank almost all night. He was a man haunted by grief, looking for reasons to destroy what remained of his sanity. Perry, not knowing how to help, followed the example of all the others in the house—she ignored his drinking.

Slowly, as the days turned into weeks, a restlessness grew inside her. She'd stand each evening on her tiny balcony watching the sun splash light along the horizon. The warm breeze would twist invisible fingers through her hair, reminding her of the way Hunter had touched her. The longing to see him, to hear his name said aloud, became a physical yearning inside Perry. She knew her feelings toward him were hopeless, but she couldn't stop them from seeping into her thoughts and dreams.

She decided impulsively to pay the Williamses a call. After studying a map in the library she discovered she could travel on horseback and reach their home in half the time a wagon could travel. The trail was overgrown, according to James, but shady. By leaving before noon she'd reach the Williamses by three, if she traveled fast. Perry loved riding and had often spent all day on horseback, so she accepted the ride as a challenge instead of an ordeal.

"I'll be back by seven and have plenty of time to dress

for dinner,'' she told Noma. Though Noma was not happy with the idea of Perry riding so far alone, she could not ride well enough to go with her.

Like most Southerners, Perry and her grandfather dined late in warm weather. In this way they could enjoy an evening breeze. Perry knew he wouldn't expect her down for dinner until eight or after.

Perry needed the exercise. Her body was well and strong, but for the last several nights she'd been unable to sleep. No matter how hard she pushed Hunter from her mind in the day, he returned at night. The memory of her lips touching his caused her many sleepless hours. Sometimes in the darkness she could feel his arms around her, his hand sliding up her leg, his deep voice whispering his pleasure as he touched her. Even when she finally fell asleep, sometimes she'd awaken with a start, ready to swear that she'd heard him calling for her. But the only sounds would be Noma's snoring from the room beside hers.

She felt a touch of guilt in realizing that the only reason she wanted to visit the Williamses was in the hope of learning something of Hunter.

Perry rode along the overgrown path, loving the wind in her hair and the feeling of being free. The dark green of summer cooled her mind. Her problems were pushed aside by the thunder of hooves beneath her. If Hunter were married, then he must forever remain only a part of her dreams. She must give him up. But if for some reason he was still unmarried, an island of hope remained in the sea of problems that separated them.

Just before three, Perry rode up to the house of John and Mary Williams. It wasn't a plantation house, as she'd expected, but a small two-story home set among a cluster of trees. Perry guessed the home had three, maybe four, bedrooms. She could see a small stream running to the left with a garden in midsummer growth beside it. The house looked warm and inviting, the kind of place Hunter, as a boy, must have loved visiting.

Mary and John greeted her as old friends. They were delighted to have Perry for company. Mary brought lemonade out on the porch and the three sat talking for almost an hour before they were interrupted.

A lone man on a huge black stallion approached from the road. He wore a dark blue uniform and his boots were shiny and oil-bright in the sun. As he moved along, the metal on his jacket twinkled, blocking his face from sight. Perry felt her body stiffen as she watched the lean horseman. It may have been dark when she had first met him, but she could never forget his wiry manner or the evil that no amount of sunlight could burn away from Wade Williams. Today his blue uniform was crisp, and he smiled broadly as he stepped down from his horse.

"Good afternoon, Uncle John, Aunt Mary. May I join your party?" Wade's smile never touched his eyes.

His step was light and casual, but Perry could feel him watching her, studying her with the same idle curiosity a boy shows an ant before he tramples it.

"Certainly, Wade," Mary said, standing to pour him some lemonade. "May I introduce our friend, Perry McLain. Oh, I forgot, Perry told us she met you once before."

Wade's eyebrow raised with an evil curve. "I'm sure I would have remembered such a great beauty as Miss McLain," he said questioningly, the professed innocence of his lie a slap to Perry.

Wade lifted her hand to his lips as Perry fought the urge to reach for his gun. "It w-was at a party in Philadelphia some time ago," she said stammering.

"Ah, I've attended many parties in Philadelphia," Wade replied, nodding his head at his uncle, as if bragging. "Do you live near my aunt and uncle, Miss McLain?"

"Yes," Perry whispered. "I'm staying with my grand-father on his plantation."

Perry said little the remainder of the hour. She was aware of Wade's eyes watching her constantly. He asked her direct questions about her grandfather and his plantation. Since Perry knew little, her responses were brief.

John and Wade talked of the many problems of Reconstruction. Both believed North Carolina would be a key state to watch, but they agreed on little else. Though John never raised his voice, his belief that his fellow countrymen had suffered enough was strong. Wade Williams took the side of many Northerners, even though his roots were Southern. He believed each state must pay and pay dearly. Perry knew men like Wade were hated even more than the carpetbaggers. He'd turned against his own kind in his quest for power. Now that the North had won, he wanted more for his Union loyalty.

Perry sat, her hands clasped tightly in her lap, trying not to allow Wade's conversation to disturb her. He was like a leech sucking blood from a wounded animal. Finally she could endure no more of the talk. She pulled on her riding gloves with a sudden urgency to be gone.

As Perry stood to say good-bye, Wade rose beside her. "I'll see you on your horse," he said in a voice that sounded a little too much of an order.

"That will not be necessary, Captain Williams," Perry replied, hoping to discourage him. His presence had already destroyed her sunny mood.

"Oh, I insist, Miss McLain. It will be my pleasure." Wade held her elbow and began guiding her off the porch.

Mary stood on the first step. "Perry, would you be able to come to lunch next Saturday?" Her musical voice drew Perry's attention. Mary's eyes smiled hopefully as John's arm moved around her shoulders lovingly.

"I'd be happy to, Mrs. Williams," Perry replied as she moved toward her horse. Perry disliked knowing Wade was only a step behind her. The thought crossed her mind to pull her knife from her skirt pocket and order him to stay back. She almost laughed aloud as she thought of the shock such an action would cause John and Mary.

Without any encouragement Wade followed her to her horse. He gallantly helped her into the saddle. "I look forward to seeing you again." As he spoke, he applied painful pressure to her hand, which was resting on the saddle horn. Perry jerked the horse into motion. She wanted to scream that he would never see her again, but she was afraid the Williamses might still be watching.

Perry rode home at breakneck speed, desperate to get away from his evil presence. Later she tried to convince herself that he was not as evil as she thought, yet her impressions were strong, as was the feeling that she would see him again.

Chapter 12

Saturday inevitably arrived, to Perry's distress. She hated the thought of running into Wade at the Williamses'. Yet she knew she must go. She liked John and Mary far too much to hurt their feelings by not keeping a luncheon date. Perry dressed with care for her visit, but the fear of Wade hung like a dark cloud over her morning. She told herself again and again that John would never allow Wade to harm her, yet the memory of their carriage ride together kept flashing into her mind.

She hardly noticed the beauty of the warm day as she rode over the fields. Most of the land had gone wild with neglect. Tall grass and bindweed covered the fields. Summer's heat had choked away most of the wild blooms, leaving the landscape painted in different hues of green and brown. But nature's gentle coloring couldn't relieve the feeling of dread mounting in her.

To Perry's surprise, however, there were no other luncheon guests. She dined alone with John and Mary and had a delightful time. They'd received a letter from Hunter, stating that he planned to visit them soon. Mary showed the letter to Perry as if it were of great value.

"Just imagine, Perry, he'll come in a balloon. Won't it be a sight?" Mary said no less than three times during the meal.

Perry didn't mind Mary's repetitive chatter, for her thoughts were the same. Hunter had never left her mind these past weeks. Late at night she could almost feel him beside her. She remembered the warmth of his lips, the way his gray eyes looked into her very soul. He was as solid in her mind as he had been the day she left Philadelphia.

After lunch Perry enjoyed the ride home. There had been no mention in the letter of wedding plans. If Hunter was married, or planned to be in the near future, surely he would have written about it to his grandparents.

In high spirits, she turned up the front drive and saw the familiar old oaks waving gently in the afternoon breeze. The day had been a relaxing change from her usual routine. Knowing that there was a chance she would see Hunter again made her smile. She longed to see him healthy and strong. She wanted to see his face when they finally met in the light. Would he recognize her? Would he remember what they'd shared in the dreamworld after midnight?

As she grew closer to Three Oaks a movement caught her attention. Perry suddenly pulled her horse up short. There, tied in the shade, was Wade's black stallion.

Anger flared within her. Wade had known she would be away most of the day. Why had he paid a visit to her grandfather? As she debated whether to turn and ride away or go in and see what he wanted, he appeared on the porch.

Perry watched as her grandfather and Wade walked out onto the drive. It was obvious they had both been drinking. Wade's uniform coat hung unbuttoned on his slender frame as he leaned against the porch railing. His usually spotless dress was sloppy today, as was his stride. The two men seemed to be visiting like old friends. Their loud, drunken voices shattered the quiet countryside.

"Oh, my fair young lady is home." Wade moved toward her as she reluctantly dismounted.

Perry refused to look at him. She could smell the liquor on his breath.

He moved close behind her and whispered sarcastically, "Do not be angry, my love. I had business with your grandfather today." He let his finger run idly across her shoulder and down her arm. The trail of his touch left an imprint in her velvet jacket. "I'll call when you're home next time."

Perry whispered back in a catlike hiss. "Mr. Williams, you needn't call on me *ever*." She jerked her arm away from his reach, brushing her sleeve to erase his sinister touch.

Wade laughed. "Ah, the woman finally shows some spirit."

Perry pushed past Wade Williams and ran toward the house. She collided with her unobservant grandfather. He stumbled across the porch and landed harmlessly in an old wicker chair. Glancing over her shoulder to ensure her safety, she then disappeared up the stairs without giving Wade time to say anything else.

Perry didn't have long to wonder what business Wade wanted with her grandfather. At dinner her grandfather seemed in high spirits. Though he'd been drinking all day, he made a great effort to carry his half of the conversation. He even asked about John and Mary, as if they were old and dear friends.

About halfway through dinner her grandfather turned to the topic of his afternoon guest. Had he not been drinking, he might have trod more lightly into the subject.

"Captain Williams is a fine man, don't you think, dear?" Ignoring her lack of response, he continued. "He'd make a fine husband."

Now Perry did respond. First with a gasp of surprise, then, leaning forward, announcing, "*No!* I don't think he would. I know *I* wouldn't marry him." She couldn't believe her grandfather, even drunk, could be so blind.

To her surprise her grandfather reacted violently. He

slammed his fist on the table, rattling the crystal as he yelled, "You'll marry who I say this time. I know best."

Though Perry was shocked, she felt a deep sadness, for she knew he was lost somewhere between the past and the present. Her words were softer than they might have been. "Grandfather, you can't mean you would make me marry a man I don't love. I don't even *like* Wade Williams."

The old man sobered somewhat, and a degree of reality touched his watery eyes. "Love! What has love got to do with anything? Your mother loved, and what did it get her? What did it get me?" His voice softened. "I will not hurry you, but in the end you will marry Wade."

"But, why, Grandfather?" Perry asked, horrified and astounded by his determination. She didn't believe for one minute that anyone could make her marry someone she detested so.

Her grandfather emptied his glass of wine, and his reply was slurred. "It would be advantageous to all. Wade has great plans to run this area and someday plans to be governor. He'll have the power. If he had a Southern wife, he'd gain the support of the people. You'd be the governor's wife someday. Also, I owe a great deal of taxes. Wade promised to take care of that for me, and in exchange the two of you would inherit this place when I die."

"If it's money, Grandfather, we can get money," Perry pleaded. However, in her mind, she wondered where she could locate any cash. Her mother's pouch, with jewelry tucked between the folds of family papers, was hidden in a barn Perry would never be able to locate again. The only thing of any value she had was Ravenwood, and it belonged to her brother too. It would be unthinkable to sell their home just as Andrew returned.

"No, it's not the money. He also made me another promise I value more than this place." He stood somewhat unsteadily and cupped her face in his hands. "You have to understand; I've buried a wife and a daughter, both dying during childbirth. He promised me there will be no children from your marriage.''

"How can a man promise such?" Perry asked, her cheeks reddening.

"Never mind, Perry. Just take your time. You'll realize I'm right about Wade. The South we know is dead. Here's your chance to survive. I plan to see that you get this chance." His eyes clouded over, and Perry knew he could no longer hear her. He picked up a half-empty bottle and disappeared into the study, as he did every night.

Perry walked to the window and stared out. The three oak trees made dark shadows on the front lawn. She watched their mournful swaying. She was angry at her grandfather for trying to manipulate her life. But he was an old man whose logic was clouded by drink. Wade was a different problem. The arrogance of his bargaining with her grandfather for her hand overwhelmed her. She walked slowly to her room, chin held high with pride and determination. Wade Williams would find he had more to reckon with than an old man if he continued with this insane scheme.

The next three weeks were a nightmare for Perry. Wade came to the house almost daily. Each time her hatred of him grew. He smiled at her and made polite conversation in front of her grandfather. However, when alone, he took great pleasure in trying to aggravate her. She thought this a strange way to try to win her heart, but it seemed in keeping with his personality.

Pondering Wade's actions for the hundredth time, she slowly dressed for a dinner party. This was the first dinner at Three Oaks in over twenty years but Perry had no wish to attend it. Wade arranged every detail of the evening with her grandfather. He even hired a girl to help with the cooking. Though Perry would serve as hostess, she felt very much like a guest. Noma was so excited about the party that Perry wished she could share some of her en-

thusiasm. Noma had spent hours cleaning the formal dining room. Invitations went out to four local couples,
including John and Mary Williams. Normally the idea of
a dinner part would have thrilled Perry. Only tonight she
faced it with dread, due to Wade's presence. Noma thought
her criticism of Wade unjust and kept laughing about
sparks of anger igniting love.

Perry tried again and again to understand exactly what
it was about Wade that fired such hatred in her. She even
tried to tell herself that he'd been doing his job when he'd
kidnapped her. Perhaps he was even unaware of how
greatly he was hurting her in the carriage? But she'd been
there, she'd seen his cruelty firsthand. In the final analysis
she knew, more than anything else, that her repulsion was
rooted in the air of evil she felt when close to him. She
disliked his way of manipulating people, but she hated the
look in his eyes when he watched her. It reminded her of
a wild animal watching his prey. Now, tonight, she would
have to spend an entire evening across the table from him.

Noma broke into Perry's thoughts with her chatter. "It's
time to go down. Now, no more nonsense about Mr. Wade.
I will not hear another bad word about the man. Didn't he
send extra kitchen help for Sarah and three stable boys to
help out back? No man that considerate would make a bad
husband. Besides, it's time you learned that every man has
his good and bad side. A woman just has to live with one
in order to get the benefit of the other."

Perry refused to comment. Noma carefully checked each
curl of Perry's ebony hair, now pulled high in a crown
atop her head. Perry stared at her reflection in the triple
mirrors, feeling very much alone. Her ray of hope remained with her brother, Andrew. He would stop this insane courtship when he returned home. More men were
returning every day. It was just a matter of time. He would
protect her from Wade's scheming.

As Perry moved down the hall she remembered her
grandfather saying he wouldn't rush her into marriage.

Maybe this obsession of Wade's would play out in time. If she could keep her grandfather from getting too upset, she could stall for time indefinitely.

With stubborn determination Perry lifted her head. She would enjoy the evening, regardless of Wade Williams. There were guests waiting downstairs, and this was her first real dinner party. She and Noma had worked all morning remaking one of her mother's dresses. The dark blue silk was now draped in flowing clouds from her tiny waist. The rich material pulled snug across her breast, broken only by the snow-white lace at the collar and bell-shaped cuffs. She wished Hunter was the one waiting downstairs and not his cousin, but Hunter had become more a dream each day.

As Perry descended the stairs she noticed that three of the four couples had already arrived, leaving only John and Mary Williams. She stood politely as her grandfather introduced her to each of their guests. They were all older, influential people in the area. Perry made polite conversation as she watched the door for the last couple.

Wade circled the room, refilling drinks and talking. He smiled each time he passed Perry, yet said nothing. His wiry grin made her flesh crawl.

To Perry's relief the Williamses arrived just as dinner was being announced. Wade hurried to greet them, as if it were his party and his home. Mary Williams said hello to her nephew, but her usual bubbling warmth was absent. John apologized for being late, explaining he had been busy helping his grandson ready a flying balloon for lift-off.

The guests turned all conversation to John as he explained Hunter's landing a day earlier not more than ten miles to the south.

Enjoying the center stage, John elaborately described Hunter's landing in a field between his farm and the old church. Everyone could see the pride John had in his grandson as he explained that the lift-off would be in sight of the church, about mid-morning tomorrow. At Mary's suggestion, he invited all for a drink of her lemonade afterward.

Everyone was interested and amazed, except Wade, who sulked quietly by the window. Perry watched him force a smile and knew Wade resented Hunter's name intruding.

Perry felt sure that people would come from miles around to see the balloon lift off. She turned to her grandfather. "May we go watch?" she asked as they strolled a few feet away from the other guests. She could feel Wade following close at their heels and hoped he wouldn't invite himself along.

Wade stepped between her and her grandfather. "Of course I'll take you, Perry. It will be right on the way to church."

Perry noticed that he addressed her informally, but she made no comment. She resented the intrusion into her conversation. Her voice was cold as she whispered, "I hadn't planned on attending church, Mr. Williams. Tomorrow is Saturday, I believe."

Wade seemed not the least discouraged. He continued as if she hadn't spoken. "Yes, dear," he whispered back, "what better day for a wedding? Your grandfather and I have been talking, and we decided a short engagement would be in order." His lips disappeared into a thin smile that framed his teeth. Clasping his hands behind his back, he rocked forward off his heels in arrogant victory.

Anger clouded Perry's vision as she fought for control. How dare he be so presumptuous! Her hands balled into fists as she fought the urge to grab his throat and choke the smug smile from his face. "I'll not marry you tomorrow—or any other day, Mr. Williams! Do I make myself clear?"

Wade grinned like an animal who'd just trapped his prey. "It's been arranged, Perry. You might as well sit back and enjoy your engagement party, for tomorrow will be your wedding day." A fire danced in his dark eyes as his smile distorted his face into an evil mask. Perry watched the small scar above his eye and wished Hunter were there to help her as he'd once helped Abram, for she felt she was about to be trampled by Wade.

Perry looked to her grandfather for support. He was just finishing his third glass of wine. She knew he could be stubborn once he'd made up his mind and had a few drinks to fortify his determination. Well, she was just as stubborn, and she was not going to marry this man. She knew women had little more rights than slaves, but she also knew she was a fighter. Wade must be out of his mind to think she would marry him—she'd see them both dead first.

The other guests were watching her. She slowly forced her hands to relax at her side. She had to control herself and think. Maybe later, when her grandfather was sober, she could talk to him. If he knew how Wade had harmed her in Philadelphia, he would change his mind. As she took her grandfather's arm and proceeded to the dinner table, her mind raced for a way out of Wade Williams's clutches.

Chapter 13

Perry remembered little of the dinner party. The guests talked around her, unmindful of her distress. Even as they said good night Perry was so consumed by her hatred of Wade Williams that she only muttered short farewells. In her mind she plotted what she would say to her grandfather when they were alone and, if that failed, what she would say to Wade.

With the hall finally empty, Perry turned to face her grandfather. "I can't marry Wade tomorrow." She fought to keep her voice calm.

His eyes were blood red with drink and anger as he stared at her. "You will marry him tomorrow. We've talked it over and we think a fast wedding will cause less problems."

"But what of Andrew? Can't we wait until he returns?" The old man shook his head.

Perry could feel herself losing control. "You promised you wouldn't hurry me. I'm not ready to marry."

"Ready or not, the time has come, my dear." He reached to pat her shoulder but almost lost his balance and had to grab the banister to keep from toppling.

Wade appeared in the study door. From his smirk Perry knew he'd been listening. "Nothing will change the fact that tomorrow is your wedding day." He handed her grandfather another glass of brandy. "All brides are nervous the night before."

"This is not the night before. I don't know how to say it any plainer. I am not marrying you tomorrow."

Wade's laughter chilled the warm night air. "You'll learn in time not to challenge me, but I swear you will be my wife tomorrow."

Perry looked from her drunken grandfather to the insane captain before her. There was no reasoning with either of them. She turned and stormed up the stairs. She had to stall for time. Her first thought was to fake illness, but she decided against that ploy. Wade might bring the preacher to the house.

The only other alternative was to get away. But where could she run? John and Mary Williams might help, but they were Wade's aunt and uncle. The only other place was Kingston. She had enough money saved from her shopping trips to last her a few days, and then she could take a job in one of the many reopened shops. Wade probably would not bother to follow her, but if he did, it would take him at least a few days to find her.

Taking a deep breath, Perry tried to calm the urgency in her voice as she opened her bedroom door. "Noma, help me dress. I must leave tonight." Perry ignored the black woman's shocked expression. "Pack a few things in a traveling bag."

Noma faced her mistress without showing any sign of following the orders she'd been given. Age lines materialized as she wrinkled her face in disapproval. "What are you talking about, Miz Perry? You're not ridin' off in the middle of the night. No, sir!"

"Noma, you don't understand. Wade Williams plans to marry me tomorrow," Perry said over her shoulder as she struggled to remove her evening dress.

The older woman's face lit up, as bright as a firefly's bottom on a moonless night. "Marry. Well, my, my . . ." Seeing her mistress frown, she added, "Now, Miz Perry, you just nervous about marryin' and I knows how you feels. But marriage is the best thing for you. To a fine man like Mr. Williams too." Noma's mind was already whirling with plans for Perry's future. She reached toward Perry to hug the girl.

Jerking free, Perry stormed toward the wardrobe. "I'm not marrying Wade Williams. I have some say in the matter. I will not!" She stopped, realizing she had no time to argue with Noma. An hour's delay might mean the difference in Wade catching up with her before she could get to Kingston. She opened the wardrobe door and pulled out her riding clothes. "I wish everyone would stop treating me like a dim-witted child. He's no good. There's bad in him, more bad than I have ever seen in a man. I've seen it. I wish I had time to take you with me, but I know how you hate riding, and I must travel fast. Wade will return in a few hours to take me to the church. By then I'll be miles away. I'll send for you as soon as I get settled in Kingston."

Noma tried again, pointing her chubby finger. "Now, Miz Perry, I knows how you is when you sets your mind to something, but this time being stubborn ain't goin' to do you no good. Every woman needs a man, and you's doin' right nice with Mr. Williams."

Perry's anger showed from the tip of her slender foot to the flashing in her eyes. "I'm getting dressed and riding to Kingston tonight. Nothing you say will stop me."

Noma walked slowly to her small room. "You can't do this, Miz Perry. You can't ruin your life," she mumbled as she went into her room and closed the door.

Perry knew Noma would always see her as a child, and she had no time to make her understand. She quickly removed her evening clothes and tossed them unceremoniously across her bed. Ten minutes later she had packed a small bag and dressed in her mother's riding habit of midnight blue. She barely glanced at her reflection as she pulled her long black curls behind her neck and tied them with a blue ribbon. .

It would be a long ride, but by dawn she'd be out of Wade's reach and free once more. Glancing at Noma's closed door, she longed to say good-bye and beg Noma to follow in a few days, but she wanted no more argument. Noma would come to her senses soon. She would just have to trust Perry's judgment this time, or at least accept it.

Resolution set her face as she lifted the bag and moved toward her bedroom door. She glanced back, taking one more look at her mother's lovely room. She felt close to her mother, saddened because she might never be able to return. Her grandfather would be so upset, he might never open his doors to her again. That was a chance she knew she must take.

As Perry turned the doorknob, opening the door into the hall, she realized it would be very awkward if she encountered anyone as she left the house. Wade was probably still in her grandfather's study drinking. She silently removed her hand from the knob. Instinctively she turned to the balcony doors. As she stepped into the night air, fear's cold fingers touched her. The ground and freedom awaited twelve feet below. Perry remembered hearing that years ago, when her mother had chosen this very route, there had been thick vines of ivy climbing close to the balcony. Her grandfather had torn them down in anger at his daughter's elopement.

Perry found the fear of staying far greater than her fear of being hurt in a fall from the balcony. She dropped her bag over the edge, hearing only a muffled thud as it landed in the tall grass. Taking a deep breath, she climbed over the rail and lowered herself until she hung by her hands. Closing her eyes tightly, she dropped onto the grass.

Cool, damp grass broke her fall, and for a moment she marveled that she had broken no bones. Then, slowly rising to her knees, she groped for her bag. Within seconds she was moving, unseen, to the stable. She would saddle her own horse, for she had no wish to trust one of the stable boys Wade had hired.

A sense of freedom and excitement filled her as she threw the latch on the barn door and stepped inside. In a few hours she would be free of Wade's evil presence. She would no longer have to endure his constant stare or hear his harsh voice. She could stay in Kingston until her brother returned. He would put a stop to Wade's crazy ideas. Andrew had seen Wade before. He know how evil the captain was without needing proof.

A low, yellow glow welcomed her from a lantern hanging in the center of the barn. Perry moved beside it and twisted the wick higher to push the darkness into the corners. As the lantern swung free on her fingers the shadows seemed to move toward her, then back with each swing of the light.

Perry hurried between the stalls, anxious to select a horse and be gone. As she pulled the first stall gate open she heard the horse's hooves stamp in front of her and the faint shuffle of footsteps behind her.

She froze, listening for any sound that might indicate danger, but only the soft melody of night blended with the wind. The horse settled down and the barn grew as silent as a crypt. Perry slowed her breathing and thought, for a moment, that she smelled brandy in the air.

As she reached for the bridle a thin hand materialized from the shadows behind her. Strong, gloved fingers smothered her mouth, cutting off her air and pulling her backward into a wall of a man's chest.

Perry fought to scream as the hand cupped her face brutally. Hard fingers dug into the soft flesh of her cheeks. Wade's voice whispered terror into her ear as he forced her painfully against him, his other arm sliding around her waist.

"Where are you going, my love?" Wade's breath brushed the hair at Perry's neck. "I know you're eager, but it isn't time to leave yet." He laughed as he released his grip upon her mouth and nose. She gasped for breath in the cool night air. Wade slid his fingers into her hair, then twisted his hand into a fist. The blue ribbon pulled free as her ebony curls wove themselves between his fingers. Tears of pain ran unchecked down her cheeks.

"I had no idea you would have the spirit to run away," Wade hissed as he smiled at the pain he was causing her. "Thanks to your maid, we'll be together on our wedding day." He enjoyed watching her eyes fill with sorrow at Noma's betrayal.

The realization that Noma had once more trusted Wade and not Perry tore at her very soul. Noma, who'd loved and cared for her all her life, had turned on her. Grief surrounded her with suffocating force, hurting far more than the agony of Wade's hand twisting inside her hair. Noma had given Perry away, fully aware of Perry's wishes in the matter.

As Perry's mind whirled in confusion Wade began dragging her backward across the barn floor. The steady pull on her hair sent lightning-sharp pain throughout her brain as she fought unsuccessfully to keep her footing. Her knees hit the ground again and again with Wade making no effort to break her fall. He only jerked her forward each time she stumbled before she had time to recover.

Wade reached the back steps as her limp body came alive. All the anger of the evening exploded within her. She kicked and fought with every ounce of energy, but Wade's hold was too secure. He slammed her face against the brick as the shadow of the building completely concealed them. Perry cried out, suddenly needing her arms to block her from the brick as he pushed her again and again against the rough wall. He pulled his arm about her waist tighter, cutting off any air entering her lungs. His fist, in her hair, tightened until Perry felt her hair pulling away from the roots. The harder she fought, the tighter his hold grew, until there was no air left in her lungs.

Exhausted from her effort and blind with pain, she stopped fighting.

As her body became limp in his arms Wade let his hold around her waist fall and twisted Perry to face him. She gasped for air, not seeing Wade raise his free hand. He delivered a smashing blow across her face with the force and accuracy of a trained fighter. She would have fallen backward had he not still been holding her hair. He straightened her with one mighty jerk, until she faced him once more.

Before she could recover, another blow struck, splitting her lip. Perry's mouth filled with the taste of her own blood. Wade released her hair and shoved her backward into the yard. She stumbled and fell, landing facedown in the dirt. As the smell of dust and blood flooded her senses she kept repeating in her mind, *This can't be happening. It must be a nightmare I'll awaken from.* Her mind flashed as she felt the force of Wade's boot digging into her ribs, almost lifting her off the ground.

"Get up, you ungrateful Southern tramp!" he ordered as he kicked her again. "No one interferes with my plans. No one! I always get what I want. I told you once before, I always win in the end. Do I make myself understood?" He lifted her head with one violent jerk. "I need a Southern wife if I'm going to run this state; otherwise I'd kill you right now."

He pulled her against him. "Now, do I win this little disagreement, or do we move back into the darkness?"

Blood filled her mouth, preventing her from answering.

Wade tightened his grip as he lowered his mouth to her neck. His kiss was savage as he pulled away her collar enough to expose clean flesh. He lifted her off the ground as he nuzzled against her throat with a lust that terrified her far more than his beating.

When he looked up, her blood was on his face and mouth. "Now, my lady, do I win—or do I get the pleasure of seeing an even greater fear in your eyes?"

Slowly she nodded, afraid to provoke the mad animal any more than she had. It was obvious her pain excited him greatly.

He laughed and pulled her toward the house.

Perry's world spun. She was only vaguely aware of Wade pulling her up the steps into the house. Halfway up, he purposely shoved her hard into the steps. She felt her cheek burn with pain as another pang shot through her rib cage. Wade pulled her roughly up beside him and slammed her body into the back door before opening it and pushing her into the hall.

Perry heard the study door open, and her grandfather appeared, his eyes glassy with drunkenness. He looked at her in the dingy hall. "Allison, Allison?" he mumbled.

Wade took advantage of his confusion. "She was running away and fell from the horse. God, the animal almost killed her before I could get to her. I'll post a man below her balcony to prevent her from trying again tonight."

Any hope Perry held for support from her grandfather evaporated as she watched him nod in agreement.

"I wanta show you something, Wade," he mumbled, then staggered back into the study to refill his glass.

Wade pushed Perry hard toward the stairs. She fell against them as she heard his order. "Go upstairs—and stay there. I want a word with you after I talk with the old man."

Perry watched him disappear into the study. Her eyes were huge with fright. She could feel the warm streams of blood trickling down her face from a cut on her forehead and another in the corner of her lip. After Wade closed the study door Perry lifted her anguished body and slowly climbed the stairs to her room.

Noma opened the door as Perry tried to turn the handle. The old woman screamed as she caught Perry's collapsing, bleeding body.

"My baby, what happened? Oh, my baby," Noma asked as she helped Perry to the bed. "I knew you shouldn't be out trying to ride at night. Mr. Williams was frantic with fear for you. He said you'd fall and get hurt. Oh, my Perry, you've never been so foolish. You should have listened to Noma.''

The swelling and bleeding of Perry's lip made speech impossible. She could only lie quietly as Noma undressed her and cleaned the blood from her face and hair. The black woman lovingly wrapped her bruised ribs and scraped hands. By now Perry's face was beginning to swell in several bluish-black mounds.

Noma continued mumbling as she worked, ''What a fall you must have had. I'll get something for your eye. It looks bad. Oh, Miz Perry, what a sight you'll be on your wedding day.''

Perry silently closed her eyes and drifted into an exhausted sleep.

Chapter 14

Perry woke to the sound of Wade's voice drifting from somewhere above her. He was talking softly to Noma. "She fell just after leaving the stable. It was a miracle I saw her," he whispered. "To think she might have lain hurt in the road for the rest of the night, if not for your help. I am in your debt, Noma."

Wade was silent for a moment before adding, "Remember, when she comes to, she may be out of her head for a time. When I tried to help her, she even fought me, as though I had somehow caused her pain. I think the best thing would be to give her something to help her sleep."

Perry heard Noma rushing to do Wade's bidding. "I'll look in the kitchen downstairs, Mr. Williams. I heard old Sarah say she keeps medicine the doctor brings her to help her rest."

As Noma's steps disappeared, Perry opened her eyes to watch Wade. He stood above her, his hands behind his back, as if he were about to address his troops. His dark good looks were twisted into a stormy, thoughtful frown. Her blood marred his cheek and coat in silent rebellion to his normally spotless appearance.

"I know you can hear me, Perry. I'm not going to touch you now; there will be plenty of time later. I've posted one of the stable boys outside your balcony to stop any future attempts at escape. Tomorrow morning we will ride over to the church and be married.'' He began to pace, planning his strategy. ''Or should you still be recovering, I'll bring the minister here for a quiet wedding.''

He halted suddenly and pointed at Perry, lying under the covers. ''Don't you ever try anything like that again. If you do, I promise you'll have more than a few slaps to remember.'' His laugh was cruel and frightening. ''I promised your grandfather I'd not get you pregnant, and I'll be true to my word. I find other games much more exciting. But we'll talk of that tomorrow, on our wedding night.''

Moving close to her bedside, he continued, ''Your grandfather showed me something very interesting to-night. I know he's a crazy old fool, but this may help you stay true, *my dear*.'' His lips curled into an evil sneer as he emphasized the last two words.

He pulled a piece of paper from his breast pocket. 'It seems your grandfather tried everything to get your mother back when she ran away with your father. He even paid a great deal of money to have this document forged.''

Opening the yellow paper, he stated, ''It says simply that your mother was the daughter of a slave and therefore property of the estate of Three Oaks. Now, Perry, you and I may know this is a forgery, but look at the damage even the rumor could do to you. Because you can't prove oth-erwise, anyone would only have to look at that beautiful black hair to wonder.'' Laughing again, he added, ''Now don't worry, my dear, I plan to keep this little secret care-fully locked up. I wouldn't want my wife to be subject to gossip.''

Perry made no motion to acknowledge that she was lis-tening. A tear ran down the corner of her eye and fell on the pillow as she absorbed his words. He was blackmailing her. What of the future? Would there be more ''acci-dents,'' until eventually one killed her?

Perry moved her lips, closing her eyes to the pain she caused herself as she whispered, "Why?"

Wade moved close. "What did you say, my dear?"

"Why me?" Perry managed with some degree of clarity.

"Why you?" He laughed. "But, my love, don't you know. First, you will inherit, when your grandfather dies, one of the most potentially profitable plantations in the South. Everyone knows your grandfather drinks, so an accident would not seem unusual after we've married."

"Second, I want a Southern wife to sit at the head of my table, for I need to make friends fast. I've seen most of the single women in these parts, and you outshine them all by far." He patted her hand in mock tenderness. "Don't worry, my love, I'll see the bruises don't show after we're married. In time you might even find my little games entertaining."

Wade straightened, remembering his lecture once more. "Oh, yes—third, I want you because you're fiery yet unprotected. I wouldn't want to fight a father or a handful of brothers."

Perry realized he was right. Noma, the only one close to her, had fallen completely into his trap. She knew even if she told Noma the truth, it was unlikely the old woman would believe her. Andrew was out of reach. Even if he did return, he might not be strong enough to fight Wade's power. Wade knew how to bend people to his will, and Andrew was already a beaten man.

Closing her eyes tightly, she forced out tears as she tried to make her head stop throbbing. She knew she must fight alone against Wade. There was no one to help her. Somewhere deep inside, that spirit which always urged her not to give up still whispered. She had to clear her head enough to think.

Noma returned with two cups of warm milk and a spoon of sleeping powder. She placed the tray by Perry's bed and added the powder to one cup. "I'll put this much in, Mr. Williams, and she'll sleep like a baby till mornin'."

Wade moved to the door, impatient to leave. "Take good care of my bride, Noma. I'll be back about nine tomorrow."

As he closed the door Noma moved closer to Perry. She lovingly arranged the covers. She was confident her betrayal was for Perry's benefit. Noma chimed softly as she worked, "Everything is going to be fine, my baby, just wait and see. Now let's drink our milk and go to sleep." Noma must have said these very words thousands of times over the years, yet tonight they held no comfort for Perry.

Opening her eyes, she stared at Noma. She couldn't hate someone she'd loved all her life, yet her trust in the old woman had vanished.

Lifting her hand slowly, she pointed to the dying fire.

Noma understood. "You must have a chill. I'll add a log. Just you rest, it'll only take a second."

When Noma moved to the fire, Perry's eyes never left her huge frame. Unnoticed, bruised fingers traveled up to the tray of milk. Silently she moved her cup backward on the tray and exchanged it with Noma's cup of milk.

Her private war had began, and she knew that no matter what happened, she would never surrender.

Chapter 15

Perry pretended sleep long after she heard Noma's rhythmic snoring coming from the other room. She knew the sleeping powder had done its job but feared Wade might return to check on her once more before leaving. She would wait and plan until the right moment.

As the ancient clock in the hall chimed twice, Perry removed her bed covers. Painfully she slipped out of bed, every muscle in agony. She slowly moved to the triple-mirrored dressing table with only the firelight to guide her. Shadowy light danced across her bruised and swollen face. A newborn sadness reflected in her huge brown eyes. She must think rapidly and very logically if she were to survive. Another foolish mistake could cost her her life. She cradled her knees under her chin and began to rock, as she had as a child. She could pretend she was curled inside her mother's arms as they rocked back and forth in a huge chair.

Her mother seemed very close to her in this room, where everything Perry touched her mother had once held and cherished. The lacy room was now a prison, and the knowledge that her mother had once escaped was the only thread of hope that kept Perry's mind bound to rational thought.

Every ounce of her being willed her to escape. Her first

problem would be getting out of the house. She knew a man slept below the balcony, so she must leave through the front. Hopefully Wade wouldn't have thought to place a guard out front.

Reaching up to touch her now blackened eye, an idea formed in her mind. There were only two people she could count on, two men who owed her favors and might be willing to repay them.

Carefully Perry pulled a few coals from the fire with a small shovel. Placing the coals on the hearth to cool, Perry moved to her wardrobe. She rummaged through the bottom of her clothes in search of the small bag Molly had given her. As she pulled out the bag she paused, listening once more for Noma's breathing. A gentle snore drifted from the small room. Digging inside the bag, Perry pulled out the rough boy's clothing she had worn when leaving Ravenwood months ago. She slipped into them silently.

Returning to the hearth, Perry tested the coals. Finding them only warm now, she began to rub the black all over her hands and face. She knew this would fool no one after dawn, but maybe she would be safe tonight. With a darkened face, anyone seeing her move in the night might think her to be only a black boy.

Perry collected her nightgown and slippers and walked to the beautiful dressing table. Opening a side drawer, she removed her small knife and placed it in her pocket. A cold determination vibrated around her. She'd need all her wits if she were going to break free.

She constructed the morning's events in her mind. Noma would search the room and find nothing missing, except her nightgown and slippers. Noma wouldn't suspect Perry of wearing the old clothes. She'd pulled them from the trash weeks ago and hidden them. At the time she decided it would be sentimental to keep them, so she'd hidden them away in the bottom of the wardrobe.

With swollen, bandaged fingers, Perry pulled the side drawer completely out, revealing Hunter's gold necklace, hidden in a small well under the drawer. She had almost told Noma of Hunter a hundred times, but each time she'd felt confused about her feelings and decided to think them out before talking about him to anyone. Now she was glad Noma knew nothing of Hunter or Abram. Perry wouldn't have to worry about being betrayed again.

Pulling her huge floppy hat low, she stuffed her gown and slippers into her baggy shirt. She would need money, but the little she'd taken before had vanished from her dressing table. Wade Williams again! Somehow she would survive. Any hardship would be an improvement over tonight. She also knew her boots would have to remain behind, for they might be missed in the morning.

In black-stockinged feet, Perry stepped out into the hall. She felt her way along the wall to the front stairs. She would leave from the front of the house, as far away from the guard below her balcony as possible.

In darkness, Perry slowly fumbled her way down the stairs to the dining room. The windows in the room faced the front of the house and would be easy to open. Her grandfather had probably drunk himself to sleep in his chair, as always; yet she moved silently past his study door, not caring if she ever saw him again. She had tried these past months to love him, but he was only a shell of a man. He was more content with ghosts of the past than with people in the present.

The large French windows of the dining room opened easily, as if in encouragement of her escape. Perry stepped from the dining room onto the porch, now shadowed from the moonlight by the three huge oaks. The ancient trees seemed to be lending their support to her flight.

Perry bore no smile of confidence, as she had a few hours ago. She knew she must now use every sense about her to escape or face death. Her swollen lip and half-closed eye were constant reminders of the danger she was in. This was no game but a fight for her life.

She stepped from the porch and turned north toward the

creek. Within a few minutes she was standing beside the slippery bank. Thanks to recent rains, the water was deeper and swifter than usual.

Pulling her gown and slippers from concealment inside her shirt, she lay the slippers in front of her, as though someone had stepped from them into the water. She ripped the collar and neck of her gown before throwing it into the middle of the stream. The gown floated like a ghost on top of the dancing water for a moment before being sucked into the current. Because of the frequent bends in the stream, the gown would soon snag on a branch or rock.

Silently she prayed this ploy would work. She had Old James and Sarah to thank for the idea, for they both loved telling anyone who would listen about a runaway they'd known who had drowned while trying to cross the stream after a big rain. Perry now hoped Wade would head north in his search for her. Wade might try that direction first, because it was in the opposite direction from the church where he planned to marry her. She doubted he would suspect that by dawn she would be in sight of the church. As he searched north, hopefully he would find her slippers and torn gown. Then he would believe she'd drowned. If she was to avoid Wade, Perry knew she must remain dead to all. She would have liked to save Noma heartache, but she could no longer trust the woman who had raised her.

Leaving the stream, she moved swiftly across the fields to the south. She knew the country well, after having ridden every day for weeks. The stars lit her way as she ran, almost invisibly, toward the Williamses' farm and the church that lay just beyond.

As dawn touched the horizon Perry saw the outline of the Williamses' home. She'd slowed to a walk almost an hour before, but her lungs still burned and her feet were too numb to hurt. Now her spirits lifted as she realized she was within minutes of her goal. John Williams had said Hunter and Abram's balloon had landed between his farm and the church. She had to find it before dawn awakened everyone. She wasn't sure how Abram and Hunter could help her, but they were her one hope.

Perry made a wide circle around the farmhouse. She guessed Hunter would be staying with his grandparents, but with any luck Abram would be with the balloon.

The pale glow of morning cast the countryside in soft, golden light. She moved as silently as a bird's shadow across the land. With the farmhouse behind her, she crossed the meadow. Within half a mile Perry climbed a small ridge and spotted the bright red, white, and blue of the balloon canvas, spread open in the field. A balloon basket sat beside the silk folds. For a moment she froze, awed by the beauty of the brightly colored material against the lush green of summer.

Rounding the basket, Perry saw a small fire and smelled coffee brewing. Her heart warmed when she saw Abram, who stood, silently acknowledging her quiet approach without surprise.

Perry stepped forward, leaving only the fire between her and Abram.

"I guess I'd know that old hat anywhere. How are you, miss?" Abram froze with his mouth open as Perry raised her eyes to his. For the first time she saw shock in the black man's face.

She shook her head slowly, too tired and hurt to speak. Silently she watched his gaze take in her black eye, her swollen lip, the dried blood caking across her forehead and at the corner of her mouth, barely hidden by the remaining traces of black coal dust. She closed her eyes, not wanting to see pity in his face.

"Miss Perry?" he finally whispered, as if he doubted his eyes.

"Help me, Abram," she pleaded as her huge brown eyes filled with tears and her legs gave way beneath her.

Abram caught her before she hit the ground and lowered

her gently to a blanket beside the fire. ''I don't know what kind of trouble you're in, Miss Perry, but I'd put my life between you and future harm.''

Perry collapsed beside the fire. Her legs hurt from walking miles, and her feet, though bloody, were numb. She stared at the torn stockings and for one foolish moment cried for their loss. She'd reached the point now where her body seemed foreign to her and even her pain was dulled.

Abram handed her a steaming cup of coffee and gently wrapped a blanket over her shoulders. A memory returned to her of being wrapped in another blanket months ago when she had slept outside a burned-out hull of a farmhouse as her brother worked on Hunter. Perry knew without asking who had covered her that night. ''Thank you,'' she whispered for the two times Abram had cared.

After half of her cup was empty, Perry tried to speak clearly through her swollen lips. ''Abram, I've nowhere else to turn.'' A tear rolled down Perry's cheek, cleaning a line of the coal dust from her face.

Abram listened silently as Perry told him of Wade and her grandfather. She paused frequently, trying to pull her swollen lip into place. As she told of the previous evening's events the last bit of energy passed from her body.

''Can you help me get away, Abram?'' she pleaded.

Crossing his arms in tightly held anger, Abram hissed, ''Wade will pay for what he's done to you. When I think of how grand you looked the last time I saw you . . . He'll pay dearly long before his soul rots in hell, but first we've got to get you to safety.''

Perry swallowed the last of her coffee. ''He must not know you've helped me. I don't want to risk your life—or Hunter's.''

''I have no fear of Wade Williams, and I assure you Hunter feels the same. He has crossed his cousin many times before and will again, but today might not be the best day to stand and fight.'' He glanced at the farmhouse, as if there were another consideration at play that she knew nothing about. "We'll get you safely away today, but then where will you go, Miss Perry?" Abram asked.

"I could go back to Philadelphia. Molly will take me in," Perry whispered. "I'll find a place to go, somehow."

Abram smiled as the idea struck him. "I'll get you out of sight for now. You need a few hours of sleep. Then you're going up in the balloon with us. We're heading north, toward home. Wade can search the countryside, if he has a mind to, but we'll be drifting over it."

Perry tried to smile but her lip hurt too much to move. This was more wonderful than she had hoped.

"Now, Miss Perry"—Abram paced as he thought aloud—"Hunter would be angry if he knew what Wade did to you. Best we wait till we're in the air before we tell him. If Hunter knew Wade beat you like that, he'd start a fight between them that might end in one of them dying." He stopped and looked at her, debating how much to say. "There are some very important reasons why Hunter must get out of here without any trouble today."

She was too tired to understand the riddle he gave.

Resuming his pacing, he went on. "If it were a fair fight, I wouldn't worry, but I've never known Wade to play fair. He'd like nothing better than to see Hunter dead— and nowhere for all the Kirkland money to go than to the next of kin. Since Hunter's an only child, guess who that'd be."

Perry's eyes filled with fear. "Abram, how can I fly off in that little basket without Hunter knowing about it?"

"I know just where to put you." He laughed. "You can sleep till we're high up among the clouds."

She followed him to the basket. Ropes lay everywhere, as did supplies. Abram lifted her into the four-foot-high basket. Even though he was gentle, every muscle in Perry's body screamed in pain until he stood her on her feet inside the basket. She was surprised at the room inside, having thought the space would be very small and cramped. About a foot below the upper rail the basket bulged slightly, then returned to the rail measurements at the bottom. This bulge made a handy storage area. Abram pulled a blanket and rope from a nearby pile of supplies. He tied the rope to the railing, then tied two corners of the blanket to the other end of his rope. Moving about five feet to the other corner, he repeated the procedure, making a blanket hammock. He adjusted the ropes until the hammock swung into the basket.

Perry smiled at his ingenuity as she crawled into the hammock. The swinging bed was just long enough for her body. Her cocoon moved into the enlargement of the basket's side and out of the way.

"You stay quiet and hidden," Abram whispered. "I'll move supplies in front of you. But you shouldn't be too crowded. When we're well away, I'll pull you out."

"Thank you, Abram," Perry answered as her eyelids closed in exhaustion.

She was only vaguely aware of Abram moving large boxes in front of her, burying her snugly in the bulging basket. She felt warm and safe wrapped in the wool blanket. Sadness brushed her last thought as she realized she'd be seeing Hunter again in a few hours. Once more he'd see her as only a boy.

Chapter 16

Sweat covered Perry like a thin coat of oil. Sweltering in the darkness, she could feel death swallowing her as she fought to wake up, closing in around her, pulling her closer and closer into its victory dance, gulping her whole into its endless, damp blackness.

A sudden jar of the basket rocked Perry from her nightmare. She tried to clear her mind, but death kept pushing her into a tomb, suffocating her as she fought to awaken. The Grim Reaper was a huge shadowy figure with a hooded cap hiding his face. He pushed her into the grave, as dirt covered her face and blocked her breath. She could hear him laughing. . . .

Another jolt brought her into reality. She must have slept a long time, for judging by the movement and noise about her, men were readying the balloon for flight. She twisted slowly in her cramped nest. Each movement renewed the pain in her bruised body. The memory of Wade's beating flashed white fire in her brain, like a nightmare that had somehow crossed into reality. Each aching part of her body reminded her of Wade's anger. He would kill her if he found her. She must keep very quiet.

Slowly she wiggled beneath the blanket until she was facing the basket wall. Abram had closed her solidly in with boxes and ropes but she could remain in darkness no longer. Not only did she hate the blackness, but the heat was suffocating.

Pulling her knife from her pocket, she cut a slit in the blanket at eye level. The opening revealed only slats of light drifting through the spaces in the weave of the basket. She could see blurred glimpses of several men running around her. From their actions the balloon must be filled and already dancing like a large pear above her. She listened silently from her concealment. An hour passed before she heard horses traveling fast toward her and guessed from the shouts that Hunter was approaching.

"Abram, is she ready to travel?" Hunter shouted as he jumped from his mount and walked toward the basket. "Lord, Abram, do you think we can get off the ground with this load?"

Perry couldn't hear Abram's response, but she could hear the laughter in Hunter's voice. He was standing only a few feet from where she lay hidden. Straining to see through the slits in the basket, she was amazed at how he'd changed over the past few months. He seemed so tall. His return to health, along with a few added pounds, made him look younger than when she had last seen him. He looked even more handsome than he had in her dreams. A gust of wind played with his wavy blond hair, and she smiled, remembering how a curl had once wrapped itself around her finger.

All traces of the wounded soldier she'd helped were gone. Hunter was strong and confident now as he talked with the men around him, explaining all the workings of his wonderful balloon. He reminded Perry of a handsome buccaneer preparing to board his ship. The white collar of his shirt stood in sharp contrast to the golden tan of his face. He'd removed his jacket and thrown it among the supplies with the recklessness of an excited child. His vest fit closely across his chest, emphasizing his narrow waist and wide shoulders. The need to touch him was as painful within her as any of her wounds.

Perry watched as the man who had ridden up with Hunter moved closer. "We enjoyed your visit," John Williams said as he stood close to his grandson. "Maybe after you marry your little lady next month, both of you could pay us a visit."

"I know Jennifer would love it here. We'll plan a trip down before Christmas."

Perry watched as the two men embraced. She marveled once again how only time distorted the mirror image. As they pulled apart, John reached inside his coat pocket and handed Hunter an envelope. Hunter slipped the letter into the top of his vest an instant later. None of the men around them could have seen the curious exchange unless they were standing between Hunter and the basket. She thought it might be interesting to see what a letter passed so inconspicuously would contain. If it had been only a casual item, the two men would not have passed it so secretively. She found it hard to believe the gentle John Williams capable of anything less than honorable. The letter must have been only a personal note, nothing more.

As the grounding ropes kept pulling it to earth, Perry could feel the balloon struggling in a tug-of-war to lift the basket. A sadness filled her as John Williams's words seeped into her tired mind. The thought of Hunter's upcoming marriage to the hateful blonde woman caused long-held tears to fall. After seeing Jennifer, Perry wouldn't wish the sharp-tongued girl on anyone. From the conversation she'd just heard, it was obvious Hunter still planned to marry Jennifer. Perry couldn't explain why she felt such pain—a thousand times greater than that of her physical injuries—welling inside her. After taking care of Hunter when he was near death, she felt he was once again in grave danger, and this time no doctor or medicine could help him.

Within the hour, amid shouts and cheers, Perry felt the balloon lift into the sky. She heard Abram and Hunter moving about as the voices below faded. The ride was smooth, like sitting in a huge swing and letting the air push gently back and forth.

Another hour passed before Hunter relaxed. "Let her float, Abram. We're finally heading right. I think we've caught the current."

Abram cleared his throat. "Hunter, I've something to tell you." He began moving the boxes away from Perry's hiding place.

"Don't tell me you forgot something." Hunter laughed.

"No, I'd have to say we added something," Abram said as he carefully lifted the blanket.

Perry pulled her hat low as she sprawled out from under the hot folds of wool. She was aware of how wretched she appeared in her old dirty clothes and covered with coal dust. Both her hands and feet were covered with dried blood, and her right eye had swollen closed while she'd slept.

Shock showed only briefly on Hunter's face before he smiled. Sparks twinkled in his gray eyes like flint striking. "Well, my lord, it's the kid. Perry, you look a little the worse for wear. What are you doing here?"

She kept her head low and pushed her small, dirty fist forward. She turned her palm up and opened her hand, revealing Hunter's necklace. The metal sparkled like a gold nugget in a muddy river. "I'm askin' for the favor back, sir." Her voice was low, barely above a whisper.

Hunter made no attempt to accept her offer as he crossed his arms over his chest and leaned back against the basket. "How could I refuse? If I said no, we'd have to throw you out like a bag of sand." Making a short bow, he added, "Welcome aboard my airship, *Northern Star*."

Perry raised her eyes to him. She saw a cringe of pain pass through him as he observed her misshapen face. "What happened to you, Perry?" he asked with tenderness and caring in his voice.

Perry lowered her face and began her planned plea.

"My grandfather beat me, so I'm running away. Can I go with you to Philly like before? I got a friend there."

"Sure you can, and kid, keep the necklace as a gift, now that we're square. We'll make much better time, if the wind is with us, than we did last time in the wagon." Hunter paused in deep thought. "I want to stop as close as we can to the barn you found me in and pick up my uniform jacket, if it's still there. I don't remember much, but I think I buried it in the hay before I collapsed." Hunter was speaking more to himself than to anyone else.

Perry nodded in agreement, even though she knew she had no say in where the balloon might float. She'd almost forgotten the leather packet belonging to her mother, also buried in the loft. If they got close enough to the barn, she could pick it up too. It was all she had left of her home or her mother. With her grandfather's door closed to her, she badly needed that last tie to home.

The wind stayed with them, blowing the huge balloon above the land along a northern course. Perry spent most of the afternoon watching the countryside drift by. She watched Hunter as he constantly played with instruments and maps. It was fascinating how Abram and Hunter maneuvered the huge balloon. Hunter explained to her that by traveling up and down in the air, they passed wind currents. He called them highways of the air. The balloon might not always travel exactly where they intended, but it didn't just drift aimlessly, as most people thought.

"How high up are we?" Perry asked, her fears forgotten as she watched miles of country passing gently below her.

Hunter shrugged. "About a mile up right now, I'd say. We could go up a great deal higher, but after a while the air gets thin and cold."

Hunter stepped to Perry's side of the basket as he continued talking. "A few years ago a couple of scientists from England decided to see how high they could go. They got to about twenty-eight thousand feet. It got so cold, the instruments froze. They claim to have reached almost seven miles up. The temperature was well below zero, and one, an older man named Glaisher, passed out. If Coxwell, his companion, hadn't been able to untangle the cord running to the gas-release valve, both men would have died. Coxwell's hands were so frozen, he had to pull the cord with his teeth.''

Watching as Hunter returned to his instruments, she decided the only times she'd heard him put more than two sentences together were the times he'd talked of ballooning. How could he ever have gotten involved with a woman like Jennifer? In her wildest thoughts she could never imagine Hunter and Jennifer arguing like the blonde and the young man in the hospital hallway had. She couldn't imagine Hunter and Jennifer together at all. A quiet goodness centered about him, deep in the passions of his work. Jennifer was a self-centered woman who obviously used her beauty to manipulate people.

Not wanting to think about them together, Perry studied the land moving slowly by, as if someone were pulling a crazy patchwork quilt from underneath them—only the quilt never ended but kept revealing new patterns to the observers above. Someday, Perry promised herself, when she was old, she'd make a crazy quilt of these earth colors. She would lie on it and dream of the day she'd spent drifting among the clouds. The pain of her body mattered little as she flew with the birds, high above all the problems of the world.

By late afternoon they'd traveled a distance that would have taken three days on the ground. The air was cooling, and clouds gathered in a deceptive tranquillity around them.

Abram recognized the terrain first. Within minutes they were lowering the balloon into the field, where only months ago Abram had fallen. From the air Perry saw the stream that she knew wound toward the barn. She guessed the walk would be not more than a mile to the barn.

The balloon touched ground several times before nesting, as if it were a huge bird testing for the right spot to stand on earth. Each bump jarred Perry's bruised bones, but Hunter and Abram were too busy to notice her cringing in pain. She silently took each jolt without a sound.

Abram heaved his huge bulk over the side and began anchoring ground ropes. The basket settled into its nest of thick grass for the night.

Hunter worked as he explained to Perry, "With luck we won't have to let out much air and can start early tomorrow. If the wind should kick up, it can really play havoc with her if she's full of air."

As soon as the balloon was tied down, Hunter stated, "I'm going to look for the barn before it gets any darker. I should be back within an hour."

Abram nodded. "I'll make camp a little ways over there," he commented as he waved Hunter away.

Perry was trying to decide whether to go with Hunter now or wait until after dark when Abram opened the picnic basket beside her. Perry stared at a huge mound of fried chicken and her decision was made. She knew she could follow the stream and find the barn, even in the dark. Hunger outweighed all else at the moment.

Abram broke her trance by softly ordering, "Go ahead, eat a few pieces. It will tide you over till supper. I know growin' boys have to eat." He laughed.

Grabbing a chicken leg, she sat cross-legged on the ground, watching Abram work. Hunter had already disappeared into the trees by the stream.

"Hunter's grandma makes mighty fine chicken, only she thinks she's feeding an army. You must be hungry." Abram talked to himself, not expecting any response.

"I'll bed down here by the balloon tonight. Hunter usually likes to move away a little. We've found over the years that if he's out of sight, it's to our advantage. Then, if someone wanders up, they're usually unaware of him until he's had time to size them up."

Abram moved closer to Perry and handed her a canteen of water. "Miss Perry, does your eye trouble you much?" he asked.

Perry shook her head as she took the water gratefully, then continued eating. To be honest, she'd been so scared and tired all day, she'd not thought much about her face. She knew the puffy eye and swollen lip disfigured her temporarily, but it would pass. She wondered if the pain of Noma's betrayal would ever stop. Her entire body ached with fatigue and bruises, but her heart hurt much more.

Abram rummaged through a duffel bag and handed her a pair of black wool socks. "Put these over your feet, Miss Perry. If you want to wash the blood off, I'll doctor 'em for you."

"Thanks, Abram, but I have no shoes. I'd ruin your socks," Perry whispered sadly as she held the pair of socks back up to him.

Abram laughed. "Better you ruin one pair of socks than your feet. Besides, they're real thick. They'll be as sturdy as some of them slippers I've seen women wear."

Perry agreed. She washed her feet in a trickle of water from the canteen, then rubbed salve on the cuts. She pulled on the thick socks over her legs to the knee. They warmed her legs. "Thanks, Abram. I've never had a better gift."

Hunter returned just at twilight with his dusty uniform jacket thrown over his shoulder. Perry watched him approach. The dying sun was shooting its last rays into his hair, turning it golden. He walked tall and confident, as a man without a care. Silently smiling at Perry, he joined Abram near the small fire Abram had started. They talked of their plans as they finished off the chicken.

She lifted herself slowly into the balloon basket to retrieve her wool blanket. After a second's hesitation she curled upon the floor of the basket to sleep. The sides cut the breeze, so her shelter would be warmer than the ground and somewhat protected.

As she drifted into sleep, she could see in her mind's

eye Hunter walking toward her. His movements were fluid and easy, and he walked in long strides. He was smiling as the sun danced in his hair. Then, in her dream, she saw him moving toward Jennifer, not her. She called, but her warnings were unheard, as he embraced Jennifer. The lovely young blonde turned her face toward Perry as she looked over Hunter's shoulder. Jennifer's features began to distort and wrinkle into an evil mask. Her lips twisted into a devilish grin at Perry as her hideously misshapen fingers moved toward Hunter's throat. Perry shouted again and again, but her warning fell on deaf ears.

A tear rolled down Perry's sleeping face as she rested curled inside her corner of the *Northern Star*.

Perry was deep in sleep before Hunter pulled the letter John Williams had handed him from his vest. He tapped the envelope to his chin as he stared into the campfire. After a long moment he slipped the envelope, unopened, into a secret pocket inside his leather boot.

Abram watched Hunter's curious behavior but, as usual, made no comment.

"Good night," Hunter said as he picked up his blanket and moved toward the shadows of the trees. "See you at dawn."

A nod was Abram's answer. He knew Hunter found his only happiness in his dreams. The black man didn't have to ask how unhappy his captain was . . . he knew. He'd seen it in those gray eyes, in the way he took risks, in the deadly game he played with the secret messages. What tore Abram apart was the knowledge that the angel Hunter spoke of in his dreams was sleeping only a few feet away, and he'd given his word to keep her secret.

Chapter 17

An hour before dawn Perry woke to the sound of a lonely owl hooting in the distance. As she stood, every muscle screamed in pain. She gently touched her face. The swelling of her lip seemed less than yesterday. However, her half-closed eye still throbbed. She knew without looking in a mirror that her face was a mass of black and blue.

The air was still and carried the warmth of summer as she moved silently out of the balloon's basket and across the field toward the stream. She knew her directions well and within a few minutes was following the small, bubbly stream as her eyes searched the blackness for the old barn. Gradually her muscles loosened, and she moved swiftly through the darkness.

In less than ten minutes Perry stumbled across an old trail that climbed upward toward the barn. With luck she'd be back at the balloon within the hour. She remembered Abram explaining that after breakfast it would take time to make the balloon ready to travel. He'd told her that they had only enough hydrogen to lift off one more time. The next time they set down, the balloon must be deflated and they would have to stay on the ground. Hunter seemed confident that they would land close to Philadelphia. Abram only chuckled and reminded Hunter of times they'd missed their mark by many miles.

As Perry stepped from the trail the dark shadow of the old barn loomed before her. It had remained unchanged by the storms of God or man. She darted across the damp grass to the barn door and forced it open. A familiar creaking of the ancient hinges welcomed her, as it had that rainy night months ago.

The barn was black inside, and Perry had to feel her way carefully. Without much difficulty she found the ladder and climbed into the familiar loft. The smell of damp hay surrounded her in the darkness, welcoming her with its familiar odor. She relaxed, letting her feet dangle beside the ladder. The last time she'd been in this place seemed like a hundred lifetimes ago. At that time she'd never known a man's touch. Now she found she longed for the feel of Hunter's body next to hers with a physical pain deep inside her. Tears threatened the corners of her eyes as she realized she would carry that unsatisfied longing for him to her grave without ever knowing its absolution.

Early dawn light touched the sky, and she felt her way to the corner of the loft—and her treasure. She moved slowly for fear of stepping off the unbanked, open edge. Having hidden her mother's bundle in haste, Perry tried several boards before the old packet was once again in her possession.

Perry hugged her mother's leather bag to her breast, longing as she had all her life for a mother's touch. Whatever its contents were, something would be useful to her because her mother had begged her children to keep it close. She remembered seeing a few pieces of jewelry tucked between papers. Maybe she could sell them if times got hard. She laughed—how much harder need they be? She had no home, her brother still hadn't returned from the war, she'd lost Noma, and she was on the run from a madman who would surely kill her if he found her. In any case, this bundle contained all her possessions—all that remained of her Southern life.

As she rose, a hand touched her shoulder, freezing her

progress as though an icicle had pierced her heart. Fear paralyzed her mind. The memory of Wade's beating washed over her in renewed terror.

"Didn't mean to follow you, kid, but my curiosity got the better of me," Hunter whispered from a foot behind her.

Perry let the imprisoned air out of her lungs. She closed her eyes, trying to calm adrenaline-fired blood as it ran wildly through her veins.

"What have you found?" Hunter reached casually for her package.

"No!" Perry squealed, backing away from him. Her nerves were still jumpy and her voice trembled in pain.

Suddenly Hunter bolted toward her, his strong arms imprisoning her and pulling her toward him.

Anger fired Perry into action as his touch sent a throbbing of discomfort through her body. *Why must every man cause her such pain?* With his arms encircling her bruised ribs, the pain of two nights before returned in full. Her body reacted like a spring too tightly coiled. She had to release her pent-up anger or snap.

Instead of withdrawing, Perry slammed her elbow hard into Hunter's chest, knocking him backward. However, his arms still encircled her, and he drew her down on top of him with such force that her hat flew off. Hunter's sharp intake of breath spoke his shock at the sight of her tangled, but still glorious, mane of hair.

She would have continued to fight, but with lightning quickness Hunter rolled over, pinning her body beneath his in the hay. Fury raced within her as she struggled helplessly to free her arms.

She could feel his body spread over her from her shoulders to her legs. His muscular weight effortlessly held her and quickly blocked any attempt she made to move.

Hunter stammered, "Easy n-now! I'm not going to take that pouch away from you. I'm sorry I startled you." He took a deep breath to relax. Perry could feel his chest rise and fall above her breasts. The rock hardness of his body molded into her softness, as it had before in the darkness.

"I only grabbed you because I saw that you were within an inch of diving off the edge of the loft," he whispered, his warm breath tickling her ear.

Perry turned her head and saw that he spoke the truth. In the half-light she hadn't realized the edge was so near. His quick action may have saved her life, but she was in no mood to thank him.

"Will you get off me, please?" she whispered, every inch of her body aware of his nearness. She breathed in the fresh, masculine scent of him as she lay beneath his hard male frame.

Hunter moved away slowly, allowing his leg to slide over Perry's body as he rolled sideways. "Sorry if I hurt you." He stood and dusted hay from his clothes, unaware of the effect his action had had on her. He retrieved her hat and slapped it against his knee before returning it. The dawn light revealed her as only a shadowy figure before him, her matted black hair covering her bruised and swollen face.

"How could I have been so dense?" The memory of her tiny, perfect body below him was thick in his mind. "Does Abram know you're a girl?"

Perry only nodded.

"So the joke's on me. I should have known. I remember a woman caring for me up here in this loft, and my mind couldn't quite accept you as a boy in camp that first day." His words came slowly as he spoke, more to himself than to Perry. "The dreams I had while I was injured made reality hard to remember for a while."

As suddenly as it had appeared, Hunter's smile vanished. "I'm sorry I hurt you just now, Perry. You look like you have enough problems without being frightened half out of your mind by someone grabbing you in the dark."

Perry turned away from him and began stuffing her hair

into her hat. "You didn't hurt me as much as others have," she answered bitterly.

She couldn't see the sadness in Hunter's eyes as she spoke. He felt a great sorrow for this poor girl who'd been treated so cruelly. He found it hard to fathom that from this rough piece of coal before him his mind had fired a diamondlike beauty, but he knew now that this frightened creature was the beginning of his fantasy. His constant dreams of the heavenly woman with loving eyes and a soft kiss had begun forming in this very loft, with this sad creature before him.

"Is your name really Perry?" Hunter asked.

"Yes," she answered, still not looking up at him.

Hunter walked over to stand above her. "Perry, is there any way I can help you?"

She couldn't mistake the sincerity in his voice. That low, earnest tone that told her he'd put his life behind his words if necessary. *Dear God,* she thought, *how I hate hearing only pity in his low voice.* But she must swallow her pride if she was to enlist his aid.

Keeping her head low, Perry stood up beside him, her hat now shading her blackened face from his view. "I have to get back to Philadelphia quickly. A man is trying to force me to marry him."

"Is he the one who hurt you so?" Hunter asked, anger flickering in his words. Perry heard the same cold steel in his voice she'd heard months ago when he'd talked with the two deserters who had tried to rob them. She knew that beneath his calm, relaxed exterior lay a caged animal. Others must feel it also. He was not a man to cross, yet she must dress her truth in lies.

"Yesterday was to be my wedding day," she answered. "I ran away once, and he beat me. He didn't think I'd have the strength to try it again. I think he'll kill me if he finds me." Her words came as fact, without emotion.

"You look so tiny, but I have the feeling you'd die rather than marry this man." Hunter moved back into the shadows to allow her to pass him. "I'll help you, Perry. I would have offered the same help if you were a boy or a girl. There was no need to pretend."

Perry could feel Hunter's kindness toward her and sense his anger at the man who had hurt her. She wasn't sure how he'd react if he knew his Cousin Wade was the vile groom she was to marry. The less said to Hunter, the better. Before Hunter had time for more questions, she slipped past him, mumbling something about Abram needing her.

Hunter watched her move silently down the ladder. She looked no more than a boy, but Hunter knew from holding her in his arms that she was a full-grown woman. The memory of her soft body hidden beneath her filthy clothes returned to him in a tidal wave. His fingers clenched into fists, then relaxed as he scolded himself and his desire. He moved to follow, then withdrew, unsure. The last thing she needed right now was to be frightened again.

Crossing the loft floor, he watched as she ran across the grass and disappeared down the trail leading to the stream. He spread his arms wide above his head and pushed on the aging beams until they creaked in strain. Now he knew that the origin of his dreams lay with Perry.

She had sparked his mind into conjuring up a vision of an angel of mercy, an angel whose form haunted his every dream, an angel who made all other beauty dim in the light of her memory. Reason told him there was no way this poor creature could be the beautiful woman he'd seen in the shadows of the night. Perry was a dirty farm girl, whereas his angel was a grand lady with a shining halo of hair. Her kiss had ignited a fire within him. His longing to see her was a hunger so great, he felt he might die of starvation if he couldn't have her.

Lately he'd questioned his sanity. For when he held Jennifer close, he longed only for the woman in his dreams. She danced like a playful nymph across his thoughts. Appearing, disappearing. Close, faraway. Sometimes she was a fierce fire he would douse from his mind. Yet at other times his arms ached with desire for her. Hunter realized his dream had been given its beginning in this darkened loft. Now this dream haunted him even into his waking hours. No woman, not even Jennifer, could clear the angel's beauty from his mind. It puzzled him how touching Perry could have brought back so strongly the desire to hold his imaginary woman. Maybe he should marry, before his longing for a dream drowned reality.

He hurried down the ladder to follow Perry, but she was already out of sight. He couldn't blame her for avoiding men if one had so damaged her face.

Slowly walking back to the camp, he tried to push the memory of his angel back in his mind. She belonged in his dreams, not in his waking hours. By the time Hunter reached the balloon, Abram was already loading supplies. They worked hard readying the balloon for flight, Perry pulling her share of the chores.

Perry avoided his glance until the *Northern Star* was airborne. Then, suddenly, the basket grew confining to her. His quick glance from Abram to Perry told Hunter his black friend knew far more than he was saying.

They sailed effortlessly in a gentle, northern current for almost an hour before either spoke.

Hunter broke the silence. "Perry, look!" he yelled as he pointed out a small farming town. People were waving frantically from below. Children danced around as their voices drifted up in contagious excitement. Perry laughed at the sight.

"They love seeing us," she said, leaning as far as she dared over the edge to return their greetings.

"True." Hunter grinned, watching her. "But we balloon flyers haven't always been so lucky. Not only did farmers mistake balloonists for monsters, but some early balloonists were beaten by the crowds if they were unable to take off on time. One French aeronaut failed to go up in Philadelphia years ago. The sightseers didn't seem to notice that winds were close to hurricane force. They rushed him from all sides. His aerial carriage and silk balloon were shredded for souvenirs. Even a mansion close by was burned to the ground by the angry mob."

"It sounds like ballooning could be a very dangerous hobby." Perry didn't look at Hunter when she spoke.

"Oh, it is," Hunter answered, his voice filled with a happiness that only showed when he talked of ballooning. "But it gets in your blood. I've dreamed of being able to fly since I was a kid. I used to build kites and tie frogs to them. The frogs never seemed as excited about being able to sail through the sky as I was."

Perry laughed. Her musical voice danced among the clouds. Hunter turned to watch her but found that her face was hidden by her hat. He tried to remember what she had looked like before her skin was so blackened and puffy. The last time they'd been together he'd been very weak from loss of blood. Those days in the barn, and later on the road, were a jumble of memories. He'd spent the time drifting in and out of consciousness.

"Perry," he began, "you don't have to wear that hat now. I know you're a girl."

Abram snorted in the background but didn't speak.

"I feel better wearing it," she lied. She longed to let her hair blow in the breeze, but she couldn't stand for Hunter to look at her blackened face again.

Hunter sensed her uneasiness and continued talking to cheer her. "You know you're not the first woman to fly. Marie Antoinette wanted to once. But an actress named Letitia Sage actually went up for about an hour in 1784. They say she was a beautiful lady, but as a balloonist, she was lacking. She was no help as a crew member and weighed over two hundred pounds."

Abram laughed, interrupting him. "She'd make two of our Perry."

Hunter noticed the way Abram spoke of Perry, as if she

belonged to them. He found this surprising because Abram usually just observed people and rarely became involved with them. However, he seemed to have adopted this poor girl. He watched her with the protectiveness of a mother grizzly.

Turning to smile at Perry, Hunter found her head averted as always. He could feel her watching him when she thought he couldn't see her, but she never looked directly at him. Maybe, if he kept talking, she would lower her guard and look at him.

"Another woman went up about two years ago. I got a letter from a friend visiting Paris in '63, telling me that a Frenchman called Nadar took his wife up for more than sixteen hours. They say he built a huge craft. The balloon could lift more than four and a half tons. He made the basket more like a small summer cottage. It even had a darkroom to develop pictures. He has this idea about developing pictures taken high up to use for maps." Hunter moved slowly as he spoke, trying to see Perry's face. She met his every advance with a withdrawal.

"Anyway, five men and one woman went. Just after dawn on the second day the six passengers were admiring the beautiful sunrise when one started worrying about what the hot sun might do to all that gas. They decided to land but encountered a storm close to ground, blocking their descent.

"The balloon went crazy, acting like a large sail, dragging the little house across the countryside." Hunter placed his hand high on the same rope Perry was using to steady herself.

"The cottage tore apart everything in its path, including telegraph poles. Finally, after fifteen miles of havoc, a dense forest caught the balloon, which, once trapped, exploded within minutes. Nadar's wife was the only one left in the basket. All the others had fallen out along the way." He moved his hand down the rope a few inches and frowned as Perry moved away slightly.

"The miracle of it all was that no one died, though all were injured." Hunter moved his hand lower once more, and again Perry moved away.

Abram broke into Hunter's story. "You're really making Perry feel safe up here."

Giving up his quest to see her face, Hunter moved back to his instruments. "We've got easy sailing today. We're moving north and there's not a cloud in the sky."

By nightfall, his words would no longer ring true.

Chapter 18

Dark, moody clouds danced their turbulent ritual in an indecisive wind as the balloon whipped first in one direction, then in another. Perry clung to one corner of the basket, absorbed in her battle against motion sickness from the constant pitching. Though the sky blackened and lightning flashed all around them, she was far too sick to be afraid.

Hunter and Abram worked together in a harmony of movement that only close friends understand. They seemed to read each other's slightest signal, which was essential now, because both knew the balloon must touch ground before the full fury of the storm broke. Otherwise the trio might be cast into the Delaware Bay.

"Brace yourself!" Hunter yelled, only seconds before the basket slammed into the earth. A sudden wind caught the *Star*, lifting them up as if they were on a giant swing, then plowing them into the ground once more. Hunter's muscles rippled beneath his white shirt as Perry watched him work, bringing new sensations to the pit of her stomach.

Suddenly, when she should have been lost in fear, she remembered the feel of him when he'd pinned her to the floor of the loft. He'd been strong and sure in his movements with no hint of the injured soldier remaining. The

memory of his muscular leg sliding across her as he'd
rolled from her was as real as the storm about her now.
Her face reddened, and she was thankful no one had time
to notice her discomfort.

Hunter began deflating the balloon with great speed as
Abram jumped out with ropes slung over his shoulder.
Both men were frantically trying to bring down the now
sagging bubble of air before darkness and the storm were
fully upon them. Perry, not knowing how to help, stood
like a stone statue propped in one corner.

A tiny light danced in the woods before her like a huge
firefly. As it moved closer, a farmer materialized carrying
a lantern. He waved in excitement as he ran toward the
balloon.

Hunter's command was a single word—"Abram!"—but
it sparked terror in Perry's heart as she watched the huge
black man spring into action. He dropped the ropes and
darted toward the farmer, as though the friendly stranger
meant them great harm.

In one mighty bound Hunter was out of the balloon.
"Climb out fast, kid!" he shouted in a tone that left no
room for questions.

She stepped on a box and lifted herself carefully over
the basket's edge. Motion sickness, bruises, and fear ham-
pered her progress. Hunter's impatience startled her as he
scooped her into his arms and ran away from the balloon
as though she were weightless in his arms.

Perry clung tightly around his neck as he darted toward
a clump of trees. His strong arms held her firmly to him.
She could hear the rhythmic pounding of his heart beneath
his cotton shirt and his breath against her neck.

As he reached the trees he slowed his pace. "Stay here,
where it's safe," he whispered as he lowered her behind
a tree. "If there's a fire, you'll be out of range."

She had a hundred questions, but she knew there was
no time for answers. She could see Abram talking with
the farmer in the distance and was relieved the huge man

hadn't attacked, as she'd feared he might at Hunter's command.

Hunter signaled Abram, then slowly walked back to the balloon, as if there were suddenly no danger in the peaceful field.

Sitting quietly among the trees, she watched as Abram and Hunter deflated the balloon by moonlight. A small crowd of farmers gathered to watch but came no closer with their lanterns.

A chilling rain began to fall by the time Hunter and Abram were finished. Perry sat cuddling her knees to her chest under a tree. Finally, through the curtain of rain, she saw Hunter walking toward her. His clothes clung to his muscular frame, and his blond hair lay dark with rain. He knelt down beside her under the shelter of the tree.

"We got the *Star* packed up, but she's had some damage to the basket. Abram's gone with the farmer to get a wagon." He slung the rain from his hair. "If we don't get her out of this field before more rain falls, it will be too late. The wagon will bog down in the mud.

"The farmer said we can bed down in his barn tonight. It'll be dry, at least. We've had to sleep in worse places. These people seem real friendly." Hunter leaned nearer and added, "I'm sorry if I startled you, but we had to get away fast from the balloon. One of the biggest dangers when you're deflating a balloon is having someone with a lantern get too close. The whole thing could go up in flames."

Leaning back against the tree, he rambled as he always did when he was trying to calm her. "Professor Wise told me that once an interested spectator ran up with a lantern while he was trying to deflate. Within the blink of an eye the balloon was a huge torch. Wise was burned pretty badly, but within weeks he was going up again."

A chill went through her at the thought of him being burned. For the first time she wished this quiet man would talk about something beside ballooning. But his low voice was soothing, and she knew they could share little more.

"Perry, you're shivering. Come over here." He opened his arms and waited. "I'd move nearer, but I have no wish to frighten you."

She slowly moved beside him. Hunter's arms gently encircled her shoulders, as though he were afraid of hurting her with his touch. Perry sensed there was no passion in his gesture, only kindness. She relaxed, lying back on his chest. A comforting feeling surrounded and warmed her.

Hunter continued talking. His low baritone voice was a melody of tranquillity around Perry, even though she didn't understand all he said. "You know, Wise and Lowe are the two best balloonists in this country. But they are as opposite as day and night. Wise is tall and spidery, while Lowe is younger and a handsome devil. Old Wise can talk to anyone on any level and loves to throw caution to the wind. Lowe, on the other hand, is cold and scientific, with a sharp tongue. President Lincoln was about the only man I've seen who really enjoyed talking with him."

Hunter searched the night for Abram. She stopped shivering and relaxed as he continued talking. "Funny thing is, Wise and Lowe both have the same dream. They both want to cross the Atlantic in a balloon. Too bad they can't work together."

She wanted to talk with Hunter, to ask him questions, but there were too many barriers between them. She knew the sooner she could disappear from his life, the better it would be for him. He was engaged to another. Besides, it would aggravate the bad blood between him and his only cousin if Hunter knew the truth about her. How could she start a relationship with a man that she'd done nothing but lie to? Above all, he was an honest man; she could feel it all the way to her heart. How would he react to having been lied to?

Yet for the moment she felt wonderful as his arms held her, molding her into the curve of his body. The clean male scent of him surrounded her, intoxicating her thoughts with dreams of passion that could never be.

The sound of horses approaching drifted through the sheets of rain, swishing her dream away as easily as morning pushed night into hiding. Hunter stood and pulled her up beside him. He darted toward the wagon, with Perry only a step behind. Hunter and Abram loaded the basket onto the wagon bed, with Perry trying to help. The balloon was neatly stuffed into the basket. Hunter lifted her into the wagon bed before climbing up beside Abram.

"The barn's only a quarter of a mile away," Abram yelled above the storm as he slapped the horses into motion. "I didn't tell 'em Perry was a woman. They call themselves 'friends,' so I'm guessing they're like those Quakers we met a few years back. Thought they might ask questions if they got too good a look at our girl."

"Good idea," Hunter shouted. "They looked like nice folks, but she'll be safer with us."

Within moments the soaked threesome pulled the wagon into a large, dry barn. The farmer's wife had left a stack of towels and blankets on a barrel just inside the door. The barn was half filled with horses. The clean, fresh smell of hay came from a haystack in one corner. Perry had heard stories of Quakers and their tidiness, yet this barn surprised her. The barn was cleaner than many farmhouses she'd seen.

Hunter handed her a towel and blanket. "You can sleep over there in the hay if you like. We'll see to it that no one wakes you." He looked away, as if not knowing what else to say. For a moment she thought she saw the uncertainty of a boy in this strong man.

Perry accepted the blanket. "Thanks," she whispered as she moved away, not wanting to see more. He was already going to be so hard to leave, she didn't want to fall in love with another side of him as well.

The men were already beginning to strip their wet clothes off, having forgotten her presence. She glanced over her shoulder and saw Hunter's damp back reflecting the lantern light with a golden glow. Her fingers opened and closed as she fought the urge to touch him once more.

Crawling behind the hay, she wrapped the blanket around herself. Her coat was damp and her hat drooped with rain, but rest seemed more important than drying out. As she drifted into sleep, Perry could hear the muffled sounds of Hunter and Abram talking on the other side of the hay. They were making plans for morning, but she was too tired to follow the conversation. She pulled the blanket tighter around her, wishing she could be in Hunter's arms.

Perry slept, curled in a ball, hardly moving all night. Just after dawn, Abram working with the horses awakened her. As she climbed over the hay she saw both Hunter and Abram dressed and ready to leave.

Abram spotted her first. "Mornin', Miss Perry. Help yourself to some of the breakfast the farmer's wife sent out." He motioned with his head to a small basket propped on a post in the corner.

As Perry moved close to the basket the smell of coffee engulfed her. She discovered an old black pot sitting on the ground under the breakfast basket.

She poured herself some of the rich brew before examining the breakfast. To her delight she uncovered huge sourdough biscuits, still warm from the oven. Each one had been split in half and a piece of sausage added to the middle. As she bit into one she found to her surprise that the sausage had been dipped in honey.

As Perry savored each bite she heard Hunter laugh behind her. "Those are mighty good. After no supper last night I believe it's the best breakfast I've ever had."

He turned to Abram. "Maybe I should ask the farmer's wife for the recipe. Jennifer could fix them for me after we're married."

Abram's voice was low. "I doubt if Miss Jennifer even knows where the kitchen is." Hunter didn't see the frown on Abram's face as he worked with the horses.

Hunter laughed. "You're probably right, Abram. Come to think of it, all the years I've known her I can't remember her ever cooking me anything."

Moving over to pat one horse, he added, "The farmer said these were all he could spare. If Perry can make the long ride, the two of you can be in Philadelphia by late tonight." He turned to stare at the top of her head. "If you like, you can wait here for a few days with me till the crew arrives. Then you can ride back in the wagon. I need to spread the balloon material out to dry so the threads won't rot. The last thing we need, the next time up, is to have her start to come apart at the seams."

"I can ride as long as need be," Perry answered. If she rode with Abram, she could be at Molly's late tonight. If she waited and traveled by wagon, it would be days before Abram could even return to pick them up.

"I thought you'd want to go." Hunter turned to Abram and continued. "As soon as you reach the house, let the crew know where I am. They'll be ready to start immediately, but you'll need to sleep. So I'll see you in three, maybe four days. There's no need for you to return with the wagon. Stay in town. I'll join you there."

"Sounds good to me." Abram gave one mighty nod of his head. "I'll just get Miss Perry situated, then wait for you."

"Have one of the men wait a few hours before leaving, so these horses can rest. Have him ride my horse out and lead these two back."

Hunter handed Abram the reins to one horse. "I should be anxious to get back to Philadelphia and Jennifer, but I want to stay in this peaceful countryside a few days. I've got some thinking to do." There was a sadness in his eyes. He was dealing with his own hell behind the calm manner he displayed.

Perry removed the horse's reins from Hunter's hand. He seemed fascinated by her tiny hand, as one might watch a spider dancing along his web. Though her fingers were dirty and covered with scabs of dried blood, he seemed to see beauty in her movement.

Hunter dug into his pocket. "You'll need some money," he said to her.

"No," she answered firmly. "You have helped me enough."

Realizing he'd hurt her pride, he added, "Perry, if you do need anything, please get in touch with me."

"I'll be fine. All I ask is that you tell no one you brought me here," she whispered.

"You have my word." Hunter helped her mount her horse. He looked into her face for a moment, then she turned away as always. She didn't want him to see her bruised face, and she couldn't look at his wonderful, expressive eyes without holding him once more in her arms.

Perry kicked her horse into motion. She could barely deal with her own pain, much less his. He must never see her again; he must never know of Wade and her. He would be married in a month and she would vanish from his memory soon. Perry knew his piercing gray eyes would haunt her forever. She knew that for the rest of her life he would be her standard for measuring other men.

Perry rode out of the barn, tears streaming down her face. She could hear Abram riding hard to catch her. As he maneuvered beside her, the horses began to move swiftly in unison.

Half an hour later, when Abram slowed his horse to a walk, Perry followed suit. He turned his sad face toward her but said nothing.

After a few minutes Perry's question exploded from her. "Why is he going to marry a woman like Jennifer?" She didn't expect an answer, she was just voicing her thoughts. The question had been in her mind ever since the night she'd seen Jennifer at the hospital.

Abram smiled, as if he knew she would ask. "They've known each other most of their lives. Seems everyone knows about Jennifer except Hunter. Nobody's got the nerve to tell him. She's all sweet around him." He hesitated, as if debating how much to tell Perry. "I've seen her other side many times over the years. Talk is, she's had several lovers during the war. Her maid told me Jennifer loves to brag about them. Says she laughs about spending Hunter's money after they're married."

Abram shook his head. "I never talk about folks, but somehow I felt you should know how it is between Hunter and Jennifer. I feel like you need to know the truth, not just what Hunter sees or what Jennifer plans. Honest, Miss Perry, I don't know what to do to stop the wedding, short of kidnapping him. But I feel all the way to my bones that their marriage will be wrong."

Perry's mahogany eyes were brimming with tears. "You've got to think of something. Hunter needs someone who'll love him. He needs a love that lasts a lifetime, like John Williams has with Mary."

Abram understood her better than she did herself. He had watched the caring and love she bore for Hunter grow each time she looked at him. Somehow the key to the solution to his problem lay with Perry, and he aimed to unlock the secret.

After a brief silence Abram asked, "Did you tell Hunter anything other than that you were a girl?"

Perry shook her head. "It's better that I didn't. I don't know if I could live if Wade and Hunter fought over me and something happened to Hunter."

"You plan on disappearing so Wade will never find you?" Abram added sadly.

"Yes. I've got no one really to care about me, anyway. My grandfather called me by my mother's name most of the time I was with him. My brother will have enough problems getting started again if he ever comes back from the war. I think Molly will welcome me. We're about as different as two women can be, but we're both alone, and that might just make it work." Perry paused. "Abram, you must promise to tell no one where I am."

Abram raised his hand, palm forward, in the air. "As before, you have my word. But I plan on keeping an eye on you, just in case you need me."

Perry attempted a smile, and Abram thought that even through the bruises she still looked very much a lady to him. In unspoken agreement they increased their pace.

Hours passed endlessly, as did the miles. She was too tired to do more than grip the reins as they rode into Philadelphia. Just after entering town, Abram stopped at the back of a massive home and asked her to wait for him. He disappeared into a side door, half hidden in the garden. Men must have been waiting, for within seconds after Abram returned to Perry a crew of men burst from the house and hurried toward the stables. "That back entrance leads upstairs. The left door is mine, the right Hunter's, if you ever need to find us fast."

"I'll be fine." Perry tried to assure herself and him. She looked up at the darkened windows of the two rooms. Somehow it was comforting to know where Hunter lived.

Abram mounted without another word and signaled for her to follow. He led until they were near the hospital, then Perry pointed the way. No one paid any notice to a black man and ragged boy moving along the darkened streets. She remembered the direction to Molly's house well as she encouraged her horse.

Within a few minutes they were at the side entrance of Molly's garden. Perry allowed the tiredness she felt to show in her posture only a moment as she climbed down from her horse.

Abram held the mounts as she moved into Molly's back gate. "I'll wait here for ten minutes to make sure everything is fine. If your friend is home, there is no need to come tell me. If not, I'll help you find somewhere to sleep."

Perry whispered back, "I see her light, Abram. Thanks for all you've done. I know you're exhausted. Go on, I'll be fine from here.'' She touched Abram lightly on the arm, wishing there was some way she could repay him.

Walking silently up the blackened path, she prayed with each step that Molly would welcome her, for there was nowhere else for her to turn.

She rapped lightly on the kitchen door. A frightened voice yelled, "Go away, I say, or you'll be dead!"

Perry realized her unexpected night visit must have frightened Molly. She shouted, "Molly, Molly, it's me, Perry!"

Only moments passed before Perry heard the bolt being pulled back. The door swung wide as light poured out onto the path. Molly stood before Perry with her arms wide and tears flooding her face. "Come in, my little lady!" she shouted.

Hearing the familiar welcome in Molly's words, Perry stepped through the doorway and into the warm kitchen. Both women were within inches of each other when they stopped, frozen. A blast from a rifle sounded in the silent night. Molly's arms encircled Perry as both women fell to the floor.

Chapter 19

Wade Williams paced the long porch in front of Perry's grandfather's house. Three days had passed since his ruined wedding. Three days and no answers. Wade had slept and eaten little, as had all the others around him. Deep lines carved his features, and a permanent frown spread across his thin lips.

When Wade first arrived at Three Oaks, he'd thought Perry's disappearance was only a plot to stall him. Confidently he'd begun to search the house, assuring himself her ploy would only cause a few minutes delay. But his confidence faded as he widened his search to include the barn and fields beyond. His anger grew with each passing minute. He plowed through each room with Perry's bewildered grandfather, a whimpering Noma following in his wake. Perry was spoiling his plans, not only for a wedding but also for owning Three Oaks. The longer he searched, the more he thought about how he'd make her pay.

Just after noon, Sarah, the black cook, came running from the creek, waving Perry's muddy slippers above her head. Tears ran down her face as she heaved for air and climbed the last few feet to the porch.

Noma spotted her first and burst into tears, exclaiming everyone's fears. "My baby! My baby's drowned!" She

ran toward Sarah and both women wailed their pain as
they hugged.

Wade had men search the creek for miles downstream.
They found Perry's tattered nightgown, but Wade continued to push them relentlessly to find her body. He wanted
to see her, no matter how mangled and bloated her body.

Now, after three days, Wade had little hope. He tapped
his leg restlessly with his riding whip. It was really too
bad, he thought, that the silly girl couldn't have done this
a few months after they'd married. She'd destroyed his
carefully made plans. Now he would have to reorganize.
His goal to run this part of the state would be delayed by
weeks, maybe even months.

Noma interrupted his thoughts as she stepped from the
house. She was sick with grief, her face swollen from crying and her voice husky from yelling Perry's name. Wade
was finding her of less and less value to him, therefore his
manner grew sharper at each meeting.

"Did you search the room again?" he barked.

"Yes, Mr. Wade. But as I told you twice before, there
weren't nothin' missin'. I know all Miz Perry's clothes,
and only her nightgown and slippers is gone." As Noma
turned to point to the slippers and gown piled on a porch
table, she burst into tears. "I don't understand why my
baby would go off like she did. It just weren't in her to do
a thing like kill herself. She always was a-fightin' death,
never headin' toward it."

Wade could stand no more of her whining. He shoved
her back into the house and resumed his pacing. Noma
was right about one thing. It just did not make sense. The
question kept pounding in his brain—why would a girl
with Perry's spirit kill herself? Though everything pointed
to suicide, Wade kept searching his mind for another answer. He would believe that she was dead only when he
saw her body.

Reluctantly he decided to call off the search. He knew
he had pushed all the people at Three Oaks to their limits.

They were a pathetic lot to begin with. He was sick of ordering them around. The old man had vanished into his study and into a bottle. Wade doubted if Perry's grandfather would ever see the light of sanity or sobriety again.

Climbing onto his horse, Wade cursed the house and its inhabitants for spoiling his plans. He rode toward the Williams farm, plotting his next step. Luckily, few people knew of his engagement. After a reasonable time he could marry another—though no other woman bore Perry's qualities. He whipped his horse in frustration.

Within a few hours Wade stood before John and Mary Williams. They'd been waiting for word of Perry. Wade was amazed at the depth of their grief when he told them Perry had drowned. John's gray eyes were filled with sorrow as he held his crying wife in his arms.

"I've done everything I can to find the body. I guess it must have washed farther downriver by now," Wade stated matter-of-factly. He paraded back and forth across the width of their porch. His boot heels tapped a rhythm to his bland voice. "With the rain, the stream was swift. She could be all the way to Cape Fear River by now."

Mary stopped crying and looked up at her husband. "Oh, John, we were watching Hunter leave that morning. To think poor little Perry was drowning." Mary was speaking to John and was unaware of Wade's reaction to her mention of Hunter.

"Did Hunter see Perry while he was here?" Wade asked the obvious question, his lips drawn tight across a facade of calmness. Only small white marks around his mouth hinted at his frustration at the mention of Hunter's name.

John watched Wade closely. He didn't know the cause of the hatred Wade bore for Hunter, but he could see it burning in Wade's eyes. John had to answer Wade's question carefully, for he was not a man to lie or give away secrets. "Perry met Hunter in Philadelphia, I think. She never said much about it, and I forgot to ask Hunter. He, or rather Abram, helped Perry book passage here just after the war.''

''Why was Perry in Philadelphia when the war ended?'' Wade's question was demanding. He had to know how much John knew about Perry.

''I have no idea,'' John stated. He turned his face toward Mary, discouraging any further questioning by Wade.

Wade knew his uncle well enough to know that even if John Williams did know the answer, he couldn't be pushed or bullied into telling. Wade's mind moved logically. If Hunter had helped her once, was it possible he'd helped her again? He'd been close enough to help three nights ago, but how could Perry have had time to let him know she was in trouble? Maybe they were secret lovers. If so, Hunter could have come to her. That would explain her reluctance to marry him. *By God, if she is alive, I'll kill her for the humiliation she's caused me.* Wade's face reddened as his thoughts raced on. He knew it was a wild hunch. He had no clue to point Perry to Hunter.

Calmly he asked, ''Who went up in that balloon with Hunter?''

John didn't seem to understand the point of Wade's question. But as always, his words were carefully chosen around his nephew. ''Hunter had only Abram with him.'' John didn't seem to want to go into detail about Hunter's visit. Wade thought it almost looked as if his uncle were hiding something—not about Perry, surely, or the grief wouldn't have been in his eyes, but perhaps about Hunter's reason for visiting.

''No one else was in the balloon? You're sure?'' Wade pressed.

''I'm sure. I walked up and looked into the basket. It was loaded with supplies.'' John's eyebrow raised as he studied Wade.

The Union captain's pace slowed. He would have to be careful or John would guess his suspicions. ''Why did Hunter come down here?'' Wade asked, interrogating

John. He could not put his finger on why, but Wade felt John was not telling everything he knew.

John shrugged. "He planned to return as soon as the war was over to visit us. Maybe he just wanted to see us before the wedding next month."

Wade knew Hunter and Jennifer planned to marry after the war, but he hadn't thought much about it. She was too much of a woman for Hunter, or for any one man. Wade had known her years ago. At the time he'd left her alone after a mild flirtation. She was more trouble than he wanted to take on. Also, Wade thought it would be fun to watch his cousin suffer after they were married. His theory about Hunter and Perry didn't make any sense, with Hunter planning to marry soon. Hunter wasn't the type to have both a wife and a mistress. Wade laughed to himself. His cousin seemed to have little to say around one woman, much less two. Unless she was a bird, any woman would have trouble talking with Hunter. His only love was flying through the air in that damn balloon.

Wade smiled warmly, transforming his manner instantly. "I think I'd best go to Philadelphia for the wedding of my only cousin." He thought for a minute before adding, "And I think I'll offer Perry's poor maid a job. With Perry gone and the old man hating the sight of Noma, maybe she'd like to stay on at my place. I haven't really had time to look for a housekeeper."

Wade's mind was plotting as he moved away. If there ever had been anything between Hunter and Perry, surely Noma would know. Also, if there was any chance Perry was alive, she would find Noma. He would have the black woman watched, even though the odds were that it would be a waste of time.

Chapter 20

Blackness engulfed Perry's mind as she heard Molly's voice calling her.

"Perry, Perry, are you all right?"

Shaking the dizziness from her head, Perry mumbled, "I'm fine. What happened?" She tried to sit up but her body seemed to fight her.

"Stay down," Molly ordered. "I'm sorry I knocked you over so hard, but at least those varmints missed us. Remember, I told you Henry's nephews was trying to run me out. Well, for the last two nights they've been using me for target practice if I step outa my door."

Perry crawled closer to Molly. She could feel the night air drifting in from the open doorway. They heard a muted noise outside, as if a large object had fallen to the ground, then only silence. Perry whispered, "Molly, your gun!"

"I've got it pointed at the door. Just let one of them creak a hinge and he'll be a dead man," Molly answered.

Footsteps sounded from the walkway outside. Perry rolled over, allowing Molly a clear view of the entrance. Both women held their breath as Molly's steady hand raised the gun. Perry's body tensed as she braced herself for the sound of the blast.

The moon silhouetted a man's frame as he stood in the doorway. His huge body almost covered the entrance.

Molly steadied her arm as the firelight danced across Abram's face. He froze when he saw Molly's gun pointed directly at his chest.

Shock struck Perry like lightning as she realized Molly was aiming the gun at Abram. For an instant her body refused to respond, and panic flooded her brain. Then, with the spring of a trap, she jumped in front of Molly's body. "No!" she shouted as the gun echoed around the kitchen.

The bullet grazed Perry's arm and lodged in the door frame. Perry whirled like a dancer into Abram's arms.

"No!" Molly shouted. "Get your hands off her, you killin' bastard." She stood and headed like a mad bull toward Abram. She raised the gun in her fist like a club and charged.

Perry raised her unharmed arm. "No, Molly. It's Abram. He's my friend. He brought me here."

Molly took another step forward before slowing. Once she put her bulk into motion, it was difficult to stop quickly. She stared at Abram, a skeptical look on her aging face. She'd seen the huge black man once before, but it had been dark and she'd been more worried about Perry's safety than trying to memorize the features of some man she thought she'd never see again.

Abram suddenly swung Perry up into his arms like a father carrying his frightened child. "The man you're gunning for, ma'am, is lying in your garden. I saw his gun blast and thought he hit Miss Perry when I saw her fall. I just walked up behind him. He never knew what hit him. If he's not dead, he'll have a powerful headache come morning." Abram's voice was calm, as if in mild conversation, yet his eyes were alert to Molly's actions.

"We'll worry about him later," the old woman stated, heaving her huge chest as if relieved of a heavy burden. "Bring that child over here and let me treat that arm." Molly's head nodded toward Perry as she stepped to the large kitchen table. Pulling her box of medicine from the

shelf by the stove, she mumbled over and over again about
how frightened she was and how sorry.

"It's only a scratch." Perry tried to smile away the pain
throbbing in her arm as Abram set her in Molly's rocking
chair. He stepped back and Molly began her work with
trembling hands.

"I'll doctor this, then we'll find you somethin' to eat.
You look like you've been on the last train to hell and
back, child."

As Molly worked, Perry watched Abram nod with his
head toward the door. He wanted to check on the man
he'd left in the garden, but trying to get a word in between
Molly's chatter was like trying to slice wet sand.

Perry smiled down at Molly. She could see the old
woman's wrinkles grow deep with concern. A trembling
hand gently touched her face.

"Child, what happened to your face?" Molly whispered as she pulled off Perry's hat. Her chubby fingers
cupped Perry's chin as she gingerly turned her face toward
the light.

"I'll explain later, Molly. First, have you got any of
that wonderful cooking of yours? We've been riding all
day."

"I haven't got much I'm afraid, only bread and potato
soup. For over a week I've been scared to leave the kitchen
for more than a minute. About a month after you left, I
started seein' men hangin' around. They've been movin'
closer ever day."

As Molly brought Perry up-to-date, she moved about
the kitchen. She put a pot on to simmer before returning
to Perry with a cool, clean cloth for her grazed arm.
"We'll worry about your belly and gettin' some rest, then
we'll tackle those bruises." She looked as though she
might start crying. "I can't tell you how glad I was to hear
your voice at my door, child."

Molly set two steaming bowls of soup on the table as
Abram reappeared in the doorway.

Abram's calm voice seemed incongruous coming from his powerful, rock-hard body. "I couldn't find any sign of the man I struck. From the tracks it looks like two men, maybe three, drug him off. I followed their tracks to the far gate. After that I lost the trail in the dark. My guess is they won't be back tonight."

"Good." Molly sighed in relief. "Now you sit down and have some soup and bread. I'm plum sorry I have no finer fare."

Abram folded his large frame into the chair as he'd been told. He sat silently, eating as Perry told Molly of her escape from Three Oaks and Wade Williams. Molly listened as she worked, first reloading the pistol, then drawing a bath for Perry.

Abram stood as he swallowed his last gulp of coffee. "I have to leave for an hour. Is there anythin' you need, Miss Molly?"

Perry was proud of Abram for addressing Molly respectfully. She knew Abram's keen eye missed little. She guessed that he already knew what Molly's profession had been, just by the way the old woman talked.

"Well, if you find a store, I need food." Molly laughed, knowing there would be nowhere to buy food at this hour.

"I'll take care of the horses and bring up my bedroll. I'll sleep against your door tonight, if you have no objections."

"No, no!" Molly shouted. "I've never been so happy to have company."

"Bolt the door behind me. I'll see you in an hour," Abram said as he vanished into the night.

Molly rushed over to do his bidding, then returned to help Perry undress. "That man looks like he could break any man in half with one hand, but he worries about you like you were a queen."

"He's a good friend." Perry pulled the bandages from her ribs.

"Well, he's one I wouldn't want anywhere but on my side." Molly helped her into the tub.

The hot bath felt wonderful to Perry's tired, bruised body. Molly gently washed the dirt and dried blood from Perry's hair. Perry was amazed at the old woman's gentleness as she doctored her arm and the tiny cuts on her body.

"You're luckier than a whore with clean sheets that I'm such a poor shot," Molly said. "This scratch serves you right for teaching me to shoot."

Perry laughed, holding her bruised ribs. "Well, at least you're a better doctor than a gunman."

Molly sobered somewhat as she studied Perry's face. "I wish I could do somethin' about your face. If I didn't know your voice, I wouldn't have recognized you on sight. You lie back and I'll put cold rags around it. Maybe that'll bring the swelling down. Then we'll wrap those ribs." She took a deep breath, enjoying the activity.

"I'd like to get my hands on that Wade Williams you say done this. I've seen men like him before in my profession. They's the ones who can't get it up less'n they's hurtin' the woman first. There ain't no amount of money worth puttin' up with them kind. I've seen them beat a woman senseless before they have their way with her. You done right to get away, Miss Perry. He would have killed you for sure next time. You can stay with me for as long as you like." Molly's promise was sincerely meant.

Tears rolled down Perry's face. This old woman, shunned by everyone, was now her only friend. She didn't have much but she was offering to share all she had. "Thank you," Perry whispered beneath the towels over her face.

By the time Abram returned, Perry was doctored and dressed in a long white cotton gown. Molly had wrapped her in a colorful shawl, almost engulfing Perry's small frame. The old woman was chatting by the fire, drying Perry's hair, when Abram knocked.

As Molly pulled the door wide, he staggered in. Both

women laughed, for he looked like a one-man market-place. He carried a large basket piled high with fruit and vegetables, hams dangled from ropes about his shoulders, and each elbow was weighted with sacks of flour and sugar.

"Where on earth did you find it all?" Perry asked as she helped him unload.

"Never mind. I'm just bringing you two a few things." He pulled sacks of apples and spices from his pockets. Then he unbuttoned his coat and handed Perry a small gun.

"I want you to keep this close by your side. That little knife of yours won't stop these men, and those dueling pistols will take too long to reload if there's a fight." His voice was firm, leaving no room for argument.

Perry accepted the gun. She wouldn't have taken it, except Molly might need her help.

Molly was rummaging through the basket like a child at Christmas. She pulled out a fresh meat pie and shouted her joy.

Abram's face twitched in a smile. "That was mighty fine potato soup, but I figure we could do with something else. Hunter's cook made several tonight; she'll never miss one."

As he spoke, Perry realized where the supplies had come from. She also knew no one in Hunter's house would have questioned Abram's actions. She watched Molly and Abram dividing the pie into thirds. A warm feeling of being home enveloped her as she joined them in the late-night feast. She was miles away from Wade and safe—for tonight.

Chapter 21

Perry tried to stand still as Molly pinned the hem of a newly made-over dress for her. This was the third one in a week that Molly had insisted she have from the seemingly endless supply in the attic. She giggled at her reflection in the mirror. The collar was high and the long double row of ivory buttons made her look very straitlaced and proper. The long sleeves hid her healing bruises. If it were not for the fear that the men who were trying to kill Molly might return, Perry would say she was happy for the first time in months.

"Hold still, child," Molly mumbled through a mouthful of pins.

Before Perry could comply, Abram's familiar full-fisted knock rattled across the kitchen.

"I'll let him in." Perry whirled across the large kitchen, ignoring the pins sticking out of her dress.

"I'll put a kettle on and see if the pie is done." Molly shoved her sewing basket aside.

As usual, Abram was not empty-handed as he stumbled into the kitchen like a heavily laden street peddler. With a racket that surely alerted every mouse in the wall, he dropped his burdens on the table.

Looking over all the items, Perry announced, "If you keep bringing us food, we'll have to open a dining house."

"I just picked some things up on the way over." He set a basket of apples down. "I was hoping Miss Molly would make some of her delicious apple butter."

All three laughed. Perry couldn't tell whether Molly loved cooking or Abram loved eating more, but his visits were welcome and probably the reason they hadn't heard from Henry's nephews.

The teakettle whistled and the smell of fresh peach pie filled the room. Abram relaxed with an at-home sigh and pulled a small box from his pocket. "Miss Perry, I checked on this pendant you gave me." He unfolded the small ornament from its wrappings. The gold-and-pearl jewelry looked tiny and fragile in his huge black hand.

Forcing her hands still in her lap, she waited with her hopes resting on the tiny piece of jewelry. She'd found the pendant in her mother's packet, along with a few rings and several legal papers. The pendant might bring several dollars to help Molly. The old woman's hospitality might be boundless, but her funds were not.

Abram leaned forward, resting his elbow on his knee. "It seems this piece is quite valuable. I talked to a man who would buy it and pay nicely."

Perry's eyes widened in hope. "Would its sale be enough to fix up the big house?"

"Oh, I think so. With a little left over to see you through a year's supply of food," Abram answered.

"Wonderful." Perry made up her mind. "We'll have the house fixed up." This was her chance to help Molly.

Molly's head was shaking so fast, her double chins couldn't decide which direction to follow. "No, child, you keep your money. Even if we fixed the house up, how could we live? We won't always have Abram here bringing us food in exchange for my cookin', and just cleaning a place like this would take several days a week."

Perry wanted to argue, but Molly was right. Opening the house would cost money, but keeping it up would be a constant drain. It had been a foolish idea. The sale of her mother's pendant would bring money for now, but what about later?

She'd racked her brain trying to think of some kind of employment she could seek. She always reached the same conclusions. With jobs hard to come by after the war, no one would hire a young woman without any references or experience. Though she had a good head for figures and had run a large plantation after her father's death, work for a Southern woman in the North might be impossible to find.

Sinking into silent depression, she stared at the fresh pie Molly set in front of her. There must be some way to make an honest living. She hadn't escaped Wade just to starve on the streets of Philadelphia. Of course, eating the best pie north of the Mason-Dixon line wasn't exactly starving.

An idea rang out in her mind like a bell. She almost choked on her pie in her sudden excitement. "I've got it. We really *will* open a dining house!" She fought to keep her voice calm while her mind picked up speed. "Molly, I've heard you say often enough you wanted to cook, and I'd be able to keep books."

Perry burst into laughter at Abram and Molly's worried faces. They looked like two grown-ups who were afraid to shatter a tiny child's dream.

"Oh, don't you see? It's perfect. The house is huge, and most of the furniture is fine. The neighborhood is full of businesses, anyway. A nice dining house will be quite the thing."

"But, Perry," Abram said slowly, "you'll need help."

"Yes, lots," Perry answered. "With all the people out of work, that should be no problem."

Abram and Molly looked at each other for a moment, then nodded in unison. They'd help in Perry's plan, not because they thought it such a great idea but because it brought back the sparkle in her beautiful brown eyes. They were both too old and wise to believe in dreams, but they

believed in her. In minutes all three had their heads together, planning Philadelphia's newest dining club.

Abram soon decided Perry's plan had promise. He'd
exaggerated the value of the pendant several fold, knowing
Hunter's accounts would meet the difference. Now, if Perry
could make the dining house a success, the profits would
provide her with an income for as long as she needed it.
Abram knew Molly's cooking would be a welcome change
to most roadhouse food.

At the end of the night's discussion each of the three
was forced into a promise. Molly would make sure the
house was respectable, with no business upstairs. She
agreed to convert four of the bedrooms into small private
dining rooms. The other two bedrooms on the second floor
would be Perry's and Molly's. The small sun room sepa-
rating the two bedrooms would serve as the office.

Abram promised Perry to say nothing about where she
was to anyone, including Hunter. In turn, Perry agreed to
stay in the background so no guest would see her. As far
as everyone would know, Molly would be the sole owner
and resident of the house. Molly was salty enough to handle both thieving tradesmen and drunken guests.

For the next three days Molly and Perry were caught in
a whirlwind of excitement. Molly found a mourning veil
for Perry to wear so they could go about town without
people staring at her blackened eye. The list of supplies
seemed endless. After several trips they realized they
would have to hire a man to help them right away. Cooks
and waitresses could wait until later, but strong arms were
needed now. It wouldn't be easy finding just the right man
to hire. He had to be someone they could trust to live
under the same roof with them.

The sun hadn't cleared the rooftops when the women
set out to find just such a handyman. As they neared a
factory only a few blocks away from home, they saw a
long line of men waiting outside the gates. The posture of

many already reflected the defeat most would receive as soon as the doors of the factory were open. One, maybe two, would be hired. The rest would wander off to stand in another line, hoping that next time would be the lucky one.

"How we ever gonna find a good one among all these?" Molly worried aloud. "If we yell job for hire, we'll be trampled right here in the street."

Perry was too busy watching the men to answer. Most were dressed in ragged army uniforms. Many bore the scars of war and were missing arms and legs. These men seemed to be outcasts of society . . . men no one wanted or needed. Many looked as though they'd slept in the streets ever since the war. The long, depressing line stretched on and on.

As the women turned the corner Perry recognized a man's broad shoulders and thick-legged stance. A dirty blue uniform jacket covered a mass of muscles far wider than that of the skeletons on either side of him . . . muscles strong enough to carry a wounded man miles without complaint. She remembered his stocky stance even before she saw his face.

"Luke!" Perry shouted as she ran toward the dusty soldier.

The giant turned a blank face toward her. He stood rigid as she neared, like a man singled out for the firing squad. The wrinkles across his forehead told Perry he didn't know her and feared she'd mistaken him for someone else. He pulled off his cap and began mutilating it in his huge hands. "I'm sorry, miss. I don't know how a lady like you'self knows my name. But I've never met you."

"Luke . . ." Perry lifted her thin veil and stared up into confused eyes.

"Y-yes, ma'am," Luke said, stuttering. His head seemed to draw farther into his neckless body, reminding her of a huge turtle frightened by the unknown.

"Luke, don't be afraid," Perry said impulsively, regretting having done so immediately. Every muscle in the man's body seemed to tighten at once.

"Ain't afraid, ma'am." Luke squared his shoulders, trying desperately to hold on to his pride.

Perry tried again. "Luke, may I speak to you for a moment?" She waited for his slight nod before whispering, "You don't remember me, but we met a long time ago. You were kind to me once, and now I need your help again."

Perry couldn't have said the words any better. Though Luke hadn't been eating regularly for days, he might have hesitated working for a woman. But helping a lady, well, that was a different situation altogether.

"What can I do for you, ma'am?" He made a small bow.

"This is Molly, my friend." Perry stepped aside to allow Luke a clear view of the older woman. "We're opening a dining house and we desperately need a man to help us. Once we're open, there will be plenty of work for you." She hesitated, aware of others around them watching. "I should also tell you before you start that we can't pay much. You'd have a room and meals, but the pay will be poor at first."

Luke's full laughter made her jump. "A meal and a bed! That sounds mighty good. Lead the way, ladies. You got you'self a hired hand."

Molly didn't budge but puffed up like a large horned toad in an ant bed. "One thing first, Mr. Luke." Her pointed finger looked as deadly as any bayonet. "There'll be no drinking or womenin' while you're workin'."

Perry almost exploded into giggles. Molly stood beside her, a pillar of respectability. Even her dress had changed over the past few days. She now looked more like an old maiden aunt than a retired lady of the streets.

Luke addressed Molly with his hands in front of him and his head lowered in respect. "I'd not do that, ma'am. I drinks a few now and then, but there be no drunkard in me."

"Good." Molly deflated somewhat before adding, "If

Miss Perry says you're a honest sort, then Lord knows we can use your help.'' Without another word she turned and marched back toward home.

Perry and Luke followed. They were at work within minutes. Luke had only enough time to remove his coat before both women began calling for his help. For the next two hours he moved furniture, lifted rugs, nailed boards, and hauled wood. Though mumbling sometimes about being caught in a tornado, he continued to work, the smile on his sweaty face genuine. He enjoyed a job that taxed his strength and not his soul. It felt good to be doing a man's work again and not a soldier's killing.

Finally Molly ordered him to rest and have lunch. After only a few bites of her cooking he announced that he was sure he'd died and gone to heaven.

As the three made afternoon plans over dessert, Abram strolled through the open kitchen door without knocking. His arms were loaded down with samples of fabric and wallpaper. Perry jumped up to help him.

''I hired three carpenters to knock those walls out and build the counters you need,'' Abram said before he saw Luke sitting at the table.

Luke stood silently, waiting for Abram to make the first move.

Perry hurried to introduce them, forgetting she'd stood between them once before. Only then they had been soldiers. ''Abram, I'd like you to meet Luke. We just hired him this morning,'' she said, then moved from between the two giants.

Abram slowly offered his hand. ''I know Luke.''

Luke shook hands in silence. His gaze never left the black man's face.

Abram was quiet a moment before making up his mind about Luke. ''I'm glad to know you're here with the women. Miss Perry and Miss Molly are very special, and I wouldn't want any harm coming to them.''

Luke nodded his head in understanding. Both men knew Abram now held Luke responsible for the women's safety.

As Luke looked first to Abram, then to Perry, he raised one eyebrow in thought. "I remember where I saw those huge brown eyes before." His lopsided smile wrinkled his stubbly cheek. "So you weren't a boy? I'll ask no questions about something that's only in the past." He glanced back to Abram. "Hope you have none for me."

"Just one." Abram's eyes were as hard as coal. "I've heard tell you've killed men in fights that had nothing to do with the war."

"Only two." Luke straightened and added, "And them two needed killin'."

Abram studied him a moment, then nodded. "I understand. I've met a few men in this life who needed to meet their maker."

Perry interrupted, not wanting to think of the one man she knew who needed killing. "Abram has been searching for carpenters." She turned to Abram, intentionally steering the conversation to safer shores. "How long will they take to build what we need?"

"Ten days to two weeks," Abram answered.

"Great!" Molly shouted. "If we can get the help hired, we can open by the twenty-third."

Abram nodded as he thought out loud. "Two days before Hunter's wedding." He turned to Perry, sorry he had said anything about Hunter.

She glanced quickly away from the others so no one would see the sadness in her eyes. Everything had been so hectic, she'd had little time to dream of Hunter. Yet he still held her in the shadows of her dreams and the corners of every day's reality.

"Two weeks. Two weeks," she whispered. Somehow she had to find a way to see him one last time before she said good-bye forever. She would wear her black veil and watch him from far away. One more memory to help her mourn a dream that would never be.

Chapter 22

The days of remodeling melded together into endless toil. Perry worked until exhausted each day, yet thoughts of Hunter still robbed her of sleep. Finally, on the eve of the restaurant's opening and three days before Hunter's wedding, restlessness overtook reason. She waited until Luke had locked up and gone for his nightly walk to the tavern for a drink, then she dressed in black and slipped out the back door.

The pleasure of being totally alone was a welcome opportunity to free her mind. She needed to walk and make herself think of all she had and not live in dreams of what might have been. She needed time to think without having to guard her expressions.

Marching along the abandoned streets, she listened to her footsteps tap a lonely rhythm against the sidewalk. Her fingers gently caressed the gun that Abram had given her, which rested in her coat pocket. The small pearl-handled weapon offered all the company she needed to face the shadowy figures in the streets. But to her relief the only people about were a few servants returning home after a late night's work and tavern keepers sweeping out their stores before closing.

The same facts kept somersaulting in her mind. Hunter would be married in three days. He'd marry without her ever seeing him again. She'd never tell him who she was or what his cousin, Wade, had done to her. She'd never speak of how much just knowing he existed had changed her life, her dreams. She must live her life without ever feeling his touch again, without ever hearing the funny way her name rolled off his Northern tongue.

Tears bubbled over her eyelashes and ran down icy cheeks. She walked without direction, lost in thought. There was something wild within her that wanted to run to him no matter what the cost. But the cost of his rejection would be too much for her to endure. He loved another. He planned to marry another.

When she dried her eyes enough to look around, she recognized the back gate of Hunter's home. Crumbling on a low bench by the stable door, she studied the house, secure in the knowledge that no one could see her in the darkness. Knowing that Hunter was inside brought her both joy and pain. She closed her eyes and let the icy wind rock her as she pressed against the wood, pretending she was somehow closer to the only man who'd ever touched her with tenderness and love.

The same wind that comforted Perry blew directly into Hunter's face as he rode down an alley a mile away. He swung around the corner and stopped to check his watch in the yellow glow of the streetlight. Ten minutes late, but the note had been vague, saying only "After midnight."

Hunter couldn't believe he'd let himself get into such a predicament. Three days before his wedding and he was waiting outside Jennifer's house like a thief. He slid from his horse and tied the animal to the iron fence that surrounded her property. He'd give whoever left the note fifteen minutes, and that was all. The whole thing was probably a joke, someone's idea of a prank. But the words sounded so desperate. "Wait behind Jennifer's stairs after midnight. Matter of life and death."

Hunter knew sleep would elude him tonight, as it did every night. So, letting curiosity get the better of him, he'd decided to make this midnight ride, even if it were for naught.

Passing through the unlocked gate into a small garden below Jennifer's balcony, Hunter's nerves tightened. He strolled toward a stairway that permitted Jennifer to visit her garden without traveling through the rest of the house. The trees lining the boundary of her garden shadowed his presence as he waited in the cold darkness, wishing he'd ignored the note. But the note took the edge off his restless mind. At least tonight he'd be fighting the cold and not some dream woman who loved him only in his mind. Tonight the wind would cool the passion in his blood that boiled each time he dreamed of his raven-haired angel whose body was soft and yielding.

A carriage slowly approached along the deserted street just beyond the gate. Hunter sank farther into the shadows, waiting, vowing to forget this mystery and return home as soon as the carriage passed.

However, the carriage didn't pass but creaked to a halt at the gate. A young couple, locked together in an embrace, climbed out. They moved through the gate and to the foot of the stairs only a few feet from where Hunter was standing. The couple held each other in a long, passionate kiss and Hunter shifted uneasily. He couldn't see her face, but she must be Jennifer's maid. Who else would be climbing those stairs at such an hour?

With a sigh the young blonde girl pulled away and ran up several steps. When the lamp light touched her face, Hunter's body jerked slightly, as though his nerves had been snapped like a whip. The muscles along his jawline tightened as he fought to remain rooted in place. His knuckles whitened, his leather gloves twisting into fists. The clear view of his fiancée showed in the moonlight.

Jennifer's whisper drifted like smoke through the air. "No further, Richard. I must go up."

The young man braved a few steps. "Oh, please, Jennifer, let me come up for a few hours?"

"No, not tonight. I don't want the maid coming in on us again." Jennifer's soft laughter was like a sword scraping the stone into which Hunter's heart had just hardened.

"But I won't see you for weeks," Richard begged again.

"Of course you will, darling." Jennifer's voice was all sweetness. "As soon as I get back from my honeymoon, I'll send word."

"But, Jennifer, don't you see? Everything will be changed after you're married."

"Nonsense, Richard. The only thing that will change is that I'll have more money to spend on you. Hunter's always going off for days with that silly balloon, anyway."

Her words grated against Hunter's pride. She wouldn't have been in such a joyous mood had she seen the stormy gray eyes that watched her as she told of all the things she planned to buy her lover with Hunter's money. He remained in the shadows, fighting for control as his blood pulsed through his temples with a powerful force.

"Before I go," Richard begged in a whiny voice that contrasted with his good looks, "say you love me once more."

"I love you, I love you, God help me. You're a worthless leech, but no man will ever make me feel the way you do." Passion throbbed in Jennifer's voice as she touched her lover's cheek with a gloved hand.

Richard captured her fingers and pulled them to his lips. "And you, my lovely lady, are a heartless goddess who delights in having everything her way."

They both laughed as Richard moved up the few steps and once again embraced her. Neither seemed to notice the cold, but Hunter suddenly felt it to his very core. He watched as they ended the kiss and ran up the stairs to Jennifer's room, too consumed with their passion even to look back at the garden.

Hunter stood in the shadows, struggling to control his

anger. His first impulse was to storm up the stairs and strangle both Jennifer and her whiny lover. But another feeling mixed with the anger, cooling it like an icy breeze. The feeling, to Hunter's surprise, was relief. He couldn't explain why, but a burden he'd been unaware of was now lifted from his shoulders. He'd carried it so long, the weight had gone unnoticed. Now he was free of her, free of the chain of honor that bound him to her. He was angrier at himself for being such a fool than at her for having a lover. He'd always found it hard to talk with or understand women. Jennifer had pushed their relationship inch by inch for years, as if with some detailed plan of attack. She no more loved him than he did her.

Perhaps he should go up and thank poor Richard?

Laughing aloud, he ran to where his horse was tied. As he swung atop his mount a figure moved among the trees. A lean form slipped from shadow to shadow, visible for only a moment. Someone else was in the garden. Someone else had seen Jennifer. And now that someone moved to watch him. Instinctively Hunter knew the other had penned the note he'd received. The informant was waiting to see the outcome of his act.

Kicking the horse into a run, Hunter turned toward home. He didn't want to share his new knowledge with another, be he friend or foe. Tomorrow would be time enough to deal with Jennifer. Tonight he wanted to be alone to sort out his feelings and file them neatly away, as he had done since his mother had died. File them away so no one could touch him, so no one could hurt him.

As he reached the boundary of his property Hunter jumped from his horse. His hand instinctively swung wide to open the stable door and be done with this night and its secrets.

He froze in mid-step as his fingers touched the cold flesh of another hand resting against the door facing.

He pulled the hand toward him and a woman stepped from the shadows. She faced him, unafraid, as though they'd touched a hundred times before and she'd never known fear. The shadows were thick but Hunter knew her. The same woman who always came to him in his dreams. The only woman who had ever touched his life, his heart, his passion.

Drawing her into his arms, Hunter let his mind believe that she was real. She made not the slightest protest as he lifted her off the ground in his embrace. There were a million questions he wanted to ask her, but all he could think about was how her lips would feel against his own. He lowered his mouth to her cold lips and warmed them with his passion. To his wonder she opened her mouth to his hungry tongue without any hesitation.

Hunter's voice was so low, it seemed a thought that passed between them. "How did you know I needed you so desperately tonight?" He gently stroked her hair. "Just when I was about to give up on all beauty, all love in the world, you appear again."

He kicked the stable door open and stepped out of the icy wind. The shed was black with night and thick with the smell of fresh hay. He wanted to see her better, but he couldn't bring himself to pull away from her, even to search the darkness for a lantern. "Shall I find a light?" he whispered against the wonder of her hair.

Her answer was in the brush of her lips against his throat. "Hold me," she whispered.

Her small hands slid up the front of his coat, her fingers twisting around his lapels. They needed no light. How many times he'd dreamed of her near, so soft, so willing in his arms. He knew her features by touch as perfectly as an artist knows his model before he paints.

"If you are only a dream," he whispered, "then dreams will be my only reality in this lifetime."

Pulling off her cap, he moved his hands slowly over the rich wool of her dress. Her hair was the silk he remembered, and the curve of her waist was the perfection of which he'd dreamed. "You'll not run away from me to-night, my dream. I need you too much."

She didn't answer but only traced her fingers along the arc of his shoulders, as though she'd longed for the feel of him as dearly as he had for her.

Hunter pulled the ribbon binding her hair and buried his face in its fullness. "Lord, how I need you." He flung her cap over a pile of straw and eased her onto it. The smells blended in his mind with another time, when she'd held him and warmed him as death fought for his soul. He'd loved her then, from the moment she'd kissed his forehead with a prayer for his life.

In the silence of the midnight hour he lay beside her, slowly covering her face with kisses. As he reached the warm flesh of her throat his fingers unbuttoned her dress. The tiny pearl buttons gave way and he slid the wool aside to reveal the thin, silky cloth of her chemise. He spread his fingers wide, loving the warmth of her flesh, with only a light curtain of material between them. He'd always been a reasonable man, but the feel of her in his arms made him know the pure joy of madness for a moment.

He could feel her body move beneath his hand, strain-ing for his touch. He lowered his face to her shoulders, pushing the material aside as he tasted her skin. There was so much that they might have said, but he was starving for her nearness. Touch would have to be his words, and pas-sion the only language spoken between them. He wanted to make love to her more than he wanted life, but tonight he needed the feel of her next to him. He needed not to be alone for a few moments in a life where he seemed always alone.

She seemed to understand, for her hands moved over his shoulders and into his hair. Her fingers stroked his temple, then moved to trace his lips with a feather-light touch. He found himself whispering words of need he'd never told another.

Pressing her body against his, she answered his cry with

kisses that knew no restraint. His mind whirled as he felt the beauty of her in his arms, a beauty so great that he knew he'd never find it in reality. He buried his face against her soft breast as his hand slid up her boot to touch the bare leg beneath her skirts. If this was the joy of dreams, the pleasure of insanity, may he never see reality again.

His angel jerked suddenly. "Hunter!" she whispered in her soft Southern voice as she pulled his face close to her lips. "There's someone outside!" He could feel the fear in her body as she curled away from him.

Hunter glanced toward the fence and saw the shadow of a man move in the moonlight. The same shadow he'd seen in Jennifer's garden, a lifetime of emotions ago. Hunter held her trembling hand. "Do you know who he is?"

"I'm not sure," she whispered. "I must go!"

"No!" Hunter answered, but she pulled away and backed into the corner of the shed.

A twig snapped in the shadows and he heard her soft cry of fear. Hunter bolted toward the intruder, resenting this eavesdropping far more than he had earlier in the garden.

He ran toward the shadow. But when he reached the fence, the shadow had vanished. And when he returned to the barn, so had his angel.

Chapter 23

Molly's restaurant opened as Molly's Place during a downpour that should have spelled disaster for a first night, but the dining rooms were packed with the curious. The rumors that Molly was a reformed lady of the streets might have drawn some in, but the fine cooking kept them through course after course.

The room had been freshly polished and cleaned until the candlelight glowed off the wood and silver. The furnishings were simple, almost elegant, in design and the prices were fair. Each bolt of lightning from the storm seemed to bring yet another carriage up the drive.

Luke, now wearing a white shirt and dark suit, stood proudly as doorman. He opened the door and seated each guest with a silent dignity while keeping a sharp eye out for any ruffians.

At midnight, with the last guest departed, Molly, Luke, and Perry finally collapsed over a final cup of coffee in Perry's small office. After paying for the food and salaries of the cooks and waiters, there was still a tidy sum stacked atop the desk.

Luke beamed with pride. "It was a good night. Most folks could barely waddle to their carriages."

"Reminds me of my working days." Laughter bubbled

from Molly's tired body. "No one left without being satisfied."

The old woman never ceased to amaze Perry. "But in
this work you have less trouble with the law," Perry added.

Molly winked. "You're right. Plus, it did make me feel
good to make a lot of folks happy instead of a few delir-
ious."

Luke's full-blown laughter blended with Molly's chuckles as Perry fought a blush. She busied herself putting bills
in a leather-lined box she'd found when cleaning one of
the rooms. Deciding it safest to change the subject, she
added, "I'll put the money here for tonight, but if we
make this much every night, we will need a strongbox."

"There's one in the cellar," Molly said, yawning. "It's
a big old rusty box I've been pushing out of my way ever'
time I store food."

"We'll bring it up tomorrow and find a place for it,"
Perry answered.

"There's a drawer in Old Henry's room with several
keys. In the morning I'll see if one fits the box, but right
now I'm taking these tired bones to bed. This honest
work's hard on a body." Molly stood and moved toward
the door connecting her bedroom with the office. Though
she'd moved her things into the room over a week ago,
she still called it Old Henry's Room, as if he might return
from the dead and have need of it. Molly talked about Old
Henry so much, Perry sometimes felt he was a third partner.

Luke also stood. "I'll check around and lock everything up before I go for a little walk." He paused at the
door before nodding respectfully. " 'Night, Miss Perry."

Perry smiled up at Luke as he withdrew. He'd proven
far better help than she'd ever hoped. He was a large,
gentle sort of man with a big heart that overflowed when
he was shown any kindness. He'd never asked any questions about their meeting during the war, but Perry knew
he'd pieced most of the puzzle together. Luke was always

near, except when he would ask to go out walking for a few hours. She could smell liquor on his breath when he returned, but true to his word, he was never drunk.

Closing her ledger book, she walked to her bedroom. She was glad she'd been so busy, for she'd had little time to think of Hunter today. As she undressed, she let her mind wander to him and the way he'd touched her in the darkness of the barn. What would have happened if she hadn't been frightened by the man outside? Why had Hunter's words of need melted her heart so completely? He was a man who had everything—money, power, adventure. Why would he cling to her like a dying man to one last hope?

"Tomorrow he'll be married," she said aloud as she circled the room. "All my life I'll think of him, and he doesn't even know who I am."

She undressed slowly, staring at the impersonal room that had become her home. The cold rain pounded against her windows, pressing a chill into the room that not even the mahogany furniture could dispel. In front of the warm fire sat a small tub, half filled with water. Since she'd moved upstairs, Molly and Luke had seen she had a fresh bath every night. Though they both worried that so much bathing might weaken her health, they'd given into her wishes; both pampering her like two maiden aunts. A huge kettle bubbled on the hearth. She poured the steaming water into the tub, letting the hot moisture caress her face with its warmth.

As she sank into the steamy water her muscles relaxed for the first time since the doors downstairs had opened for business. Reaching, she wound a small music box Molly had found while cleaning. As the charming lullaby drifted around the room she closed her eyes, remembering another cold, rainy night a month ago. Hunter's arms had encircled her as they waited beneath a tree for Abram to return. She could almost feel his hard frame molded along her back. From the depth of her being she knew he was thinking of her at this moment, just as she was dreaming of him.

Hunter spent a sleepless night thinking of the woman he'd held in the darkness. She'd been heaven in his arms and exactly what he'd needed after witnessing Jennifer's betrayal. But her appearance reinforced the worry inside him that he might be going mad. How could a woman feel so wonderful and only be a dream, an imaginary lover he'd pasted together from the memory of all the good traits he'd seen in every woman he'd ever met?

When he finally rolled out of bed, he was greeted by a day as gloomy as his mood. The icy wind of midnight had brought in a cold rain that drizzled so slowly, it seemed to hang in the air, as heavy as a milk cloth full of cream.

A nagging logic kept tapping at his mind. Someone had wanted him to find Jennifer and her lover last night. The same person must have left the note, then followed him. But why? How could anyone profit from his knowledge of Jennifer having an affair? Was the person who'd been hiding in the shadows his friend or foe? A friend might want to save him from a bad marriage. But an enemy, knowing his sense of honor, might hope he'd react violently. If he'd killed Jennifer or Richard, Hunter probably would have hanged for murder. There was also the chance Richard would kill him in a fight. Hunter could think of only one person who hated him enough to wish him dead . . . Wade.

Evening brought with it heavier rains and the realization that he had to deal with Jennifer. Hunter waited until Abram retired, then rode over to her house with little thought of the weather. A carriage would have been more comfortable, but he wanted to see if the shadowy figure would follow again.

Within a block Hunter had his answer. One lean rider on a black stallion stayed well behind, convincing Hunter the man meant harm. He disappeared as Hunter knocked on Jennifer's door, but an hour later, when Hunter returned, the man was waiting half a block away.

The argument with Jennifer had left a bitter taste in Hunter's mouth. He stopped at a small tavern, wanting to settle his raw nerves with a strong drink and hoping his pursuer would come close enough to be identified.

But the tavern was as poorly lit as the street, with layered clouds of smoke blurring his vision. Hunter found a table facing the door and sat waiting. He paid little heed to the filthy tables or the rough language that surrounded him. The stranger who'd tailed him was about to feel the wrath of his bottled-up anger.

The tavern door opened with a gust of damp air just as a barmaid blocked Hunter's view. He heard the voices of several men entering, but they mixed with the crowd before he could study them.

"What'll it be, mister?" the barmaid's rough voice bellowed as she leaned over the table toward Hunter, displaying her cleavage like a peddler showing his wares.

"Whiskey." Hunter raised one sandy eyebrow. "And see that my glass is never empty." He felt a chill all the way to his bones that had nothing to do with the weather. Jennifer had taken the time to inform him of his every shortcoming. She'd reminded him repeatedly of his cold manner. In the end she'd even thanked him for saving her from having to share a bed with such a heartless man as himself. Hunter downed the drink and waited for the girl to pour him another. Maybe Jennifer was right. Maybe the only woman who could put passion in his soul was a figment of his imagination, a dream who fired all the warmth within him just by her nearness.

"Be you wantin' some company in your drinkin'?" the barmaid asked as she smiled, revealing yellowed, stubby teeth. Her breasts swung in her loose blouse like two overripe melons and her rounded stomach rose to meet the bottom of her chest.

"Thanks, but I've some thinking to do," Hunter answered as he handed her a coin. How different she was from his angel.

He swore under his breath and downed another glass. Must he compare every woman to her? His arms ached to hold her. There could be no substitute. Not Jennifer, not the barmaid. He would hold his angel or he would hold no woman. She had stolen all passion, all need, and left him a lonely hull of a man. Maybe he was destined to live the rest of his life unmarried, with only his dreams to give reason to living.

Hunter scanned the room for the shadowy figure he'd seen following him. Half of the men in the bar would have qualified, for most wore dark, wet coats.

He downed his third glass of whiskey, angry at the world and not really knowing why. He should be happy. He'd lived through the war, his father had left him enough money to do whatever he wanted in life, and he'd just been saved from marriage to a leech. Then why did he find it so hard to smile? Why was he so lonely?

Deep in his own thoughts, he was unaware of the men who talked around him. Rough voices rumbled and rose at the next table like a pot beginning to boil over. Four men shoved chairs across the room, clearing a space on the floor. They suddenly began to swing at one another in anger. Hunter lifted his glass and stood, uninterested in the quarrel. As he turned, a fist plowed unexpectedly into his chin. His drink showered several onlookers as another fist hit him in the side. In an instant he found himself in the middle of a barroom fight. Though he'd had a few drinks, he was clearheaded enough to realize the men were ganging up on him, deliberately fighting him, not each other. To this small band he must have looked an easy target to rob.

Anger flashed in Hunter's eyes as he fought. He was a skilled boxer, and Abram had taught him a great deal about street fighting. In a few minutes two men were sprawled unconscious on the floor. The other two quickly lost some of their bravery.

Hunter watched as one of the men backed away, preparing to rush at him. The man stopped in mid-stride and turned his eyes upward above Hunter's head. His glance followed the man's eyes but he had no time to react. A second later a chair slammed into Hunter's skull. He saw a flash of bright light before darkness overtook him and he crumpled to the floor.

A man in a dark, rain-soaked coat moved over Hunter's body. His voice was a low hiss, full of malice. "If I hadn't stepped in with this chair, he'd have beaten the lot of you.

"Pick him up and tie him up out back. Then come back in and wake up your friends. I'll need all four of you to help." With these orders Wade sat down at the table and began to plan his next move. This was his chance to get rid of Hunter once and for all. His only cousin was an ever-present blow to Wade's pride. The money Wade might inherit was a minor detail. All of his life Wade felt he'd been compared to Hunter and come up lacking. Now was his chance to end it once and for all. Always before, Abram had stood near like a guardian angel, but tonight Hunter was alone. It was really quite a shame his cousin hadn't reacted over Jennifer as Wade had planned. Now he'd have to resort to something more direct.

Wade scribbled down directions, unaware of the huge man who'd observed the drama from a corner seat at the bar. As the two hoodlums returned from dragging Hunter out, the huge man stood and quietly left through the back exit.

Wade slapped one of the men on the back. "Take care of this for me and I'll see you're paid well. If there was one thing I learned in the war, it was how to cover my tracks. See that there is nothing on the man out back that could identify him. Should someone find the body, he'll be just one of many the police have no name for.''

A few minutes later, when Wade and his four hired ruffians stepped out in the alley, Hunter was gone.

Chapter 24

Luke carried Hunter's unconscious body swiftly through the rainy streets toward Molly's place. He laughed to himself at having spoiled Wade Williams's plan. He'd hated Captain Williams after serving under him during the war and could imagine how angry the short-tempered captain was at this instant. From the looks of the gutter rats who were huddling around Wade in the tavern, they were up to no good. It had been so simple for Luke to slip from the tavern, untie Hunter, then vanish into the rainy darkness. Wade would have no clue.

The kitchen door rattled on its hinges as Luke entered. His huge boots left puddles with each step as he hurried toward the fire, left unattended to die in peace.

Luke shifted Hunter's body on his massive shoulder as he kicked a rug close to the fire. There'd be hell to pay come morning for trailing mud all over the kitchen, but right now he had to see how badly the young gentleman was hurt.

The rocker creaked in the darkness, freezing Luke's muscles into rock hardness. Molly's plump form materialized.

"Luke, what's that you got there?" she demanded as she stood, spilling the cat onto the floor.

"I found him, Miss Molly. He was beat up by some

fellers in the bar.'' Luke lay Hunter on the rug at Molly's feet. The firelight danced across the blood on Hunter's face, reflecting its light in sparkling diamonds of red.

''Now, Luke, you can't go bringin' every stray you find on your walks,'' Molly scolded as she knelt beside the man. Though her voice was rough, Luke watched wrinkles of concern twist around her eyes. ''He's a fine-lookin' fellow, ain't he?'' Molly brushed the blond hair from Hunter's forehead. ''But none of our concern.''

''But, ma'am, this is the man I saw with Abram during the war. The first time I saw Miss Perry, she was with this gentleman and he weren't in much better shape than he is right now. She was dressed like a boy and this man was a Union officer.''

Molly's eyes widened as she studied the unconscious man with renewed interest. So this is Perry's Hunter, she thought. Then she commended Luke. ''You done right, Luke, to bring him here.''

''Yes, ma'am. There was a group of men beatin' him up. Looked like they planned to kill 'im. I'm thinkin' he's more hurt than drunk.'' Luke nodded his head continuously, proud of himself for his actions.

''I'll doctor his head first.'' Molly reached for her small medicine kit. ''When I'm finished, you take him upstairs and put him in Old Henry's room. Then you go after Abram. My guess is he'll want to know about Hunter bein' here. He may even want to send for a real doctor.''

Luke continued to nod for several seconds. He warmed himself by the fire and watched Molly work on the cut in Hunter's scalp. ''You're up late, ma'am,'' Luke said, more as a statement than a question.

''I have trouble sleepin' when it's dark. Too many years of being awake all night,'' Molly said, a slight flavor of her Scottish accent showing.

''Yes, ma'am.'' Luke watched her closely. He'd heard about what Molly had been; so had everyone else in town. But as long as she was square with him, he would give her all the respect she asked. Besides, he genuinely liked the old woman.

"There." Molly stood and closed the medicine box. "Be gentle with him, Luke, and don't let those big feet of yours go wakin' up Perry."

Luke cradled Hunter in his arms and eased through the main hall and up the stairs. He knew his way, even in the dark. Part of his job was to check out the house a few times each night. The womenfolk were still afraid one of Old Henry's nephews might try to return. The first night, Luke had stumbled into furniture, bringing Molly storming down the stairs waving a dueling pistol like a pirate boarding a king's ship. Since then he'd been careful to follow a precise path through the house in the dark.

As Luke laid Hunter on Molly's bed he mumbled, "By the time I go fetch Abram, I'm gonna miss my night's sleep."

To Luke's shock Hunter's eyes opened. The two men stared at each other as though both had just regained consciousness.

"Who are you?" Hunter mumbled, rubbing his head and trying to sit up.

Luke smiled like a new father. "Well, it's glad I am to see that chair didn't leave you permanently senseless. You're safe at Molly's Place. Luke's my name. I fetched you out of the alley after a fella name of Wade Williams slammed a chair into your head. Up till then, I was bettin' on you holding off all them gutter rats."

"Molly's Place? That's a new dining house, isn't it?" Hunter sat on the edge of the bed. He twisted his neck, testing the limit of his pain.

"That it is, but there are a few bedrooms up here. You rest and I'll go get Abram." Luke moved toward the door.

"How'd you know about Abram?" Hunter asked, the cold, steel gray of caution touching his eyes.

"Molly told me to go fetch him," Luke said as he opened the door and vanished into the darkened hall.

Hunter tried to clear his buzzing head. He'd heard of a prostitute named Molly opening an eating place, but he was sure he'd never met the lady. How could she know about him and Abram?

Hunter sat in the darkness thinking over the recent strange events and wishing he'd gone to bed and ignored the fateful note last night. One good thing had come from it—he wouldn't marry Jennifer. Her voice was still ringing in his ears. She'd said every hateful thing she could think of to him, but the announcement that his touch made her freeze bothered him the most.

Smiling, he remembered how she'd reacted when he told her that he knew all about Richard. *Poor, whimpering Richard*, Hunter thought. *I'd never beg my way into a woman's bed.* How could Jennifer prefer Richard to him? How could she say he was void of passion and Richard set her afire? Hunter shook his head. Her choice hurt his pride more than his heart. He'd known Jennifer for most of his life and thought she knew him better than any other woman. It hurt to know she was only interested in his money.

He held his throbbing head in his hands and wished he'd told Jennifer of the woman in his mind who'd set his blood on fire and warmed his heart as no other woman could ever do. How would she have reacted if she'd known he also cared for another?

As Hunter sat in the darkness a melody drifted through the night to him. A melody so soft, he could barely hear it above the rain tapping on the windows. Curiosity drove him to search for the sound. The door by the windows opened into a small office. Lightning lit the room long enough for him to cross to a half-opened door directly across the office.

Hunter froze in the door frame at the sight before him. A vision purer than any dream filled his eyes with unbearable beauty. His angel sat on the floor beside a newly kindled fire. She was slowly, almost absentmindedly, brushing her long black hair. The silken strands billowed around her like a black cape, in sharp contrast to her white cotton gown. He watched the vision study the firelight, unaware of how beautifully the lights danced across her skin and set fiery highlights in her black curls. He was afraid to move, for fear she might once again vanish. He'd never seen her so clearly, and from this dream he never wanted to awaken.

The music box stopped playing and his angel turned toward him. As she saw him she smiled, as if she thought him only a figment of her imagination. As though she'd thought of him coming to her many times and now he finally had.

Moving slowly toward her, he knelt beside her on the rug and gently lifted her face in his hands. Her skin was as warm and velvety soft as he remembered. He could hardly believe she was real, not a dream. He drank in her huge brown eyes, her creamy skin, her slightly pointed nose. Moving his thumb slowly across her cheek, he touched her lips. The angel he'd seen was flesh in his hands and as real to his touch as she had been the night before. Only now he could see her, every perfect part of her.

Unable to restrain himself, even as he saw the puzzlement in her eyes, Hunter bent forward and lightly touched her lips with his own.

"Hunter?" she whispered. "How . . ."

"Yes, angel." His words caressed her ear as his arms encircled her and drew her up to her knees.

"Hunter, what—" She couldn't finish, for his lips were smothering her words. He was drowning in a new ocean of feeling. Each time they touched, the need between them had grown until now all his world was here with her this moment.

"Don't talk," he whispered. "Just let me hold you before the world finds us again and I must return to sanity."

Tears ran down her cheeks, spilling against his throat and shoulder. His face moved against her hair as he felt its warm silkiness. Her heart pounded beneath her breasts, keeping rhythm with his own. There would be time for questions later; now all he needed, all he wanted, was in his arms.

She pulled her head back, looking full into his face. "This is no dream," she whispered in her Southern voice, which reminded him of all the gentleness of his mother. Raising her hand, she touched his cheek and jawline and he wanted to laugh with pure joy. The firelight danced in her warm eyes and set aflame his need.

Hunter bent and kissed Perry deeper than before, his mouth parting her lips. As the kiss lingered, he felt her body mold against him with its own longing.

The flame traveled down her face, burning her cheeks as it moved to her breasts. She ached with desire for him. She spread her hands into his hair and laughed with ecstasy. How many hundreds of times had she longed to touch him? Now he was beside her. "It's not a dream," she whispered again, finally glad he could know she was real.

Hunter's hands moved slowly up and down her back, sending through her a pleasure so great, she feared she might explode from it. With each stroke Hunter's hands went lower, until they covered her hips with fire. His muscular body molded into her softness and Perry felt the need of his manhood press against her stomach.

She sensed Hunter pulling her to him as his hands rested on her hips. She knew nothing of lovemaking, but she knew she wanted him. She wanted him in the very depth of her being. Her body pressed instinctively against him, drawn to the warmth of his body.

Putting his hands on her shoulders, he pushed her a few inches from him. "I'll love you on this rug if you like, but we'd be more comfortable in bed." Passion had made his voice low, and she found it both exciting and frightening. She shivered as he stood and pulled her up into his arms.

Her mind refused to think rationally. For one moment in time she wanted to float on the passions of her dreams. Closing her eyes, she rested her hand on his shoulder as he played with the buttons of her nightgown. They gave willingly to Hunter's touch, as willingly as she came to him.

She heard his sharp intake of breath as he opened her gown. Looking up, she saw the fire of his desire in his smoldering gray eyes.

He reached down, cupping one breast lovingly in his hand. "My God, how can one woman be so beautiful? My mind tells me I'm awake, yet my eyes tell me I'm dreaming. I can still hardly believe you've been so near and I thought you were only a dream." He bent and kissed each breast before returning to Perry's lips with a demanding kiss.

She heard his low moan as his tongue circled her lips and tasted her mouth. Perry opened to him as a flower opens to the sun. His kiss grew more demanding as she pressed against him, wanting to melt into him. Wanting to be as much a part of him physically as she had been emotionally for every moment since they'd met.

Hunter lifted her into his arms and walked the few steps to her bed. He carefully laid her down, as though she were a priceless doll. "Now isn't that better than the floor, Molly," he said as he began unbuttoning his shirt, never taking his eyes from her.

Perry raised on her elbow, a look of worry on her face. "My name's not Molly," she began. Why would he call her by another name?

"Now there's no need to play coy. I've figured it all out. It doesn't matter to me how you earned your living during the war. I want you so much, I'm willing to pay whatever you ask. Lord knows how you can keep those innocent eyes." He continued undressing. "I met a poor farm girl with eyes like yours once. Until a few minutes ago I thought you were only a fantasy. When I stepped to your door and saw my angel sitting before me, I could not believe you were real. So name your fee, lady, it's yours."

Hunter turned to place his shirt on a chair. His hand was trembling with the excitement of being near such a flawless wonder. He really didn't care that she was a prostitute; he had dreamed of her since he'd been injured. He realized now he must have seen her sometime before, and her image had become his model for perfection.

When he turned back to the bed, she was gone. For an instant he thought she still might have been only a dream.

Glancing around, he saw her standing by the windows beside a large dresser. Relief was evident in his face as he watched her draw something from a desk. She turned to face him, her huge brown eyes filled with pain, a small gun in her hand.

She didn't know what kind of game Hunter was playing, but she wanted no part of it. "I'm not Molly. I nursed you when I found you during the war. I lay beside you in the barn loft to give you my body's heat. I fought death with you. Last month I had to leave my home and you helped me." Her words were coming in gulps now as she backed away from him like a frightened animal. "You are the only man who has ever touched me. I thought I was bound to you—that we were forever a part of each other. I cannot believe I almost made love with you when I mean nothing more to you than a paid attraction."

Hunter's mind spun. The whiskey, the bump on his head, Jennifer's unfaithfulness, and now this. He tried to think of what to say. "Does it matter? You're here and I've dreamed of you for so long. I want you like I've never wanted another woman. I ache now from wanting you."

Hunter moved toward her. He watched her clutch her nightgown tightly together with one hand as she held the small pistol in the other. Her beauty intoxicated him, drawing him to her. The danger mattered little. He could still taste her kiss on his tongue, and he knew he was drunk on her loveliness.

"Stay back, Hunter," she said. He could see the hurt in her eyes, the fear, and something else . . . determination. The pain in her eyes shot through his very heart, hurting him far more than any bullet she might fire at him.

"I'll shoot you if you come any closer," she said as she lifted her chin and blinked the tears from her eyes. His hard chest glowed in the firelight and she longed to run her fingers over the soft hair covering his body. But she could not, would not, give herself so cheaply.

"What do you want from me?" Hunter asked, frustrated. The muscle rippled over his jawline, reminding her of his strong will.

"I wanted your love, but now I only want your absence," she ordered as they heard voices from Molly's room.

In an instant she vanished from Hunter's sight. In complete darkness she ran through the connecting door to the small office, across the office, and into the hall.

Hunter heard Abram calling him as he darted after her.

"I'm here, Abram!" he shouted as he grabbed his clothes and began dressing. Abram and Luke appeared in the doorway. They were both rain-soaked and muddy.

"Where's Miss Perry?" Luke demanded as his eyes searched the room.

Hunter nodded at Abram, noticing Abram did not return his greeting. Stone-faced, both men stood in the doorway watching Hunter dress.

"Sir, I asked you a question. Where is Miss Perry?" Luke drew himself up and clenched his fists. "If you've harmed her, I'll break you into so many pieces, they'll not find enough to bury."

"Slow down, Luke," Abram said as he placed his arm across the other man's chest. Luke's anger vibrated from his huge frame. "We'll get the answers."

"Is this man a madman? Need you hold him back, Abram?" Hunter asked as he buttoned his shirt. "Surely he can't be seriously thinking to do me harm."

"No, Hunter." Abram's words slapped Hunter. "I'll not hold him back unless you answer his question. If you've hurt Miss Perry, I'm planning to help him. I know you well, but it looks very bad with you standin' here in her room putting your clothes on."

"Now I know you're mad!" Hunter backed up until he sat on the bed. He lowered his head and thought for a long minute. What a crazy night this had been, and now his best friend was about to turn against him. As Hunter realized how badly he had misjudged Perry, he couldn't blame Luke and Abram for reacting so violently. He raised his gray eyes to the two men before him and spoke honestly. "I wish you both would knock some sense into me. I won't even fight back. I mistook Perry for another kind of woman. I hurt her very deeply. She ran out of here crying. Before you beat me to a pulp, can I find her and at least say I'm sorry?"

Luke and Abram looked at each other. A part of each man wanted to slam a fist into Hunter, but both saw the pain he already felt. Abram saw just how much Hunter cared for Perry, knowing his friend was the kind of man not given to hurting anyone. He'd help him talk to her, but Hunter had better make it right.

"We'll help you find the little lady, but if she doesn't forgive you, I'll have my turn with you," Luke said.

Hunter stared at Abram. "Why didn't you tell me Perry was here?"

Before Abram could answer, Molly stormed between the two pillars of muscle blocking the door. "Where's Perry?" Molly's keen eyes surveyed the room, but it was Hunter's face that told her all she needed to know. Stomping her bulk to within inches of him, Molly waved her chubby finger in his face. "You be either a filthy swine like your cousin, or a fool for sure. Perry made you out to be a god, and here you sit showin' what an ass you be. You're no better than any other man. Perry's an innocent lady who needed a slow, loving awakening. From the looks of it, you stormed in, threw the curtain back and started yellin'. Blast your hide, I'd like to—''

Hunter caught Molly's flying hand. ''You'll have to stand in line. There's two ahead of you.'' He moved his head toward the two still blocking the door.

Molly glanced at Luke and Abram. Hunter lowered her hand to her side. He stood up, tucking his shirt into his pants. ''You must be Molly,'' he stated, rubbing his forehead. ''I wish I'd met you half an hour ago. But right now we've got to find Perry. I've got to talk with her.''

''I saw the front door ajar when I came up,'' Molly lied. She had heard the attic door close but had no intention of giving Perry's hiding place away. ''I'll stay here in case she comes back.''

Hunter grabbed his cape, bolting through the door and disappearing before Abram and Luke could even move to follow. For a moment the two giants struggled for the same space in the door frame.

''Hey, leave me my door, boys!'' Molly laughed at the comic pair. Despite her ranting of a few minutes ago, she was in a jolly mood. Molly had seen the passion burning behind Hunter's eyes. She knew he had looked at Perry as a woman. Call it lust or love—he would burn for Perry until the fire was quenched. Judging from the depth of his flame, it might take a lifetime to quench.

Chapter 25

Perry silently tiptoed up the dusty attic steps. Reaching the top, she jerked Hunter's necklace from around her neck as though it were burning her flesh. She threw the shining disc as far into the dark attic as it would sail and had the satisfaction of hearing it hit a wall and fall to the floor. Feeling her way to two large trunks, she slid between them like a frightened child hiding from the world.

She waited, listening for footsteps. Slowly, as the moments ticked by silently, Perry relaxed. Curling her knees to her chin, she wrapped her slender arms around her legs and buried her face in her lap. Emotions churned within her like beans in a coffee grinder, colliding into one another until all were split open and raw. Love and hate ground together with a newfound feeling: passion.

Nothing had felt more wonderful than being in Hunter's arms. The warmth of his mouth exploring hers had been explosive, as were his strong fingers moving over her body, setting a fire wherever they touched. Yet how could she forget the pain that shot through her when he thought he could buy her love?

Ten minutes passed before Perry heard a sound. She lifted her head to listen to the familiar sound of Molly's steps. After pausing to catch her breath, the woman emerged carrying a chubby candle and two steaming mugs.

The candle spread its pathetic light in a small semicircle in front of Molly as the steam from the cups floated the aroma of chocolate in the air.

"Miss Perry," Molly said briskly, "better crawl out of your hole and take one of these mugs of hot chocolate before they burn all the fat off me fingers."

Rising, she joined Molly and accepted the mug gratefully. "Thanks. Did anyone follow you?" Perry didn't even try to hide her tearstained face from Molly's sharp eye.

"Naw," Molly answered. "I sent all them men on a wild-goose chase. It'll cool their blood to tramp around in the rain." Molly took off her multicolored shawl and placed it around Perry's shoulders.

"Now, child, you sit over here and let's have a little talk." She led Perry to a corner of the attic where furniture was stored. Pulling out two paint-chipped chairs, they sat down.

"But, Molly, won't you be cold?" Perry was reluctant to take her shawl.

"No, no." Molly shook her head. "I've got enough meat to warm me through two winters." She patted Perry's knee, thankful that Perry cared about her. She'd seen many a lady take everything that folks did for them as if it were their due. Perry always worried about Molly. The old woman had never had such a love given to her.

"Don't know why you'd come up here," Molly mumbled as she settled into her chair like a hen squatting over a full nest. "This place always smelled funny to me, but I never have been able to figure out why."

"Probably all these old sea trunks." Perry downed half the dark liquid in the cup and waited for the old woman to speak her mind.

"I saw your man, Hunter," Molly stated, never one to ease into a subject.

"He's not mine," Perry lifted her chin. "I never want

to see him again." The words sounded hollow, even to her.

"Do you love him, child?"

"I don't know," Perry whispered, more to herself than to Molly. "I know he's in my thoughts most of the time. But what he feels for me is not love. It's only lust." Her sad brown eyes looked at Molly for an answer.

The old woman drew herself up as straight as a schoolmarm. She thought for a long minute, then replied. "Now listen, dear. I don't know nothin' about books and the like, but you might say this here is my specialty. Love be somethin' that strikes a body now and again, sort of like the flu. Every once in a while someone gets this love illness bad, maybe even till death. Near as I can figure it, not all people got the same amount of love inside 'em. But as far as how you know you really love someone, there's only two tests. If you care more about him than you do yourself, it's love. If he feels the same way about you, then you'll be one of the few people who can tolerate each other through a lifetime." Molly patted her fat knee as though congratulating herself on a fine speech.

Perry decided it was none of her business, but she had to ask. "Were you ever in love?"

Molly rippled with laughter. "Oh, hell, child, I used to fall in love ever' time I was exposed to the disease." She stared into the darkness as though looking back through time. "But I said there were two tests. The other is time. That was my problem. I'd love some man a powerful lot, and the next thing you know, I couldn't stand the sight of him. It was like that with my first husband."

Perry moved closer to her and put her arm around the old woman's shoulders. "I didn't know you were ever married."

"Oh, sure. I was fifteen the first time. He was twenty and farmed next to my folks. My dad said he took my virginity, so he might as well take me. As I remember, I

gave him my virginity, but I was in love, and marryin'
sounded good at the time.

"After a year of cookin' and cleanin' his cabin I began
to wonder how I'd ever loved him. Everything he did
started to bother me, till I thought maybe I was going
crazy. I lost a baby that year. The doctor said I wasn't full
grown and couldn't carry it. Guess it hurt me inside, 'cause
I never got pregnant again. You would have thought I was
just a cow that wouldn't give milk, the way he treated me
after that. He wanted kids real bad, I guess. He wouldn't
even talk to me." The sadness in her voice told Perry how
much the loss of a child had hurt her.

"So I just walked out one day, and kept walkin' till I
reached Philadelphia. I reckon he must have felt the same
way about me, 'cause he didn't follow me."

"But it weren't six months till I fell in love again. This
time he was a handsome sailor. He's the one who taught
me to cook. He was a mighty good cook, the opposite of
my first husband. No two days with him were the same.
We did some wild living in those days. Times got bad and
he couldn't find a ship to sign on with, so he took it out
on me. He'd get drunk and come home. He'd either beat
me or rape me pretty near every night. Well, I figured I
could do better on my own. Hell, if I'm going to have sex
with a drunken brute every night, I might as well get paid
for it." Both women laughed, and Molly could see that
her chatter had taken Perry's mind off her own problems,
as she'd planned.

Molly rose and stood by Perry. "What say we get a
good night's sleep and worry about matters of the heart
tomorrow?"

"Sounds good." Perry hugged Molly as she stood. She
knew it would be hours before she slept, but at least Molly
could get some rest. The old woman had cheered her
greatly. Sometimes it seemed that people who got knocked
down the most in life got back up the quickest. Molly was
a fighter and made Perry herself feel stronger.

At the attic stairs Perry halted and turned around. "Wait just a second!" she yelled over her shoulder as she headed in the direction in which she'd thrown Hunter's necklace.

Molly followed, curious as to what Perry could need in the attic. She held the candle high, for she had never ventured into this part of the storage area. Stacks of paper lay between broken furniture and old wicker baskets. "I'm beginning to think Henry and his wife never threw anything away." Molly grumbled as she maneuvered her bulk between the stacks.

Perry could see the glittering gold of Hunter's necklace behind a broken bed frame propped against the far wall. "I threw my necklace over here," she whispered. This part of the attic was a dusty graveyard of abandoned items. A chill ran through her as she moved across the icy floor.

"You be careful, now. Don't want any of this junk tumbling down on us," Molly called as she followed. "I'll have Luke carry out some of this and burn it tomorrow. I won't sleep good knowing all this might fall through the ceiling on me."

Perry reached between the wood slats to retrieve her necklace. Her fingers dangled just above her treasure. "Molly, could you set the candle down a minute and help slide this bed frame out of my way, please?"

"Sure," Molly answered. As they strained to push the frame aside the candle cast shadowy, deformed replicas of the women on the wall behind them. Molly grunted and the frame slowly scraped across the dusty floor. A screeching noise set both women's nerves on edge as they moved the huge oak bed frame.

Perry grabbed the chain tightly into her fist. "Got it," she said, laughing a little nervously.

Molly arched her back and groaned. "Thank God I was never meant to be an ox, even if I look like one." She leaned her back against the attic wall to catch her breath.

Perry glanced at the necklace just as Molly's scream rattled the air. She looked up in time to see Molly's huge body fall backward, disappearing as a panel in the wall gave way. Papers and dusty wicker baskets flew everywhere, cluttering the air and burying Molly completely in useless rubble.

A voice shouted from the heap, "Perry! Perry!"

Perry hurried to Molly's aid, grabbing her fluttering hand and pulling her back to her feet. "Are you all right?" she asked as she dusted off her friend.

"What happened?" Molly asked. Both women turned to examine the fallen wall. It was obvious that this was not a wall at all but only a panel placed to close off a corner of the attic. Long ago someone had sealed off this small attic space and purposefully designed the panels to conceal the existence of the room within.

"Get the candle," Molly whispered to Perry, as if someone might overhear. "Somebody's trying to hide somethin' up here and I aim to find out what it be."

Lifting the candle, Perry moved toward Molly. A flicker of fear flashed in her mind. It might be better to wait until morning, but curiosity, mixed with the adrenaline in her veins, pushed her forward.

Both women stepped together through the opening left by the crumbled panel. A dusty, foul odor surrounded them as they brought their light into the small chamber. Perry held her candle high and the yellow light spread in beams around the room. A modest table and chair stood before them. The spiderwebs were thick, forming a fine, lacy netting over the table. The chair was turned toward the table, away from the women. It seemed occupied with a bundle of dust-covered clothes.

Molly stepped forward first, for a closer examination. Perry glanced around the room, wondering how anyone could leave such clutter behind. Trash lay covering the floor like a thick carpet. Many of the papers looked as if they had been torn from a book years ago.

Perry's gaze fell on Molly in time to watch her face blanch. Her fingertips buried themselves in the candle wax as Molly shattered the ancient air with her scream. Terror seemed to ricochet off the aging walls, disturbing years of quiet neglect.

For several seconds both women stood like statues frozen in time. Slowly Molly's blood returned in abundance to her stout cheeks and her breath came in short puffs, sounding like a small, overworked engine. "Come no closer, child." Molly's order came too late, for Perry moved the few steps to join her.

Perry braced herself for a shock but was unprepared for what she saw. The dark bundle in the chair was not a pile of old clothes at all but the decaying body of a man. The rotting flesh, once wrapped in layers of blankets, now looked with a dead stare up into eternal darkness. Perry found that she couldn't pull her eyes from the face that had once held human life. The skeleton now sat patched together with remaining bits of tissue and muscle. A spider glided along an invisible tightrope from the hair of the corpse to the tabletop.

Feeling a mysterious weight pushing up out of her lungs, Perry stifled her screams. She couldn't get blood and oxygen to her brain, and her mind began to spin. She fought fainting with every ounce of energy she could muster, but her eyes couldn't pull themselves from the ghastly guest before her. After all these years of fear and fighting, Perry now found herself looking at death's face. Here, only a foot away, sat an enemy she had fought all of her life. Here was the face of the shadowy, hideous figure who haunted her dreams and laughed each time someone around her died.

As she stared, a worm crawled out of one eye socket and slithered into the other, curdling her blood with horror.

The candle slid from Perry's grasp. As Molly shouted, the candle splashed into the trash on the floor, splattering fire around both women. Molly scanned the attic for something, anything to slap the fire out as Perry remained hypnotized by the form before her. She didn't notice the fire dancing around her feet but remained motionless until her knees buckled and she fell into total blackness. Neither woman heard three men clambering into the attic.

In seconds Hunter was through the panel opening and beside Perry. With lightning quickness he removed his rain-soaked cape and wrapped it around her. He lifted her into his arms as Abram and Luke began pounding the flames with their wet coats.

Hunter showed little interest in the room. His main concern lay cradled in his arms. "Get out of here, Molly. I've got Perry. They can get the fire out faster if we get out of the way!" he shouted above the noise. He held Perry tightly to him as he waited for Molly to pass through the opening. Flames lashed out at his muddy boots. Molly moved faster than he thought her capable.

He followed the old woman down the stairs and along the hall to Perry's room. Kicking the door wide with his foot, he issued commands to Molly, who was already throwing the bed covers back. "Get some brandy and something for her feet."

Molly nodded. "There's some downstairs. I'll be right back."

Hunter placed Perry on the white sheets. Her glorious hair spilled over the lacy pillows. For a minute he stared at her loveliness while she lay as if in sleep. In all his life he'd never seen such a wonder of beauty, nor felt such fear when he realized how close he'd come to losing her. Every nerve in his body had felt as if it were exploding when he'd topped the attic stairs minutes ago. From the hall he'd heard Molly's scream and the noise of the panel falling. He had reached the top of the stairs at the same time Perry dropped the candle. His heart nearly stopped as he watched the fire spring up around her, a moment before she crumbled into the flames. Had he been any later, she could have been badly burned or even killed. He tenderly brushed a few strands of hair from her face, unable to hide his smile at the relief—no, pleasure—that this was a real face and not just a figment of his imagination.

Molly appeared beside him. She shoved a half-filled glass of brandy into his hand and turned her attention to Perry's feet. Though her gown hem was blackened in several spots, her legs did not seemed badly burned. "Hold her head up when you give her a little brandy. She's had quite a shock, but it will bring her around," Molly ordered as she covered Perry's legs with a blanket.

Hunter sat on the edge of the bed, very gently lifting her head. As the warm brandy passed over her lips Perry's eyes opened slightly.

"Molly!" she whispered in fright. "Molly, are you all right?"

"I'm fine, dear. How is the little lady?"

Perry's hand rested on Hunter's chest. In spite of his treatment of her, she felt safe from her nightmares in his arms.

"All you need is some sleep and you'll be good as new in the morning," Molly said as she moved away. She could hear Abram and Luke in the hallway. "I'll go check on the others."

Perry watched Molly disappear into the hallway before closing her eyes. She heard her friend directing Luke and Abram to the kitchen. The brandy had burned its way down her throat, relaxing her from inside. She pushed the horrible vision of the body she'd seen from her mind and relaxed in sleep.

Hunter held her for several minutes, feeling her relax in his arms. He gently laid her back among the pillows and drew the blanket up to her chin. As he moved her arm to put it under the covers, something fell to the floor. Bending, he retrieved his medallion. He smiled to himself as he lifted her hand to his lips. Turning her palm up, he saw the small scar running across her hand and remembered when she'd slashed it to save them. He kissed the scar tenderly, as if to take away the pain. The beautiful woman before him and his angel were one. Placing the gold disc in her hand, he closed her fingers around it. "How could I have been so blind?" he asked himself. "Why could I not see beneath the dirt and old clothes? How could I have ever thought this tiny beauty to be a boy?"

As he kissed her forehead he remembered how a month ago her face had been swollen and blackened. Wrinkling his brow, he realized how badly she must have been hurt the last time he'd seen her. He strode to the door. How could anyone have beaten such a lovely creature? He hurried to find Molly and the answer to his question.

Chapter 26

Hunter found Abram and Luke huddled at the kitchen table, with Molly standing above them as she halved a pie.

The old woman looked up at him and pointed her serving knife. "Well, speak of the devil. We was thinking we might have to come up and check on you." Mischief twinkled in her eyes. She wasn't the least frightened by the storm in his gray depths. She'd seen a great deal of life and had long ago learned the difference between anger and concern in a man's eyes.

Luke rose awkwardly. "I wish to make my apologies, Captain Kirkland, for my rash actions earlier when I found you in Miss Perry's room. I didn't know you were the lady's serious beau. Miss Molly explained it to me. I had no right interfering with two people in love."

Lowering his head, Luke missed the sharp look Hunter shot Molly. The old woman grinned like a fat cat after Sunday dinner, knowing he couldn't say anything. If he denied her claim, he'd reignite Luke's fuse, which seemed short where Perry's welfare was concerned. Hunter wasn't sure he could deny the charge, anyway. He realized the feelings he had for her were deeper than anything he'd ever felt for a woman.

In defense, Hunter glanced at Abram, only to find his

236

friend smiling at his discomfort. "Why didn't you tell me Perry was here?" Hunter snapped.

Abram raised an eyebrow. He'd rarely seen Hunter upset, even when in danger. Never had he found the young captain's temper so amusing. "Miss Perry asked me not to tell anyone where she was. At first she was running away and afraid you'd take rash action if you knew why. Later she was afraid of what you'd do if you knew who she was."

"And who is she?" Hunter asked, thinking she could not be worse than he'd guessed her an hour ago. She'd been so many things to him now, the truth couldn't add any more surprises.

Abram looked down, not wanting to answer Hunter's question. "I promised her I wouldn't tell you anything about who she was or who beat her up."

Molly waddled around the table and crossed her arms over her ample breasts. "Well, I didn't make no such promise, and I'm in a mood to speak my mind." She didn't even blink as Hunter looked at her with his stormy eyes. "But before I tell you anything, I want you to think about that poor child up there and not just your anger."

"Agreed." He placed his fists on his hips and waited, none too patiently.

"Best as I can tell, her father blamed her for her mother's death, the Union army ran her off her land, and her grandfather thought she was her mother come back from the grave. Then up pops a snake name of Wade Williams who almost beats her to death for not wanting to marry him." She jabbed her fat finger into Hunter's chest. "Then, along you come, almost raping her tonight. From what I see, it's a wonder the girl even speaks to the whole male population."

Every muscle within Hunter tightened in anger. "She was to marry my cousin, Wade?" His words were a low whisper between clenched teeth. All his life Hunter had held his emotions under tight control, but he now felt them snapping. "He beat her!"

Molly looked away, suddenly unable to watch the pain her words were causing. "Pretty near killed her for trying to run away. If Abram hadn't hid her in that balloon of yours, I don't wanna even think what might have happened to my little lady."

Her final words were snuffed by the slamming of the kitchen door as Hunter bolted from the room. The three remaining occupants stared at one another.

Abram slowly stood. "I best go with him."

"Don't guess there's much doubt where he's going." Luke reached for his coat.

Abram nodded. "Least I can do is see it's a fair fight. Guess I always knew it would come to this someday."

"Mind if I tag along? I'd like to be there when Wade Williams gets his due." Luke turned to Molly and added, "We can't do nothing about the body in the attic until morning, anyway."

As Abram passed Molly he handed her a letter. "This came for Hunter yesterday, but I don't think he'd mind Perry reading it." He paused for a moment. "You know, Molly, he loves her. I could see it in him when he talked about her."

"Yes, I know." Molly followed them to the door, mumbling, "I only hope he stays alive long enough to realize it."

Dawn was hesitantly lighting the sky as Luke opened the kitchen door. Molly was still in her rocker by the fire with Herschel curled on her lap. She raised sleepy eyes and asked, "Did Hunter find Wade?"

Luke plopped down on the long bench and pulled off his muddy boots. "Nope, but weren't from lack of trying. We tromped through every boardinghouse in this town. Finally found where he'd been staying. The clerk said he'd packed and rode out not an hour before we arrived. He told Hunter that Wade left bragging about getting back South in time to claim an inheritance.''

''Well, that's that, then. We won't see him again.'' Molly rocked back in her chair. ''How does a stack of buttermilk pancakes sound for breakfast?''

''You're after my heart, woman.'' Luke stretched his tired body and rubbed his stomach.

''That and a few other parts of men seem always available.'' Molly chuckled as she stood. ''While I stir up breakfast, why don't you get the old strongbox from the cellar.''

''Sure, but don't know why anyone would leave a locked strongbox in the cellar.'' He pulled his boots back on. ''Seems like he'd have stashed it under his bed.''

''Maybe Old Henry figured under the bed would be the first place someone would look?'' Molly answered, more to herself than Luke.

''Well, nobody but a cook would fall over it down there.''

''That smart Old Henry,'' Molly squealed, startling Luke. ''He knew I'd find it there.'' She clapped her hands. ''Get the box, Luke. I'll run up and get the keys.''

Luke cocked his head in confusion. For the life of him, he couldn't explain Molly's actions. She must have been tripping over that box for two years. Why was she so fired up about opening it now?

In less time than he thought possible, Molly returned, her apron filled with keys that danced in a nonmusical tune as she waddled. She spilled the keys onto the table and announced, ''If one of these don't work, we'll blast the lock off.'' She laughed in nervous excitement.

Selecting key after key, she tried each in the lock as she chattered. ''Henry must have left somethin' in this box. He knew I loved to cook. So he put it where I'd fall over the blasted thing daily. Those ignorant nephews of his must have never bothered to look in the cellar.''

Molly's excitement was quickly melting into impatience as she threw useless keys across the room in disgust.

Finally her reasoning registered on his sleepy brain, and Luke moved to her side. As a key fit and turned in the lock, they both smiled in anticipation of untold riches. The lock fell away and Molly pulled the lid off the strongbox, staring in disappointment at its contents. "Papers!" Molly shouted loudly. "Ain't nothin but papers and maps in the damn thing."

Luke poked around the items. "Looks like some mighty nice maps in here." He lifted out an envelope between his beefy fingers. "This here looks like a letter to you, Miss Molly."

"I can read my own name, man. Give it to me," Molly ordered, then laughter bubbled from her ample frame. "Trouble is, that be about all I can read. How about you?"

Luke echoed her laughter with his own. "Truth be known, ma'am, I was just guessin' that letter was to you. I never had the time or the patience to learn reading."

Molly stuffed the letter in her apron pocket, which already bore the outline of another envelope. "I was planning to let Miss Perry sleep, but I might take her some breakfast and ask her to read it to me."

"Oh"—Luke slapped his forehead with his palm—"I forgot to tell you, Hunter said he'd be here at ten."

"Well, why didn't you say so? I'd best wake Perry." Molly rose and began preparing a morning meal. "Luke, take that box up to the office. I know she'll want to look in it. Maybe she can make somethin' out of all those papers."

Minutes later Molly clambered into Perry's bedroom, carrying a large tray of food. Perry smiled sleepily from beneath the covers, knowing Molly was trying to be quiet. "Be you awake, little lady?" Molly whispered.

"Yes, Molly, I'm awake. What time is it?" She yawned and sat up in bed, unaware of how lovely she looked with her hair spilling in a dark cloud around her shoulders.

"Near eight, I think," Molly answered. "I need you to do some readin' for me. Luke and I found this letter in that old strongbox that was in the cellar."

Pouring a glass of juice, Perry crossed her legs in the middle of the bed. Despite all the excitement of last night, she had slept well and felt rested. "Hand me what you found, Molly. I'll be happy to help."

Molly pulled the two letters from her pocket and debated a moment over which to give her first. But curiosity outweighed duty, and she handed Henry's letter to Perry.

With great care Perry opened the letter marked "To Molly—Important." She studied the poor penmanship until she understood the impact of the letter. "Molly!" she shouted suddenly. "I know about the body in the attic. This letter explains it all."

"Well, tell me what it says. I'm gettin' nervous just knowing he's still up there." Molly shivered as she sat on the bed and helped herself to the biscuits she'd brought for Perry's breakfast.

"The handwriting is very poor, but according to what's written here, the body must be Henry's partner. This is not a letter but some kind of confession stating that Henry's nephews killed his partner during a robbery. The nephews were unaware of Henry's presence in the back room at the time. Henry heard them plotting to kill him after Henry took over his partner's half of the business. Only Henry decided to hide the body and stall for time. He knew his nephews wouldn't kill him until they were sure they would inherit all of the company. He thought you would find this before you found the body." Perry glanced up to see if Molly understood.

"Old Henry was no fool. That's why he wanted no servants in the house," Molly said, nodding her head as the pieces of the puzzle began to fit. "Poor old soul. I guess it would drive anyone to drink knowing there was a dead man sitting in your attic and that a corpse was the only thing keeping your kin from doing you in."

"He put this letter in the strongbox, hoping you'd find it before the nephews did. I'll bet they're still wondering how the body of the man they killed had disappeared."

Molly laughed, rocking the bed with her chuckles. "They must have had a few sleepless nights thinking of what they could do about it. They couldn't go around asking if anyone had seen a body. They must have known Henry was lying about his partner disappearing, but what could they say? There was no one but the killers and Henry to say if the partner was alive or dead."

Molly's eyes filled with sadness. "Henry knew the law wouldn't declare his partner dead for seven years. He told me himself that the doctors didn't give him more than two years to live, and that only if he stayed away from the bottle." She shook her head. "Why should he have stayed sober with his only kin plotting to kill him? That's why he let his business go to ruin. By the time he died, the company was worthless."

Molly stood and dusted the crumbs from her dress. "I'll go tell Luke to find the sheriff, then I'll be back to talk with you while you dress." She stopped after only a few steps. "Oh, I almost forgot. I've got another letter here that Abram gave me. He said you might like to read it." She tossed the letter to Perry and hurried to find Luke.

As Perry picked up the second letter her eyes widened in surprise. The envelope was addressed to Hunter. The letter within hung halfway out. She debated a moment before pulling the pages out and opening them.

Glancing at the last page, she read Mary Williams's neat signature. She knew Abram must have brought the letter to her because he guessed how hungry she was for news. An ounce of guilt for reading Hunter's mail was outweighed by a ton of curiosity.

She was unaware of how long she'd been sitting staring at the letter when Molly interrupted her once more. "Well, Luke's gone for the law." Molly laughed. "We'll be rid of our silent partner soon."

The old woman wrinkled her forehead. "What is it, dear?"

Perry lifted the letter as though Molly could read it for herself, than lowered the paper to her lap. "Most of it doesn't concern me, but Mary Williams does mention that my grandfather died only a week after I left and that my brother has been at Three Oaks for several days. She also writes that her husband, John, is very ill."

Folding the paper carefully, Perry placed it back in the envelope, as if she were also folding away her memories. She remembered the way her grandfather had been sitting in his old chair by the fire when she walked in on him.

"I'm sorry." Molly patted her hand.

"I should be sorry too," she confessed. "But I'm more saddened by John Williams's illness. My grandfather and I were not very close."

"Do you want to go home?" Molly whispered, almost afraid to ask.

"No," Perry answered. "I'm glad my brother is safe and I'll write him today, but this is my home now."

"For as long as you like." Molly was having trouble getting the words out. She pushed her emotions aside with a loud clearing of her throat. "Well, enough talk. You'd best get dressed. Hunter left word he'd be here at ten to call on you."

Perry rose slowly. "I don't think I can see him again." She stood by the window, staring out but seeing nothing. "He cares nothing for me, I'm sure of it. He wanted to sleep with me last night without even knowing my name." Her voice was as low as the wind across open grassland. "He plans to marry another tomorrow."

"Now hold your horses, little lady!" Molly shouted in as scolding a voice as she could muster. The Scottish accent thickened her tongue when she was angry. "I don't know what happened in here last night, but he saved your life in the attic. As for marrying another, you'd best ask *him* about that. I think the least you can do is talk with him. If you still don't want to see him after that, I'll personally help you bolt the door. But one thing I've learned to do over the years is to size up a man fast. I'd bet your Mr. Hunter Kirkland is a man to reckon with. I don't think he'll take no for an answer when he calls.''

Perry stared out the window at the trees, still heavily laden with rain. The morning sun shone bright, turning the moisture into sparkling diamonds. "All right," she agreed, unable to fight both herself and Molly. "I'll receive him in my office."

"Good." Molly waddled toward the door. "I'll go down and get the cooks started on the pies, then I'm going up for a little nap."

Perry wasn't listening. Her mind was spinning with all the things Hunter might ask when he arrived, and how she could answer him.

Chapter 27

Yellowed maps covered Perry's desk, whispering of worlds she'd never known. She tried to make her mind focus on them as she heard her office door open.

Luke stammered, "Miss Perry, y-you've a visitor."

Without looking up she answered, "Thank you, Luke." She heard the door close and knew Hunter was in the room, but she couldn't bring herself to look at him.

He stood silently just inside the door for several minutes, watching the morning light play off the halo of black hair atop her head. She was wearing a navy dress with a white lace collar and cuffs that made her look every bit the lady he now knew her to be. If it were possible, she looked even more like an angel than before. After all these months of caring about her, of dreaming of her, he suddenly found the few feet between them an impossible canyon to cross.

"May I come in?" Hunter asked awkwardly, thinking she might never acknowledge his presence.

She lifted her head, but their eyes met only briefly before she lowered hers. "I'm sorry, Captain Kirkland. Please come in and sit down."

The last thing Hunter wanted to do was sit down across the desk from her, but he knew he must move slowly. Every ounce of his being wanted to storm around the table and pull her into his arms. He wanted to finish what he'd started last night, before his unjust words had broken the spell. Yet he sat down, allowing reason to hold him temporarily in check.

Perry tried to keep her movements fluid as she absently closed the maps. He was wearing a freshly pressed blue uniform, and though he looked very handsome, the coat reminded her of a war that would always stand between them.

"Do you think you could call me Hunter? The *captain* will vanish in a few days when I return to civilian life, and you haven't used my last name since we've met."

His low voice made her feel like the room was suddenly running out of air.

When she didn't answer, Hunter continued, trying to stay on safe ground. "I learned that your grandfather died, and I wanted to say how sorry I am for your loss."

"Thank you," she whispered as she turned slightly toward the windows.

He twisted his hat in his hands to keep from standing and closing the space between them. "Abram told me all about why you left your home and how you were running from a treason charge. The war's over now, and no one will hold you to account for your crime."

Perry didn't answer but turned away as she tried to control the anger mounting inside her. She didn't view her actions as criminal, and she didn't want to look at him now, for all she'd see would be the Union blue of his jacket.

Mistaking her silence for shyness, he continued, "I also understand you were engaged to my cousin. My grandmother wrote that his fiancée died. You planned your own death, didn't you?"

"Yes." Perry lifted her head. "I had to make sure no one would follow me. I am sorry, though, that I brought sadness to your grandparents. They are a wonderful couple and so very much in love." She remembered the way John

Williams's wrinkled fingers would reach over and pat Mary's hand every now and then, as though reassuring her of his love.

Hunter slapped his hat against his leg. "Why?" he asked. Then when she looked at him, puzzled, he added, "Why were you engaged to Wade?" The one question had haunted him all night as he'd searched for his cousin. "Couldn't you see what kind of man he was? Or were you blinded by his insane ambition for power?"

"I was never unaware of Wade Williams's character." Perry resented his questions. What right did a man who was marrying a woman like Jennifer have to ask questions of others? "He asked my grandfather, not me, for my hand. I have no wish to talk about your cousin, Mr. Kirkland."

"Nor I," he answered, wishing he could erase Wade from his life. They'd never liked each other, and Hunter aimed to see he paid for what he'd done to her. But now he wanted to talk of other things with her. So far everything he'd said had been wrong. He could feel her anger mounting toward him. He wanted to talk to her of love, not war and pain, but he wasn't sure how to begin.

The silence grew between them. When finally his voice came again, it was softer. "You fell asleep in my arms last night."

Perry turned toward him, shocked at his words.

A flicker of passion echoed as he continued. "I enjoyed watching you sleep." His eyes moved from her face to run the length of her body. He smiled, remembering her soft fullness and the way she had molded to him. Beneath the wrappings of this lady was quite a woman.

Perry felt her cheeks redden as her anger rose. How dare he talk to her of such things when he was marrying another tomorrow? First he calls the burning of her own fields a crime, then he questions her judgment, and now he looks at her with his wonderful, passion-filled eyes and thinks she'll forget he's about to be a married man.

He saw her anger grow and knew he'd somehow said something else wrong. Laughing, he thought how easily he could talk to important men, even the president, yet this little lady made him feel like he was still in short pants.

Misreading his laughter, Perry exploded into action. Before she thought, she raised a glass paperweight from her desk and sent it sailing toward him. "Get out, Captain Kirkland! How dare you laugh at me! I'm not a child or a loose woman. Go marry your Jennifer and stay out of my life!"

Perry looked down at her desk for another object to throw. "What do you want of me the day before your wedding?" When she lifted an empty china cup and glanced back up, she saw that Hunter was missing from his chair. Before she could find him, his arms encircled her from behind. He grabbed at the cup and pulled her against him.

Anger surged through her. "Let me go!" she shouted as the pain of Wade's, not Hunter's, arms returned. In her mind she was plunged back to the night a month ago at Three Oaks. "Don't touch me!" She fought with all her strength. "Don't hurt me!"

Hunter dropped his arm instantly, moving out of range as he saw the fear in her huge brown eyes. He was confused and angry with himself. Why hadn't he listened to Molly's warning? He'd stormed in again where he should have tread lightly.

Backing to the window, he raised his hands in the air. "I'll not touch you again. I won't hurt you, Perry. If you will talk to me, I swear, I'll stay the entire distance of this room away from you."

Perry took a deep breath and calmed down slightly. She saw the seriousness in Hunter's gray eyes and knew he was trying very hard to talk with her. Before she could answer, the door burst open.

Luke stormed in. He looked first at Perry, standing by

the desk; then at Hunter, over by the window. All seemed in order. "I'm sorry, Miss Perry. I thought I heard a scream." Luke spoke to Perry, but his eyes never left Hunter, leaving no doubt that he'd break Hunter in half if he bothered Miss Perry.

"I broke a glass, nothing more, but thank you, Luke. It's good to know you're near if I need you." She shot Hunter a silent look of warning.

Luke swelled with pride. "I'll be right at the foot of the stairs." He bowed slightly and backed out of the room.

Hunter didn't miss the devotion in Luke's manner. It reminded him of the way Abram spoke of Perry. But Hunter didn't want to line up behind Luke and Abram as Perry's guardian. He wanted to be more, far more, to her.

Turning his back to her, he tried to think. He'd spent little time around women, but she fascinated him. He had trouble getting his words into sentences when he looked at her.

His fingers idly toyed with a small gun on the table by the window. She must have left it there when she'd run from the room—and him—the night before. He recognized the handle as one having belonged to his mother years ago, but he wasn't about to mention it to her lest she refuse to keep the gun for protection. He stared out the window and stated, "Thanks for not having me thrown out. I wouldn't have liked fighting the man who brought me here last night and very well may have saved me from a planned accidental death."

He heard Perry's sharp intake of breath and continued. "I think someone was trying to kill me." He slowly turned to face her. "The fight I found myself in, in the middle of last night, was planned. Had Luke not found me, I'm sure my body would have washed up on shore this morning." Hunter was shocked by the concern in her face. This woman was a great mystery to him. A few moments ago she'd been hurling objects at him, and now her brown eyes reflected concern.

He took a step toward her, then froze as she backed away. "Perry, I swear I'll not touch you against your will. I'm not so much a gentleman to lie and tell you I don't want you. I *do* want you." He'd never been good at the games men and women played. He had to tell her how he felt. "I've wanted you so much, I've dreamed of you."

She bit her bottom lip, wishing he'd say something about loving her and not just wanting her. She didn't want to be afraid of him. "I believe you. Please sit down and I'll pour tea."

Hunter pulled out one of the chairs by the window and Perry sat, trying not to brush his hands. Every part of her was aware of his nearness. She tried to keep her hand from shaking as she poured.

He accepted the cup with disinterest and placed it down on the table, his eyes never leaving her face. "There is one thing I should clear up. Jennifer and I are not planning to marry. It seems she's found another."

Perry swallowed the warm liquid, trying to hide her surprise. "You don't seem like a man who just lost his bride the day before his wedding."

Hunter didn't answer her question. He hadn't thought about it, with everything else that was happening, but Perry was right. He wasn't upset. His angel had haunted his every dream, driving all thoughts of Jennifer away. All morning he'd thought about seeing her, and now he couldn't find the right words to say. He wanted to blurt out all his accomplishments to prove himself, he wanted to share with her all his dreams of the future, and most of all he wanted to hold her.

They sat drinking tea for several minutes before Hunter broke the silence. "I'd like to ask you something, but I don't want to upset you." He sat his cup down. "Molly probably wants to keep all her china intact."

Perry folded her hands in her lap, embarrassed by her outburst.

"My grandfather is very ill and I must go to North

Carolina. I want you to go with me.'' He hesitated a moment, awaiting her reaction. When none came, he continued. ''I have a small ship, the *West Wind*, that has been making trips along the coast since the war ended. I sail in the morning.'' He wanted to tell her how desperately he needed her beside him, but he didn't know what she'd say. ''I thought you might like to visit your brother.''

Perry hesitated. The invitation was tempting, but she was needed here. Besides, she knew Wade would be waiting for her if she went south again. ''I'm sorry, I must stay here.''

''I could arrange for my bookkeeper to help Molly.''

''No, thank you.'' Perry didn't want to think about what Wade would do if she arrived in North Carolina on Hunter's arm.

The strong set of her chin told Hunter she wouldn't change her mind. She was as stubborn as she was beautiful, and if he was honest, she was probably safer here. ''Then I'll see you upon my return.'' He stood slowly, too proud to ask again.

As she stood, she brushed dangerously close to him. He closed his eyes as he breathed in the sweet, honeylike smell of her. Last night he'd wanted her, but today she seemed as vital to his life as air. His voice was suddenly low, speaking his mind. ''You will be in my thoughts and dreams until I return.''

She looked into his gray eyes, now clouded with desire. A deep yearning filled her, yet she held back, wanting more from him than just his passion.

Luke's loud knock shattered the moment. He poked his head in and shouted, ''Beggin' your pardon, miss, but Molly needs you bad in the kitchen.''

''I'll be right there,'' Perry answered as Luke withdrew. Turning to Hunter, she whispered, ''Give my love to your grandparents and tell them my prayers will be with them. I'll see you when you return.'' On impulse she stood on her tiptoes and kissed him lightly on the cheek. A heartbeat later she was out of his reach and vanishing from his sight.

Hunter stood alone for several minutes, thinking over all they'd said to each other. How could he keep his promise not to touch her? If she'd stayed another moment, he would have crushed her to him. Maybe it was good that they would be apart. How else could he get this summer storm of a woman out of his blood? Out of his mind? Out of his heart?

Chapter 28

Shouts rattled from the back of the house as Perry ran down the stairs. A scream echoed through the hallway, quickening her steps toward the kitchen, fear mixed with concern for Molly. With only a moment's delay Perry stopped at the entryway table and pulled one of the dueling pistols from its hiding place. If she was going to face danger, she didn't plan on doing so unarmed.

When she reached the kitchen, Luke was blocking the door to the storage room. Molly's shouts filled the kitchen with colorful language.

"What is it?" Perry peeked around Luke.

Molly stood in a pile of ruined supplies. "Someone broke in last night." She lifted a handful of sugar mixed with coffee. "They cut the bags on all our dry goods." Perry stepped aside as a stream of syrup passed by, and Molly continued. "It was them nephews, I just know it. I had a feeling we hadn't seen the last of them."

"But when?"

"Probably while we were upstairs. They couldn't run me out by frightening me to death, so now they're planning on starving us out."

Perry lifted an empty bag of flour. She'd learned during the war not to spend energy crying over what had already happened. "We don't have much time. Molly, make a list

253

of everything we need. I'll go change, then Luke and I will go shopping.''

''All right, but when the sheriff gets here, I'm adding this to their crimes. Killing an old partner in the slave trade is one thing, but destroying good food . . . well, that's quite another.''

Within an hour Perry's boots were tapping along the wooden steps toward the market. Luke followed closely in her wake, swinging a large basket under one arm. They had only an hour to buy the items on her list and return home in time to cook everything for tonight. Luckily the streets were packed with carts and merchants displaying their wares. Many were local farm families who traveled into town once a week to sell their crops and buy supplies.

Most of the farmers had no special market cart but merely sold out of their wagons. To disguise the drab work wagons the farmers often hung colorful ribbons from the sideboards, making the marketplace seem festive and gay. As husbands sold their goods, wives visited with their neighbors, and the children played chase, threading their way in and out among all the people.

After half an hour of shopping, she sighed. ''That's everything but the coffee, Luke.''

Luke smiled from beneath his cumbersome load. ''That's good, I'm about ready to start back.''

Perry was aware of Luke's slower pace. She knew if she'd stopped for more than a moment at any one stand, he would've fallen asleep while still standing. ''I'll get the coffee and catch up with you within a block. You go ahead and start home.'' Perry smiled up at him, wondering if he'd even been to bed the night before.

Luke turned, juggling the purchases in his arms. She watched him move slowly away and knew she would have no trouble catching up with him. Lifting her skirt a few inches to move more freely, she hurried across the street to a store where Molly always bought spices and coffee.

As she opened the door into the shop the owner greeted

her warmly. "Welcome, Miss Perry. What can I do for you today?"

Standing for a time in the doorway, she let her eyes adjust to the shop's darker interior. The old store had an almost cavelike atmosphere, with blinds pulled closed and dark bags lining the walls and hanging from the ceiling. Moving inside, the wonderful aroma of spices met her. The old shopkeeper's skin was the color of ground cinnamon, and his voice belied a foreign origin. "May I have five pounds of coffee beans, please, Samuel?" Perry placed a coin on the counter.

"Yes, miss." The owner moved to scoop the dark brown beans into a bag.

Perry wandered behind a counter, reading the labels more clearly and loving the smells that seemed to seep through the pores of even the wood and glass that housed each spice. As she scanned the shelves a shadow fell between her and the sunshine as someone stepped into the doorway. Samuel greeted the new customer as Perry glanced up with only mild curiosity.

She felt his evil presence even before the light shone on his face. As her gaze moved down his lean, wiry body a sense of dread turned to fright in her stomach. He was dressed in dark riding clothes and highly polished boots pulled to his knee. His wrist impatiently slapped a gold-handled riding whip against his pant leg as he squinted, peering into the darkness.

Perry's eyes widened in fear as Wade Williams's stare fell upon her. His face blanched slightly when he found himself face-to-face with a ghost. "Perry . . ." His mouth whispered what his eyes would not accept.

She watched the disbelief in his tired eyes slowly ebb away as anger fired within him. His face reddened, except for the small scar over one eye, which grew milky white, like the moon in a midnight sky. For the hundredth time she wished that Hunter had killed Wade and not just scarred him. His hands now clenched into fists as his shoulders rose and fell between jagged breaths. He fought to control his anger and shock.

Samuel broke the heavy silence. "You the Captain Williams that sent word for me to pack a travel portion of that special coffee?"

Wade glanced at Samuel as if he hadn't understood a word the man had said.

Perry took advantage of Wade's shock and confusion. She lifted her skirt high and darted past him, her coffee beans completely forgotten. His hand grabbed the air only a hair's breadth away from her shoulder and she passed.

Darting like a child between the colorful stands, she mixed in and out of the mob of people along the side of the street. She was afraid to look back, terrified she might see his black-gloved hand reaching toward her. He was always in control in public, but she'd seen him slipping just now, and she didn't want to risk being within his grip again. She guessed it must be hard for him to maintain a sane pose when insanity bubbled in his blood.

Terror throbbing in her throat, she ran for several blocks before darting behind the stores and reversing her direction. She was in clear view one minute, then disappeared from sight around a corner or between two carts.

When Perry was sure she hadn't been followed, she turned toward home. She caught up to Luke just as he crossed the street to Molly's house. Luke glanced back, hearing her steps, a smile ready to greet her, but one look at her flushed cheeks and huge, frightened eyes told him of her distress.

"Luke," she whispered, "I saw Wade!"

Luke froze in his tracks. "Did he see you?"

"Yes." Perry took a deep breath and placed a small hand to her pounding heart. "I don't think he followed me through the crowd."

"You run on home, Miss Perry. I'll wait here for a few minutes to make sure." Luke's exhaustion was completely forgotten as he turned a sharp eye back up the street. He was a simple man, and over the years he'd cared little for most people, yet he'd risk his life to stand between Captain Williams and Miss Perry.

She didn't hesitate. Without another word she ran toward home. The memory of the night she'd left Three Oaks pounded in her head, along with her footsteps. He'd given her more than bruises to remember. He'd taught her the meaning of terror. The taste of it was thick in her mouth, like the blood and dirt had been a month ago. She wouldn't allow him to hurt her again. She would die fighting first.

For the remainder of the afternoon Perry went about her work, her nerves as sensitive as burned flesh. Luke kept a constant eye on the street and saw nothing. Still, she couldn't relax. Every little sound made her back stiffen. Even Molly's constant reassurance did little to relieve her nerves. She knew that somewhere in Philadelphia, Wade Williams was looking for her. From the hatred she'd seen in his eyes, he wouldn't stop until she was dead.

As darkness grew, so did Perry's fears. Wade seemed to her a creature of shadows. Even after she locked herself into the small study and people began to fill the restaurant, she couldn't relax. She knew Luke stood at the foot of the stairs and would allow no one to venture up. Yet she kept up her pace. Now that Wade knew she was alive, he wouldn't stop until he found her. She knew his pride would fan his anger into an all-consuming fire. If he found her, he would see her dead this time, as well as all those who tried to help her.

A light tapping on her door interrupted Perry's thoughts. "It's me," Molly announced. "Open up."

Perry dashed to the door and turned the lock.

"I brought our supper up." Molly stated the obvious as she labored with the heavy tray through the room and set their dinner on the small table. "You wouldn't believe the people downstairs. Seems the word's out about a body bein' in our attic. You'd think that would discourage folks,

but it seems to fascinate them.'' Molly laughed. ''Tonight
we not only provide the food but the dinner topic as well.
And everybody is so nice to me. They even ask me to sit
and talk with 'em. Like I was a lady.''

''You've always been a lady to me,'' Perry answered
honestly.

''Maybe to you, child, but not to the rest of the world.
You know, I think folks treat me nicer just because you're
around.''

''I'm not downstairs.''

''Yes, but you started it somehow, I just know you did.
I lived my whole life without so many people treating me
good as they have this last month with you here.''

Perry pulled a chair away from the window and examined the dishes before her. ''You make me feel safe.
Maybe I was overly frightened by Wade this morning.''

Molly patted Perry's hand. ''You're not defenseless now.
Luke and me will take care of anyone coming around
bothering you.''

Perry lacked Molly's confidence but tried not to show
it. She remembered Wade, the way his eyes burned in
anger when he'd seen her. Somewhere out there in the
night he was still looking for her. She could feel him coming toward her. She bit into a piece of bread and stared
out the window into the backyard. She could feel him
coming the way a farmer feels a storm.

Molly chattered, unmindful of Perry's lack of response.
''If I thought there be any chance of him findin' you, I'd
see you packed away from Philadelphia. Maybe on that
boat leaving at dawn tomorrow with Hunter. Though I'm
not sure about that Mr. Kirkland. He looks like he would
see after your welfare, but you never know how a man's
gonna act without land under his feet.''

Hunter's name drew Perry's attention. ''Oh, Molly,
Hunter would be a gentleman.''

''Now, Perry,'' Molly answered between bites, ''I've
known a great many men in my day, and one thing I be-

lieve is that underneath every gentleman is a man. Heed my warning: If you push a gentleman too far, you'll see the man.''

''I guess you're right,'' Perry whispered, more to her reflection in the window than to Molly. ''I know the gentle, even-tempered Hunter from months ago, but the man beneath frightens me.''

''There's time enough for you to get over your fears.'' Molly helped herself to another spoonful of potatoes. ''Fear's a funny thing. I've always been scared to death of lawmen, but today, when they came to pick up the body, they was real polite-like to me.

''They said there's nothin' to worry about with the nephews, but just to make me feel better they put a guard out front to watch for them.''

Staring into the darkness, Perry heard Luke's heavy steps moving up the stairs. His familiar knock shook the walls as always. A second later the knob turned and he entered the office. ''Beg your pardon, ladies, but the sheriff just sent this note over.''

Perry almost ran to Luke, but Molly waited patiently for Perry to read as she sopped the last bit of gravy from her plate. Notes were not so exciting to someone who couldn't read.

A smile spread across Perry's face as she read. ''They've caught the nephews, and both gave detailed confessions.''

She waved the note in a large sweep about the room as Luke let out a hoot and Molly clapped her hands together. ''This calls for a celebration,'' Molly ordered. ''Luke, go down to the cellar and get a bottle of the special wine Old Henry had. I'll check and make sure all's well downstairs. We can all meet in Old Henry's room in a few minutes and have a toast to our health.''

Turning to Perry, Molly added, ''You best stay up here. We'll be back in a few minutes.''

The room was suddenly empty. Perry moved to her desk and folded the maps she'd spent the day looking over. She decided that when Hunter returned, she'd ask him to take a look at the yellowed maps. Who knows, they might be of use to someone somewhere. They were certainly doing no good here. Molly hated sailing, and Perry had only been out of sight of land a few times in her life.

Placing the maps back in the strongbox, she picked up her lamp and moved into Molly's bedroom to wait for the others. The fire was out in the room that Molly always called "Old Henry's room." Perry placed the lamp on a side table and moved back into the darkened study to retrieve her shawl. As she covered her shoulders she looked out the window. Luke moved toward the cellar door in a slow, even pace. She smiled as she watched him, remembering how he'd carried Hunter over his broad shoulders all those months ago.

As Luke bent down to pull the heavy door open, Perry noticed a movement in the shadows behind him. For a moment it looked as though the shadow of the shed extended suddenly toward him. Then a dark form broke from its concealment and the outline of a man moved toward Luke. The creature's cape blew gently in the evening breeze, revealing a thin, wiry form beneath its folds. Gasping for air, she recognized the stride of Wade Williams even without seeing his face. Before she could move, the figure in black stepped behind Luke. The shrill screech of Luke pulling the cellar door open blended with his low moan as Wade struck him from behind. Luke tumbled headlong into the cellar, as lifeless as a bag of potatoes.

Frozen against the window, Perry watched as Wade pushed closed the latch to the cellar and melted back into the shadows. Two other dark figures moved from the cover of trees to join Wade. They were dressed in ragged clothes and looked as though they had just crawled from some gutter.

A tiny shrill cry escaped her lips as the door behind her opened. With trembling fingers she gripped the gun Abram had given her. Slowly she turned to meet her intruder.

"Lord, little lady, what's gotten into you?" Molly stared at her in confusion. "You look like you just seen a murder."

"I may have," Perry whispered. "Wade is in the back-yard with some other men." She was suddenly afraid that her words might drift down to him and give her hiding place away.

"Are you sure, child?" Molly joined her at the window.

"I just saw him club Luke and lock him in the cellar. I'll get the other guns," Perry whispered in panic as she ran to her room.

"Now settle down," Molly ordered as she followed. "There be a house full of people downstairs. My guess is he's waitin' till later, when the crowd dies down. He may be figuring to get us one at a time." Molly's bright eyes came alive in thought. Many times during her life her survival had hinged on her ability to think fast. Now the talent jumped into action like a horse ready to run full out.

"I've got my gun, and with your dueling pistols I can stop him and his friends." Perry's voice showed more confidence than she felt. She paced back and forth as Molly looked around the room thoughtfully. The old woman folded her arms over her breasts and patted her elbows, as if encouraging herself to think.

"No, you can't go out in the dark shootin' nobody. First off, we don't know how many men he's got out there, and second, they might shoot back." Molly plopped on the bed and planted her chin firmly on her fat fist. "We gotta get you outa here."

"How?" Perry asked with interest. "He's probably got someone watching the front door."

"I know he does. When I was comin' up a few minutes ago, I glanced out to see if the sheriff's man was still there. He was gone, but another man stood boldly watching the front door. He was a ragged lowlife varmint, and from the way he patted his gun handle he was just lookin' for a fight. I was gonna tell Luke to scare him off before he robbed one of the customers.'' Molly scratched her chin. "I'll see to Luke later—his head's plenty hard enough to take one whack. First we gotta get you safe and away from here."

Perry was pacing, feeling like a caged animal. If Molly hadn't stopped her, she would've faced Wade here and now. It would have been foolish—two women and three guns were no match for who knows how many men. She was willing to risk her own life to fight Wade, but it wouldn't be fair to put Molly in more danger.

In the typical fashion of a woman who'd spent most of her time alone, Molly continued thinking aloud. "Way I see it, there's just one way out, and that's with a ruckus. You can figure that man out front is watchin' for a lady to leave. Wade Williams has probably told him just what you look like. So we got to make such a ruckus, he doesn't notice who you are."

"What!" Perry exclaimed, totally lost from Molly's logic.

"Years before the war, I used to work in a house full of girls. We traveled around some, and not all places welcomed us. Ever' now and then a mob of righteous citizens would storm us and put an end to our night's work. I soon figured out that if I just threw on my cape and walked out the front door, no one usually bothered me. They was too busy chasin' the girls crawlin' out the windows and under the beds."

Molly giggled. "Tonight, little lady, we gonna do the same thing for you. You change into some travelin' clothes. Then pack a big bag only half full. I'll be back in a minute."

Molly left in a flurry of instructions. For several seconds Perry stared at the door through which she'd vanished. There was the possibility that Molly had completely lost her mind, but for lack of a better idea, Perry followed her instructions. A plan, even a crazy one, was better than none.

Within five minutes Molly was back. She waddled in, locking the door behind her. A bright red cape lay over her arm. Perry could tell, even in the poorly lit room, that the cape was cheap and gaudy, as well as being none too clean.

"Are you packed?" Molly asked as she threw the cape down on the bed.

"Yes," Perry answered as she slipped her small knife into her skirt pocket.

"Good." Molly let out a long breath before continuing. "I sent one of the girls down to the corner to get a carriage. There's usually one for hire this time of night. Our fella's still outside watching, but it's gettin' good 'n' dark, so he won't be able to see clearly."

She lifted Perry's half-filled bag and handed it to her. "Hold your bag close and I'll tie it to you. It would be a dead giveaway if he saw a lady leaving with a bag. But if I strap it around you and put the cape over you, you'll look like a fat little whore."

Perry gasped in surprise at Molly's plan, but she held the bag tightly as Molly tied it around her middle with a few of Perry's ribbons.

Ten minutes later both women stood at the top of the stairs. Molly gave Perry one last hug. "You take care of yourself and write when you're safe. I may not be able to read, but I'll know you're fine when I get the letter."

Tears formed in Perry's huge eyes. "You be careful here. I'll send the police as soon as I get away, but don't misjudge Wade."

"I'll be fine. You've no cause to worry about me." Molly lifted the ugly cape hood over Perry's hair and pulled it low. "Throw this thing away when you're finished with it. That part of my life is over."

"I'll be back," Perry promised, wondering if she spoke the truth. "I love you, Molly."

Tears bubbled from Molly's eyes and crisscrossed down the wrinkles on her cheeks. "I never had no children, but if I had, I wouldn't have loved them more than I do you, child.''

Both women hugged once more, then silently agreed the time was at hand. They moved together down the stairs. As they reached the last step Molly grabbed Perry's arm and shoved her toward the front door.

As they stepped out into the night air, Perry held her head low so no one could see her face. She knew that as soon as she could get away, Molly would be safer.

Molly propelled Perry toward the waiting carriage. She yelled in a gruff voice, ''You get yourself outa my house! I runs a respectable place here and I won't have any of your kind drummin' up business inside my place.''

Perry stepped into the carriage as Molly continued yelling and pushing. Molly shouted at the driver, ''Take this trash back where she belongs! I never want to see the likes of her again!''

Glancing out the carriage window, Perry saw Molly standing with her feet wide apart and her hands set on her ample hips. Aware that she was watching, she yelled all the louder, ''I don't wanna see your face again, you trash!'' Perry knew her meaning and pulled the hood lower over her head.

The man Molly had described was laughing from across the street, but he didn't move as the carriage pulled away from the house. He made no attempt to stop Perry or to report her leaving. Perry laughed, for she knew Molly's plan had worked.

The carriage traveled through the streets swiftly as Perry untied her bag from around her waist and removed the red cape from her shoulders, revealing a blue cape of her own. She shoved the red cape under the seat and leaned forward to direct the driver.

When they stopped at the sheriff's office, the driver seemed in shock as he watched a slim young woman step from the carriage. He looked inside for the old fat lady he'd picked up, but there was no sign of her. Scratching his head, he mumbled something about having too much to drink as Perry politely told him to wait for her.

She caught the sheriff just as he was leaving his office for the night. He was happy to stop and talk with such a lovely young lady as she begged him to go to Molly's aid. She described Wade and his gang as robbers. After having just solved a major crime, the sheriff was anxious to assist. It was not every day that he put two killers in jail, thanks to Old Henry's letter to Molly. The talk of Henry's partner being murdered and his body left in the attic was all about town, and the sheriff welcomed the attention. This next problem might add even more color to his stories.

As the sheriff helped Perry back into the carriage he assured her he would round up ten men and be at Molly's side within the hour.

Turning her brightest smile toward him, she asked one last favor. "I would greatly appreciate it if you would keep a close eye on Molly. Should she need anything, please contact Hunter Kirkland's house."

Surprise showed on the sheriff's face. "She's a friend of Mr. Kirkland?"

Perry didn't miss the respect in his tone when he said Hunter's name. She decided a lie might provide added protection for Molly. "Yes, she's very dear to him, and he would be very upset should something happen to her. I'll tell him you will see to it nothing does."

"Thank you, miss." The sheriff beamed. "You tell Mr. Kirkland I'll watch after her as if she were my own mother."

The sheriff hurried to do his job as Perry waved the driver on. They moved through the streets toward the dock. A tear slowly drifted down her cheek as she thought of Molly. She would miss the dear old woman. Quietly she mumbled the last words the sheriff had said. ". . . as if she were my own mother."

A few minutes later Perry stepped from the carriage. After paying the driver she moved along the docks in search of the *West Wind*. Even in the moonlight she recognized the familiar lines and walked the plank to board. She hadn't known Hunter owned this ship when she'd last sailed.

A guard moved in her path as she stepped onto the ship. "May I be of some service, miss?" he asked politely.

"Yes, you sail in the morning, right?" Perry asked, keeping her hood low. It would be better if no one knew who she was, though she doubted any of the crew would remember her from months ago. On that first voyage she'd stayed to herself and had never even spoken to the captain except for a few words the last day.

"Yes, miss," the guard stated without moving from his post.

"I wish to come aboard early. I hate getting up at dawn. I'm—I'm," Perry said, about to lie for the second time in an hour, "I'm Mr. Kirkland's cousin, and he invited me to sail with him." Seeing the guard's confusion, she added. "Please show me to my room. I'm catching a chill."

The guard shuffled his feet as if forgetting his manners. "Yes, miss, please come this way. I'm sorry, miss. We weren't expecting any passengers 'cept Mr. Kirkland this trip."

Within a few minutes Perry was settled into one of the tiny staterooms. She undressed and crawled into bed. The room was the same one she had had so many months ago, when she had sailed home and away from Hunter for what she thought would be forever. The room had been drab and sad, as was her heart. Now the room seemed cozy and welcoming. With covers tucked tightly around her, she drifted between worrying about Molly and thinking of her future. In a few days she would be back at Three Oaks with Andrew. When this business with Wade ended, she would return to Molly.

"If it ever ends," she whispered into the darkness. For she knew the only way would be when either she or Wade was dead. She touched her gun beneath her pillow and fell asleep.

Chapter 29

The thunder of a fierce pounding echoed across the tiny cabin, awakening Perry. For a moment confusion clouded her mind as she focused on her unfamiliar surroundings. Slowly the cabin took form with a rhythmic rocking, telling her the ship must already be sailing.

Jumping from the bed, Perry pulled her cape on. She hadn't had space to pack a wrapper; however, the cape served her needs well. She closed her fingers around the small gun in her pocket and moved cautiously to the door. The fear that Wade had somehow found her suffocated all other thought.

Throwing the latch, she stepped back and lifted the gun in greeting.

An instant later the door flew wide open as two men burst into the room. Both froze in mid-stride as they saw the little lady standing before them with a derringer pointed at their heads.

Perry breathed a sigh of relief as she recognized Hunter and the ship's captain.

Hunter straightened as his eyes registered the beauty before him. She stood, draped in dark blue, her wonderful hair flowing to her waist. Her eyes were huge with fire and fear. For a moment he could think of nothing to say. There

267

was nothing in the world that mattered but her standing before him.

The captain raised his hand as though his fingers might ward off a bullet. "I'm sorry, miss. I'm not meaning to do you harm. You can put the weapon down." For years he'd thought there was no more deadly animal than a woman with a gun.

Perry held the weapon steady. "Is this your usual way of awakening a guest who sails with you?" A smile touched the corner of her mouth.

"No, miss." The old captain shuffled in embarrassment. "We heard you were Hunter's cousin. We thought you were his Cousin Wade. The guard who saw you come aboard is asleep. He left only a message saying that Hunter's cousin boarded last night." The captain fumbled with his hands as though they had suddenly doubled in size and would no longer fit in his pockets.

"That'll be all, Cap," Hunter said. "Thanks for standing by me, but this is one cousin I can handle."

The captain turned toward the door. "I'll tell the cook there will be one more for breakfast." He vanished.

It took Hunter another moment to recover fully from the shock of Perry's presence. He casually folded his arms across his broad chest. From the smile on his face she never would have guessed how much sleep he'd lost because of her. Twice during the night he'd decided not to sail, but to stay close to her. But at dawn, duty prevailed. Though he was needed in North Carolina, he'd dreaded the few weeks away from Perry as a man dreads a jail term. Now she stood before him, even more beautiful than he'd remembered. Her hair, tousled from sleep, stirred his desire to hold her.

"Perry." He wondered once more how she had the power to make him tongue-tied. "I didn't mean to frighten you. I never expected to see you here. I'm glad you changed your mind and decided to sail with me."

"I didn't really change my mind. I was forced to leave,

thanks to Wade,'' she answered sharply, seeing the hint of fire in his gray eyes. "I hope I can rely upon your word as a gentleman."

"I don't give my word lightly and I will not break it lightly. You may put your gun away." He purposefully stepped toward her as he spoke. "Have you seen Wade?" he questioned. "I was told he left town."

"You were misinformed." Perry's voice broke into soft sobs, tearing at Hunter's heart. He moved closer but dared not touch the angel before him.

In a low caring tone he whispered, "I've a shoulder to cry on, but you'll have to come to me."

She glanced up with wide, tear-filled eyes and saw only sympathy in his face. She closed the space between them as he lifted his arms in welcome.

Cradling her face into his chest, she let her tears flow unchecked. She cried for her lost home at Ravenwood, and Three Oaks, and now Molly. She felt afloat in a raging stream, with no direction to her life. She wished she'd returned with the sheriff to Molly's to help him catch Wade so she would know that this was over. Sick of being afraid, she allowed all her pain to flow out with her tears.

Hunter held her close, drinking in the fragrance of her hair as she pressed against him like a frightened child. Never in his life had a woman so captured his very soul. He longed to take all the hurt from her, yet all he could do was vow to add no more pain to her life. Lightly he stroked her hair, mumbling inaudible words of comfort.

Finally the tears ceased and her breathing grew regular. "Thank you," she whispered. "I've never cried like this before. I'm sorry."

"Don't be sorry," he answered, almost drowning in a single tear that clung to her dark lashes. "I'm here whenever you need me. I'll see that no one ever hurts or frightens you again."

He clenched his teeth. Here he was swearing his allegiances to her like all the others. He didn't want to be her guardian. He wanted to be her lover, but her only touch was to push him away from her softly. He could see it in her eyes; she was not a child looking for protection. She was a woman with her own mind. He'd said the wrong thing *again*.

For an instant he resisted her leaving his arms. But he'd given his word and he wouldn't break it. Once he chose his course, Hunter stepped away quickly, trying to hide his disappointment. "I'll wait for you down the hall," he said.

With one swift movement Hunter vanished, leaving Perry brooding. She was sorry for having let him see her cry. Though he held her gently, he'd escaped at his first chance. "He probably thinks I'm a weak-kneed female," she mumbled as she dressed, deciding his obvious hurry to leave was a clear indication of his dislike for a whimpering women. "I'll not let him see such a display again," she swore as she opened her door and stepped into the small passageway.

The morning was spent in pleasant conversation as they watched the banks of the Delaware River drift by. Perry and Hunter were the only passengers aboard the small craft, manned by a crew of four. Hunter and the cook added a hand when needed.

He made no apology for his casual dress, and in truth Perry enjoyed watching him. Without a coat she could see his wide shoulders and the outline of his muscles as he moved. He was a far cry from the thin soldier she'd nursed months ago. His attire was much like the other men's aboard, white open-collared shirt and dark trousers, except his boots were highly polished black knee boots. He took to the rock of the ship like a seasoned sailor. Perry soon realized he was in command, with the captain gladly serving as first mate. As she watched the wind blowing his blond hair and pulling at his shirt, she thought he'd make a dashing picture of a pirate.

His voice came as low as the rumbling thunder along

the far horizon. "My father often took me with him overseas. Cap was younger then, and always served as captain on my father's ships."

"Where is your father now?" She wanted to hear his voice, but suddenly there was a sadness in his tone.

"Since my mother died, he spends most of his time in England. The war was hard for him to understand. He still chooses to live abroad. I haven't seen him in years."

After a long silence Perry moved the conversation to calmer waters. "Why didn't Abram come with you?"

He looked relieved that she'd changed the subject. She remembered Abram saying Hunter had lived alone when he'd first met him. It seemed to her that when Hunter's mother died, his father abandoned him. He could not have been out of his teens at the time.

Hunter interrupted her thoughts. "Abram hates the sea. He never took to the water. Spends most of his time leaning over the rail losing his last meal. I sent him overland with the *Northern Star* packed in a wagon behind him. He should arrive a few days after we do. To tell the truth, I don't think he likes going up in the balloon with me much, only he thinks I'd kill myself if I went alone."

The sleek little ship moved out into the Delaware Bay as night fell. Hunter and Perry enjoyed a relaxing dinner in the small dining area off the galley. She found the food simple but well prepared. They both laughed as she related her departure from Molly's Place.

"I looked very much the fat little lady of the evening." Perry's laughter filled the room like music.

"How could anyone think you such?" Hunter teased, loving the way she smiled.

"You once did," Perry answered. It seemed hard to believe that only a few nights ago Hunter had thought her to be Molly.

Hunter's face grew serious. "I'll try never to misjudge you again." His eyes looked deeply into her own. "You're a puzzle to me, but I'm learning." He leaned back in his chair. "I've enjoyed today." His voice was suddenly lower as he gazed at her.

Perry glanced around nervously. If she looked back at him, she'd fall into those gray eyes. He might discover how deeply she wanted the passion he offered. But she wanted his love also, and it never seemed a part of the offering he was willing to give.

Hunter was half drunk on her beauty. The more he talked with her, the more lovely she became. He loved hearing her soft, gentle Southern accent. When she'd climbed the stairs, her slender waist and rounded hips disturbed him greatly. He enjoyed watching her face change expression, for her moods were as varied as the seasons, with each lavished in its own beauty. Her moody pout when she felt challenged contrasted with her free, sunny laughter. Her stormy anger flashed hot and proud, yet when she was teased, her cheeks reddened in a spring blush.

As the evening grew late Hunter was reluctant to leave her side. He kept her talking and laughing in the narrow corridor for as long as he dared.

"I wish this day would never end. I've enjoyed your company immensely," he whispered as he moved closer, due to the cramped surroundings.

"I've enjoyed the day also," Perry answered, suddenly nervous at his nearness.

Hunter moved away. He didn't need to be reminded of his promise. It had haunted him all day, stopping every advance. He now lifted her hand to his lips. "Sleep well," he said softly as he pressed his lips to her small hand. For a moment he moved her fingers slowly past his half-open mouth to his cheek.

"Good night," Perry whispered breathlessly. She moved inside her small cabin and closed the door. Her cheeks burned and her hands shook slightly as she took a deep breath to calm herself. She wanted him to hold her and make love to her. Yet she couldn't give herself lightly. She had to know of his love, for without it she was no

better than the whores she'd seen during the war. She had
to know he felt as strongly for her as she did for him. For
Perry knew, no matter how long she lived, that she would
love him even if she never voiced her feelings.

Hours later Perry awoke to a violent tossing of her bed.
She jumped from her covers in fright before realizing the
entire room was rolling back and forth. Holding on to the
bunk's frame, she moved around the bed to gather her
cape. She couldn't stay here in the darkness like a frightened child. She had to see what was happening. If the
ship was in danger, she must know. After several tries she
tied her cape. Opening the door, she moved into the passageway on bare feet. The pitching slammed her from side
to side as she fought her way to the stairs. The wind lent
assistance when she pushed the hatch open. Then the
storm's breath tried to rip the wood from her hands as
Perry crawled out onto the deck, using all her strength to
close the opening.

She ran the few steps to the railing and watched the
fierce drama before her. Huge waves rolled high, breaking
in the wind, as if challenging the sky. The moody atmosphere responded with thin, bent fingers of lightning and
a rolling, brooding thunder. Nature's battle raged, unmindful of the tiny ship in its midst. Mighty fists of waves
hammered against the hull as water spilled over the deck.
The sky, not to be outdone, pushed black clouds almost
within reach of the boat, then dumped sheets of rain in a
sporadic mixture with icy wind.

Perry clenched the railing with both hands frozen. She
didn't dare let go to return below deck. The wind might
catch her cape and send her sailing into the angry ocean.
Her feet were numb and the spray had quickly soaked her
cape and gown. The water splashing on deck seemed to
pull at her feet. Horror filled her as she felt herself shake
with cold. *What if I can't hold on?*

Her hands grew numb. Suddenly the thunder became
the low laughter of death's voice. Perry, afraid to move

and questioning her ability to continue, stood immobile. The wind pushed her hard toward the churning water.

Suddenly, large hands covered her own. Hunter's harsh voice screamed above the storm in almost equal fury. "What are you doing above deck! You'll be washed overboard."

Hunter pried Perry's fingers from the railing and turned her around, pulling her into his arms. His wide stance held them firmly on the rolling deck. She barely noticed his harsh tone, only welcomed his strong arms encircling her. Her fingers moved around his neck and held tight as she buried her face in his chest.

"Come on, I've got to get you below!" he yelled again as he lifted her drenched body. The storm seemed to be fighting him for each step.

Another man appeared at Hunter's side. "Open the hatch!" Hunter yelled to the dark form. "I'll be back in a few minutes."

As he stepped sideways into the passageway, silence suddenly surrounded him. With Perry clinging tightly, he moved down the hall to her cabin. He kicked the door wide and stepped inside.

"You fool, you could have been killed!" He spat the words out.

Perry said nothing. She knew he was right. She could feel his anger as he tightened his arms around her. Her only excuse was her lack of sailing knowledge. Yet somehow that seemed flimsy.

As he dropped her onto the bunk, she looked at his face. An angry fire raged out of control in his gray eyes and his jaw was rigid.

The next roll of the ship caught Hunter off-balance and shoved him down on top of her. His wet body covered her, pushing her deep into the covers.

"You could have killed yourself," Hunter mumbled an inch from her face. His arms, on either side of Perry's head, held him above her. Yet his chest rested heavily against her breasts and she felt his weight press down on her body. He moved his face an inch closer to her and whispered in agony, "I might have lost you."

For an instant she feared he might strike her. She closed her eyes to brace against the blow. She was totally unprepared as his lips came down upon her own, afire with anger and passion, sending a flame through her that warmed her completely. His mouth demanded a response as his hands moved to either side of her face. Hunter's fingers pushed Perry's damp hair away from her cheeks in a gentle gesture that contrasted with his savage kiss. Any thought of resisting was swept away by a need deep within her.

As Hunter's kiss continued endlessly, the anger within him ebbed away and a fierce passion blew in. She felt his body moving slowly above her. For a long minute they were lost in each other. For them there was no storm outside, for the tempest raged deep within them.

The thought that he might have lost Perry kept scorching Hunter's mind. He wanted to draw her to him and hold her forever. He was driven mad by the way her body moved timidly beneath him. Without question she was as much a part of him as bone and blood. His hands moved down her neck to push way the damp clothes and rest on her warm shoulders. Her skin was soft and yielding to his touch. The feel of her was passion's dream in reality.

Against her cheek she felt a sharp intake of breath as his warm hand slid off her shoulder and onto her breast. Her gown gave willingly to his touch. He held the soft mound possessively as his lips tasted her flesh. She moved instinctively beneath him as his thumb slowly circled the peak of her breast. Running her fingers into his wet hair, she was lost in the wonder of pleasure. With each movement he taught her of a new world, and she responded as a willing student.

He moved slightly to one side, allowing more freedom as he gently pulled her gown to her waist. His kiss parted her lips and he tasted the full wonder of her as his fingers roamed freely.

She arched slightly as his hand caressed her, sending fire to every nerve ending. His fingers moved masterfully from her thigh to her shoulder in unrestrained bliss. She could hear his low moans as he took possession of a dream. With each movement his need to explore grew greater.

From an eternity away, both heard Hunter's name being shouted. Agonizing, he pulled free of her lips and let his head fall on the pillow beside her. He kissed her breast gently, then lifted smoky gray eyes to stare deeply into her own. "Stay here," he whispered. "I have to go or this ship will tear apart." His voice was thick with passion. "It tears me apart to leave you."

He lifted himself off the bed. He was not making love to this lady but consuming a basic element necessary for life. He realized a simple fact as he stared down at her flushed beauty. Holding her wasn't a luxury he wanted but a vital necessity. He'd play no silly games of love with her. She was a part of him, a staple of his life. He didn't just need her to be happy; he must be with her to be alive. From the way she moved within his arms, she must feel the same.

Hunter stepped to the door. "Get those wet clothes off. I'll be back later."

In an instant he was gone, and Perry grew cold in his absence. She lay shivering in the damp bed for some time, marveling at the power he had over her. Slowly she crawled out of bed and removed her clothes. She rubbed a towel briskly across her bare skin until her body was warm and glowing. Because she had no other nightgown, Perry put on her camisole and petticoat. After spreading her gown and cape out to dry, she rummaged through the drawers for dry bedding. She paid little attention to the constant rocking of the ship, for the turmoil inside her seemed as great. Moving slowly around the bunk, she put dry sheets and blankets on. Her heart seemed to be fighting her in any effort to think clearly.

Perry blew out the light, locked the door, and crawled into the newly made bed. Every cell in her body wanted to wait for Hunter to return, yet her mind needed time to think. Slowly a great sadness covered her in the darkness. He had made no mention of love in his advances toward her. In fact, his words had been harsh and demanding. He'd yelled at her as if she were a weak-minded child. Perry's anger grew at Hunter and at herself. She was no street woman to be bedded at will. He'd given his word he would behave as a gentleman, yet his first night he'd lain in her bed, handled her as he'd promised he wouldn't. She knew what would have happened if Hunter hadn't been called away. She slammed her small fist into her pillow, knowing she'd wanted him with a passion equal to his need for her. "But I'm a lady," she kept repeating in her mind, "and the door will stay locked until I gain control of my own feelings."

Perry tried to sleep, but the memory of Hunter's touch haunted her.

Chapter 30

Hunter worked hour after hour with his men to keep the ship afloat. The storm gradually wore itself out and the ocean settled into a fitful sleep. As he relaxed at the wheel, the first ribbons of light whispered dawn on the horizon. The men slowly crawled off in exhaustion, leaving Hunter and Cap alone on deck.

"The storm seems to have blown us in the right direction," the captain said between puffs of his pipe. "We weathered her without much damage."

Hunter was impatient to return to Perry, now that the storm didn't demand his full attention. As he watched the old seaman he knew the storm had taken its toll on the man. Cap would have retired years ago, but he couldn't leave the sea he loved. He'd contributed his share during the storm, but now his energy was spent.

"Why don't you go get a few hours sleep, Cap," Hunter ordered. "I'll sail her for a while."

The captain moved away and Hunter smiled to himself. He'd give Perry a few hours more sleep before awakening her. All night, even in the midst of fighting the storm, she'd never been far from his thoughts. He could almost feel her body now. He remembered her soft full breast in his hand and the way she'd grabbed his head, forcing his kiss down to her. He'd never wanted anyone the way he wanted her. Women had always been an extra in his life. After his mother died and he'd seen what love had done to his father, he made up his mind never to be bothered by such feelings.

He kept telling himself he was infatuated with Perry. She was so small, like a fragile china doll. Yet the fire within her surprised him. He'd have to handle her with care, but handle her he would. What did Abram's and Molly's warnings matter once she was in his arms? She responded with zeal to his every move, with a fire equal to his own. They were both two starving peasants at a banquet. Today they would have their fill of one another.

The two hours passed slowly as Hunter thought of the lady who waited below. He almost bolted and ran from the wheel when Cap appeared to relieve him, not even noticing the captain's smile as he dropped below deck.

A moment later Hunter turned the door handle to Perry's room. He'd hoped to find her still asleep so he could study her beauty in the morning light. To his surprise her bed was neatly made and she was nowhere in sight. He stepped across the hall, thinking she must have spent the night in his bed. But again, to his disappointment, there was no one in the cabin.

Hunter moved rapidly down the small corridor to the galley and dining area, impatience showing in his stride. He stepped into the small dining room and in frustration snapped, "Perry!"

"Yes?" Her musical voice drifted from the galley as she stepped to the door. Her blue dress was almost completely covered with a large cook's apron. Her hair was pulled neatly to the back of her neck by a long blue ribbon. She held both flour-covered hands palms up in the air as she looked at him.

"Hunter," she answered in a low voice, "sit down and I'll finish cooking your breakfast. It seems the cook needs sleep, so I volunteered to make breakfast for anyone awake."

Hunter sat down at the end of the long table. Food was not foremost in his mind, but he was polite. Through the open galley door he watched her as she moved skillfully around the kitchen. He could smell the hot biscuits and ham she was cooking. Five minutes passed before she set a plate of food in front of him. The appetizing aroma surrounded him, and Hunter suddenly realized how hungry he was after a hard night's work.

When she handed him a cup of coffee, their fingers touched and he smiled up at her. Without responding, she moved to the other end of the table and sat silently, drinking her own coffee. She'd spent most of the night thinking of what she would say, but now, as she watched his gray eyes caressing her, she was speechless. His hair was windblown and half covered his forehead. He looked younger, and his smile came quickly and easily as he glanced up at her between bites.

She felt herself tearing apart at the seams. Half of her demanded she stand by her principles. She had little left but her standards, and if she cast them away, her pride in herself would be tarnished. Yet watching him, she so wanted to close the distance between them. Even in the morning light she could still feel his warm hands moving slowly over her. But she must have his love, not just his loving. For without love their physical union would be cheapened.

Hunter pushed his empty plate aside and lifted his coffee mug. "That was a very fine breakfast." He smiled, willing to play her game for a time. After all, they had all day.

"Thank you," Perry whispered as she stood and removed her apron. She folded it neatly and began her planned speech. "About last night . . ."

If Hunter had known more about women, he might have hesitated instead of rushing in. "Perry, come here," he demanded in a low voice seasoned with passion. "Come closer." He pushed away from the table and opened his arms, indicating she should sit on his lap. He'd waited long enough for her to be near him. Whatever she had to say could be said as he held her close.

Anger fired within her. He was ordering her around as if she were a child. He wasn't asking but telling. Every fiber within her rebelled. Why was it men always treated women as children, to be coaxed and pampered?

Perry stood her ground. "About last night . . ." she tried again as he folded his arms and leaned back in his chair. "I realize there were many factors contributing to what happened. The storm, my fright, your anger." She hesitated. She must finish what she had to say without looking into his eyes. "I want you to know I don't hold you entirely responsible. However, today is another day, and we can start again as if last night never happened."

The front two legs of Hunter's chair fell to the floor with a thud as he stood. He couldn't believe what he was hearing. "Perry?" He moved toward her. "Are you saying you wish to forget what we both felt last night?" If he could but touch her, he'd make her little speech worthless.

Stepping around the table, Perry widened the distance between them. "Last night never happened, Hunter. I hold you to your word as a gentleman." She lifted her chin in pride and stubbornness.

"Damn the promise!" he shouted as he shoved a chair out of his path. "I want you." Passion filled his voice. "And you want me!"

Perry's eyes widened at his frankness, and she could find no way to deny his statement. Yet anger flared once again. He spoke not of love but of need. "You said you'd not touch me until I came to you. And need or no need, Hunter Kirkland, I'll not come to you." Her hands balled into fists at her side as she backed away, keeping the table between them.

He moved closer. "Perry, you couldn't have been so warm in my arms a few hours ago and now be made of stone. I—"

Shaking her head, she cried, "I'll not listen to you!"

"If I can touch you," Hunter answered, "you'll hear me."

Perry matched his every advance with retreating steps. They moved as fixtures on a merry-go-round with the table always between them.

"You'll understand my promise was folly when . . ." He couldn't believe she was shattering his dream.

"Need I carry my pistol to keep you away? For I assure you, I'll not hesitate." Anger flashed in her eyes. "Are you so like your cousin that I must fight or bend to your will?"

Straightening, he backed away. Perry's comparison of him to Wade stung like a slap. He pushed his eyebrows together and studied her. "I'm not like Wade." His voice was cold and firm. "You wound me, madam, even to make the comparison. You shall have your wish. Last night never happened, and I'll make no advance toward you." He stared at her with icy, pain-filled eyes. "You've no need to carry a weapon. Your demands injure me far more than a bullet."

Hunter opened the door. "If you will excuse me, I must get a few hours sleep. I find my dreams much less painful than present company. Good day."

With a slam of the door he was gone, and Perry was alone. She'd won, yet where was the victory? She'd talked him into making no more advances toward her. She'd erased his smiling, confident manner to watch a cold, controlled mask return. Perry slammed her fist on the table in anger. "Why do I have to love such a man?" she whispered. "Why couldn't he just once speak of love and not of need?" She had to be more than just a woman he bedded. She'd settle for nothing less than being the one he loved.

Perry wiped tears from her flushed cheeks. Let him sleep, she would busy herself in the small kitchen. She might know little about sailing, but she did know how to cook. Attacking her job with an energy born of frustration, she stayed in the galley all morning. She was relieved when the cook finally awoke to serve a late lunch that she'd prepared for the crew. As the men gathered around the table she wandered above deck for some fresh air. The morning's work had dulled her anger.

A cool breeze greeted her as she opened the hatch. She welcomed the fresh air to clear her thoughts. Casting her gaze around, she met a sky that mirrored her mood. The clouds hung low as rumors of rain whispered in the wind. She climbed up to the open deck where the captain stood idly smoking his pipe. He smiled a greeting before continuing his study of the sky.

"Are we in for more storms?" Perry asked in an effort to make conversation.

"Appears we might be. But I'm figuring by the way those clouds are moving over yonder"—he pointed with his pipe—"that we are just skirtin' the storm. If we're lucky, a little rain is all we'll have to worry about."

The captain reminded Perry of a piece of driftwood. He was weathered and wrinkled beyond his age, yet there was a solidness about him. He stood watching her with wise old eyes, as though he were reading her as he did the weather.

Perry blushed slightly under his stare but welcomed his company. "Do you and Hunter sail often?" she asked.

"He has another ship—a fine, big lady. We've sailed on her many times but not lately." The old seaman wasn't accustomed to idle conversation. He'd spent a lifetime at sea and felt ill at ease around womenfolk.

She liked the old man and felt a need to be honest. "I'm not Hunter's cousin," she stated, wondering what he would think of her.

"I know," he commented without hesitation.

"Did Hunter tell you?" Perry asked, wondering.

"Didn't have to." The captain smiled. "No man looks at his relative like he looks at you." Perry's cheeks burned as he continued. "This is a small ship, and when voices are raised, everyone on board hears."

Perry lowered her head to stare at the sea. "Thank you for the warning, Captain," she whispered.

"What warning?" Hunter's voice sounded from behind her.

Perry turned in surprise as he stepped onto the small deck to join them. Though he was smiling, there was a tiredness in his eyes. She wondered if he'd slept at all this morning. He had changed into a clean white shirt and dark brown slacks, but he hadn't bothered to shave. His whiskers formed a light brown covering over his strong jaw.

Since Perry seemed deaf to Hunter's question, the captain stated, "We been talkin' of ships and weather." He dumped his cold pipe ashes out, tossing them to the wind. "I think I'll go have a bite while you're up top." He nodded to Hunter and moved away.

Perry and Hunter stood for several minutes, as if they were frozen statues. He watched the wind whip at her hair. He'd spent the morning thinking, finally deciding that the pain of being with her was no greater than the pain of not seeing her. Now, as he watched her standing proudly before him with her chin high, he wasn't sure his decision was correct.

Moving a step toward her, he rested his back casually on the railing. From this angle he could watch her closely as she seemed to be studying the waves. "I can answer any of your questions about sailing, Perry."

She didn't miss the change in his voice as he said her name. There was only the barest hint of passion in his tone. Perry knew he was holding himself closely in check.

"I have no more questions, thank you," she answered curtly. "Except, when will we arrive?"

"Can't wait to be rid of me?" Hunter asked, an odd smile forming on his face. He realized that his presence bothered her as much as hers tormented him. He stepped closer and studied her as he added, "In a few days you'll be rid of me and never have to see me again."

Perry glanced up and saw his smile. He must be counting the hours, she thought. Aloud she stammered, "G-good. I'll not have to be manhandled by you or your cousin again, once I'm under the protection of my brother."

Hunter moved back a step. "You need no protection from me. Your barbed tongue lashes like a whip."

"And you, sir, are as true to your word as a Yankee snake."

"And you, madam, are a poison in my blood. Would that I could cut myself and bleed until I am rid of you." Hunter's gray eyes turned stormy.

"You wouldn't bleed long, for you have no heart! You carry your needs like a banner, completely void of feelings!" Perry shouted. She knew others on the ship could hear her, but her anger wouldn't allow her to stop.

"And you, Perry, you feel? Tell me, what do you feel?" Hunter was within inches of her now.

Perry stared wide-eyed at him. His gray eyes looked into the very core of her. "I feel, I feel . . ." She could not continue. She whirled around to face the sea, gripping the railing tightly as if choking back words. How could she tell him she felt anger and love for him at the same time? How could she say to him how much she wanted and needed him, when his words would not be of love?

Hunter placed his hands on either side of her, yet he didn't touch her. She could feel his body only an inch behind her. His voice was low as he whispered, "What do you feel, Perry? Do you feel within you the same longing I feel? Does the temperature in your blood rise just a little when I'm around? Do you long for my arms to hold you as dearly as I long for you?" Hunter knew his words were tormenting her. He knew she was as aware of his nearness as he was of hers.

"I'll hear no more." Perry whirled and pushed him

back a step. She would have run, but his movements were swift.

"Wait, Perry." Hunter stepped to the ladder, blocking her path. He took a long breath to clear his thinking. He knew he'd chosen the wrong path and now must retreat before all was lost. "I didn't plan to fight with you." His voice was low and serious. He'd planned on being polite and distant to her, yet after only a few minutes they were shouting again. Hunter set his jaw in determination. "Hear me out."

Perry nodded, unable to trust her words.

"We must be together for a few more days. For the sake of my sanity, could we declare a truce?"

"You will hold true to the truce?" Perry questioned, raising her eyebrow in doubt.

"I will," Hunter answered. "If you will agree to stay below in bad weather."

Perry thought for a moment. She couldn't endure much more fighting. "I agree."

"Then for the next few days we won't fight but relax and enjoy each other's company." Hunter stepped away from the ladder and swept his arm across it to allow her to pass. "I'll see you at dinner, Miss Perry."

She walked to her cabin, her mind eased somewhat by Hunter's truce, but she couldn't help wondering how long this lull would last before another storm erupted between them.

And the next storm might drown them both in its fury.

Chapter 31

The next few days passed peacefully. Hunter saw Perry at meals and in the afternoons when they talked on deck. Each evening he'd walk her to her cabin and politely say good night. It bothered him that after she closed the door he'd hear the bolt being pushed. She didn't trust him. He'd always prided himself on being a man of his word. Each time she threw the bolt, he swore to convince her of his good character. It was vital for Perry to trust him again—as vital as trusting himself.

They anchored in the same cove where she'd been put ashore months ago. Amid the music of the sails being lowered, Perry hurriedly dressed and packed her belongings. She'd just begun tying her hair back when Hunter knocked.

Opening the door, she struggled with her ribbons. "I'm almost ready. Please, give me minute." She picked up a brush and combed back her ebony curls.

Hunter leaned against the door frame, showing no signs of impatience. "I'll wait all morning if I can watch." He'd grown in his belief that there was no more beautiful woman than this creature before him. With this knowledge in mind, he studied her movements.

Glancing over her shoulder, she became very aware of

the intimacy of her act and her fingers suddenly became clumsy.

Hunter stepped up behind Perry. "Let me tie your ribbon?" he asked at her ear.

In an effort to save time she agreed. His large hands tried to wind the ribbon around her curls as she held her hair together at the nape of her neck. Within a few minutes the ribbon was twisted and knotted while Perry's hair hung in a messy tumbling of curls about her shoulders.

She looked in the mirror at Hunter's confused face behind her and burst into laughter. "Have you ever tied a ribbon, Mr. Kirkland?"

"Well, no," Hunter admitted, twisting the ribbon around his long finger, "but it didn't look all that difficult."

Perry turned to face him, and for an instant she saw the boy within the man. She gently pushed him until he backed into the only chair in the room. "Sit down and wait. I'll do it myself." Her laughter filled the cabin, and he leaned back, content to relax.

With renewed purpose she pulled the end of another ribbon from her bag. "I have another ribbon," she said as she tugged, wishing she'd packed more carefully.

Finally frustrated, she yanked on it. Several items tumbled from her bag. Her mother's pouch landed on the floor between Hunter and her.

He slowly reached down and lifted the old leather pouch, a question in his eyes. She made no move to take it from his hand. He knew, of course, that it was the same one she'd fought to keep away from him in the old barn.

She stared at the leather in his hands. "It's all I have left of my home. It belonged to my mother."

Hunter smiled, realizing she was trusting him with her secret. "You needn't tell me."

"I don't mind." She worked her hair into place. "My mother, for some reason, made my father swear he would keep this pouch with me always. All it contains is a few rings and several old papers, but it was all we saved from the fire and the Yankees.''

"What kind of papers?'' Hunter asked curiously.

"Oh, nothing unusual. The kind all families keep. Birth certificates, baptismal certificates. There's even a letter from the doctor who delivered my mother.''

Hunter seemed lost in thought as he stared at the leather. Slowly she closed her fingers around the top of the pouch and pulled it from his grip. "I'm ready.''

Looking up, he said, "You look like a vision.''

Perry suddenly burst into laughter. "I hope I don't frighten anyone.''

"What?'' he asked, confused.

"Everyone in these parts thinks I'm dead.''

"I'll step ahead of you and tell everyone you're very much alive.'' Hunter bowed, like a knight offering his services.

Perry curtsied before disappearing through the door, and he wondered, even now, if she weren't more a vision than a reality. For he couldn't help but fear she might vanish from his life at any moment.

Twenty minutes later, when they stepped out of the rowboat and onto the dock, they were met by John Williams's hired hand, Hank. He greeted them with a twitch of a grin and sadness in his eyes.

After Hunter introduced Perry, Hank cleared his throat several times. His large, calloused hands twisted his slouch hat. "Mr. Kirkland, I'm glad you're here. We got your telegraph wire yesterday. I've been coming down every four hours since.'' His face was as gray as the day.

"How's my grandfather?'' Hunter words were as tight as his grip on Perry's elbow. She could feel him bracing himself for whatever Hank answered.

"He's mighty bad, sir. They didn't think he'd make it through another night.'' The hired hand lowered his head, not wanting to see the pain in young Kirkland's face. Hank had known Hunter as a boy, and he'd always liked and respected him.

"Let's go." Hunter moved toward the wagon.

Hank followed with the bags. "I didn't know you'd have the lady with you, sir. I brought you a horse in case you wanted to travel faster. The lady is welcome to ride with me and the bags back to the house, or, if you like, I'll ride the horse."

The man was obviously confused by Perry's unplanned presence. He grew confused and frightened when everything didn't go as planned. Hank had suffered greatly because of John's illness, for there was no one to tell him what to do. He'd been glad to hear of Hunter's coming. Now he could resume his accustomed pattern of life. Hunter would tell him what to do, and he'd follow without question. To Hank there were only two kinds of people, those he believed and followed and those he avoided. He'd tried the army at the beginning of the war, but he'd become too baffled trying to decided whom to trust and whom to avoid. In his first battle he'd injured his arm in a fall before the first shots were fired. The army sent him home to sit out the war.

Placing his arm on Hank's shoulder, Hunter's tone told how well he understood the older man. "Hank, I want to get to my grandfather faster than that wagon can travel. You did right to bring the horse. I'll ride and you bring the bags."

Hunter swung into the saddle and looked down at Perry. "The lady will ride with me." He offered his hand down to Perry and removed his foot from the stirrup. "I've seen her ride, and this will be no challenge for her."

He wasn't ordering but asking. He could have easily lifted her into the saddle, but he awaited her decision. She hesitated only an instant before lifting her skirt and stepping into the stirrup. As her hand touched Hunter's he pulled her into his arms so that she sat sideways in front of him. He held her close to him as he turned to Hank, who was staring, somewhat shocked, at the pair.

Hunter laughed. "I assure you the lady may look fragile, but she's able to ride. We'll cut across the fields and be at the farm an hour before you."

Within minutes they were out of Hank's sight, riding swiftly across the winter fields toward the Williams farm. For safety she slid her arm around Hunter's waist and rested her head against the rock-hard wall of his chest. The pounding of his heart thundered in her ear, and she remembered accusing him of having no such organ.

Finally Hunter slowed his horse to a walk as they moved through trees. Branches, barren in winter, lashed out at the unwanted visitors. Perry buried her head lower into his chest, as strong arms came up, shielding her from harm. After several minutes they emerged on the other side of the trees and into a shallow stream. "My grandfather showed me every shortcut through these woods years ago," Hunter explained.

His thoughts were suddenly filled with memories of his childhood. The old man had always had time for him. They'd spent many evenings talking of all the wonders of the world. Here, on this farm, Hunter never felt alone, not even after his mother died. Now John Williams was dying. Hunter instinctively tightened his grip around Perry's waist. He kissed her hair softly. "Thanks for coming with me." His words were barely heard above the splashing water.

Perry understood. She sensed Hunter's loneliness. He needed to know she was near. His need for her now stirred her far more than his independence had.

They were within sight of the house before he spoke. "No matter what happens, I want you with me."

"I'll be there if you need me," Perry answered. She knew there would be time enough to get in touch with her brother, Andrew. Hunter was alone, and she owed him the favor of standing alongside him.

He rode to the front steps and jumped down. Lifting Perry to the ground, he grabbed her hand and pulled her up the steps.

As their feet rumbled across the porch the door flew open, and Mary Williams hurried into the morning light. Her puffy eyes and hollow cheeks showed the impact John's illness had had on her. She'd aged ten years since Perry had seen her. Now the old lady had eyes only for her grandson as she cried joyfully and ran into his arms.

Hunter lifted her off her feet as she shouted, "Hunter, my dear Hunter!"

He set her to ground and whispered, "Grandfather?"

"He's resting quietly, but he's had a hard night. I thought I lost my John more than once." Mary cried softly, "I'll tell the doctor you're here."

Hunter cradled Mary under the protection of his arm. "Grandma, I brought someone with me."

Before he could say more, Mary glanced around him and saw Perry standing in his shadow. "Perry!" she shouted, "Can it be true? Perry?" Surprise lit Mary's eyes.

The old woman threw her arms around Perry and wept for joy. "We all thought you were dead."

"I know," Perry cooed as she stroked Mary's head. "But as you see, I'm very much alive. I'll explain everything later. First, I'm worried about John and you."

"I'm fine, dear, just a little tired. John started out with only a cold," Mary explained as she led them into the house. "It settled in his chest and grew worse. The doctor has been here every day, but each day he grows weaker. I'm worried sick." Tears bubbled over her tired eyes.

Perry wrapped her arms around the old woman and patted her gently on the shoulder. "Now you just stop your worrying, Mary. Hunter and I are here. We'll take over the worrying while you rest. You can take care of John when he wakes."

Hunter watched as Perry coaxed his grandmother over

to a comfortable sofa. Her gentle concern touched his heart.

As Perry talked with Mary he looked around the large living area that was so typical of his grandparents. Unlike most farmhouses built forty years ago, it had only one large room. John hadn't wanted his house to be divided into a maze of little rooms, so he'd built one huge room running the length of the front of the house. The only other two rooms downstairs were a dining room and a large kitchen. Hunter smiled as he remembered his grandfather sitting in one corner behind his desk, trying to work, as Hunter and Mary played checkers by the fire.

He could almost hear his grandmother saying, "If you'd build a study, John, you could have it quiet enough to think."

John always replied, "But I couldn't watch my beautiful wife all day."

Hunter knelt beside the woman John had never stopped calling his beautiful wife. "Grandmother," he whispered, "I'll sit with Grandfather. If he wakes, I'll call you." Her eyes were already growing heavy as her head rested back on the pillows.

Perry sat on the edge of the couch, talking softly to Mary, reassuring her that they would do everything that needed doing if Mary would only take a short nap.

Mary mumbled a soft thanks and drifted into sleep as Perry drew an afghan over her. Hunter bent and kissed his grandmother's cheek.

As he stood, he whispered to Perry, "We got here just in time. I don't know how sick my grandfather is, but my grandmother is completely worn-out."

Perry nodded and moved with him toward the stairs. "She just didn't want to leave his side until she was sure he had someone who loved him close by."

Hunter took a step by the stairs. "It may be a long day sitting with him." He moved up another step.

Perry knew what he was asking. "I'll stay," she said

simply. "There'll be plenty of time to let Andrew know I'm here later."

He held his hand out toward her. She accepted his silent invitation and they walked up together. He was slowly learning about this little Southern lady. She was a woman with her own mind, not to be ordered or bullied and steadfast in her loyalty when times were hard.

As Hunter turned the handle to his grandparents' bedroom the doctor stepped onto the landing. Dr. Moore was a country doctor whose years of watching human suffering showed in his face. He was worn-out and should have retired years ago. But the war had called away all the younger doctors; and someone had to see to the people back home. Now his eyes were disheartened because he knew he was losing a lifetime friend. These young folks wouldn't understand, he thought, but John and he had been young together. They'd both courted Mary, even though there had never been any doubt which one she'd pick.

How could he explain to Hunter that after sharing a lifetime with a friend like John Williams a part of him was dying too? So the old doctor just smiled his sad smile at Hunter, knowing they wouldn't realize it, but to Dr. Moore, John would always be remembered as looking very much as Hunter did today. Dr. Moore knew Mary also saw John as young and strong. Sometimes God seems to bless a couple, the doctor thought, with a special kind of blindness. All their life together they saw only the beauty in each other and never the aging.

"Dr. Moore," Hunter asked, interrupting the old man's thoughts, "how is he?"

"He's weak, I'm afraid. To be honest, son, it's just a matter of hours till he goes to meet his maker." The doctor's face was solemn. The hardest part of his job was not watching the dying but helping the living to let go.

Perry let out a soft cry and turned toward Hunter's shoulder. He encircled her with his arm and drew her to his side. "Thanks, Doc, for being honest with me. I'll sit with him for a while."

The doctor nodded, and Hunter stepped inside the bedroom. Perry turned to Dr. Moore. "I'm Perry McLain. I want to do anything I can to help." She lay her hand on the doctor's arm. She could see that his pain was great.

"Thanks, miss, but there ain't much anyone can do," he muttered. "You any kin to Andrew McLain?"

"He's my brother." She was surprised the doctor would know her brother.

"I've heard of a Doc McLain moving in at Three Oaks. Hope he'll help me out with the doctoring," he stated. "Didn't know he had any kin left alive."

The old doctor started down the hall. "I'll be here most of the day. Call me if John stirs. Otherwise I think I'll sit out on the porch for a while."

Perry watched his slow movements down the stairs, then joined Hunter in the dying man's bedroom.

Chapter 32

Hunter sat on the edge of his chair as the last rays of sunlight slid through the shutters of his grandparents' bedroom. Even though he'd been there for hours, he found it impossible to relax. Every few minutes he paced the room, standing at the sickbed, then at the window, only to see the same problem in his mind's eye.

There was no comfort for him in the warm friendly room, decorated with a lifetime of memories. He needed to talk with his grandfather, to feel the old wrinkled hand grip his own. But John was battling between one world and the next, with no time left to help Hunter.

Perry's silent footsteps moved in and out of the room. He was aware of her serving meals and taking care of the normal running of the house, for the two maids, Eva and her daughter, were almost useless with grief. They'd been with John for years and couldn't control their sorrow.

To all within the house the evening drifted by in slow agony. Friends dropped by to check on John. Their visits were well meaning but trying on a household consumed with worry. Mary greeted them but allowed no one upstairs except the minister, Reverend Cleland. He prayed for almost an hour, then finally left, to everyone's relief. He was new to the area and had learned little about giving comfort to the dying. He was more concerned with his new title than with John's illness. When Perry closed the door on him, he was in the midst of listing all the important people's deathbeds he had attended. She could see no sense in being polite to someone whose realm of concern passed no farther than his nose.

She was careful to stay in the background. By nine, when she'd seen no one whom she'd met before, she relaxed. The household accepted her as one of the family, and she was happy to help, knowing Mary had all she could think about with John upstairs growing weaker each hour.

Darkness covered the farmhouse, and all prepared for another sleepless night. Mary stepped out of the room to tell the maids to go home, leaving Perry and Hunter sitting on either side of John's bed. As Perry wet a cool cloth and placed it on John's forehead, his eyelashes flittered.

"Hunter," she whispered, bringing him instantly close.

They waited as John's eyes slowly opened. His glassy gray eyes surveyed the room. A smile slowly spread over his wrinkled face as he saw Hunter beside his bed. "My boy," he whispered, "come go fishing one more time."

"Anytime you're ready," Hunter answered, his sadness almost breaking his voice. He reached across the bed and closed his hand around his grandfather's fingers.

"I'm a little tired right now. But after I rest a few hours . . . a few hours . . ." John's voice was far away, as was the look in his eyes. He drifted into sleep once more for a few minutes. When his eyes opened again, he looked at Perry and smiled. "Perry, I had the funniest dream. I dreamed you were going to marry Wade."

She kissed the wonderful old man on the cheek, not trusting herself to speak. How different her life would have been if her grandfather had shown this concern. She looked across the covers at Hunter. He seemed hypnotized by a tear drifting down her cheek.

John continued. "Wade's no good for a fine girl like you."

"Yes, John, I know," Perry whispered.

A violent coughing spell consumed him. When he finally grew calm, she lifted his head, allowing him to drink.

"Mary," he whispered in a voice raspy with illness and age. "I need to see Mary."

Hunter moved to the door to call his grandmother but found her already heading up the stairs. She must have known John needed her. She hurried into the bedroom.

"John." A smile creased her damp cheeks. "John, you're awake." Mary propped on his bed and held his large hand in both of hers. Tears rolled down her wrinkled face, blocking out all awareness of anyone else in the room. Hunter moved his grandmother's rocker close beside the bed so she could sit more comfortably.

John looked up at his beautiful wife of almost fifty years. "You know, Mary, I wouldn't have traded a day of my life with you."

"Nor I," she whispered.

"I've loved you every minute since I first saw you in that pink bonnet at church." Though John's voice was low, his words were clear.

"I know, John. You don't have to talk, you need your rest." Mary kissed both of his cheeks as she pushed the gray hair off his damp forehead.

John shook his head from side to side. "Darling, I've never lied to you and I'll not start now. I have no more time. From the first I've always prayed that if God saw fit not to take us together, He'd take you first. I never wanted to leave you alone."

Tears were running down Mary's old cheeks like tiny rivers through rocky soil. "No, John. No, don't leave me." Mary's words tore at Perry's heart. She knew she should leave this couple alone in their last few minutes together, but the power of their emotions had overwhelmed her.

John's hand patted Mary's softly. "You got to understand. I'm going first, but it's not bad." He stopped to build his strength, then continued with little more than a whisper. "I'll wait for you just beyond. I'll be there when you need me. I'll be waiting, I promise. Hold my hand tight. I'll be with you through this."

Mary held his hand with both of hers as he whispered, "Now don't you be afraid, my love. I'm only stepping through the door ahead of you. I'll be on just the other side waiting. I wouldn't want to go into heaven without my Mary at my side." As his voice faded, so did the life within him. Mary let out a gasp of pain as half of her being died within her.

"John!" Mary cried. "John?" As she cried softly, Hunter and Perry watched John's face relax in eternal sleep. After a moment Hunter dropped to his knees and buried his face in the covers of the bed.

Perry instinctively reached to stroke his blond hair. He wasn't crying or praying. It was as if John's death had pulled all the energy from the room. She moved beside Mary's slumped body and encircled the old woman's shoulders with her arms. Mary looked up into Perry's face. "My John's gone," she whispered. "He's waiting for me now."

Tears ran unchecked down Perry's face. "I know," she whispered. "I heard him promise."

After a long minute Mary turned with tear-filled eyes to Perry and Hunter. "I'd like to be alone with John for a few minutes. Hunter, would you go tell Hank what he needs to do? Perry, I'd like you to speak with Eva, if she hasn't left yet." Mary paused as she saw their worried looks. "I'm fine, I just want to rest here a minute with John." Mary was still holding his hand. "Please ask that no one come up until I call."

Hunter stood and crossed to his grandmother's side. He bent and kissed her cheek before moving away. As he passed, Perry saw unshed tears in his eyes. Yet his fists were tight as he fought for control.

Without a word she followed him to the hall. As they

stood together in the darkness Perry sobbed. "I'm sorry, Hunter."

He placed his arms around her, but he seemed far away, in his own private grief. She could feel a wall between them. He didn't want to share his pain with anyone.

"I'll go down and make the arrangements." He moved away. If she hadn't seen the pain in Hunter's eyes when John died, she'd have never known how deeply he felt his loss.

An hour later both the doctor and the minister were downstairs waiting for Mary. The minister seemed impatient and displeased at having to wait. He showed his displeasure by frowning at Perry as she poured his third cup of coffee. He mumbled to the doctor, "I feel sure Mary will want to make a large donation in John's name to the building fund."

The old doctor knotted his mouth into a wrinkled prune and refused to speak to the reverend.

Hunter made all the arrangements and put Hank to work on the coffin. He stood tall and silent by the windows, staring at the winter night. Perry wanted to comfort him, but his rigid stance held her back. It said to all that he needed no one. He made no effort to talk with the doctor or the minister but cocooned himself in silence.

Dr. Moore finally broke the vigil. "Perry, perhaps it would be better if you and I went up and checked on Mary. She's been up there a long time."

Perry was hesitant to break Mary's wishes, but the doctor added, "I'll just look in on her."

Reluctantly she followed the old doctor up the stairs. He listened at the door for a moment but heard nothing. As he opened the door they saw Mary sitting in her rocker, by John, still holding his hand.

"Mary," Dr. Moore said as he stepped into the room.

She didn't move as the doctor neared. Perry reached for a shawl to cover Mary's shoulders, for the night and death's hand had chilled the room.

"Mary?" Dr. Moore's words were laced with a lifetime of friendship. "Are you all right?" He touched her shoulder in concern.

Mary's body slumped forward, first half onto the bed, then melting toward the floor. Both Dr. Moore and Perry dropped to her side, fearing she'd fainted. The doctor lifted her head gently with old, unsteady fingers and lovingly closed Mary's eyes.

"*No!*" Perry shouted, not believing what she saw. "No!" She screamed, moving beside Mary, trying desperately to awaken her.

The doctor stopped her efforts. "It's no use, Perry. She's already cold; she's been dead some time."

"No," Perry sobbed.

The old doctor lay Mary's head down lovingly and put both his hands on Perry's shoulders. "Perry, don't you see? It's the way they wanted it. Mary's heart has been weak for many years. She just couldn't live without him."

Both turned as Hunter burst into the room. For a moment he looked confused, not believing what his eyes told him. He darted to his grandmother and lifted her into his arms, holding her tenderly, as a father carries a sleeping child.

"I'm sorry, Hunter," the old doctor whispered through his tears.

Hunter placed her on the bed beside his grandfather's body. He stared down at her in disbelief.

Something fell from Mary's lap as he lifted the body. Perry bent and picked up a tattered old pink bonnet and handed it to Hunter. He turned the old hat in his hands as if examining a great treasure. "He said he fell in love with her when he first saw her at church in this." He lay the bonnet beside Mary.

"Hunter," Perry whispered, "I'll go downstairs and tell the others."

He nodded sharply as she watched his self-control stretch tight. He stood at the edge of the bed, staring at the bodies of his grandparents. "They were my shelter from the world when I was a child. I thought they would live forever."

Stepping away, she was unable to watch the pain in Hunter's face any longer. She moved slowly downstairs, in no hurry to share her heartbreaking news. Her mind ran over all that must be done. She knew that Hunter and Wade were the Williamses' only living relatives, so there was only one to notify except those already in the house.

Midnight had passed to the steady pounding of Hank's hammer in the barn by the time all the plans were made. Perry instructed Eva and her daughter to begin cooking for any company who might come in tomorrow. They were thankful for something to do. Perry said good night to the doctor and returned to the main room.

Hunter sat in a comfortable chair, staring at the fireplace. She admired how he had handled the minister earlier. Hunter had been much nicer than she could have been.

Kneeling at his knee, she whispered, "It's very late." Her hand rested lightly on his leg. She could feel his leg muscle tighten to her touch, as if he resented her closeness.

For a moment he looked at her as though she were a stranger he remembered seeing somewhere. "You need to go up and get some sleep," he said matter-of-factly. "The room at the end of the hall, on the left, was my mother's. You can sleep there." With a tired sigh he leaned back, resting his head against the back of the chair. His handsome face was outlined in gold by the firelight. The desire to touch him was a deep ache within her, but there was a coldness about him she'd never seen before. She'd seen the young boy of years ago in Hunter's face. Gray eyes so capable of fire showed only the frozen coldness of steel now. He must have withdrawn like this when his mother died. He would cry out for no one, and no one would touch him.

"You need some rest too." Perry's words were soft and

filled with concern. "The minister will be back in the morning. You handled him wonderfully."

"I learned a long time ago never to antagonize a fool. You never know which way he'll react. He'll be useful tomorrow to read over the graves. Then we can forget him."

Hunter grew silent once more. When he spoke again, his voice sounded far away. "My grandparents told me years ago where to put them to rest. At the time I never thought much about it. There's a little hill a few hundred yards up the stream. Grandmother used to have picnics up there. I remember playing by the stream as they sat on the grass watching me."

"That sounds like a wonderful place," Perry added, not knowing what else to say.

He reached over and covered her hand with his own. "Thanks . . . for being here."

"I cared for them a great deal . . ." She wanted to add, "and for you," but she wasn't sure he'd welcome her caring now.

He spoke into the fire. "It's very late." He seemed to have pulled away into a shell. "I think I'll sit here for a while."

Perry moved away, knowing Hunter wanted time alone. She climbed the stairs. Suddenly the house seemed cold and bare. She found her room and within a few minutes was curled into bed. The room was small but homey. A large patchwork quilt was spread over the bed and a shelf of poetry books lined one wall. A worn, overstuffed chair sat beside a small table by the window. Perry guessed Hunter's mother must have spent hours reading in that chair. Perry could picture in her mind what this farm must have been like thirty years ago. Love must have warmed the house as death cooled it now. Maybe Hunter was right, Perry thought. Pulling away from people is less painful in the end.

She'd have to wake up very early to get everything ready

for the funeral, but sleep eluded her. She kept listening for Hunter's steps on the stairs but they never came. Finally Perry fell into a fitful sleep.

By five the next morning, Perry was dressed and ready to go downstairs. She heard Hunter moving about in the room across the hall from her and wondered if he'd slept at all. With Mary gone, Perry quietly supervised the running of the house. She felt strange doing so, but she knew there was no one else to do it. The two maids were lost in grief and barely any help at all. Some people bear their grief on the outside, Perry realized, while others, like Hunter, hold it deep inside.

As the sun marked almost noon without giving any warmth, the funeral passed like a slow-moving dream. The small procession walked from the house, following the wagon carrying the coffins up the hill. Though the day was cloudy and cold, all except the minister were too numb with grief to comment. The maids cried in waves, first wailing loudly, then whimpering and sniffling. About the time everyone believed them quiet, another wave of wailing would resound.

As the minister read from the Bible and prayed, Perry glanced around her. In spring this spot would be beautiful, with trees shading it on the left and the stream babbling on the right. Her attention was brought back to the funeral by Dr. Moore blowing his nose. She knew not a day of his life would now pass without him remembering and missing John and Mary. He had not enough time left on this earth to build another such friendship.

As the little group walked slowly back to the house, Perry silently slipped her hand into Hunter's. She needed to touch someone, even if he didn't seem to need her. He looked at her in surprise, as though he'd forgotten her presence. She could feel the distance between them even as they touched.

Hunter's hand was warm to Perry's fingers. As they walked, he brought her hand to his face and blew his warm breath over her icy fingers. Though his actions were caring, his mind seemed far away.

After an almost untouched lunch he began pacing the large living area, as though he'd been assigned it as duty. One by one the neighbors came to pay their respects, each telling of his own sorrow. Hunter listened quietly and thanked each for coming; yet he remained detached. Perry stayed in the background. She had Eva serve tea and greet the guests while she moved about in unnoticed silence.

By mid-afternoon, clouds covered the sky, the wind grew colder, and the visitors stopped coming. When a door slammed somewhere in the front of the house, Perry moved to the kitchen window in time to see Hunter heading toward the barn. In another minute she watched him ride out like a man being chased. He vanished into the foggy gray air.

She worked around the house the rest of the afternoon, making an early supper, then sending the exhausted maids home. They were anxious to reach their small cottage before the dark clouds began to vent their wrath. Perry told them to sleep late tomorrow, for she would prepare Hunter's breakfast.

As night came, so did a steady rain, slamming into the house with vigor. Perry paced in front of the windows after she'd given up all other efforts to keep busy. Minutes dragged by as she studied the darkness for any sign of Hunter.

At ten Perry gave up waiting downstairs and decided to go up to her room and read. Hunter may have stopped somewhere for the night, she reasoned. Maybe he didn't want to return to this house filled with memories. Whatever his reason, Perry thought, he probably would be no more interested in seeing her tonight than he had been all day. She felt she'd been of little comfort to him.

Removing her shoes, she curled her legs underneath her in the comfortable chair in her room. She picked up one of the books of poetry and began to read.

The old clock in the hall was chiming midnight as she heard the front door open and close. At first she sighed with relief at Hunter's coming in from the storm. Then the thought occurred to her that it might not be him. Suddenly the realization that she was alone in the house struck her.

Slipping silently off her chair, she reached for her derringer on the nightstand. A noise echoed from across the hall. She moved out of her room and into the darkened hall without making a sound. What if someone had been watching the house? They might think this is a good time for a robbery.

She saw a dim light coming from the room across from hers. She cautiously moved to the half-open door. Peeking in, she breathed a sigh of relief. Hunter sat by the small fire, his legs spread wide as he relaxed in a chair. He'd removed his boots, and a soaked coat lay on the floor beside him. His hair was wet with rain and his face as stormy as the clouds outside his window. He watched the fire, studying its every pattern.

After a few minutes he glanced up at her with tired gray eyes. "Come in if you wish," he said flatly. Looking down at her gun, he laughed without humor. "Planning to threaten to shoot me again with my mother's gun?"

Perry looked surprised and lowered the gun. "Oh, no, I thought you might be a robber." She moved closer. "I didn't know this belonged to your mother."

"I didn't tell you because I wanted you to have it." He stared into the fire, yet his body seemed oblivious to its warmth.

"You're dripping wet." She grabbed a towel from the washstand. "You'll catch cold." Moving behind him, she rubbed his hair with a towel. "You need to get out of those clothes. I'll get you something warm to drink."

An iron hand grabbed her wrist, stopping her. He pulled her arm down, away from him. "Something hot to drink would be nice, but don't mother me." He almost spat the words.

Anger flared in Perry. "I'm not mothering you, but someone needs to take care of you. You haven't slept in two days, and then you go out riding in the middle of a storm—"

"Stop!" Hunter shouted as he stood and leaned close to the fire. His clothes clung to his hard, muscular body as he gripped the mantel. "I don't need anyone feeling sorry for me."

Perry threw the towel down. "Fine, Hunter Kirkland, don't let anyone feel anything for you." Her hands balled into fists at her side "You've made it plain you don't need anyone, so good night."

"And you've made it plain that you only take people on your own terms," he shouted at her retreating back.

Perry whirled to face him, her eyes wide in anger. "If you weren't so headstrong, you'd see that I just want to help. Why is it so terrible to believe someone cares for you?"

"Cares? Cares on your terms," Hunter said, his anger flashing. "I'll not come begging for handouts of caring. Every time I've looked up today, I've expected you to say you were leaving. I thought you would be gone by now, glad to have a damned Yankee like me out of your sight."

"What do you want of me, Hunter?" Perry asked, exasperated.

"No, madam, the question is, what do you want from me?"

A long silence fell between them as Perry's heart burned with a mixture of pride and pain. Finally Perry gave up any hope of understanding. "I want nothing from you, Hunter. Nothing you are capable of giving."

She would have moved away, but she heard Hunter whisper to himself, "I want you to stay with me. But you'd accuse me of trying to molest you again."

The sadness in his words brought tears to her eyes. His loneliness mirrored her own as he stared into the fire, unaware he had voiced his thoughts. He'd lost two people he loved dearly, and he was too tired to fight with her anymore. He moved across the room to his bed, threw the covers wide, and dropped on his back onto the sheets.

Perry turned slowly. "It's cold in here," she stated matter-of-factly. She crossed to the fire and put another log on, then waited for it to catch. She moved to his wet jacket and carefully dropped it over the back of a chair.

Hunter watched her with a frown, resenting her kindness. He placed his hands under his head but made no comment. No matter how tired he was, he would never tire of watching her move. Even through his anger and grief he was aware of her beauty. She seemed so kind and caring, yet he knew that if he touched her, she'd vanish like a dream.

To his shock she didn't leave, but stood for a moment beside his bed. Then, with a determined suddenness, she crawled, fully dressed, into the other side of the bed and reached for the covers he'd thrown aside. She spread the blankets carefully over them both and lay down on the pillow opposite him.

When she turned her face toward him, he didn't miss the challenging look in her eyes. She was daring him to say anything. Her chin was high and her eyes were bright in the firelight. As usual she'd made her decision and would stand by it. She was telling him by her action that she cared and, more importantly, that she trusted him.

Hunter slowly pulled his arm from under his head. She lifted her head off her pillow and moved under his arm to lie closer to him, her head resting on his shoulder. Hunter's body tensed as her warm breast pressed lightly against the cool dampness of his shirt. He reached with his free hand and pulled the ribbon binding her hair. As he gently spread her curls over his arm and onto the pillow, he whispered, "Are you sure you hadn't rather sleep with a bolted door between us?"

Perry's voice was soft, barely audible. "Do you need me here, Hunter?"

He lay silent for several minutes, holding her in his arms. He wanted to say he needed no one, but he couldn't lie. If he admitted how totally, truly, and desperately he needed her, he might frighten her away. Finally he stopped the battle within him by whispering against her velvet hair. "I need you, my angel, as dearly as man needs air."

In response she molded closer to his damp clothes, sending a warmth through him that no fireplace could provide. Placing her arm lightly over his chest, she whispered, "Good night," and her body relaxed next to his.

Hunter lay awake, trying to understand the woman at his side. Finally from lack of sleep, combined with the warm feeling surrounding him, he closed his eyes. There would be no need to dream tonight, for all his fantasies lay beside him.

Chapter 33

Early morning sunlight drifted through an opening between the curtains as Perry awoke. At first she was only aware of how wonderfully warm and rested she felt. Then, slowly, she realized where she was. Hunter's arm rested across her as he lay on his stomach beside her. She turned her head slowly to watch him sleep. This strong, complicated man looked so open and boyish now. His tight jaw was relaxed, his mouth slightly open. His sun-bleached hair curled across his forehead and along his neck. As she touched a single strand she realized how very much she loved him. Closing the inches between them, she lightly kissed his cheek. "I love you, Hunter Kirkland," she whispered as he slept. Someday maybe she'd say the words when he was awake.

Perry snuggled close in contentment and gazed lazily around the room. She had no wish to leave her warm nest or the man sleeping at her side. The room obviously had been Hunter's when he'd stayed here as a child. Though the toys were removed, books remained, lining the shelves along each wall. A beautiful pair of swords were crossed on one wall above the dresser. Perry could almost see him as a boy, fencing with his shadow. He could have fought many an imaginary pirate with such grand swords.

Wiggling around to see the other side of the room, she

found sleepy gray eyes watching her. She loved the look of wonder on his face before he fully awoke, blocking out all his feelings from the world.

He moved onto his side and pulled her closer. Wordlessly he bent and lightly kissed her nose. When she didn't object, he allowed his lips to glide hesitantly across her cheek to her ear. "Good morning, my angel," he whispered. "Did you sleep well?"

"Very well, thank you," Perry answered without moving away. "And you?"

Hunter's tongue brushed her upper ear. "Except for your snoring, I rested well." He smiled.

"My snoring!" Perry pouted, knowing he was teasing her and enjoying the game. "I do not snore, sir."

Hunter couldn't resist the full, pouty lips; he closed the inch between them and kissed her softly. "You're so soft and warm beside me. I could live a lifetime waking up with you." He propped his head up and stared down at her flushed face. "Was sleeping with me so bad?"

"It was not the sleeping I feared," she answered. "I've slept with a man before."

Hunter's eyebrow arched, questioning.

Perry hastened to continue. "Many months ago in a barn loft. You were far different then." She touched his once wounded shoulder.

Hunter watched her closely. "Pull my shirt aside if you doubt my identity."

The game excited Perry, and her cheeks warmed under his gaze as she unbuttoned his shirt. With trembling fingers she pulled the shirt wide and brushed his warm flesh. Though he made no attempt to help or resist, his breath grew short as her hands moved shyly over the soft hair of his chest.

She removed the shirt from his shoulder and lightly traced the scar. His muscles rippled beneath her touch. The feel of him was like liquor to her already hazy mind. As her fingers moved, she felt the explosive atmosphere that always surrounded him, only this time she was the one playing with the match. She was the one setting him afire, and his warmth was burning through her fingers into her very core.

"It appears you are the same man I've slept beside," Perry teased as she timidly moved her hand back across his chest. "The wound has completely healed."

Hunter closed his eyes and absorbed her light touch like a man taking in the warm sun after a cold winter. Finally he whispered, "And how do I know you are the same woman who slept with me in the barn?"

His hand traveled from her shoulder to her waist, pulling her nearer. "She molded so perfectly against me, giving me her body's heat."

"Like this?" Perry leaned against him, laughing at his sudden loss of breath. As she moved slightly, allowing her soft curves to torture him, she added, "Do you believe I am the one?" Her fingers slid over his scarred shoulder. "Or need I move aside and let some other audition?"

The movement of her breasts against his chest as she breathed drove him mad as he answered, "You're the one."

She watched his eyelids slowly open and was shocked by the passion reflected there. No matter how long she lived, she'd never forget the first time she'd looked into those fathomless depths.

He studied her face, seeking an answer. "Lady, you're a puzzlement to me that makes my life both a heaven and a hell." He nuzzled his face in her hair and savored the fragrance of her tossed curls. "Could we not be honest with each other for a few minutes?"

"Completely honest?" she asked, knowing she was playing with fire just by being this close to him. Yet the flame fascinated her.

"Yes," Hunter whispered as he kissed her forehead and allowed his hand to slide just past her waist. "Completely honest."

"Who goes first?" Perry studied him. This could prove to be a very interesting game.

"I ask the first question, but you must speak the truth, totally. Swear." Hunter insisted.

"I swear." Already questions filled her mind. "I have nothing to hide."

Hunter's tone grew serious. "Did Wade rape you?"

Perry was shocked by his question. She never thought he would mention Wade. Would it matter to him if Wade had? "No," she whispered. "He pulled me across the yard while hitting me several times. It happened so fast, I don't remember how many times." Perry's whole body shivered. "He slammed me against the stairs. Each time I cried, he laughed, as if hitting me were great sport." Her words echoed the pain of remembering. "He was so angry that I would try to leave, I think he would have killed me if he'd caught me a second time."

Hunter's arms tightened around her, pulling her close. "It's all right, darling. I didn't want to bring back painful memories to you, but I had to know."

She cuddled closer to Hunter's warm chest, trying to block out her fear of Wade, but the nightmare couldn't harm her now, not while she was in Hunter's embrace.

They lay in silence for a while. Finally Hunter moved his hand slowly over her shoulder and down her arm to her hand. He lifted her fingers to his lips.

Perry looked up. "Now it's my turn to ask the next question."

Hunter nodded as he continued kissing her fingers.

"Why weren't you upset over losing Jennifer?" The question had been in her mind for days. How could he give up his fiancée so lightly? "Didn't you love her?"

Hunter smiled. "One doesn't love someone like Jennifer."

"But you were two days away from your wedding."

"I'd known for days I wouldn't marry her. Richard just solved the problem of why."

"But—" Perry began, only to be stopped by his fingers gently touching her lips. He traced her mouth with one finger, stopping a moment to pull slightly against her bottom lip. When her lips parted, she shivered against him and watched his mouth move in hunger for her. His finger pressed against her lips in the silent promise of the kiss that would soon follow.

"It's my turn now." He didn't remove his finger from her lips. "Only one question at a time."

Hunter's question came softly in her ear as he blanketed her with his chest. "Do you want me?" He moved, his entire body feeling her beneath him, then he settled once more to his side. He hesitated a moment, as though giving her a chance to flee. When she didn't move away, he boldly pulled her against him.

Before she could answer, his hand slid into her blouse and softly caressed her breast through her thin camisole. Her body arched to his touch and his exploring grew bolder.

"Don't!" she ordered as his mouth moved down her neck and shoulder.

"The truth," he demanded huskily as his fingers pulled the undergarment away and his palm moved in circles over her breast.

Perry sighed, knowing she could stop him by moving away, for nothing held her to his bed but her own need. She wanted to be closer to him. Her silent answer came as she timidly moved her hands to his neck and pulled his face to her hungry lips. His mouth explored hers lightly at first, teasing her until she twisted her fingers into his blond curls, pulling him closer.

A long kiss stirred the passion within them and fulfilled a promise. It grew savage with need and tender with desire. His mouth demanded her lips as his fingers explored her body.

Finally he pulled an inch away, laughing as he moved

under the covers, replacing his fingers with his lips against her full breasts.

Perry cried out with delight as his mouth gently tugged at her flesh. How could she lie to him when her body gave her away so totally? She sighed with pleasure as his hands moved over her, pulling at the blouse that separated his touch from her.

After what seemed an eternity of pleasure he returned once more to her lips. At first his kiss was slow and tender, then his warmth turned to fire. He delighted in her breathlessness. "Answer me, lovely angel!" he ordered in a passion-filled voice. "Do you want me?"

She stared into the handsome face above her, then pushed him slightly away. "Yes, but . . ." She turned her face away, knowing she was denying herself the heaven of his lovemaking.

"But what!" Hunter shouted, suddenly angry that she would pull away from what they both needed, both desired. "The truth, woman, no more games."

Tears trickled down the corners of her eyes and fell untended into her hair. "But not without your love." Her words echoed with pain and anger. "I'm not the kind of woman who can give myself without love, and I'll not accept less."

"Lord, you want my body *and* my soul." Hunter lay back on his pillow, her words as cooling to him as a spring stream.

Perry's anger flared. She couldn't understand him. How could he show such tenderness yet never speak of it? "It's my turn," she said, sitting up in bed and pulling her knees to her chin. "Do you . . . do you care for me?"

Hunter folded his arms behind his head and stared at the ceiling. "This was a silly game. We get along much better when we're not talking."

Perry waited for his answer.

"I've never played any childish games of love. I always thought it brought more destruction and pain than joy,"

Hunter said, avoiding the question. "I remember my father after my mother died. They were very much in love. The pain of her death left him only a hollow shell." He couldn't look at her. "His suffering left no room for life within him."

"The truth!" Perry ordered. "Do you care for me?"

"You're a demanding wench," Hunter snapped, and his anger allowed him the willpower to look at her.

"You swore you'd speak the truth." Perry moved her fist to her waist.

The movement revealed the beautiful mound of her breast where her blouse gaped open. He saw the gold medallion he'd given her, nestling in her cleavage.

He reached for the chain. Perry squealed, hitting his hand away. "Answer my question, Hunter Kirkland."

He knew he was no different from his father or grandfather, in that he'd fallen hard for one woman, but he'd be damned if he was going to let her badger him into admitting it. He rose to his knees and with a sudden jerk pulled her beside him. "I'll answer your question!"

His mouth was fully on her lips as his hand twisted into her hair and held her still. His free arm pulled her against him. Her struggles only excited him as they pressed against each other. After a moment she clung to him, and he allowed his hands to roam freely up and down her body. Her wrinkled clothes did little to hamper his progress. When he'd kissed her until he felt her body melt completely against his, he raised his mouth and stared down into her face. "You are my heaven," he whispered against her cheek. "There are no games, no questions between us."

He cupped her face in his hands and kissed her. They were so lost in each other that the knock on the front door seemed a million miles away. Moments later the downstairs door opened and slammed closed, drawing them both from their dream.

Jumping from the bed, she started buttoning her blouse as she heard her name shouted from the hall.

"Andrew," she whispered. "It's my brother, Andrew."

She was halfway across the room when Andrew burst through the door. "Perry!" he shouted with joy, then froze at the scene before him. Hunter was shirtless on the bed, and it was obvious that Perry had just left his side.

She started toward Andrew, then stopped when she saw his shocked face. For a moment she couldn't understand his strange expression. Never had Andrew failed to open his arms wide to his little sister. Now he just stood watching her, as if he had never seen her before.

Moving a step closer, Perry whispered her brother's name once more.

Andrew turned to her, his face filled with anger. "I couldn't believe my ears when I heard from Dr. Moore that you were alive. Now I can't believe my eyes. Look at the disgrace you bring to our name. What kind of trash are you to let this Yankee bed you?"

Too shocked to speak, Perry glanced from Hunter to her brother.

Andrew would have tread more lightly if he'd seen the anger in the Yankee's face, but he had time and words for no one but his little sister.

Deadly calm, Hunter moved off the bed.

The redheaded doctor grabbed his sister's arm as she tried to move past him. He pulled her toward the door. "You're coming home with me!" His fingers dug into her arm as he shook with anger. "I'll not have any sister of mine playing whore to a Yankee."

"No!" Perry screamed. "No, Andrew!"

He couldn't see Hunter's approach, but Perry did. With lightning-quick force Hunter slammed his fist into Andrew's jaw. Andrew let go of her and whirled around, colliding with the wall. He heard Perry's scream as his eyes rolled back and his legs slid out from under him. Shaking his head from side to side, he tried to clear his brain. As his vision cleared, Andrew found himself staring at a sword pointed directly at his heart.

Perry stood frozen, watching as Andrew forced his sight past the weapon to the man beyond. Fiery gray eyes bore into him with such hatred, Andrew grew white with fear.

Hunter's voice was low yet crystal clear. "You are alive, sir, because you are Perry's brother. Do not challenge your luck, for I will not consider the kinship again."

Amazement showed on Andrew's face as his tiny sister moved fearlessly beside this blond madman and gently laid her hand on his arm.

"Hunter," Perry whispered lovingly.

Hunter didn't move his gaze from Andrew or lower his sword. "No one, sir, takes Perry from my side." His eyes burned in anger. "Anyone who touches her against her will shall not live another day on this earth. Do I make myself clear?" Hunter's voice was deadly earnest.

Andrew was obviously too frightened to speak. He nodded slowly and breathed a sigh of relief as Hunter lowered the sword.

Perry moved to help Andrew up as Hunter returned the sword to its place on the wall. "Andrew, I'm no longer a child. No man orders or owns me." Perry hoped Hunter would heed her words also.

Andrew straightened his clothes, trying to gain back a few ounces of his self-respect. "If you stand beside such a wild man, perhaps you need no protective big brother. I will not tempt fate again by accusing you of anything." A newfound respect echoed in his words as he addressed his sister. "Even in shock and anger I never meant to hurt you, Perry."

"I know you didn't, my gentle Andrew." She smiled, her thoughts full of Hunter's words. Though he had spoken in anger at Andrew, he told of how deeply he loved her. He might not have said the words of love, but she knew he felt them.

She moved beneath his protective arm, sliding her hand

lovingly around his back and resting her fingers at his waist. She bore no shame for being with Hunter, and she wanted Andrew to understand this. "I would've wished the two of you to meet under less violent circumstances," she said, trying to ease the tension. "Hunter, my brother saved your life once. Do you think you could give him another chance?"

Hunter's eyebrow raised. "You were the Confederate doctor in camp?" His anger was vanishing with Perry's touch. Though Andrew paid no notice, she was slowly moving her fingers up and down Hunter's side as they talked. He found himself hard-pressed to think of anything but her fingers sliding along his skin.

"Yes, I treated you at Perry's request." Andrew straightened, pulling his shoulders back.

Hunter's anger diminished. He saw a defeated man standing before him, only tiny threads of pride holding him together. "I can't hate a man for loving his sister, even if you were harsh in your attack. Perry speaks of you with admiration." Hunter slowly extended his hand to Andrew. "I thank you, Dr. McLain. When I reached Philadelphia, the doctor said if it hadn't been for your excellent care, I'd have lost my arm, if not my life."

Perry smiled up at Hunter. She knew he was giving Andrew back a fraction of the pride the war had torn away.

"Dr. Moore tells me we could use a doctor with your skill. Will you consider staying at Three Oaks?" Hunter asked.

Gaining control of his voice, Andrew answered, "I like it here. Maybe it would be better to start somewhere new, now that the war is over." He coughed and attempted to make the question show only casual interest. "Do you plan on staying on here?"

Hunter laughed at his question and winked at Perry. They smiled, both knowing Andrew would be hoping for a negative answer. "I would like to, but my work is in Philadelphia and Washington. I plan to visit here often, however. I'm very concerned with the politics of this area. The election of the next governor in a few days may prove very interesting.''

Perry watched as Andrew became more relaxed when the subject turned to one of his favorites, politics. "It will be a close race between Worth and Holden. Many of the men I've talked to are not even going to bother to vote. They say with either man as governor, North Carolina is in for a hard time.''

"President Johnson has a special interest in this election, what with Raleigh being his birthplace and all,'' Hunter said, all too aware of Perry's stirring as she pulled from beside him and moved toward the door.

She smiled first at Andrew, then at Hunter. "Do you think you gentlemen could continue your discussion downstairs? I'd like to freshen up, then I'll cook you both breakfast.''

Hunter bowed. "Yes, angel.'' Then, turning to Andrew, he added, "I'll show you to the kitchen, and maybe between the two of us, we can find the coffee.'' He bent casually to pick up his boots as he stuffed his shirt into his pants with his free hand.

The men moved down the hall as Perry crossed to her room. She removed her wrinkled blouse and skirt, deep in thought. She began absentmindedly combing her hair as she tried to remember everything Hunter had said that morning. Finally her hair was shining and beautiful. Perry removed all but her light camisole and began washing from the cool water at her nightstand. Pulled out of her thoughts by a light tapping at her door, Perry lifted her dress in front of her and said, "Yes?''

Hunter opened the door quietly and stepped in. "Perry, I have to talk with you.''

"Not now, I'm dressing," Perry answered firmly. Even unshaven, he was by far the best-looking man she had ever seen. His blond curls were a mass of golden disorder, and she loved the morning look of him.

He smiled as his eyes rested on her bare shoulders. "If I promise to turn my back, may we talk?"

"Your word?" Perry questioned.

"My word," Hunter said as he slowly turned around and showed Perry only his back.

Timidly Perry lowered her clothes and began washing each part of her body with care. She kept one eye on Hunter's back as she bathed.

"I needed to tell you that Abram will arrive sometime today. I also must ride to Raleigh and see my grandfather's lawyer. He left small plots of land to each of the help. I need to clear up all of his paperwork."

"Is there anything I can do to help?" Perry asked as she slipped off her camisole and reached for a clean one.

"No, I don't have time to explain, but I need to be in Raleigh for the election. I thought you might like to ride back to Three Oaks with your brother." Hunter stopped, as if in thought, leaving Perry to wonder if he was trying to say good-bye. "I would like to call for you in three days. We have much to talk about."

"If you like, I'll stay here and run the house. There is much to do. I need to talk with you about what you would like done."

"No," Hunter answered sharply, "I don't want you here alone. If Wade returns, this will be the first place he will come. I'd feel much better if you were at Three Oaks with Andrew."

Perry slipped into her dress. "I'd better pack," she said, more to herself than Hunter.

"No." Hunter's order surprised her. His next words told her a great deal about the way he felt. "You have everything you need at Three Oaks. Leave your things here. I want to know part of you stays."

"All right," she answered, knowing she was getting into his blood.

"I'll tell Andrew you hadn't enough time to pack," Hunter reasoned. "I've already asked Hank to saddle a horse so you can ride back with your brother after breakfast.''

Perry slipped her knife into her pocket in an action that had become habit.

''You'll need to carry your gun also, until we are together again,'' Hunter added.

Perry's head jerked up to study Hunter's back. ''How . . . ?'' she whispered, then realized he was watching her in the mirror on the wall in front of him.

She stormed toward him. ''Hunter Kirkland, you were watching me all the time.'' She raised her fist to strike him.

He easily dodged her swing. ''Sorry, madam, but I kept my word. My back was to you.''

''Hunter!'' she squealed as she raised her fist to his chin.

''Take your best blow, lady, for I assure you the pain will be little to endure for the pleasure I've received.'' He laughed as she fumed.

''Or if you think me unfair, I'll let you watch me change clothes, and then we'll be even.''

She burst into laughter at his plan of repayment for the crime.

He pulled her into his arms and lifted her off the floor. ''Will I ever get enough of you?'' he whispered into her hair. ''Is there enough time in eternity for me to grow tired of the look of you?''

His lips found hers, and for several minutes there was no world outside his arms.

An hour later Hunter gently lifted Perry onto her horse. Andrew watched the way his eyes held hers. His hand covered hers as he spoke to Andrew. ''Take very good care of my angel, Andrew.''

Andrew thought the way they acted was improper, but he knew he would never again comment on their behavior. He felt sorry for any man who dared.

Chapter 34

As the three old oaks came into view Perry felt a sadness engulf her. The memories of Noma's betrayal and Wade's beating suddenly and painfully returned. The place looked much the same as it had months ago when she'd first arrived. When her horse stopped beside Andrew's mount, she stared at the long French windows through which she'd made her escape, and all the pain of that night came back to her.

Andrew helped her from her horse, unaware of her hesitation. "I haven't properly welcomed you back to the living." He hugged her tightly. "When I rode to Ravenwood and found only ashes, I was disheartened. When I reached here and was told you had drowned, I thought life and this war had finally broken me. My only hope lay in the fact that they never found your body, and I remembered how strong a swimmer you were."

Sarah and James came out of the house shouting like sinners on the last night of a revival. When Sarah calmed down enough to speak, she mumbled between sobs, "We kept your room just as it was. Noma made us. Said there was so much sorrow in that room, nobody was ever goin' in there again."

"You've seen Noma?"

Andrew nodded. "She came by a few weeks ago. She

works near town for a Union officer named Williams."
His tone lowered as Wade's name flavored his voice with
disgust. "Seems he was real nice to Noma after you 'died,'
and Noma went to work for him. I invited her to come
back here, but she said she couldn't stay at the place with
you gone. I'll ride over and tell her you're back."

"No," Perry answered, wishing she had time to tell
Andrew all that had happened. "Wait a few days." The
last thing she wanted was Wade's entire household knowing where she was. There would be time enough to tell
Noma after Hunter returned from Raleigh.

Andrew watched her, reading her sadness. "Come on
inside. You must be tired. We can talk at dinner."

She was thankful he allowed her the afternoon alone.
When she joined him in the newly decorated dining room,
Perry felt she was finally ready to face his questions.

But to her surprise they didn't dine alone. An attractive
widow, Victoria, whose husband had been Andrew's friend
during the war, joined them. She was warm, and her voice
was soft and friendly. She'd been helping Andrew redec-
orate the house and mend the wounds of war. As they
talked, Perry watched her eyes and knew she would someday erase Andrew's scars of war with strokes of love.

When they moved from the dining room to the newly
painted study, the thunder of horses silenced all conversation. Andrew patted Victoria's arm and excused himself.
Perry moved to build a fire to warm the study. Her brother
often had late visitors before the war. It usually meant
someone was hurt and in need of a doctor. With the cold
night his visitors would welcome a fire.

Just as Hunter lifted his hand to knock, Andrew opened
the door. "Andrew"—Hunter's voice blew into the hall,
along with the cold night air—"I know it's late, but I must
see Perry."

Andrew stepped aside and held the door wide. He could
see just beyond the porch that a huge black man waited

holding the reins of their horses. Andrew indicated the study door. It never occurred to him to deny Hunter's request. In truth, Andrew knew Hunter was stating his plans and not asking permission. Despite Hunter's temper, Andrew liked him and had decided, after a day's thought, that the Yankee was probably an equal match for his headstrong sister.

Hunter stormed into the study and stopped in mid-stride as he watched the vision before him. Perry was kneeling beside the fireplace trying to add more logs. Her dress was a dark wine red, which made her skin seem even more lovely. Her hair streamed down her back in long waves the color of midnight. He wondered, as he moved closer, how she could grow more beautiful each time he saw her.

He was almost across the room before she looked up. "Angel," he whispered as he pulled her into his arms. His lips met hers as his name formed on her mouth. He held her close to his body, as if they had been separated for a long time. Her softness molded into his hard frame as his mouth whispered of his need. His hands moved over the velvet of her dress in hungry urgency.

After some time she pulled away slightly. "What are you doing here so late?"

"Trying to make love to you," Hunter answered as his hands roamed her back in caressing strokes.

"No." Perry laughed. "What has brought you?"

He released her long enough to throw his hat and heavy coat aside. "When I see you, I forget all else but my need to hold you." He reached for her, but she darted from his touch.

"Hunter, this is my brother's house."

He moved toward her slowly. "I'm aware of that fact. Why else would I be restraining myself?" A devilish twinkle danced in his gray eyes.

"You're a lost cause." Perry moved away, loving the way he followed.

"Agreed, lady, completely lost," he whispered before

sobering to his duty. "I came to warn you of something. Abram arrived this afternoon and reported Wade may have reached North Carolina ahead of him. He said several people along the road reported having seen a man of Wade's description, traveling fast."

"Wade's here?" she whispered as she unconsciously slipped her hand into her pocket and encircled her knife.

"I've spent the past few hours looking for him but with no luck." Hunter walked to the window, as if searching the darkness. "He has a house between here and town, but he isn't there."

Hunter turned suddenly to face Perry. His voice was cold with determination. "I must go to Raleigh tonight. It's very important. I've come to tell you to stay inside and be careful. Go nowhere until I return."

"Ordering me?" she asked, placing her fists on her hips as she faced him. When would he learn to stop treating her like a child or a servant?

"Yes, damn it, I'm ordering you!" he shouted, suddenly tired and torn between staying with her and doing what must be done.

"Well, I'm through with running away from Wade. Let him find me. I'll shoot him for the dog he is!" Finally all the fear within her changed to anger. "I can't spend the rest of my life running from him."

Hunter raised his finger. "You will stay safe. I'll not have you confronting Wade alone." His anger set fire to his stormy eyes. He'd seen men freeze at his wrath, yet this little lady stood her ground.

She lifted her chin. "And who are you to tell me what to do? No one owns me, and I'll do as I please."

Hunter moved toward her, his frustration showing in the muscles along his jaw. The door to the study opened before he reached Perry.

"Oh," Victoria said, ignorant of the drama she had walked in on. "I'm sorry. I didn't know anyone was in this room."

Perry introduced Victoria, loving the way Hunter fought to control his anger as he addressed the lady. "I hope you'll excuse us, Victoria," Perry urged. "We were in the middle of an argument."

Andrew stepped into the room just behind Victoria. He watched his sister and the Yankee closely as the widow politely said, "Oh, we can't have you two arguing. I'll bring tea and we'll talk over any problem."

Andrew almost burst out laughing. Gentle Victoria, who'd been sheltered from the war, would be unprepared for these two.

Hunter bowed politely. "I thank you, but I can fight with Perry quite successfully without refreshment. If you and Andrew will excuse us, I have a few things to say to her, and I feel they must be said without an audience."

Victoria looked at Andrew for direction.

"Does my sister wish us to leave?" He watched Perry.

"I'll be quite safe." Perry smiled at Andrew, wondering what he would have done if she'd demanded he stay.

Andrew nodded and took Victoria's arm. He closed the door behind them without another word.

"Safe?" Hunter raised one sandy eyebrow as he moved toward her.

"I'm not afraid of you or anyone else." She stood her ground by the fireplace. He seemed so tall in his black riding boots and dark gray slacks.

He put his hands around her waist, encircling her as he lifted her off her feet and stood her upon the brick hearth. Now her face was equal to his as he studied her in the firelight.

"Perry.' His voice was low, without anger. "I must go to Raleigh tonight. I would feel much better if I thought you safe. This morning you asked me if I cared for you." He was only an inch from her nose. "I care for you very deeply." His words came slowly, as though being pried from him.

Perry laid her arms lightly on his shoulders. "And you

think your caring gives you permission to order me around?''

She loved his words, but she had to be honest. ''I'll not be ordered or bullied by any man. Not even you. You can't take what must be given.'' He would accept her as an equal or not at all. She would not be one of those women who lived in fear of a man's orders.

He ran his fingers through his hair. He had to convince her of the danger she was in, but he found it hard to reason with her hands gently moving across his neck. Finally he shoved his fists into his pockets and looked deep into her eyes. He saw the warmth and fire of a woman he would hunger for all his life. ''Come here,'' he whispered as she stood only an inch away.

Perry closed the space between them and lightly kissed him. ''I'll not be ordered.''

He closed his eyes in agony as she slowly moved her lips over his face. She ran her fingers through his wind-blown hair, yet he made no move to withdraw his hands from his pockets. He was waiting for her to agree to his request. It was unthinkable that she might try to face Wade alone.

''You'll stay in the house until I return?'' he asked, not moving as she slid her hands along his shirt.

''And if I say no, what will you do?'' she whispered as she kissed his ear.

''Will you take care?'' His body stood in agony as she moved beside him, pushing her breasts lightly into his chest as she kissed his cheek. The vision of her dressing only hours ago floated over his mind like a fog.

''I will,'' she mumbled as she boldly kissed his face. Her velvety lips moved along his skin with maddening slowness. ''You need have no thought of my safety.''

''Thoughts and dreams of you are all I ever have,'' he whispered as she swayed against him.

''I'm not a thought or a dream now,'' she answered.

Finally he could stand no more of her torture. He pulled

his hands from his pockets and broke his vow to talk without touching her. "You're driving me mad," he said, pulling her into his arms. Moving one arm under her knees, he lifted her against his chest and carried her to a chair. As he fell into the large chair he pulled her into his lap.

"I've never met the likes of you," Perry said with a giggle. "I'm beginning to think my brother's right—you are part madman."

"It's true, my love. I'm quite mad." He moved his hand up her bodice and began pulling at her blouse as he slowly kissed her neck.

"No!" Perry squealed. "Andrew is probably at the door."

"Then we must be respectable." Hunter laughed as she rebuttoned her blouse. "I have to go. I've a long ride ahead of me. But first I'll hold you once more, for your memory will warm this night."

"We will continue our argument when you return."

"Ah, lady, and more." He pulled her close. His kiss was long and deep, exciting her with its promised fire. His hand moved up her leg, under her skirt, and to her bare thigh. As her eyes opened in shock he moved his hand boldly up and down the soft flesh of her leg. Suddenly she was lost in a whirlwind of ecstasy. With each new touch her yearning for him deepened.

Finally he pulled away to study her face, glowing with the fires he had kindled. He knew he would never tire of her. He watched her eyes close in pleasure, and she leaned back against his arm as his hand moved slowly beneath her skirts. Her lips parted and he leaned to catch her cry of joy in his mouth. She was his as surely as he had lost his heart to her.

When he was able to break their kiss, he whispered, his voice low and thick with passion, "I must leave. Promise you'll wait in safety. I have much to say to you, and now is not the time or place." She pulled his face to her, and he was lost once more in her kiss.

She pulled away and whispered, "I'll be careful."
Standing, she looked at him, her mahogany eyes telling
him all that he needed to know about how she felt.

Hunter wanted to stop time's passing, but he couldn't.
He wanted to stay with her forever, but honor and duty
demanded he leave her once more. In silence he grabbed
his coat and led the way to the porch.

They didn't say a word to each other on the porch but
only held each other tightly for a moment. Then Hunter
and Abram vanished into the darkness.

Perry stood staring into the night. Finally, when the
cold had seeped into her bones, she returned to the house.
She walked silently to her bedroom and curled up amid
the covers and her thoughts.

The next few days passed like feather-light clouds over
an endless sky. Andrew hired new servants and retired Old
James and Sarah to a little house out back. They still came
over every morning out of habit. Sarah planted herself in
the kitchen and spent the day telling stories. James tried
to make himself useful by sauntering through the house
making announcements. He shuffled from room to room
like a town crier, calling that dinner was served, or that
the wind was changing, or other news everyone already
knew. He often answered the door when folks came to see
the doctor. He'd wander around announcing their ailments
to everyone. Perry found his manner hilarious, but Andrew didn't share her opinion.

On December twelfth they heard that the election for
governor went to Jonathan Worth by only five thousand
votes. Perry knew Hunter would be coming soon.

James had just finished sweeping the porch the next evening when he stepped into the hall. "Rider coming," he
announced in his usual serious tone.

Perry jumped to her feet and ran to the door. Her heart
was pounding in the hope of seeing Hunter again so soon.
Far down the road, she watched a lone rider moving fast.
The setting sun was shining in her eyes, so it took her

several seconds to recognize the form drawing near. "Wade!" She whirled around and ran into the house.

Colliding with her brother in the hall, Perry tried to slow her words enough to make sense. "Andrew, it's Wade. I don't wish to see him."

"All right." Andrew didn't need to ask questions; he could read her eyes and find all the answers he needed. "Go upstairs and I'll take care of him."

As Perry climbed the stairs she wished she'd told Andrew more about Wade and how dangerous he was, but the time had never been right to reopen all the wounds he'd inflicted.

Running to her room, she pulled her derringer from the dresser drawer and shoved it into her pocket, then moved to the top of the stairs. Here in the shadows she could see everything as she stood unnoticed.

Andrew answered the pounding politely. "Yes, may I help you?"

Perry froze when she heard Wade's voice: "I understand Perry McLain is visiting here. I wonder if I might have a word with her. We're old friends." His voice sounded casual, as if he had just dropped by for a visit. "I'm Captain Wade Williams." He extended his hand to Andrew.

Andrew took Wade's hand, knowing the Union officer didn't remember the bearded Confederate doctor he'd once insulted. But Andrew would never forget Captain Williams and the small Union camp. Wade had only been in charge of the prisoners for a few weeks, but during that time many of the wounded had died. Andrew remembered that if it hadn't been for the bargain Abram made for supplies, many more would have perished. At the time Andrew had wondered how Captain Williams could care so little for his fellowman. Not only didn't he value the prisoners' lives, but also he cared little for his own men. The only thing all the soldiers in camp had in common was their hatred for Williams.

"Captain, I'm sorry, but my sister is not receiving guests."

Wade's voice grew cold. "I've ridden a long way to see her. I'm sure she can find the time." He placed his arm on Andrew's shoulder and pushed slightly to make his point.

"I'm afraid not. Perry has no wish to see you, sir." Andrew's voice was nervous. "I'll have to ask you to leave."

"You can't stop me from seeing her." Wade's tone was sharp with rage. "I'll tear this house apart—and you along with it."

"No. I can't allow—" Andrew never finished his statement, for Wade's fists plowed into his face. Andrew was unprepared for the sudden violence and fell backward like a puppet whose strings suddenly had been dropped.

"I'm not in the habit of allowing anyone to stand in my way." Wade kicked Andrew with his boot. "Now, if you'll tell your sister I'm here, we'll avoid any more unpleasantness."

Andrew stood, swinging blindly toward Wade. The captain showed no mercy. He pounded into the doctor with the power of a trained soldier. Blood streamed from Andrew's nose and mouth, and still Wade drove his fist into the gentle doctor. Finally, as if suddenly bored, he stepped back, allowing Andrew to crumble into a puddle of blood.

Wade moved toward the stairs without a backward glance at the damage he'd done. He was smiling at his victory and looking forward to more of such pleasure to come.

As he reached the foot of the stairs a gun being cocked cracked the silent air. Wade froze, irritated at another delay.

"Back up, Captain!" Old James's voice rang from beneath the stairs.

Wade took several steps backward as James moved to

block the stairs. The old black man stood taller than he was, an old rifle in his hands pointing directly at Wade.

Shock and rage blended in Wade's face. "You old fool. You don't want to point that antique at me. I doubt it would shoot, anyway." Wade would have laughed off the attempt to stop him, but the gun was pointed at his middle. At this range the old man just might hit him.

"It'll shoot." James's voice was solid, though his body shook with nerves.

"You'll hang if you shoot a white man."

"I knows that, but I figure I don't have much time to lose, anyway. I saw what you did to Miss Perry that night, and I have to stop it from happenin' again. I may die for killin' you, but at least the likes of you won't be around pesterin' good folks like these."

Perry pulled her gun from her pocket and moved down the stairs. "It will be hard to tell if my bullet or James's took your life." She stood on the steps just behind James. Her hand held the gun solidly and Wade knew her aim would be true.

He backed away. "Perry, I only came to say I'm sorry for all the trouble I've caused you. If I'd known you were serious about not marrying me, I would have stepped aside. In Philadelphia I only wanted to talk. I didn't even hurt anyone at that restaurant. The guard you had only got a bump on the head. But thanks to your telling the law, I almost got thrown in jail. So it is I who should be angry." His movements reminded Perry of a snake as he backed to the door. "Luckily I have friends in government who owe me favors."

Andrew moaned from the corner, drawing Perry's glance for an instant. Wade darted from the door and disappeared. She ran around James to the porch, but he was already riding away. Lifting her gun, she fired, warning him never to return. If he did, he would find them prepared.

Chapter 35

Perry dug with a vengeance at the brown weeds in the garden. Three days had passed since she'd seen Wade, and still there was no word from Hunter. She'd done everything she could to stay busy. Finally, when the house was spotless, she turned her nervous energy to the overgrown garden. She cared little that spring was far away and the day cold. At least here she could be alone and think. Andrew had hired several extra men around the place, and all wore holstered guns as they worked. He'd given the order that anyone seeing Wade on the grounds was to fire one shot. Perry found herself praying that that one shot would pierce his heart and put an end to her fears.

The order and the guns should have made her feel safe and protected, but instead she was on edge, half expecting a shot to ring out at any moment. She felt like a prisoner being constantly watched.

The sun melted into the dormant earth, giving the ground a golden glow. Storm clouds huddled to the north, dressed in radiant violet hues. But she hardly noticed, for she dreaded another night without Hunter. She was like the cold earth and he was her sun. When he touched her, life had a golden glow, yet when he was gone, life seemed cold and dead.

Finally she stretched and looked over the garden wall.

Two of the men Andrew hired to help out were coming slowly toward her. They were rough, hardworking lads who seemed thankful enough for a job. The country was running over with men now, compared to only months ago, when most had been away fighting. From the look of them these two were brothers. Except for one being several inches shorter than the other, they were a matched set of grimy bookends. Both wore filthy uniforms and bored, lifeless expressions that seemed engraved into their faces. As they approached the garden's edge they both waved their hands in a childlike gesture to catch her eye. Perry remembered someone calling the shorter one Brub, a nickname given him by his younger brother, Cleve.

"Miss Perry!" Brub yelled. "Miss Perry, could we speak with you a minute?"

Perry smiled at the two oafs. Since one carried a large bag over his arm, she guessed they must have found something of interest. Probably a rabbit or a turtle. From the silly grins on their faces she could tell they were planning to scare her. Dropping her hoe, she grabbed her cape and moved closer, prepared to play along with their game. It would be something interesting to tell Andrew at dinner.

As she stepped over the ruins of the garden wall she asked, "May I help you?"

"Please, miss," Brub said, "me brother, Cleve, wants to show you somethin' we found."

Perry turned to Cleve as his beefy hands pulled the opening wide. For a moment she was too repulsed by his dirty fingers to look past them into the bag. Whatever the contents of the sack, it couldn't possibly be as ugly as his filthy, misshapen hands. If bathing brought on illness, as many believed, these two must be very healthy.

To Perry's surprise the sack was empty. She glanced up at Cleve in time to see him nod at his brother. "Now, Brub!" he yelled, the smile gone from his dirty face.

Both men sprang toward her. She opened her mouth to scream. Before her cry could escape, Brub grabbed her and stuffed a soiled rag in her mouth. Cleve slid his huge hands down from her shoulders and pinned her arms firmly against her sides. The sun passed uncaringly beneath the horizon as she struggled between the two men.

Fear flowed through her like quicksilver as she realized she was being abducted. Her mind whirled, searching for a reason to their madness. She knew times were hard, but surely these men realized Andrew didn't have enough money for ransom. In panic she looked around for help, but no one was in sight.

With every ounce of her energy she kicked at Cleve's legs. He danced in front of her, yelling each time her foot met its mark.

"Quiet down, you dummy!" Brub ordered. "You makin' too much noise. Get the bag over her head and let's get outa here."

Cleve pulled burlap over Perry, cloaking her world in darkness. She continued to struggle and kick, but he only grunted at her attack. The dirty smell of the sack, mixed with the filthy taste of the rag in her mouth, drove her to fight even harder.

In a sudden movement Perry was thrown over Cleve's shoulder like a load of grain.

"Get her in the wagon," Brub whispered as they jogged across the grass toward the trees.

Within minutes she felt herself being lifted off his shoulder and placed on her stomach in the bed of a wagon.

"Cover her with hay," Brub ordered, and Perry felt the wagon sag with their weight as they climbed in. A moment later she felt the jolt as the horses were slapped into action.

The wagon rocked across the uneven ground as she battled to free her hands. The coarse ropes dug into her flesh, and each time she twisted, her wrist grew raw with pain. She kicked at the hay around her, knowing she must be knocking some out of the wagon and hopefully leaving a trail. Her mind kept returning to the weapon in her pocket.

She struggled until she lay on her side, but she couldn't reach the knife. The wagon bumped along for what seemed hours, bruising her shoulder and cheek without mercy.

Eventually, when they were well away from the plantation, Brub broke the silence. "With the money we get for this little lady, we can make a nice start in California or Texas."

"Ya, we'd have to work a year to make this much," Cleve answered. "She's quite a looker. She's a lady, too, not like the others we've taken him."

"That's why we're gettin' so much."

"What you reckon he does with these girls we keep bringing him?" Cleve's voice was low, almost childlike.

"Ain't none of our business. We gets paid well, don't we? He don't kill 'em or nothing. I think he even gives 'em money to help their families out when he turns 'em loose. Whatever he does to 'em, the girls keep their mouths closed about it."

"Who knows? Maybe they likes it." Cleve laughed in a hiccuping sound that sent cold terror up Perry's back.

"He may keep this one a little longer." Cleve's voice grew loud. "She's small, but I seen the way her chest pushes out. She's a ripe one, that's a fact. Ready for the pickin'."

Fear froze her mind for a moment, blocking out all other thought. She could do nothing but listen to the two men above her.

"You think he might let me have a turn after he's finished?" Cleve asked excitedly.

"No," Brub answered sharply. "We'll need to get on the road, won't have time to wait. You know sometimes he takes two or three days to get his fill of a girl."

"How about we pulls off up here and have a little fun with the lady *before* we deliver her? Couldn't hurt nothin'. I seen some men once during the war tie a nigger gal spread-eagle in a wagon. They was sharing with anyone who wanted some. The girl didn't even scream after a few times. She just laid there wide-eyed, like she didn't care anymore. Why, some of the fellers even took seconds, and she didn't say nothin' or even try to fight them.''

"I don't know . . ." Brub hesitated. "It looks like it might rain any minute." Yet to Cleve's delight he slowed the wagon."But I guess you're right, couldn't hurt nothin'. You ain't gonna give the lady nothin' she ain't gonna get plenty of where she's going.''

Cleve was so excited, he was hiccuping again. "Captain might thank us for warming her up for him.''

Perry cringed in fear as the wagon stopped and she felt one of the men jump down. She could hear Cleve telling Brub all about what he was going to do.

She lay very still as Cleve's hands felt in the darkness for her form in the hay.

"Now, Miss Perry," he said, laughing in his excitement, "don't you fret none. I ain't gonna do you no real harm. I'm just gonna get you ready. We taking you to a gentleman who likes young girls, and we'll just have a bit of fun with you for a while. Then he'll let you go home with enough money to buy yourself a real purty dress.''

Cleve jerked the sack off Perry's face. His huge fingers hooked her collar and pulled downward. Buttons flew as her blouse tore open. She moved her head from side to side in agony, not believing what was about to happen. His beefy hands pulled at the material of her blouse, trying to get beneath her clothes. The rag in her mouth held her screams inside her mind, blinding all else from her thoughts.

"Cleve!" Brub yelled nervously. "Don't mess with that, just pull up her skirts and get on with it. We don't have all night.''

Cleve grunted in disappointment. "I was looking forward to squeezing a ripe one. It's been so long since I had my hand full of somethin' soft." He rubbed his hands down her blouse, trying to satisfy himself. Grabbing her breast, he pushed hard and rolled his palm over her blouse.

When she jerked, he repeated the action like a child torturing a tiny animal, unaware of any pain he caused.

Perry tried to roll away, but he pushed her against the rough wagon floor. "You be still, little lady. I'll be finished in a minute. We ain't gonna hurt you more'n we have to." Grabbing her ankles, he pulled them toward him.

He shoved her skirts up almost to her waist in one movement. She heard his sharp intake of breath as the moonlight shone across her bare legs.

Perry studied his outline in the darkness. She could hear him fumbling with his pants. When he looked down at his belt buckle, her mind and body reacted. With all her strength she kicked her leg. Her boot flew toward him with a quick swishing sound. If she missed, there wouldn't be another shot.

She hit the mark solidly and Cleve fell backward in shattering pain. Blood squirted from his nose like a fountain, splattering her clothes with crimson.

"What is it?" Brub yelled as he ran to the back of the wagon.

"She broke my nose!" Cleve whined as blood filled his hands. "The little bitch broke my nose!"

"I thought you said you knew how to do it." Brub pushed his injured brother. "I knew this was a bad idea." He seemed more upset about the waste of time than about his brother's bleeding.

"Blood's comin out fast!" Cleve cried. "Whatta I do?"

"Get back in the wagon," Brub ordered in disgust. "We'll get her delivered and go find some cold water. Serves you right for thinking."

Brub slapped the horses into action as Cleve whimpered like a two-hundred-pound baby. Within a few minutes Perry felt the wagon slow once more. She tried to recognize her surroundings, but it was too dark. All she could tell was that they were at the back of a house. She could see no other homes nearby.

Brub whispered above Cleve's sobs, "You wait in the wagon. I'll take her in to the Captain and get our money."

Brub went around the wagon. He pulled the sack back over her head and shoulders, then lifted her up into his arms. He walked up the steps and kicked the door with his foot.

"Come in," a voice snapped, and Perry saw dim light through the burlap.

"Stand her up at the bedpost and tie her to it before you remove the sack," the voice whispered. She thought it sounded familiar, but her heart was pounding so violently in her throat that she wasn't sure of anything but the biting ropes at her wrists.

Brub checked the ropes, then jerked the bag from her head. Terror exploded in her mind like fireworks as she blinked in the sudden light.

The room was large and richly furnished. A man dressed in black stood in the shadows, smoking a cigar. The tip of the cigar pointed toward her as the man whispered, "What's all this blood?"

"She's a wildcat, Captain." Brub saw no reason to tell the truth. "She broke Cleve's nose while we was puttin' her in the wagon."

A cruel laugh sounded from the corner, filling the room like a foul odor. Perry's eyes widened in terror. She recognized his voice even before Wade stepped into the firelight to pay Brub.

His evil gaze never left her. "She's a woman worth taking."

Brub nodded, more interested in the money than in any woman. "You want me to take the gag off?"

"No, I think not. I need her to keep quiet for now." He moved closer, as if examining his treasure. "I love seeing those huge eyes so full of fear," he whispered into her ear. "I've had my fun with several local girls, but I've never killed one. You, my dear, are going to be the first." He smiled as if he'd just paid her a compliment.

Wade turned, remembering Brub. "You may go."

Brub hesitated. "You ain't going to hurt her, are you, Captain?"

"No. I'm just going to detain her for a few hours. Don't worry. In a little while I'll send her home. Here." He pitched her cape to him. "Lay this across the railing outside so Miss Perry can retrieve it as she leaves. And make sure the lantern is left outside the door."

Brub nodded, then disappeared.

Wade moved closer. "Well, I'm glad you decided to drop by tonight." He slowly blew smoke from his cigar in her face. "You'll forgive the lie I told to that idiot. You and I both know you'll never leave this room alive."

He moved a few inches closer.

She could smell the whiskey on his breath. A spark of insanity lit in his eyes as he rambled on.

"My original plan was to disgrace you and have Hunter shot as a traitor in Raleigh, but somehow he escaped. My guess is that he'll ride straight to your brother's house. If I know him, and I do, he'll go wild when he discovers you've vanished. He'll have no trouble following the trail those two dullards left."

Wade stepped away and moved back into the shadows by the door. "This time there will be no mistake. I'll personally see that Hunter dies."

His voice was that of a madman, utterly pleased with his own cleverness. "Hunter will see your cape and break the door down. He'll see you here in the center of the room, tied up and frightened. As he runs to his love I'll cut him down from the darkness."

The cold steel of Wade's gun flashed in the firelight. She realized that if Hunter rushed in from the darkness he'd only be able to see her, no more. Wade would kill Hunter before he even realized his cousin was in the room. Tears spilled over and rolled down her cheeks as she saw how carefully Wade had planned Hunter's death.

Wade laughed as he moved nearer. "I'll leave your lover

bleeding on the floor while I bed you,'' he taunted as he moved the tip of one gun barrel along her jaw.

"Tomorrow I'll explain to the authorities how Hunter found us and killed you. Then, of course, I killed him.'' He delighted in seeing her tremble.

He studied her carefully. "I need to make sure he sees no one but you when he breaks in.'' Wade moved his hands to her blouse and ripped off the material, leaving only her white camisole to cover her breasts. She was breathing rapidly in fright, and for a moment he watched her breasts moving up and down. In haste he jerked the band of her skirt and it ripped free. With it went her only hope of escape: the knife.

"That looks better.'' He smiled. "All white, like you would have been on our wedding night.'' He rolled the torn clothes up and moved into the darkness.

Perry heard the door creak open. "If you'll excuse me, my love, I'll get rid of these,'' Wade said, leaving the room.

She twisted violently, not caring that the ropes were digging into her flesh. She had to get free. But the bonds were impossible to break, and she only succeeded in causing herself pain. From somewhere outside the door she heard Wade call Noma's name.

Perry listened as she heard him order her old servant to get rid of the rags. Tears rolled down her face as she heard Noma's voice. For a moment she prayed the woman would help her, then she prayed Noma wouldn't discover her. For Perry knew it would only mean Noma's death as well.

Wade dismissed the servant and returned to Perry. He paced before her, slapping his fist against his open palm like a fighter impatient for the round to start. "We have a few hours to wait. Much as I'd like to have my fun with you now, I feel your cries will be so much more meaningful when your lover lies at the foot of our bed.'' He moved closer so that his words stung her damp cheeks. "With the rumors I've spread about you today, all you'll be fit for is whoring. And tonight you'll be my whore while I spread Hunter's blood over you.''

Perry fought to keep from throwing up as he whispered all his plans in her ear. He didn't touch her. He didn't have to. He was whipping her senseless with his words.

Chapter 36

Moments ticked by in heartbeats as Perry waited. Each low roll of thunder halted her breath. She listened for Hunter's approach, praying the storm would somehow keep him from coming to his certain death. Her wrists were caked with blood, but still she twisted, trying to break loose. If one hand were free, she could pull the gag away in time to warn him. But her task was impossible.

When a low pounding of hooves sounded above the rain and drew nearer, Perry knew time had run out. Horses screamed to a halt and footsteps hammered across the porch. She could do nothing but wait for her world to end.

Abram's voice shouted above the storm, "Wait, Hunter, it might be a trap!" Perry's body jerked, and she wished she could add to Abram's warning.

But Hunter slammed his entire body into the door, blasting through like a cannonball fired at close range.

In agony, Perry strained against her ropes, trying to pull herself away from the terrible reality before her. She closed her eyes the moment she saw his face, unable to bear the sight of Wade's bullet blasting into Hunter's body. It was enough that she saw the worry and rage in Hunter's eyes as he looked at her. She couldn't remain sane if she saw him fall.

The door to the room creaked, blending with the storm's cries, rolling in from the open back door.

"No!" a woman's voice screamed from the darkness near Wade. "Stop!" she shouted as a round from Wade's gun shattered the room. For a moment the room seemed to be in the heart of a storm cloud, the sound of the rain punctuated by the thundering cry of a weapon and the bright flash of fire.

Recognizing Noma's voice, Perry opened her eyes and searched the darkness in the corner. The black woman was standing directly in front of Wade's smoking gun. Her large frame had blocked the bullet's path to Hunter.

Noma stood rigid for a moment before she slumped forward, and then blood covered her chest like a huge scarlet flower. "Don't you . . . hurt my baby," she whispered between clenched teeth.

Perry watched in horror as Noma's body melted to the rug. The old woman reached toward Perry, a fist clutching the small pearl-handled knife. "My baby," she mumbled as a crimson stream flowed around her. Then her stare turned cold in death.

Tears raced down Perry's cheeks as she realized Noma had given her back her life. Above all else, Noma had loved her. In the end she'd loved her enough to face Wade *and* death.

Wade looked surprised and irritated that Noma had stepped in his way. He raised the gun again, cursing under his breath.

Taking advantage of Wade's moment of hesitation, Hunter flew into him, deflecting his arm as the second shot sounded. Wade growled in an animalistic rage. His fist slammed into Hunter's stomach, knocking Hunter backward. Perry struggled feverishly as the two men landed blow after blow on one another. This was a fight unlike she'd ever witnessed, for both were war-hardened soldiers and each knew it was a fight to the death.

As they fought, destroying the room in their wrath,

Abram moved behind Perry. He slid a knife between her cheek and the rag. With one jerk he cut it.

"Help him!" she begged.

"He'd not have it," Abram stated calmly as he worked at the ropes around her hands. "This fight has been brewing since they were children. They must settle it." Abram knew it would end in one of the men dying. He hoped it would be Wade; but should he kill Hunter, Abram would make sure Wade didn't live long enough to enjoy his victory.

The two cousins rolled in and out of the darkness. "Abram!" Perry shouted as Wade pulled a gun from his boot. The silver barrel flashed, only a blink in the firelight. Before Abram could move, Wade pulled the trigger.

Hunter twisted out of the line of fire. Wade aimed again, sighting his adversary with the steadiness of a trained marksman. But the darkness Wade had so carefully planned on to aid him now concealed Hunter.

As Wade searched for his mark a cane chair flew from the shadows, catching Wade's leg and knocking him off-balance. Hunter's body slammed into his full-force, and they moved together back into the darkness.

They became only shadows in a terrible dance of death. Perry couldn't see the gun but knew it rested between the two. She pulled at the ropes, trying to hurry Abram's progress and free herself.

A sudden blast shook the room, light flashed between the two men. They fell together to their knees. For a moment they faced each other in what was almost a farewell embrace. Perry held her breath as Wade's lean form stood in the darkness. A scream clawed its way up her throat as Wade turned toward her, his eyes wide in shock. He stepped into the firelight, gripping his stomach with both hands. Blood oozed out between his fingers like warm molasses. A look of confusion crossed his face just before he fell headlong at her feet.

Perry stared at his lifeless form. His body relaxed as

blood drained from him, mixing with Noma's, which was already soaking the rug. The evil twist of his face smoothed in death, returning the handsome profile that his thoughts had distorted.

"Hunter!" she cried, at last jerking free of her bonds.

Opening his arms, Hunter pulled her to him and swung her around. For a moment there was no one in the world but the two of them. They'd come so close to hell, so close to losing each other.

"I love you." Perry sobbed softly.

"I know, darling," he answered. "I—" The sound of approaching horses stopped him. He pulled her close as he listened. Within seconds shouts came from the front of the house.

"They've caught up with us," Abram announced as he lifted several of Wade's loaded guns. "You get Miss Perry away and I'll distract them."

Hunter draped Perry's cape over her shoulders. "Trust me," he whispered. Then, turning to Abram, he added, "I'll take the back way to the farm. It's longer, but safer for her. Meet me at the *Star* as soon as you can."

Abram wrapped the guns in a quilt and threw them into the fire, then followed his friends.

When they reached the horses, they could hear men pounding on the front door. Hunter lifted Perry into the saddle and swung up behind. He turned his horse toward the trees while Abram turned toward the road.

Within a minute they were in the shadows of the trees. He slowed slightly as the sounds of shots rang from Wade's room. "Hold on tightly, darling. Those burning guns won't give us but a few minutes head start."

There were a thousand questions in Perry's mind, but all she cared about right now was being with Hunter. They were safe, and Wade could no longer hurt them—that was all that mattered. She leaned her head against him and relaxed.

• • •

They rode for an hour through the trees. The storm blew cold splashes of rain against them, but Perry felt warm in his arms. Hunter knew his way amid the brush as only a man who'd memorized a path in boyhood could. Finally, when all was quiet around them, they stopped by a stream and he lifted her down. The night was dark and stormy, making them appear as only silhouettes to each other.

"Why are we stopping?" Perry whispered, as though the other shadows might hear.

"I want to wash your wrists," he answered as he knelt beside a stream.

"It's nothing." She wished to see his face. With an exhausted sigh she sat on a huge rock beside him.

He worked gently, washing the blood away. After rummaging in his saddlebag he wrapped each wrist with a dry cloth. "Those men are chasing me because they believe I'm a traitor. If we're caught, I'll be hung."

"How could they think such a thing?"

Only the rumbling wind answered Perry, then Hunter let out a sigh. "I suppose to some in the South I am a traitor. I didn't come to North Carolina just to see my grandparents. Both times I've brought papers from President Johnson. There are men on either side who want peace to come, and others who know only hate. The president is worried about the way Reconstruction is moving. He fears radicals will bleed the South dry. He asked me to meet with whomever became governor. There are many, North and South, who don't want the pain of the war to end."

He knelt beside her. "There's already talk about refusing to seat Southern congressmen when the House resumes. If North Carolina resists, so will the other Southern states. The wound left by the war will fester and bleed for years."

Perry touched his hair with her fingers. "Why are you telling me this?"

Hunter captured her hand and kissed it tenderly. "You

have a right to know. I'm putting you in great danger by loving you. I want you to come with me, but if we're caught—"

"You have papers with you now!" It wasn't a question.

"Yes." Hunter's words were direct. "And I'll die before giving them up, but I have no right to put you in such danger."

"Do you want me with you?" She was almost afraid to ask.

"More than life," came his reply in only a heartbeat. "I want you with me forever. When I realized you'd been kidnapped, it was like someone had ripped a part of me away." He pulled her into his arms. "You asked me once if I cared for you. You're my world, all the happiness in my life. You're my dreams and my reality. I love you beyond the definition of the word."

"Then I will go with you," she whispered, knowing her home would always be in the circle of his arms.

Hunter didn't kiss her but gently lifted her back onto the saddle. He held her tightly as they moved on through the endless shadows of trees. There were no more questions between them, no more secrets. They loved each other, belonged to each other as completely as if they'd said wedding vows in the darkness.

Just before dawn, they reached the end of the trees. Hunter lowered her to the ground. "We'll go on foot from here." He unsaddled the horse and turned it loose. "Granddad's place is just over the rise. We can hide there. In a few hours we'll raise the *Northern Star* and float over any traps set for me."

They moved in silence to the barn. Perry was beginning to feel the lack of sleep and the cold night air, but she said nothing. Hunter opened the plank door a crack and stepped in, pulling her in behind him.

The barn was clean and mostly bare. The red, white, and blue silk of the balloon waited, ready to be unrolled, but the basket lay upside down. "We should be safe in here. Those men were from Raleigh and have no idea which way I may have been traveling." Hunter lifted one side of the basket. "It's not as grand as the loft, but we can hide in here."

Perry slid across the straw and into the overturned basket. Hunter followed, lowering them into darkness. Waiting for her eyes to adjust, she moved to the other side and listened to his breathing in the silent closed space. The darkness and the smell of hay welcomed her with the knowledge that she was once again alone with the man she loved.

"Angel?" he whispered, knowing she could be only a few feet from him. "Dear God, Perry, don't be afraid of me."

She stretched her hand in the darkness and touched his searching fingers. "I'm not afraid," she answered.

He pulled her to him and they sat against one corner of the basket. "We are in great danger, yet all I've thought about for hours is holding you." He kissed her forehead lightly.

Rising to her knees, she removed her cape and spread it across the hay.

"You'll be cold." He pulled off his coat and draped it over her shoulders. "Use this as a blanket and try to get a few hours sleep."

Pushing him down against the velvet layers of her cape, her soft laughter filled the tiny space. "I've no wish to sleep."

As his body slid next to hers the memory of another night in a barn loft flooded his senses. He'd thought he was in death's grip when she lay beside him, giving him her warmth. He'd been past caring about life, then she'd moved her body against his, showing him what he'd miss if he gave up. When the pain had been too much for him to bear, he'd reached for her, and the warmth of her body next to his had given Hunter reason to fight.

Now she pulled his hands around her, cuddling against him, her body wanting more than just warmth. "Darling, what are you doing? Much as I'd like to, we have no time."

She lifted his hand and laid it across her lace-covered breast as her lips burned across his cheek.

"We can't do this now!" Hunter's voice was low with passion. All the time he'd wanted her, and always she'd pulled away. Now she was giving, and his rational mind ordered him to stop. "We can't . . ."

In answer she shoved his hand lower, pushing the lace from the velvety globe of her breast so that his fingers were filled with her flesh. Her mouth covered his protests as her hands slid beneath his shirt to glide over his chest.

Finally, when Hunter could pull his lips from hers, he mumbled, "We must stop. This is madness, angel." She was kissing his face, ignoring his protests. "We'll be in Washington soon. I'll make love to you in a proper marriage bed."

She laughed at his hesitation. Pushing his hands over her hips as she knelt above him, she slowly untied her camisole. The morning light had turned the inside of the basket from chocolate to milky gray. When the first tie lay open, she worked on the second. "Tell me to stop, my love, and I will." She'd been so near death a few hours before that now she wanted only to taste life. "Just say one word. Order me to stop."

Hunter was silent.

"Tell me you haven't longed for me in your dreams as dearly as I've longed for you." The second tie fell free, opening Perry's very heart to this man she'd loved from the moment she'd seen his face. "Tell me you don't love me and I'll stop this torture." She twisted the bow loose on the next tie. "From the moment we met, we've never known how much time we would have together." Perry pulled the last ribbon free and the camisole fell open. "But we have this moment, and for me it is my lifetime."

Hunter watched her with passion-filled eyes, loving,

wanting, and cherishing her all at the same time. She lowered her mouth over his and began driving him mad with her feather-light kisses. "Tell me to stop, my love," she whispered against his open mouth, "or make love to me." With her final demand she lowered her bare breasts against his chest.

He surrendered willingly, twisting her in his embrace until he lay atop her. "I'll make love to you, my angel, now and for the rest of my life."

There was no more time for words as he undressed and lay beside her. Gently he kissed her body and moved his fingers over every inch of her flesh, forever branding her as his own. His fingers glided as smoothly as the balloon crossing a cloudless sky. The taste of her was as clean and fresh as mile-high air over snowcapped mountains. He was drifting into a passion that spanned his life's horizons and to which there'd never be a setting sun. He'd reached for an angel and captured perfection in his arms.

She followed his lead, loving the way his muscles tightened beneath her touch. Running her fingers over the scar on his shoulder, she remembered every time he'd held her, every moment his lips had touched hers, but none were as sweet as this moment, this time. There was no taking in his actions but only a giving—a giving of all the love he'd banked for a lifetime.

When he entered her, she didn't cry out in pain. All the discomfort was drowned in a flood of pleasure. They were together as one, and he found the piece that had always been missing from his life. He belonged to her as completely as she belonged to him. As he moved within her they floated to heaven and sealed for eternity a bond between them.

Stretching with the sweet pleasure that filled her, Perry drifted back to earth. She curled beneath Hunter's arm and fell asleep. No matter what happened, she knew he loved her, and that, somehow, was all that mattered.

Hunter lay awake, loving the way she felt in his arms.

A tight knot twisted in the pit of his stomach. He loved her, totally and completely. When she'd given herself to him, it had been Hunter who'd surrendered his heart. He had sworn never to care deeply for a woman, but she'd broken down all his defenses. And now she was at the very core of him.

He smiled finally, understanding his father and grandfather. He wanted a lifetime with Perry, but even if he had only this one moment, it would be worth all the pain of losing her.

Hunter leaned to kiss her sleeping forehead as the sound of the creaking barn door reached his ears, shattering the peace from his mind.

Chapter 37

"Get dressed!" Hunter whispered as footsteps shuffled through the hay outside the basket.

He silently pulled on his clothes. The barn door creaked again, louder, bolder. Hunter jerked on his boots and listened.

"What ya doing in here?" a man shouted.

Abram's voice was calm. "Don't see that it's any of your concern, Preacher, but I'm getting this balloon ready."

"Where is Hunter Kirkland?" It was obvious the minister saw no need to waste time being polite to the huge black man.

"I haven't seen him in a while," Abram answered.

Hunter gently touched her shoulder, warning her to be silent.

Cleland's voice snapped, "What's that you got there?"

"Supplies."

"Well, if you see Mr. Kirkland, you might tell him I'd like to speak with him before he leaves. I'll be back later."

Abram's voice was frigid. "You do that, Preacher."

As the side door slammed behind the minister, Hunter casually slid from beneath the basket. "Morning."

"Morning." Abram showed no surprise at Hunter's sudden appearance. "I brought you and Miss Perry some

354

breakfast." He lay a basket on the workbench. "Biscuits with sausages dipped in honey."

Hunter accepted one. "Let's give her some privacy while we spread the balloon out between the barn and the house." Hunter was having trouble controlling his smile. He wanted to shout across the heavens. He was the luckiest man alive. But he cleared his throat and tried to sound calm. "I'm ready to get back to Washington and a normal life."

"Me too." Abram studied his captain. "Is the little lady coming with us this time?"

Hunter faced his old friend. "She'd be safer here, but I love her too much to leave her behind."

Laughter bubbled from Abram. "It sure took you long enough to realize it. I was beginning to think you hit your head when you fell from the sky the last time. There isn't a place on this earth that little lady will be safer than between us."

Hunter ignored his teasing as he worked. "What happened with the men at Wade's place?"

Abram lifted the ropes and followed. "I stayed back and watched for about an hour. The house caught fire during all the shooting. They were waiting around for the blaze to die down. My guess is they'll identify Wade's body as yours and proclaim themselves heroes by the time they get back to Raleigh."

Hunter agreed, knowing that the kind of men who hunted in gangs were usually not long on bravery, nor intelligence.

By the time the balloon was ready for flight, the minister reappeared like polecat stink after a rain. He hurried toward Hunter, obviously a man with a mission.

"Mr. Kirkland!" he shouted. "I would like to speak to you before you leave."

Hunter nodded, having already decided to donate the land close to the church for the new building to stand on.

His dislike for the reverend had been the only thing that had kept him from making the announcement.

As Reverend Cleland skirted the balloon Hunter looked toward the barn. He was unprepared for the beauty that stepped into the sunlight. Her hair tumbled around her like sunlit ebony, and her cape flowed around her like royal robes.

She walked toward him, and he suddenly knew that in fifty years she'd still look the same to him. She was all that was perfect in the world, all that was beauty.

Perry smiled. "Is something wrong, Mr. Kirkland?"

"Yes," Hunter whispered. "Marry me."

"Now?"

"At this moment." Suddenly Hunter could wait no longer to share his name or his life. He pulled her toward the balloon.

"Reverend Cleland, I must leave, but I want you to know that I left the acres beside the church to the building fund."

Cleland clapped his hands. "Oh, that is wonderful. Just wonderful."

Hunter interrupted his celebration. "I ask only one favor. This lovely lady and I wish to be married."

Cleland's face dropped suddenly. "That's impossible. I was led to understand she was your, well, your"—he didn't dare say what he thought—"your houseguest." The thin man began to sweat. "That was bad enough, but marrying her . . . well, that just can't be done."

"I don't care what you thought, but you best take care with your speech." Hunter's eyes turned a cold gray. "The lady will be my wife. You *are* licensed to marry folks?"

"Certainly." The reverend moved a few feet away. "Only if you wed this woman, you'll be arrested."

"What!" Hunter exploded. He grabbed the man by the lapels and almost shook religion from him with one mighty jolt. "You'd better explain, for I assure you, sir, I do plan to marry this lady."

"I wasn't planning on mentioning this." The minister pulled a paper from his pocket. "But your cousin came by to see me a few days ago. He feared something like this might be attempted, and he wanted to protect you. He gave me this document, which states that Allison McLain, Perry's mother, was the daughter of a slave from Three Oaks. There's even a letter here from Allison's father testifying to the fact."

Cleland looked up, as if the papers were somehow a shield. "As you know, Mr. Kirkland, in North Carolina it is illegal for a white man to marry a woman of color."

Hunter's anger reached a point of deadly calm. He moved toward the preacher slowly, deliberately.

"Hunter!" Abram shouted. "Riders coming."

They all glanced far to the north and saw a cloud of dust moving fast. Hunter grabbed Perry and lifted her into the balloon. "Hold this," he whispered as he shoved his Colt into her hand, then turned and shoved the minister into the basket.

"Take aim on our guest!" Hunter shouted loud enough for Cleland to hear. "If he moves, shoot him!" He turned toward the frightened preacher. "Don't worry about her being a good shot. If she fires, we'll all go up in flames."

Abram threw the grounding rope over and hopped into the wicker gondola. Within moments the basket broke loose from the ground and they moved upward, as if someone in the sky were pulling them into the clouds.

"You can't do this!" Cleland whined. His eyes were darting about him like a man who'd just been thrown in a snake pit.

"Just taking you nearer to heaven," Abram said solemnly. " 'Course, if you don't want to come, you're welcome to climb out."

Cleland glanced over the edge for help, but the men below were too far away to hear him. His hands gripped the basket tightly as he watched his world grow smaller below him. "What kind of insanity is this?"

"My plan is unchanged. I wish to marry Perry, and nothing you can say will change my mind." Hunter faced him with cold directness. "What better church than the heavens? You may perform the wedding service now, or you can start flapping your arms and pray you learn to fly before you hit the ground."

The reverend hesitated. He might have called Hunter's bluff, but he felt Abram's massive hand on his shoulder. "I have no Bible and you have no rings."

Abram's grip tightened, lifting him off the floor of the basket.

"All right!" The reverend reconsidered. "I'll marry you!"

"Thanks, Abram." Hunter winked. "The minister seems to have received some divine guidance. Set him down."

Hunter pulled Perry close. "Abram found your bag at the farmhouse, my love. If you'd like to dress and comb your hair, the wedding can wait a moment." Then, to the others he added, "Gentlemen, if you'll turn around and allow my future wife a few moments of privacy . . ."

Abram and the minister turned their backs as Hunter helped Perry open her bag. Abram began telling the minister of the workings of the balloon, as if he were a willing guest and not a prisoner in the small craft.

As Perry removed her cape she looked up shyly into Hunter's love-filled eyes and whispered, "Aren't you going to turn your back while I dress?"

"Not on your life," Hunter answered. "You might as well understand something from the first, Perry Kirkland. I plan to spend the rest of my life watching you."

Perry shrugged her slender shoulders and smiled at him honestly. She pulled her dress from the bag as her mother's pouch fell to the basket floor.

Hunter picked it up. "Did you say there were old papers in this?"

"Yes, and a few rings. Perhaps we could use them."

Hunter opened the pouch. "We can buy rings in Washington. I want you always to wear that medallion I gave you." He smiled as the gold disk reflected the morning sun. "Many a night I've thought of my name carved into the gold of that small disk. My name nestling lovingly in a place I long to lay my head."

Perry blushed scarlet, and not even the breeze could cool her cheeks. "Hunter," she scolded, "we're not alone."

"That fact has never evaded me. Were we alone, I would tell you far more." He laughed as she turned her lovely back to him.

"The crest on the front of that necklace is about all that remains of the Kirkland family. Several generations ago the clan left England for America. As far as I know, I'm the only one left. But we'll change that very soon. I'm looking forward to many dark-eyed, black-haired Kirkland children."

Perry refused to look at him as she combed her hair. He thumbed through the papers in her bag. As the contents of the letters registered on his mind, Hunter gave them his full attention.

Perry finished, then turned to find him reading the papers. A smile spread across his face as he read.

"Reverend Cleland!" he shouted. "Would it relieve your mind if I could show proof that your document from Wade is a forgery?"

"How?" Cleland glanced over his shoulder without letting go of the basket edge.

"I have here birth documents of Perry's mother and of both Perry and Andrew McLain. Hunter held the papers tightly in the wind. "Perry's mother must have feared that old forgery might turn up."

All aboard the tiny craft gathered around as Reverend Cleland examined the documents. After several minutes he huffed. " 'Pears to be in order. I fear I may have been tricked by Wade." He hated admitting his error but saw no point in insisting he was right when the evidence was so obviously on Hunter's side.

A few minutes later he married Hunter Kirkland and Perry McLain among the clouds somewhere over North Carolina. Then they gently lowered the balloon and set him aground several miles from his church. Though he walked many hours to reach home, the reverend never stopped thanking God his feet were on solid ground.

Epilogue

Perry awoke to church bells sounding outside her window. She looked around for a moment, confused. She remembered the long balloon ride, then climbing onto a horse and traveling several hours. Finally, when she could no longer hold the reins, Hunter held her in his arms. Vaguely she remembered being carried upstairs and tucked into bed.

"Good afternoon, Mrs. Kirkland." A woman appeared from the doorway. "I hope you slept well. The mister left orders for a bath to be brought in as soon as you awakened."

Perry looked up, confused.

"Mrs. Adams." The woman pointed to herself. "I'm the housekeeper. Mr. Kirkland has gone to see the president. He'll be back soon."

Perry couldn't believe the beauty of the room before her. Everything was exactly as she would have dreamed a perfect room to be. The walls were sky blue and the furniture dark mahogany with one wall lined in bookshelves. All the curtains were pale blue, trimmed in ivory lace. A warm corner fireplace welcomed her.

When Mrs. Adams went to fetch the bath, Perry jumped from the bed and walked through the open connecting door. A master bedroom greeted her, this one decorated

361

in mahogany and midnight blue. The room could belong to no one but Hunter. Every book, every map posted on the walls, reflected his personality.

She couldn't resist curling into the huge wing-back chair by the fire. She pushed into the velvet and closed her eyes.

"Mrs. Kirkland," the housekeeper whispered, "would you like your tea now, or after your bath?"

"I'll wait for my husband," Perry answered, and heard the housekeeper withdraw.

There was a long silence before the door closed. "Your husband is home," came a low voice from behind the chair.

Perry opened her eyes as he pulled her up into his arms. The look of love in his own gray depths left her speechless.

He carried her to his bed and laid her down gently. "I told you once, whatever your price, I'd pay it." He straightened and removed his shirt, his eyes never leaving her face.

"I ask no price but your love."

Hunter lay beside her and pulled her into his embrace. "Before I met you I thought there was no freedom and joy, except in the *Star* when I was among the clouds. Now I know my heaven is here in your arms. I love you beyond any limits."

Perry delighted in his touch as she rolled close to him. "I love you, but there is one thing we must clear up."

Hunter raised on an elbow and studied her. "And that is, my wife?"

Perry brushed his bare chest with her hand. "You should know one thing. I plan on having only blond children with gray eyes."

Hunter pulled her beneath him and whispered against her ear, "We'll talk about it in the morning, my angel. Right now I plan to give all my dreams wings."